The Game

Parker Felterman

Galaxie Publishing — Patterson, LA
ISBN 978-0-692-06525-9
Library of Congress Card Catalogue Number 2018902133
The Game | Felterman, Parker
Available Formats: Digital | Paperback distribution

Table of Contents

Acknowledgments

To Gam and Granddad, who inspire me every day with their faith, love, and encouragement.

To Tim and Grandy, the latter of whom I've proven right that "any fool with a typewriter can write a book." Grandy: consider this the last version of *The Game* for you to read. Thank you both. For everything.

To my parents, Jody and Beth, without whom *The Revolver* never would have been published, and thus *The Game* never would have become a reality.

To the faculty of the Louisiana School for Math, Science, and the Arts, in particular Dr. Pat Widhalm and Dr. Bradley Bankston, who gave me the honest feedback needed to bring *The Game* to fruition.

To "The Revolver Committee": Joe Busse, Mary Grace Hymel, Tyler Lambert, Michael Martin, and Olivia Orlando, who all spent countless hours selflessly promoting *The Revolver*. Your loyalty and friendship is something I can never fully repay.

Perhaps most importantly, to Josh Bagwell. Without you, Josh, *The Game* never would have been a reality. From your initial character suggestions to always keeping me on task, you were undoubtedly a crucial part of *The Game*'s five-year journey.

Lastly, to all players of The Game, past and present, who inspire me with their passion, ingenuity, and ambition. Thank you.

Figures of Note

Los Angeles Criminal Underworld

- Andy Shapiro- Beppo Family *Consigliere*.
- Antonio "Tony Spits" Spitolli- Beppo Family *Caporegime*.
- Bobby Mancuso- Beppo Family Made Man.
- Chad Black- Black Outfit captain and Johnny Black's cousin.
- Dillan Kamenev- Vasiliev *Bratva* enforcer and part-time mercenary.
- Don Luigi Beppo- *Mafia* boss.
- Eddie Maroni- Beppo Family Made Man and con artist.
- Jimmy "Pips" Palermo- Beppo Family associate and thief.
- Joey "Fours" Gregario- Beppo Family Made Man and hitman.
- Johnny Black- African-American biker gang leader.
- Jose Cortez- Drug *Cartel* CFO and Luis Cortez's younger brother.
- Leonardo Bianchi- Semi-retired counterfeiter.
- Luis Cortez- Drug *Cartel* boss.
- Marcus Dean- Johnny Black's number two.
- Murray Gigante- Loan shark with minimal mob ties.
- Peter Richardson- Exiled *Fratres Criminis Praetor*.
- "Uncle" Donnie Scarlatti- Murray Gigante's debt-collector.

The Washicha Family and Squadron

- Captain John Washicha- Pure Gore Fighting Company member and ex-Washicha Squadron leader.
- Chief Petty Officer Jesse James Washicha- Decommissioned Navy SEAL; John and Katy Washicha's youngest son.
- Chief Petty Officer Terrance Washicha- Decommissioned Navy SEAL; John and Katy Washicha's middle son.
- Corporal Carl Lowry (Deceased)- Ex-Washicha Squadron rifleman.
- Damion Occhipinti- Public defender; John and Katy Washicha's eldest son.
- Katy Washicha- John Washicha's assumed widow.
- Master Sergeant Dustin MacManus Washicha- John Washicha's half-brother and ex-Washicha Squadron sniper.
- Staff Sergeant Brett Castle- Ex-Washicha Squadron heavy gunner.
- Staff Sergeant Justin Walker- Ex-Washicha Squadron sniper's spotter.
- Violet Washicha- John and Katy Washicha's youngest child.

Other Figures of Note

- Alexei Pomerov- *Fratres Criminis Praetor* and mastermind of Russia's largest crime family.
- Clare Angelou- Waitress working her way through law school at USC Gould.
- District Attorney Isaac Fuentes- Los Angeles politician working to cripple organized crime in his county.
- Special Agent William Vasquez- The FBI's top expert on organized crime.
- Vice Admiral Matthew Sanders- Naval officer and friend of John Washicha and Peter Richardson.

"At the end of the game, the king and the pawn go back in the same box."

-Italian Proverb

John's Prologue
Home at Last

John. June 6th, 1987.

Some say the road is the only home for ol' boys like me. After this last stint, I was about ready to upgrade. Soon I'll be reunited with the ones I lost. The ones I loved and never stopped loving.

I sat on my old Model 841 Indian, the most trusted bike I've ever owned. It hummed none too quietly, preventing me from being alone with my thoughts as I traveled down Airline Highway—alone. I passed an electronic sign toting the explanation for the empty road—2:05 AM, June 6th, 1987. One year, two months, and fifteen days since I had been deemed Missing in Action after the op in Afghanistan took a wrong turn. The details were still being worked out by the suits in the Pentagon. The truth, though, would be kept between five men. Only four of them still breathing.

The humid night air whipped my face. I had finally returned home to the States a month ago, but had owed some indentured servitude to the mercenary organization that smuggled me and my squad across the pond. If Castle hadn't called in some favors, I doubt we would have made it this far.

As far as Uncle Sam is concerned, we never made it back. Just a handful more soldiers left for dead in a hopeless struggle. The mercenaries smuggled us, smelling like sand, goat, blood, and war, into New York Harbor. The memory still burned my nostrils. What made it unbearable was the Middle

Eastern garb we had to wear; all it did was remind me of the enemy. But now I was finally away—away from those who hated rather than loved me.

Thankfully, Castle's friends were nice enough to eventually get ahold of some civilian clothes for us. For a price, of course. But that was expected from guns for hire. The ones who killed for a paycheck. No honor. No loyalty.

We made the long journey South just the four of us: me, Castle, Walker, and Dustin. We made quite a team. Always had. But a shadow hung over us as we entered Richmond. We should have been coming home with Carl. Now… now Carl is waiting for us elsewhere.

Richmond had been our ship-out point. Our vehicles were impounded there with my officer uniform, though it didn't take much to get them out. It appears the Department of Defense doesn't live up to its namesake on all fronts.

That was where we parted ways. We had families to get back to, after all. Except Dustin, but he had his own personal mission to take care of. I wasn't going to stop him. I knew my brother well enough to not fight his stubbornness. Our appearances didn't reveal that he was my half-brother, for he certainly didn't share my rugged good looks. No, those who knew us could tell because we share the MacManus determination that my mother's family crafted over countless generations.

After far too long, I made it to my home city, the same one in which my family had been patiently awaiting my return: New Orleans. I turned off the highway. A few more streets and I'd be home. My real home. Not this artificial one of gravel and dirt, though I'd lived here all my life. Katy is my home. My sons are my home. And, I had to remind myself, my youngest that I had never laid eyes on. The day I was shipped out, I had hugged a crying and pregnant Katy good-bye. Now this child, whatever their name may be, is over a year old.

I could already see Katy in front of me: piercing green eyes that held a special sparkle, like twin emeralds. Her deep-throated laugh she made as she shook her head softly when I messed up, usually in the accompaniment of one of our sons. Her soft lips as I kissed her in the morning.

I wondered how the boys had been. Terry with his shy awkwardness. Jesse James and his knack for annoying Terry. Damion, the eldest, who, not unlike his old man, had developed an interest in Poe. All three, each so different from one another, hold a special place in my heart.

I had promised them all when I left that after this op I would be hanging up my beret. No more heading to foreign nations no one's ever heard of. No more crawling around deserts and jungles and who-knows-what. I had promised them too late, all things considered. I had never been away half as long. Not even when I was captured in Vietnam.

I turned onto our street. We had been living here for ten years, ever since Damion was born. I finally made it back to the familiar street I had traveled up and down innumerable times, the street I taught my sons how to ride bikes on (and soon will teach the newest addition to our family), the one where I went on strolls with Katy. The moments that mattered. My heart sped with the anticipation of being able to continue those moments.

An unfamiliar silver minivan was in the driveway. Understandable. Katy's Pontiac never would have been able to hold four kids safely.

I parked my bike in the driveway, next to the minivan, and sprinted up to the front patio, bounding up the steps like a child on Christmas morning, until my own front door loomed over me. I had told myself I would control my emotions. I had wanted to seem cool and collected. Strong for my family. Now I wasn't concerned with how I looked. I stooped down and picked up the mat. The key was gone.

I nodded to myself. Smart girl, Katy. I'd warned her before that the neighborhood was getting dangerous. She could take care of herself—and granted I taught my boys how to shoot—but the baby would be too defenseless if there was a break-in. That would be taken care of now that I'm back and here to stay.

I rang the bell and held my breath. Hopefully I wouldn't wake up the baby. They weren't expecting me; I hadn't been able to contact them since I'd left. I'd wanted to. Badly. But it was impossible. The mission was too risky as it was without communicating with our loved ones back home, and once we were back we couldn't risk being found by the men in the suits.

A light flicked on, shining through the window. I eagerly awaited the door to be thrown open, Katy to rush into my arms. I heard the bolt being pushed back and the chain undone. The door clicked as it was unlocked. It swung inward.

I faced...a stranger. He was still dazed from sleep, with a robe haphazardly slung around his shoulders. He waited impatiently at the door, one hand behind him. I stared, my mouth agape.

No. Not my Katy. I'd heard stories from other units about soldiers getting back and finding their wives with other men. This couldn't be. I stared down at my bronze biceps and then at his pasty... arms. Yet here he was, beer belly and bald, standing in front of me.

"Can I help you?" he asked impatiently, not bothering to hide his annoyance.

I snapped, grabbing him by his throat with my right hand,

barging my way into my own house. The baseball bat he had been hiding behind his back clattered to the floor.

"Listen up," I growled, "all I want is my wife. Where is Katy?" Realizing what I had done, I set him down. I had to remain calm, despite the flood of emotions I felt deep in my chest, forming a lump in my throat. This was surely nothing more than a misunderstanding. I took a deep breath.

"Katy?" he seemed confused. I licked my lips, trying to control my anger.

"Katy. The woman who lives here." A spark of recognition entered his eyes, momentarily masking his fear.

"You must mean Katy Washicha," he said, rubbing his throat, inching toward his bat.

"She *is* the woman who lives here."

"No, she *was*." I stared at him, dread forming in the pit of my stomach.

"Did something happen?"

"You could say that. She sold this home to my wife and me. Four kids in a house this size? I don't think so." The dread began crawling into my chest. Katy would never move without letting me know somehow. I pushed back my scraggly hair, my leather jacket and hair combination suddenly making me very hot.

"Where?" I was anxious. Confused. He chose my apparent uncertainty as a time to grow a backbone. He shakily gripped the bat.

"Look, Buddy, I don't know who you think you are, and it's none of your business, but she said something about moving out West. California, I think," he sized me up and down. "You look like Hell."

"I've seen Hell. This doesn't even come close." I turned, ready to leave the way I had come. Time to head West.

"Who *are* you?" he asked. Something in his tone suggested

that I should answer. If he called the cops, a run-in with the law could be detrimental to an MIA soldier. I turned my head slowly, to where my chin was just over my shoulder.

"John. John Washicha." From the corner of my eye, I could see his lips press into a thin line.

"Look, I don't know who you are, but that's not funny."

"What's that supposed to mean?" The dread was back.

"You can't be John Washicha."

"And why not?" I faced him.

"Because if you are…"

"Spit it out." I braced myself for the blow.

"You're dead."

Peter's Prologue
Fratres Criminis

Peter. April 12th, 2009.

It has been said that some of the greatest men in history were once pariahs of their people. The latter is certainly true of me, yet I could by no stretch of the imagination be considered a great man. I have no qualms, for I never strived to be anything other than what I am: a criminal. A thief. A gangster. The world's most powerful underworld figure, all in one five-foot-eleven package.

I refused to look at the bleak stone walls of the chamber. Instead, I stared at the man sitting across from me. He is many things: my captor, my interrogator, and—before the coup—my friend. Half a foot taller than me and a hefty build of pure muscle, it would be nearly impossible to overcome him in a physical brawl. Not that I could even attempt to fight him, anyway: I've had handcuffs chaffing my ankles and wrists since the moment I arrived here. Wherever "here" is—though I have my suspicions. I'd been dragged out of my bed in the middle of the night by the same men who used to work for me. My many security protocols for just such an incident had failed. I knew they would. Not even an army can protect you from *Fratres Criminis* if they're interested in you. And they had plenty reason to be interested in me.

I shook my handcuffs, rattling the chains connecting them to the bolted-down table between me and the gangster I had trusted too much. I remained focused on him, with his very harsh yet attractive features. Piercing black eyes. Black hair. My mental clock said he'd been sitting here with me for the past six hours, but it was difficult to discern for certain. In that time, I had been "persuaded" to sign all sorts of paperwork: real estate deals, financial statements, even a legal document to change my name. I'm now Peter Richardson. That was already what I went by. Just not my legal name. The reason behind that one was still unclear, yet it made one thing certain: they plan on letting me live. Penniless, but alive. And I have a habit of bouncing back. Give it six months, and I'll be back on top. Besides, I still had my secret bank account in Zurich.

He handed me one final document: my secret bank account in Zurich. I didn't show my surprise. I refused to give him the satisfaction. "You know the drill," he told me.

"Someday, Alexei," I said as I signed away the last of my wealth, "someday the meek will inherit the earth," he didn't respond. "So… do you come to southern Siberia often?" I asked. He gazed coolly.

"How do you know we're in Siberia?"

"Well, it was just a guess, but combine the length of the plane ride with arriving in a large city, then driving in a UAZ jeep several hours that caused the air to grow thinner and warmer, we could be in only so many remote areas. The bank transfer here shows my money is being funneled through Zurich to Moscow, while this symbol here is the insignia for the First Bank of St. Petersburg, so we're clearly in Russia. The guard standing directly behind me is wearing a parka, but not one that speaks of a heavy cold. He has been adjusted to this through a lifetime of it, and has distinctly Cossack features. We passed by a very large body of water on the way over here, but the air didn't taste like salt water. In fact, the air was cool and crisp, like in the mountains. That pinpoints us to Lake Baikal in southern Siberia, probably in some sort of underground bunker. That, and you just admitted as much." I sat back as far as my chains would allow, fairly satisfied with myself. Alexei looked unimpressed.

"What makes you think you're always the smartest in the room?" I smirked.

"No one has ever shown me otherwise." I had distracted him for long enough. The pen I had used to sign everything had done its job in picking the lock on my handcuffs. My hands free, I leaned back, my chair kept from falling by the chain at my ankles. My hands went over my head to the holstered pistol at the guard's side. I snatched it from him before he could react, ramming my head into his stomach. I fired the weapon at my chains, breaking them. I jumped up. The guard, bent over in pain, groaned. I slammed the butt of my gun into his head. He fell. I turned to Alexei, who stood with a gun of his own. He still showed no emotion. He didn't have to. I smiled widely, waving the pistol. "I have a gun now," I said. I waved it in the air, taunting him in case he hadn't noticed. Meanwhile, my hand was feeling for the door behind me. Grasping the knob, I flung it open, backing out. I waved the weapon in a "what are you going to do about me?" kind of way. Suddenly, it went off, blowing a hole in the roof. Alexei and I stared at each other a moment, unsure what to do. I slammed the door shut and started running.

Being a secret hideout in the middle of literal nowhere, I doubt they needed much security. Still, the lack of guards was surprising, coming from Alexei. As the new *Praetor* of the most powerful criminal alliance in history, he has a reputation to live up to. *My* reputation. I grimaced. I had been deposed only a few weeks ago. It was foolish of me to believe they'd just let me be. I wouldn't make that mistake again.

I shouldn't have run. I had nowhere to go. I had just signed away my estates, and had no way to get to them, anyway. Still, I had nothing to lose.

An alarm blared. I would have expected it about 10 seconds ago. Alexei must not have had his bearings yet. If he didn't ensure his control soon, his own Brutus may appear. I could hear yelling from deep within the bunker. Or maybe it was from the top. Sound bounded off the walls in all directions. Not that it mattered: what they said remained a mystery. I spoke five languages, but my Russian had always been a bit rusty. I stopped at an intersection. The door ahead read either "Exit" or "Freezer." I couldn't tell which. I decided to take my chances and shouldered the door. A wave of pain went through my body. I grit my teeth. The door was locked. My mind racing, I grabbed a nearby fire extinguisher off the wall and threw it against the doors. I backed away and fired the gun, covering my face as the fire extinguisher exploded. When the debris cleared, the doors were open. I ran through. As I took in my surroundings, I cursed. The sign had read "Freezer." I heard the pounding of boots behind me. I looked around. The only doors were the one I just opened and another open one leading to a meat locker. I hid behind a crate of vodka. The room was very dark; maybe they wouldn't see me.

In came three soldiers. At least, they might as well have been soldiers. Each carried an assault rifle, and looked like they intended to use them. I removed a bottle of vodka from the open crate and slid it across the floor. It went into the meat locker and crashed somewhere inside. The soldiers ran over. I sprinted across the room to the door and closed it. Since it was a meat locker, my pursuers couldn't get out from the inside. I had always wondered why: it wasn't like the meat would walk out. I made my way to the exit.

They began pounding on the door. Another walked through the crater of an entrance I created. No, this wasn't a soldier. It was Alexei himself. I pressed my gun to his temple. He froze. I grinned. Then, he did the last thing I would have expected. He smirked.

"Go ahead. Pull the trigger. I'll be dead, you can hide those papers, and you'll be back on top. Just twitch that finger." My smile faded. My hand shook. I hated this man, but I couldn't kill him. And he knew it. I aimed away and fired at the crate of alcohol instead. Thankfully, vodka doesn't fully freeze. It instantly caught fire. The flames began to spread immediately. I used the distraction to run. I didn't make it far before—as I glanced back—I hit something hard. I fell, my gun bounding away. I looked up at Johnny Black in all his biker glory. Alexei walked up behind me.

"Not so smart now, are you?" Johnny, always wearing sunglasses, removed them as he placed a pistol against my forehead. My heart thudded in my chest.

"Any last words?" Johnny rumbled. I licked my lips, my mind searching and scanning for a way out. I smiled, a hair away from death.

"Parlay?"

One
The Match

Peter. October 23rd, 2009.

"Los Angeles. Tourists flock here like pigeons to crumbs without a damn clue how poisoned it is. The gang bangers and celebrities alike think they run this town. They don't run a thing. The gangs answer to whoever controls their supply and the celebrities, with their fake noses and glamour, answer to the unions. Who controls that? The Families. The mob. My boss." I took a sip of wine.

"It's your move," my annoyed opponent casually mentioned, though his voice was so used to command that "casually" wasn't really in his vocabulary. I glanced at the board and moved my knight to E3.

"Checkmate," I said as I swiped his vice admiral hat off the table. I carelessly plopped it on my head with a grin as he gaped.

"You… my hat," he whined.

"Won't the Navy give you another?" I said.

"It's not about the uniform, it's the *hat*. My lucky hat."

"Don't bet something you're not willing to lose," I told him.

"Come on, Peter… what do you want for it?"

"Well, covering the bill would be nice." His face fell.

"But I had two beers… You got wine and a steak." A lumpy one, at that. I shouldn't have expected much more from a dive bar with its steaks between "Buffalo Chicken 'Wings'" and

"Jalapeño Poppers."

"And, let's not forget, your hat," he sighed as he pulled out his wallet. I checked my watch. "Right on schedule," I said as I stood and put on my Italian leather jacket. I walked toward the bar's exit and placed Matt's lucky hat on his head in passing. He shelled out a few bills despite his plethora of credit cards; he was too paranoid about being recognized with a known criminal. National security or something.

Despite his stout legs, Matt quickly caught up with my longer stride.

"Are we taking your Lexus?" I asked as we left the bar.

"The fight's only a block away. We'll walk," he said as he took the lead.

"You sure you can make it, old-timer?"

"I'm only sixty-five."

"Twice my age." I scoffed.

"And twice the muscle mass." I didn't bother responding that being 5'7 gave him certain muscular advantages that weren't naturally afforded to men, such as myself, who were 5'11. "So how much did you bring?" he asked.

"All of it." I responded. He cleared his throat.

"All of it?"

"All the cash I've saved up." Translated: not much.

"May I ask why?"

"Well, even if I somehow lose, it's on you," he flashed a smile.

"The point is to lose," he responded. I frowned as we entered a warehouse that functioned as a fighting arena and may have been a part-time club. Or a club that may have been a part-time fighting arena. Heavy metal pounded from unseen speakers—unseen because fog machines gave the whole building a hazy aesthetic that made it impossible to see from one wall to another. The perfect atmosphere in which to fix a fight.

"We're late," he said. "Fighting is about to start. Here, give me your wager. I'll place it against our loser, *Swamp Thing*, while you grab us some seats." *Swamp Thing*? I gave Matt my money. He took hold of it with my left hand, his right holding his own bet. It was a much smaller amount. Maybe he had fallen on hard times? I grimaced, glancing at his polished black shoes.

The crowd cheered as the next fight began. There was so much booze, sweat, and hormones in the air, I felt like I was back at my old penthouse in Fiji.

I took a side door to cut around and find some seats close to the ring. Instead, I ended up walking down a long corridor as the pulsing music from the arena gently throbbed. At the end was an open door with a black-clad man beside it. I studied him. He didn't move. I began to walk inside, but then he shot out his arm.

"Woah, Buddy. Only fighters past this point," he sized me up. "You don't look like a fighter." I looked past him to where men were applying makeup and accessories. I watched one guy, almost seven feet tall, have the back straps of a robot outfit applied by an assistant. An idea occurred to me.

"Look," I said, "you're gonna want to let me through. I'm a recruiter."

"Yeah, you and every other drunk slob."

"My boss won't be too happy if I can't see *Swamp Thing*…"

"Who's your boss?" he asked, uninterested.

"Johnny Black." Now I had his attention.

"Johnny Black, the gangster?"

"Well he's not a baseball player. He's looking for a new bodyguard. The old one… well, I'm sure you've heard about

Johnny's temper," he crossed his arms.

"How am I supposed to believe you work for Johnny Black?" he asked apprehensively.

"Because I'm not stupid enough to make something like that up." His fear for his job battled with his fear for his life.

"He goes on in a few." I nodded and brushed past him. All I wanted was meet the one making me money.

The man pointed out was bare-chested, showing his well-toned, well-muscled body. Early fifties was my guess, but it was hard to tell with the makeup. He sat on a stool in a corner, fist to chin. There was something off about him. Something dangerous. He wasn't too big relative to some of these monsters. Tan, grizzled, with black hair greying at the roots and a square jaw, and significantly less stage makeup than the rest of these clowns.

He didn't look up at my approach. I cleared my throat. Still nothing. I cleared my throat again, louder this time. He sighed, but glanced up. We stared at each other a moment. He grunted a greeting. I pursed my lips.

"*Swamp Thing?*"

"You the contact?" he rose. He was taller than I had thought, at about 6'3. I had a sharp intake of breath. With people like this, it was best to choose your words carefully. And to show no fear. They can smell fear.

"I'm a friend of your friend, yes. Peter. Peter Richardson." I extended my hand. He took it and crushed it with the firmness and grace of a log. He spoke in a deep, rumbling voice with an accent I couldn't quite place.

"Is that your real name?" he didn't let go of my hand. I continued shaking it. I had faced worse brutes than this one.

"Of course it's real," he increased the pressure to my hand. I bit the inside of my cheek,

4

"Son, don't lie to me. I don't like liars."

"It's real enough for you." I replied, my voice stronger than my hand felt. He let go with a grunt. I nursed my hurt hand behind my back.

"You better be worth all this," I said. He grinned, a glint in his eye.

"Oh, I am." I met his stare. His eyes were cold, devoid of both malice and kindness. Empty. Unsure of who (or what) I was facing, I nodded my good-bye. The supervisor gave me a curious glance on the way out. I kept walking, sparing only a glance back at the fighter. He was back to sitting on his stool, fist to chin. Staring right at me.

Matt was waiting for me outside the corridor.

"Eh, ya *goombah*, you were supposed to grab our seats."

"I met our 'contact.'" He started with surprise.

"I… you're uninjured, so I guess he likes you." I noticed I was still cradling my hand. I stopped. "Come on, let's get our seats."

We sat on the second row of folding chairs. Matt placed his admiral cap in his lap. I smiled inwardly to myself.

"Where's he from?" I asked as the next fight began.

"What's that?" Matt mumbled, all attention on the fight.

"*Swamp Thing*. Where's he from? He has an accent."

"N'Orleans," Matt said. I nodded to myself.

"N'Orleans, Louisiana?"

"No, Alaska," he replied absently. The fight ended as a *mook* was pummeled to the ground.

Swamp Thing and some other *mook* were called to the ring. Or the box, or square, or whatever they call it. It wasn't round, so it couldn't be a ring. A bell dinged and they circled each other a few times. *Swamp Thing*'s opponent was much bigger, maybe as much as half a foot taller. Suddenly, they rushed at one another.

I leaned forward in my seat. It wasn't some drunken barroom brawl. I knew a thing or two about fighting, and what they were doing was martial arts. A roundhouse kick was met with an elbow block. A "sweep the leg" by *Swamp Thing* ended with a returning palm-heel strike.

I was close enough to see our boy wasn't too happy. He gave a flying kick and hit his target's chest. The target, *Shark*, flew back. He jumped up and made a lunge at our fighter, who gave him a clean swipe to the nose. I could almost hear it break.

If this moron didn't lose, I was dead. He had to lose. But looking at him fight, I didn't think he would. He gave a few jabs at *Shark*'s stomach, who then doubled over as if to vomit. Instead, he wiped away some blood from his nose and swiped at our guy. Our meal ticket ducked and jumped up, kneeing him in the chin.

Shark put his arms in front of his face, disoriented. He attacked *Swamp Thing* like an animal, with rapid punches and kicks. Our boy fell almost automatically. He didn't get back up. The referee slapped the floor and it was over. I jumped up. Matt did the same, snatching his hat before it fell.

I vigorously shook his hand. "What's his name?" I asked suddenly.

"Whose?"

"*Swamp Thing*'s, ya *goombah*!"

"His name?" Matt looked at me, a strange apprehension clouding his features. "It's John. John Washicha."

Two
Peter Richardson

John. October 23rd, 2009.

I sipped my sweet iced tea. I had been part of the Company long enough that my beverage preference didn't garner strange looks; iced teas don't give off the tough-guy image supposed to be displayed by Pure Gore Fighters. I didn't care. Alcohol would drain my senses. For now, I needed those.

I did my best to ignore the revelry. *The Pub*, the only name given for the establishment, was a regular hangout for the Company after matches in the city. I didn't understand how they could bear the music if their heads pounded from the blows as hard as mine did

The front front door opened. Normally, a ringing bell would accompany it. I'm sure it still did, but I couldn't hear it.

In strolled Admiral Sanders and his friend who called himself Peter. I casually put my head back down, seemingly pining over my injuries, searching for an answer for it all in my iced tea. From what I could see, they were searching too. For me.

It was the pretty-boy in his smooth jacket who spotted me. We made brief eye contact. He didn't point. He didn't have to. Next thing I knew, he was bringing the Admiral over with him to my booth. The one that called himself Peter brushed past *Razor*, as usual dressed as a bottle of shaving cream. "Peter" halted and scowled before continuing onward, brushing off the possible germs on his shoulder. He was too proud for the way he dressed. No hood rat could walk into a room where everyone was a foot taller than him and act like he owned the place. Yet he managed it. He managed it all too well.

The kid slid into the booth, Admiral Sanders after him. I usually appreciated a good leather jacket, but the kid's had too nice of a cut, a leather too smooth to be good for anything other than fashion.

Admiral Sanders shook my hand. His friend seemed prepared to do the same, then thought better of it. I smiled inwardly. The Admiral threw down a small wad of cash. I didn't acknowledge it. He nudged his friend, who grudgingly fished in his pocket and pulled out a much larger wad, throwing it on top the other. I didn't look down at the money as I scooped it up and slid it into my own pocket, careful my teammates didn't see.

I grimaced. Losing a match for cash didn't weigh heavily on my conscience; cash was cash and I needed it to stay alive and searching. It wasn't my own wrongdoings that irritated me. It was seeing an officer in the United States Navy not only watch but participate in something illegal that got on my nerves. Especially one as seemingly-upstanding as the Admiral.

The goon next to Admiral Sanders made eye contact with me yet again. I glared at him. The Admiral cleared his throat.

"You two have fun. I'm going to get a drink," he excused himself. I frowned slightly.

I studied him—the gangster sitting across from me—with a feigned disinterest. He hadn't made a strong impression on me earlier: dark brown hair combed to the side. Dark brown eyes that didn't sparkle so much as shine in the light. Olive skin two shades lighter than my own tanned hide. Nothing to look twice at. I could see that some women might find him attractive in an almost-fragile way, yet it wasn't his lean build. And he *was* lean, verging on skinny.

"If you keep your face like that, it'll freeze," he smirked. I growled. He had an accent I hadn't fully picked up on earlier, a sort of Jersey-hood-meets-Hollywood-executive. He was entirely impassive. Unreadable. Then, to my surprise, he cracked a smile. I did the same.

"That was nice work you did back there. Could have won." I shrugged.

"Money wouldn't be the same, though."

"A man who has his priorities in order." I took a sip of tea and grimaced. Three packets of Splenda and it was still too weak.

"I have other priorities. I just can't find them," he chuckled. I didn't. He saw my expression and his mirth came to an abrupt halt. We sat in awkward silence for a few moments, his eyes traveling everywhere but near me.

"So…" he began, his fingers drumming on the table. "you skim points often?"

"This was a first. The Admiral asked a favor, and he's not a man I turn down."

"And, like you said, the money wouldn't be the same," he pointed out. I shifted uncomfortably.

"So how do you know the Admiral?"

"He was a friend of my father's," he said.

"A Navy-man?"

"Yeah," he scowled. "A good one, too." I cleared my throat.

"I was in the Army for a while. I know what it's like… having a family back home. Not a second goes by you aren't thinking of them. Wondering how they're doing. Wondering if they miss you as much as you miss them."

"So you're a family man?" I sipped my tea, unsure how to answer. For all I knew, my wife had remarried. My sons are grown and could be anywhere in the world.

"Yes," I replied, "I have a family. I just haven't seen them for twenty-three years," he gave me a strange look.

"Did she find out you gave another girl the same model Corvette? Because that will do it."

"No, nothing like that. When I was in the 'Berets-"

"What was that?"

"What?"

"Did you just say 'Berets? As in Green Berets?" I sighed.

"Yeah. If you stop interrupting, I'll give you the full story. As much as I can, anyway. Back in the '70s and '80s, I was in Special Forces." I paused, reflecting on the years I gave to a country that in return denied my existence and left me for dead. "To most, these operations never happened. To others, them never happening was wishful thinking. I know how it looks: I killed people I didn't know in places I didn't know for reasons I didn't know." I took a sip of tea. He stared and, after a beat, slowly nodded.

"'God created war so that Americans would learn geography.'" He sounded as if he were quoting something.

"Didn't you agree to not interrupt?"

"Actually, I didn't. You just told me not to. Besides, it wasn't interrupting."

"You could be a lawyer," he nodded, acknowledging the fact as if it were a badge of honor.

"Thanks. I am, as a matter of fact. Paperwork and everything."

"That wasn't a compliment. Was it an online college?"

"I'm pretty sure the degree says Berkeley. So you became a fighter...?"

"I tried a few different trades that suited my skills. Worked for a mercenary group awhile. A carpenter. Longshoreman. Construction worker. I run a gun store for my brother. But fighting ended up being the one that suits me best. I'm getting too old, I've been told." Peter shrugged. "It's true, I know." I sighed. "Fifty-four years old. Can you believe it?" Another shrug. Between the shrugging and the staring, I was getting a little impatient for him to start talking. "So what about you?" he stared at me.

"Waddya mean, what about me?" Suddenly, he was more Jersey hood than executive.

"What's your story?

"What are your kids' names?" he asked suddenly. I didn't push it. If the kid didn't want to talk, he didn't have to.

"Damion, Terry, Jesse James. And... the baby."

"They as ugly as you?" I scowled, but played along.

"Hopefully not. Though I haven't seen them in two decades."

"So pictures wouldn't help me get a better idea?"

"I have some of when they were kids. My mental image of how they are now probably isn't too accurate." Peter—I might as well accept that name—leaned in close and licked his lips conspiratorially.

"What if I found them for you?" I grimaced.

"Good luck. I've been searching for quite a while. Nothing."

"Ever heard of the Internet?"

"Rings a bell," I answered flatly. "I told you: two decades of searching. Not even worth you trying," he pressed his lips into a hard, flat line. I didn't know why he would help, anyway. That sort of service usually has a hook in it.

"I'm not the type you should underestimate," he said coldly. I took his word for it.

"I'm just saying I can handle this on my own."

"And I'm just saying that isn't working out too well, now is it?" I sucked in air through my teeth.

"What's in it for you?" he nodded, tongue in cheek

"The people I work for... they're not nice people. To anyone."

"I never would have guessed," I said, dry as paper.

"Look: I've been asked to do a small job for them. It's nothing big; just collect a debt off some *mook*." I blinked. That's a word I hadn't heard in years.

"Off some what?"

"Some *mook*. Ya know... in the Old Country, it would be *malook*, except no *mook* here is worth the extra syllable. It's like *goombah* only harsher."

"My mother called me a *goombah*."

"I'm sure she did." I tensed.

"What's that supposed to mean?" he shrugged.

"It can be affectionate. So look: I gotta take from this *mook*, except my expertise isn't in physicality, ya know what I mean?" he indicated his unimpressive physique. "My boss has been trying to get rid of me, but there's this understanding... well, let's leave it at that. So I was thinking, after seeing you fight, that maybe I could use a hand. You'd be compensated for your efforts. Not much, but you get out what you put in."

"So you're asking me to be a criminal?" I asked bluntly. He held up his hands, palms to the ceiling, like a balancing scale. Morality versus greed.

I didn't know a thing about this guy. He was clearly small-time. Loan shark? Gambler? Gangster? All of the above? His friend is a high-ranking naval officer and he dresses like he's from a Scorsese. Talks like Mario Puzo and Michael Bay are his golfing buddies.

It wouldn't hurt to shake someone down if it means a possible lead. Wouldn't be the first time, won't be the last.

"I'm in," I said confidently. He gave me a curious look, studying me. Sizing me up. He nodded to himself, satisfied with whatever he saw. "What are you thinking? Don't give me that beating around the bush, either. No politician's hot air." I said, wondering why he would need help picking up some money.

"That you're big enough for any trouble we may encounter," he answered simply. "I hope that wasn't too much hot air for you." I grinned.

"Just the right amount, actually," he flashed a grin back. His features slowly returned to normal, eyebrows knit together in thought. He had delicate, dark eyelashes, slightly curled. His nails, surely at least touched-up by a manicurist, drummed on the table.

"Matt here," he motioned to Admiral Sanders at the bar, drinking a beer. Several empty bottles were in front of him on the counter. "usually keeps good company. I hope that's the case with you."

"You're not going to ask if I'm a rat?" he eyed me.

"You're not a rat."

"How do you know?"

"A rat wouldn't draw attention to possibly being a rat."

"Well, how do I know *you're* not a rat?" he stared a moment, then shrugged and placed his hand over his heart.

"I solemnly swear that I am not a rat."

"Good enough for me. When are we doing this whole debt-collection thing?"

"Tomorrow. What's your number? I'll give you a call in the morning." I waited for him to pull out his phone. He stared, unmoving. "What?

13

"You just want me to tell it to you?"

"Yeah. I'd rather stay away from records for now. Expect that call to be from a payphone. You can pay me back tomorrow." I told him my number, to which he yawned in response. I stuck out my hand. Hesitantly, he took it. I grasped it lightly as we shook. I could feel his hands. Harder than expected, yet still soft.

With that, he went over to Admiral Sanders at the bar, who had ordered pancakes and appeared to be flirting with the Aunt Jemima syrup bottle. His efforts seemed unsuccessful.

Three
Owing Johnny

Peter. October 24th, 2009.

"They had gone missing back when I was still a captain," Matt said over the phone. I kept walking through the Los Angeles State Historic Park: an official-sounding name for an official-looking park. To be blunt: it tried too hard. The park was meant to be a reminder of the rugged landscape that surrounded the city, but it missed its mark. The brush was too evenly distributed, the trees too varied in height.

"Look: his wife never wanted him to leave for that mission in the first place. She would have wanted to get as far away from the military as possible. You were using the wrong people to try and find her."

"Peter…" he paused. "What about the kids?"

"Who knows? They would have followed their mom at the time, but they're all grown up now. John is a strong character. Run the names in your server. Not Army."

"Why not?"

"They would want to be like Daddy, not follow in his footsteps. So try the other branches."

"You got it, Boss. Listen, I really gotta go…"

"Sure, no problem. I have a few other leads to follow up on. Have a nice trip." I hung up as I approached John sitting on a rustic bench. He swung a pocket knife on a chain around his finger, wearing an unzipped black leather jacket with a white t-shirt and jeans. Neither of us spoke as we studied each other. Finally, I broke the silence.

"Sorry Danny," I greeted him, "but Sandy already left for the dance," he rolled his eyes.

"You're not paying me for my fashion sense. Couldn't you have chosen somewhere more discrete? Like your apartment?"

"We're not that far into the relationship, Bud. But if you keep up the good work you did today as my muscle, maybe sometime soon." I took a seat and pulled out a white envelope from within my own brown leather jacket, handing it to him as I looked at the landscape.

"This was a one-time thing. I was helping out a friend of the Admiral's. I'm done." From the corner of my eye, I saw him jolt in surprise as he peered within the envelope. "Is this a joke?" I sighed.

"I wish. My boss… well, he has the firepower to take as big of a cut as he wants."

"This isn't a tenth of what we took from that guy."

"I know."

"Who's your boss?" I pursed my lips. In the distance was the rumbling echo of motorbikes.

"Someone you don't need to know just yet."

"I have a right to know."

"You're acting like a rat," I said.

"Maybe I am," he shrugged.

"First off, if this was a racketeering or illegal gambling infiltration, you'd go after the high-ranking naval officer, not the street thug. Second, last night you gave me what I'm assuming are the highlights of your story. If you were a fed playing a part, you'd have given me your life's story down to your Social Security and mother's maiden name. Third: you

16

said you're not," he nodded slowly, taking it all in.

"I want to know who just stole from me," John replied.

"He didn't steal-" I realized the rumbling was growing louder. John and I turned and saw the hood of a white van about to make impact. John swung his arm around my shoulders and propelled us to the side as the van crashed into the bench we had been sitting on just moments before. Three motorcyclists trailing the van broke off, circling us as the van made a wide U-turn. John had out a revolver. I took out my own pistol, my head swiveling from rider to rider as they slowed down. John and I put our backs together; the van parked on the outskirts of the riders' circle. Two black men got out the front. The riders stopped and dismounted. We were surrounded, though none of them were armed. They didn't have to be.

"Peter," John murmured, "your side only has one guy. You take him out, and we can run for it." My hands shook.

"Yeah."

"So do it. Shoot him." The five began closing in. I took a confident step forward, gun raised, silently willing the biker to flee.

He didn't. "*Shoot him,*" John hissed. The biker strode toward me, grabbing my gun with one hand and punching me across the face with the other. I crumpled to the floor, turning in the grass to see the same biker throw his arms around John, who dropped his gun. John instantly grabbed hold of his assailant's arms and tossed the biker over his head onto the ground. The other four met him head on, forcing John to take up defense. I scrambled to my feet and joined the fray.

"What the Hell was that?" John asked as he blocked a sucker punch and delivered his own uppercut.

"We're in public. There are kids," I replied.

17

"What kids?!" John spared a glance at the park and was hit with a brass-knuckled fist. He went down. Two bikers grabbed my arms. A third kneed me in the stomach. Hard. I groaned. Wordlessly, they dragged me to the van. As one biker opened the back doors, another forced my hands behind my back and applied what felt like a zip-tie. I sighed.

They threw me in the back. My face to the floor, the distinctly metallic scent of blood hit my nostrils. We weren't the first passengers this van has seen.

A moment later, John, also zip-tied, was thrown next to me. The doors shut. Shortly thereafter, the van lurched forward. John glared at me.

"What?"

"You didn't shoot him."

"I told you: kids."

"There were no kids, Peter."

"Then why didn't I shoot him?" he opened his mouth to respond, then realized there was no point. We were trapped in the back of a van either way. We hit a major bump, causing us both to fly into the air. I grunted as we reunited with the floor.

"My pocket knife is in my front jacket pocket," John whispered. My eyes widened.

"You want to break out of here with the van moving?"

"You have a better idea?" I looked around, noticing that every few seconds, the passenger would look over his shoulder at us.

"Actually, yeah. Look ahead." John stared at the two seats ahead of us, separated by a black screen. "They'll see us trying to cut our way out before either of us are free."

"So what's your plan?" We hit another bump. As we flew into the air, I planted one leg beneath me, turning so my other foot could turn the back-door handle.

"This," I said as I opened the door wide and jumped out. Wind whistled around me as I hit the hard asphalt. I instantly rolled to the side, though no cars were coming. I grunted not from the pain, but from how this will affect my Florentine jacket. John had wriggled his way out a few dozen feet in front of me. I slowly got to my feet and ran over. He sat up. I bent over and began feeling around for his knife.

"Could you not squat so close to my face?" he asked. The van had screeched to a halt. The bikers were already coming our way. My fingers wrapped around his knife and opened it, going to work sawing off my own zip-tie first. Once free, I sliced through his with ease. The bikers were almost on us. I surveyed our surroundings.

We were on our way out of the city, but not on the highway yet. Meaning there was nowhere for us to run. I sighed. It was a valiant effort.

John, on the other hand, refused to give up. He began running from the bikes. I ran along side him.

"It's okay," I asserted, panting, "they're not going to kill us."

"You know these people?!" John asked as he snatched his knife back.

"They're associates. Business partners, of sorts." I felt a weight against my shoulder blades. I fell with a yelp. Looking up, I saw one of the bikers had a baseball bat outstretched. I didn't have to see it to know it was metal. I sucked in breath through my teeth. Another biker stopped beside me and picked me up. The van reappeared, and the process started all over again. John, struggling against two bikers, was brought back. Zip-ties were reapplied. This time, they pulled two coarse bags out of the van.

"We shoulda done this the first time," one of them muttered

as the bags went over our heads. We were shoved in the van. I heard the doors slam shut and the van rumbled to life. Minutes later, we stopped again. For a second, so did my heart. I knew exactly where we were. We waited to get pulled out. We weren't.

"What's going on?" John asked, his voice muffled.

"Someone's coming out to meet us."

"Why?" I swallowed.

"I don't know." The van's back doors opened. A moment later, they shut again. I could feel there was more than just the two of us now. My bag was ripped off. I stared at a man wearing a silk shirt as dark as his skin, unbuttoned three buttons too low, in addition to an eyepatch that I knew to be for show.

"Hello, Marcus."

"Peter," Marcus rumbled, "so glad of you to join us."

"I didn't really have much choice." Another thug stood behind John. Marcus nodded, and the thug removed John's bag. Marcus grinned, staring right at me with his one visible eye.

"Now," Marcus said, taking out a gun and putting it to John's temple, "let's chat." John stared at me, unmoved by the metal against his skull. I blinked.

"Is that a nail gun?" I asked. I instantly regretted asking. Marcus's grin widened.

"Sure is. You know Johnny: never pays for more than he has to. My .357 costs 35 cents a bullet. Fifty pounds of nails is seventy bucks."

"But you had to buy the nail gun."

"Trust me," Marcus said, finally looking at John, "this baby has paid for itself many times over." John stiffened.

"Son," John said, "think about what you're doing."

"I know what I'm doing," Marcus replied. "I'm offing a rat." His finger tightened around the trigger.

"Marcus!" I yelled. "He's not a rat!" Marcus lowered the nail gun.

"How do you know?"

"What, you think I can't tell these sorts of things?"

"No," Marcus responded, the nail gun going back to John's temple, "I don't."

"Marcus, stop! I swear on my life he's not a rat!"

"Your life?" Marcus asked, the gun never wavering. "What's that to me?" I licked my lips.

"We both know you've wanted to get rid of me for years, and we both know why you can't. John being a rat would overrule parlay."

"You're putting your life on the line for this deadbeat?" I made eye contact with John, who stared back defiantly. I sighed.

"Yeah, yeah I am." Marcus put his makeshift weapon beneath his belt. I breathed a sigh of relief.

"I want my gun back," John said. The biker behind him grabbed his hair and forced his neck back. Marcus wordlessly hit John across the face with his nail gun.

"You live above a gun store, don't you? Get another one. Besides, we did you the favor of bringing your chopper. We would have done the same for Peter, but..." but I didn't own a car.

"What's this about, Marcus?" I asked, tense.

"First, it's about your little side job rigging fights and not giving Johnny his cut."

"I was going to-" I felt a hand grab my hair. I hadn't realized there was someone behind me. As I processed this, Marcus swung. I yelled in agony, feeling my jaw trying to dislocate from my skull.

"You're going to give us the whole cut for the last match, and next time we're taking seventy percent. That's what you get for stealing." I could have argued that they, in fact, were stealing from me, but I doubted it would be worth the pain.

"There's not going to be a next time," John said.

"Oh, yes there is. We hear you're good, Washicha. Johnny's interested in what you can do."

"Johnny Black?" John asked. Marcus gave me a wry smile.

"You didn't even tell him who he's working for? Classic Piet-"

"What's the second thing?" I interjected. Marcus barked a laugh.

"We'll let him tell you himself." I inhaled sharply as I was hauled to my feet. I barely felt my zip-tie being cut. I just stared as Marcus and his goons left the van, leaving us a path to follow as we went to see Johnny Black.

Four
Johnny Black

John. October 24th, 2009.

Johnny Black's fights had reached my ears before. It had never been major news, just that about once a week someone would make him angry and end up in the hospital. Or the morgue. I had known plenty of people like him back in the Special Forces. Well, not "known" so much as "assigned to." Thought they owned the world. I showed them all how things really work. All except one.

"Look: when we go in there… just let me do the talking." I shrugged. "I mean it, John." I sighed, but nodded. What could I say, anyway? Peter briskly walked in the same direction Marcus had gone, raking his hair with his fingers in the process, and then combing it to the side with the same fingers.

I followed close behind him, examining my surroundings. Johnny Black was supposed to be one of the biggest crime bosses in the state. I found that hard to believe when I saw what he surrounded himself with: a biker bar that was more a worn tenement out on the highway on the outskirts of the city, AKA in the middle of nowhere. It fit into an alcove in a hill facing a rundown part of the beach. Neon signs advertising popular beer brands lit up the windows. Not fitting the scene were about three dozen bikes, sleek and new, parked in a single line against the building.

We entered. As soon as Peter closed the door behind us, I

blinked. The lighting was so dim I could barely see more than the bare outlines of people. Which wasn't difficult, considering the place was filled with them. The lighting probably didn't bother any of the patrons. It seemed like all of them wore dark sunglasses and embroidered leather jackets not nearly as smooth as Peter's. Every table and booth was brimming with bikers. My kind of place, except these bikers weren't the type to include outsiders. Most weren't, but these in particular. They gave off the wrong kind of biker vibe.

The only light came from a flickering bulb above a pool table in the middle of the room. Behind it to the right was a long bar extending to the wall. Next to the bar on the left was a stairway with walls on either side.

We walked over to the bartender. I felt eyes in the room follow us. Marcus was nowhere in sight.

"Mr. Black should be out in a few," the bartender said in a distinctly Haitian dialect, "have a seat." We each took a stool: two of the only chairs unoccupied. The feel of the place—the violence brewing below the surface, the stale beer, the roadhouse grease that permeated the wooden floor—was faintly reminiscent of Bourbon Street at three a.m. It was hardly noon.

The bartender looked down to his right and moved aside. As if out of thin air, a large man rose from below the bar. He must have been coming up from a basement. As opposed to the black leather of the rest, the newcomer wore an executive's suit and tie, though still wore the trademark sunglasses. His hands and sleeves were wet. A metallic scent hit my nostrils. Blood. They were wet with blood. The bartender handed him a white towel. He grasped it. Within seconds of wiping his hands, the towel was drenched in dark red. He handed it back to the bartender, who took it and knelt behind the bar as if this

24

were regular operating procedure.

I studied him, the most wanted man in the city, as he removed his suit jacket. An inch or two taller than me, he was only slightly above average height relative to his companions. He wasn't lean. Big wasn't the word. Just muscular. He had no hair other than long black sideburns reaching down to his square chin, a detail hard to notice against his skin, along with a white scar crisscrossing his right ear. I could feel his glare beneath his sunglasses.

He flung his suit at the bartender and flashed a smile at us. His pearly whites shone in the dimness of the bar.

"Guy thought he could leave the Outfit," he answered the unasked question, "so I helped him go," he licked his thin lips as a low chuckle sounded in his throat. The man who I assumed was Johnny Black removed his sunglasses, showing eyes that were the color of coal, without the warmth.

I extended my hand. "John Washicha," he grasped my hand firmly. He met me with an iron grip, which I returned with my strongest. If my grip surprised him, he didn't show it. "Johnny-"

"Mr. Black," he cut me off. With the look he gave me, I wouldn't be surprised if we got into one of his famous brawls. I wouldn't have minded. I let go.

"Mr. Black," he flashed what could have been a smile. I knew it wasn't.

"All right then. I wanted you to give me one simple answer, Richardson: can you vouch for Washicha here?" Peter hesitated. "Well, Richardson?"

"With my life."

"Okay then. Richardson, Washicha: nice job with the pickup. No problems?" Peter swallowed.

"No. No problems."

"It's always nice to hear you didn't screw things up for once, Peter." I gritted my teeth as he turned back to talk to the bartender. We stayed put. Finally, Johnny turned back around to face us.

"Can I help you with something?" he asked Peter. He didn't seem inclined to actually help.

"Just waiting on that job you promised would come." Johnny sighed.

"You want a job?" Peter curtly nodded, all business.

"He doesn't just want one," I added, "he deserves one." Black snarled at me, but seemed to take my words into consideration.

"Fine. You can have a job. One with a nicer payout than playing IRS."

"What's the op?" I asked, interested. I received twin glares from Black and Peter. I wanted my time's worth of money. That meant more of it.

"Well, Rambo, I have a business associate with whom relations have been… strenuous. He wants to muscle me out of his operations due to… differences in management style. Break into his mansion out in Bel-Air Crest, 1454 Cobham." Peter's eyes shot up. "Problem?" Peter slowly shook his head. "Let him know we can get to him: ransack his study and steal what you can to make it look like a regular B and E, like he's no better than anyone else in this town. You can keep half of the stolen goods' worth through my seller. I'm choosing you guys because I know you can be discreet. So be discreet." More like he was choosing us to be stool pigeons in case things went wrong. "There won't be much security: this is only one of his houses, and Halloween night he's gonna be out the country. Think you can handle all that?" I was prepared to nod. Peter was more hesitant.

"What do you mean 'not much security?'" Black shook his head like it was obvious.

"I mean no one guards the place. His private security travels with him. The mansion has cameras, a security alarm, and a locked door. Some of the more valuable stuff may be in a safe." Peter bit his lip, but nodded. I nodded more enthusiastically, reassuring both of them that we could get the job done.

"Will I need a piece?" I asked. For some reason, that made Johnny bark a laugh.

"Adese, soldier. It's breaking and entering, not Vietnam." I blinked a few times to clear the images that came to mind. I licked my lips.

"Don't you tell me about Vietnam." I whispered hoarsely. He took a step toward me. Our faces were inches apart.

"Can you handle it, or not?"

"Of course we can," Peter replied. I tried shaking hands with Johnny. He stared at it like it was a venomous snake. Slowly my arm went back to its side. I guess he shook it the first time to show off his strength. I clenched and unclenched my fists. Peter grabbed me by the shoulder and marched me out of there.

"Why do you let him do that?" I asked as we headed toward my Harley.

"Do what?"

"Let him scam you like that."

"Not much choice. Besides, he hadn't even been expecting me to come back from that job. The money still isn't bad, either. Johnny surprisingly knows what he's doing: he pays well, but not too well. Leaves you wanting more, and you know he has more. Lots more. That's part of the reason why he's-" Peter froze. I glanced at him.

"Why he's what?" Peter seemed unsure how to answer.

"Why… he's the leader of the biggest syndicate in the state. Most firepower. Admittedly, it doesn't have the brains or loyalty of most of the others. But firepower works for Johnny." I nodded slowly. He was rambling.

When we got to the bike, I noticed a long, thin scratch. I sighed as I put on my old Vietnam helmet, and offered Peter the my spare. He took it and hopped on. Neither of us spoke as I took off. Motorcycles make me feel so free.

"Looks like I'll be seeing where you live after all," I said. The entire ride, he only spoke to give directions.

When we stopped at Peter's apartment, he jumped off so fast I didn't have time to ask what him and Johnny's story was. Once he was off and walking inside the building with the promise of getting in touch soon, I rode off back to my own place above my brother's gun shop.

When I opened the glass door, a bell went off. I took in the smell of fresh sawdust. Saying hi to Vince, who was sweeping the floor, I strode upstairs.

At the top of the stairs, I opened a door with a Jimi Hendrix poster plastered across it. I walked over to the couch in the center of the room and plopped down, admiring my old M16 in the corner. I put my feet on the wooden table in front of me, narrowly avoiding the many gun parts, ammo, and crumbs strewn across it.

I picked up the apartment's only photograph off the end table next to the couch. When Katy left, she took everything. All I had to remember my friends and family by were the faded photos in my wallet, and this picture of the five of us — Castle, Walker, Carl, Dustin, and I — from Mardi Gras thirty years ago that Dustin had left behind.

I already felt exhausted. I headed to my bedroom, the bed

covered with gun parts I would need to put back together if I planned on sleeping there again soon. The closet door hung open. I pushed aside the sparsely-hung clothing and picked up the outfit on the end. I carefully hung it on the closet door as I undressed. I put on the outfit, donning my green beret last. I turned to the mirror against the bedroom door.

I saluted an officer of the United States Army.

Five

Clockwork

Peter. October 28th, 2009.

"I told you," Matt said over the phone, "it'll be like clockwork. He's meeting you there, right?"

"Again: I'll call him to make sure."

"Just be sure we catch him by surprise."

"We will. Don't worry." I hung up.

I walked over to the toaster and placed the checklist inside, next to my life savings. I didn't use banks. Not anymore. I know who runs them.

My phone rang. I flipped it open. I didn't use a landline; they were too easy to trace if anything were to happen.

"Yeah?"

"Pete, it's me." Pete?

"John. I was about to call you." No answer. "John?"

"Sorry, I was… you still want to head over to *The Pub*?" I grinned. If only he knew what I had planned.

"Sure. What time?"

"Now." I blinked. I checked my watch. Almost three.

"I'll be right there."

"Good," he hung up. I sighed and put my phone away as I went out the door, making sure to lock the door behind me. Too many thieves in this neighborhood to not be careful. I walked out the building and hailed a cab.

The cabbie pulled into *The Pub*. I paid the fare and got out.

30

He immediately sped off in search of other customers. Unsurprisingly, the parking lot was almost empty. Except for a lone bike.

As I entered, I noticed a rustic ringing that I missed last week amid all the… celebrating. John was in the same corner booth as last time, drinking what appeared to be another iced tea, strangely enough. He seemed like the drinking type. We made eye contact.

John Washicha. A soldier let loose in the concrete jungle of Los Angeles. Who I vouched for with my life.

I shivered. I had been in my fair share of fights, scraps, knife fights, and shootouts. It was part of the job. Yet there was something about John's methodical approach to battle, something about his pragmatic pragmatism of wanting to shoot bikers in broad daylight that made my blood run cold. In the Old Neighborhood, there were shootings, but you do it when you're alone, behind closed doors. I approached slowly.

"John."

"Pete, have a seat." I did. "Do you have a time?"

"I'll pick you up at six on Halloween night."

"You cased the joint?"

"It's a gated community, hard to monitor well. Johnny was wrong about the guards: there are two not part of the private security force, one at the community gatehouse and one patrolling the grounds. There's also a gardener who comes at least every third day, and a maid who shows up at noon.

"As near as I could tell, there were cameras at all entrances and exits into the main building. The alarm system was coded yet slightly outdated."

"Materials?"

"Everything from ski-masks to sticky notes. I have it under control; we're slightly under-funded, but we'll make do.

Johnny's lending us a van, at least."

"Speaking of Johnny… you two have history?" I rubbed the back of my neck.

"We used to be friends."

"I'm going to need more than that."

"Is this why you invited me down here early?"

"That's not an answer." I grinned. He was good. But conversations are like chess: you have to think a dozen steps ahead.

"He used to work for me." John gazed coolly.

"The tables have turned." I shook my head.

"Further than you would think," he didn't ask what I meant by that and I didn't tell him. "Why do you dye your hair?"

"The next time I see my family… I know they won't look how I remember them. But I want them to see me as if a day hadn't gone by. As if I never left." I nodded understandingly, even though I didn't understand. He cleared his throat. "Did you find out whose house we're knocking over?"

"No. At least, not the real name. It's registered to a Russian corporation. One that doesn't exist. I triple-checked." Quintuple-checked, actually.

"Typical Russia."

"It's not all bad."

"You've been?" he seemed to be recalculating me, reappraising my value. If only he knew the truth.

"On business."

"I can't say much for their food." My eyes widened in surprise.

"You must've tried the wrong stuff."

"I suppose 'Boar in a Can' is wrong, then?"

"Very wrong," he cracked a smile. The waitress, slim with straight, light red hair that cascaded down her shoulders,

32

hurried to the table. I flashed her a smile. She showed some teeth. "It won't help," I told her.

"I'm sorry?"

"Rushing out of here to study for that exam tomorrow. Cramming the night before won't do you much good. Besides, we both know you already know the material. But not studying isn't what put you at the top of your class," her light eyebrows creased with worry.

"Are you psychic or a stalker?"

"Observant. You hurried to take my order when the only other customer is sitting across from me: you want us out of here so we don't hold up your shift. Your jeans are fashionable yet very creased at the knees; you've had this job since high school, when you lived in the neighborhood, and didn't want to give it up to go to college, so you commute. Your eyes scream that you are usually full of life but have spent too long reading large books with tiny print in the library. You walk with confidence but not arrogance. So you're a working-class girl paying her way through either law or medical school. You're too warm to have seen lots of bodies, so that puts you as a law student at UCLA."

"USC Gould," she began walking away.

"Clare," I said. She whipped around.

"Okay, how did you know my name?"

"You have a nametag. And I'd like a water, please," she pursed her lips as she nodded and walked off. John leaned in.

"Really?" he hissed. "You could not have made that more obvious." I blinked.

"Make what more obvious?"

"You're into her, but you're either creeping her out or annoying her." I narrowed my eyes.

"I was messing with her," I assured him. He scoffed.

"Keep telling yourself that. Look, here she comes." My head snapped toward the direction of the kitchen. No one was there. I glared.

"That wasn't funny," he chuckled.

"Really? 'Cause I'm laughing," he took a sip of iced tea.

"And I didn't creep her out. I intrigued her."

"Intrigued me?" Clare said as she set my water down on the table. I inhaled sharply. "You'll have to try harder than that to intrigue me."

"How about you being especially close to your mom, which is why you stayed in LA?"

"Lots of girls are close to their moms."

"But not all girls receive offers from schools all over the country and choose to stay close to home. I'm not into living in this city, either."

"What *are* you in to?"

"Plenty. Law. The unequal distribution of wealth between New England aristocracy and the working class. Chess."

"Oh," she walked away, eyes downcast. My shin felt a light pain.

"Ow! What was that for?"

"First, because you're acting like a teenager," John said, "and second, because if you're going to act like a teenager, at least be cool about it. You had her. Then you shut her down, just like that," he snapped for emphasis.

"Relax. I know what I'm doing. She'll think over what I said and try harder to engage me in conversation."

"You've done this before?" he seemed doubtful.

"Plenty of times."

"If it doesn't work, you pay for drinks."

"You're on," he stuck out his hand. I gingerly shook it. His tanned, callused hand went easy on my slightly less tan, smoother one. "Why do married men always think they're experts on women? Most of the time, they're out of the game for good."

"Maybe because they've won that game."

"You won?"

"I did," he nodded gravely.

"So where's your prize?" he gave me a flat stare. I winced. "Too far?"

"Way too far." Clare returned carrying a metal pitcher beading with condensation. She began to fill John's almost-full glass, keeping her eyes on her work. I remained still. Something about her made me slightly off-balance. I wasn't sure what it was, but I liked it.

"So," she began as she finished. I perked up. "You said one of your interests is law?" I cleared my throat.

"Yes, that's right. Peter Richardson, attorney-at-law." I stuck out my hand. She awkwardly shook it with her free hand.

"Another semester and hopefully I'll be in the same boat.

"What field?"

"Criminal defense, though I'm thinking of changing it."

"My advice: don't. This city is the perfect place for it," she smirked and walked away. I shot John a look. "Ready to pay for my water?" John shook his head with a grin.

"Nice job, but that wasn't the deal. We only agreed that if you lost, you'd pay. Nothing was said about if you won." I stared at him, dumbstruck. I reconstructed the conversation in my head. Unbelievably, he was right. "So tell me: what color are her eyes?"

"Light brown, like almonds. Why?"

"Just the fact that you noticed speaks volumes."

"Of course I noticed," I said indignantly. "Did you not?"

"I can honestly say I paid absolutely no attention to her eye color," he gloated. I glared.

"Is there a problem?"

"Not at all. Just wondering how, with all these time-consuming criminal activities of yours, you managed to go to law school."

"I had a friend speed along the process. It's more about the degree than the actual education, anyway."

"So you don't know law?"

"I know plenty. Just you wait and see. Someday your veteran self will land in jail for gunning down bikers, and you'll need me to get you out," he snorted. The front bell tinkled. I twisted in the booth. I made a sound in my throat. He was late.

His head swiveled on beefy shoulders, scouting the place out. His eyes rested on us. Dark eyes; soft. They were the only part of him I'd describe as soft, though. He wore a muscle shirt and jeans, so that I could see the muscles ripple in his abdomen, in-shape as only someone in their late twenties can be, with square shoulders that hardly moved as he walked briskly toward us. A military walk. His skin was not quite to John's darkness, perhaps a shade lighter than my own. His hair was close-cropped, to the point where although it was probably a light brown, the lack of it made it look dirty blonde.

John looked up, studying this man. The newcomer did the same, the angular features of his face unmoving as his eyes lazily moved about. Not wanting to be a part of what was about to happen, I slid out the booth with my water in hand and moved to a nearby stool at the bar.

"Do I know you?" John asked the apparent stranger.

"I... yeah."

"Care to tell me who you are, then?" I glanced over. The

younger soldier studied the older one, unsure what to say. I didn't blame him.

"It's me, Dad. Terry. Your son."

Six
Meet the Family

John. October 28th, 2009.

My son. Standing before me was my own flesh and blood. It had been twenty-three years, but now, staring at this hardened man where had once stood an innocent boy, I could see that this was indeed my son.

Terrance Washicha. He stared at me with those startlingly gentle eyes. No man who had been in active duty should have eyes like that, and he clearly had been. He sat across from me.

"What'll it be?" Our waitress asked as she walked to the table, less rushed than before.

"What're you having?" he asked me.

"Iced tea."

"I'll have the same."

"Unsweet okay?" she asked. He sighed.

"Yes," she left.

"A few packets of Splenda works wonders." I assured him.

"I don't remember the last time I've had one of those."

"I don't remember you having hair that short," he blinked.

"Things are different, now." I winced.

"They don't have to be," I told him, my eyes pleading for us to go back to that house in New Orleans and forget about the last twenty-odd years.

"Yes, they do, Dad. You had been dead. If I hadn't gotten that call-"

"What call?"

"Yesterday I got a call asking who my father is. I was getting ready to tell the caller off… but then he asked if I wanted to see you again. He told me to be here at this time. I figured something was up, so I brought JJ with me. He's out front."

"Who…" I stopped myself, turning in my booth to face Peter at the bar. He was flirting with that waitress, who had an iced tea on a tray. He caught my stare and broke into a smile, wiggling his fingers at me. Clare brought over Terry's drink. I gaped at Peter. He returned to flirting once she went back to him. As if reuniting me with my family was no big deal. I cleared my throat as I turned back to Terry. "So Jesse James is out front?"

"Sure is."

I slowed my breathing. "Think you can bring him in?" Terry nodded and got up, crossing the room in only a few steps. He was only an inch or so shorter than me. He opened the front door and stuck his head out. A few seconds later, he opened the door wide to reveal a slightly taller man, though gangly. Together, they had a powerful image. The two walked shoulder-to-shoulder back to the booth. Terry slid in first. The other remained standing, staring at me.

He was slim, with darker skin than his brother and black hair in the same military cut, and… his mother's eyes. A pair of shining emeralds. He also had on jeans, yet in his case they were accompanied by a t-shirt with a picture of a clock and the words "Father of Tim" on the front. I broke into a smile.

"Who's Tim?" I asked. JJ looked down at his shirt, as if contemplating where it came from, and then looked back at me with blank eyes.

"Father," he whispered. I nodded. He walked over and

patted me on the shoulder before taking his seat next to Terry. My eyes followed him. Where Terry had the strength of a lion, JJ moved with the deadly grace of a panther. "You are a good man," he spoke with a strong, low tenor. Soothing, in a New Orleans jazz kind of way. I nodded at his compliment. He beamed.

"Don't think we haven't missed you," Terry began, "this is just a lot to take in. We haven't seen you in so long... Mom doesn't even know."

"Has she..." I made a sound low in my throat.

"Remarried?" Terry asked. I nodded. "No. She was crushed, Dad. Really crushed. She had told you not to go. We all did." His eyes held no accusations. Only remembrance, and the hurt that went along with it. I most likely held that same look. He leaned forward, a yearning in his eyes. "You can imagine how much we missed you," he said, soft-spoken, "Damion and I did our best to step up and take care of the others, especially Violet."

"Violet..." I tried the name out on my lips. My little girl.

"She's something, Dad. Right now she's at UCSB, but when she hears..."

"That's a nice school," I commented. I didn't have to say the unspoken word: expensive. Terry shifted in his seat.

"We got a check a few years back, no name, only a Russian bank. Five figures. We all thought it came from you, but Mom didn't want us getting our hopes up..," he left the question hanging. I shook my head. Vince received checks every month from Russia, but they didn't come from me. "JJ and I were in the Navy SEALS awhile, in Iraq and Afghanistan, but now Damion is the one keeping us afloat. We're still looking for work. Doesn't seem there is any to be had."

"I may be able to help with that." Vince worked so hard.

40

The least I could do is lighten his load. "So Damion is doing well?" Terry froze. JJ whimpered beside him.

"Damion..." Terry sighed. "You mean Damion Occhipinti?" I blinked.

"He took his mother's name?" Terry swallowed.

"Yeah. As soon as he turned eighteen. He, uh, has his own place saved from his ATF days, so that's good. Last year he became a public defender." That sounded like Damion. To Damion, everything was black and white, good or evil, legal or illegal, right or wrong. Seems some things never change. "He's also a Prius-driver." I sucked in my breath through my teeth. That was a blow. Still, he is my son, no matter his last name. "Kind of reminds me of that guy in the too-smooth leather jacket at the bar over there. Like anyone who doesn't work in an office is beneath them. The kind that scoff at guys like us but need us to fight their wars," he jerked his head at Peter. I grinned.

"He's the one who called you here." Terry's eyes widened. I shook my head. How could I introduce someone like that? "What about my wife? How's Katy?"

"She's an older Violet. Or, I guess, Violet is a younger her," he reached into his pocket, taking out a leather Indian wallet similar to my own. He removed a fairly-recent photograph and held it in front of me. I gently took hold of it between my thumb and forefinger.

Terry was right: there was quite a resemblance between mother and daughter. Both had striking green eyes and dark black hair that went perfectly with their olive skin, though Violet was lighter than Katy. I analyzed every detail I could in the photograph; this was the same Katy I had envisioned in my mind for the past two decades. I held out the picture. He shook his head.

41

"Keep it." I smiled, stashing it away in my wallet with the rest of my pictures.

"May I see her?" I asked, training my gaze on my son.

"You're asking me for permission? She's your wife."

"My wife I haven't seen in a long time. You have."

"Well then yes, yes you may. My bike's out front. JJ rode with me, so I figure you can give him your keys and he'll drive yours back while you come with me."

"Why can't I just ride my own bike?"

"Because I haven't had alone time with my father since I was eight."

"Fair enough." I rose, taking out my wallet and removing a generous number of bills. I placed them on the table and headed over to Peter as I set my wallet back in my pocket. I stood behind him. He swiveled on his chair to face me, annoyance plain on his face as his waitress-friend left.

"May I help you?" he asked.

"I think you already did," he broke into a grin.

"Hey, that's what friends do, right? Favors? You got me my first meaningful job in… I don't even remember." I nodded my appreciation and turned to join my sons heading out the door. So Peter and I were friends.

We headed out the front door into the parking lot. Next to my bike, a black 1990 Harley Fatboy, was a bright blue 1996 Harley Dyna Super Glide. I tossed JJ the keys. He caught the ring between his teeth.

"She looks nice." I motioned to his bike.

"Modified," Terry said, "I replaced the old handle bars with a Sportster's, made a couple of adjustments to the engine, changed out the exhaust pipes."

"Impressive." Terry hopped on his Dyna.

"I'm your son. Let's go." I picked up the spare helmet and

traded with JJ, who had begun to analyze mine with a neurosurgeon's intense concentration. Once I strapped it on, Terry took off.

"JJ hasn't gotten any better, has he?!" I asked over the sound of the roaring wind. Terry shook his head. I had suspected as much: Jesse James always had been different. I loved him to death. His mental state just set him apart.

"Who was that friend of yours?!" Terry yelled back.

"Who, Peter?! At the bar?!"

"Yeah! It was easy to tell he was a crook! Lawyer?! Banker?! Hitman?!" I chuckled. He could feel my body vibrating. "What's so funny?!" I decided to keep my theory about Peter to myself for the time being.

"He's a lawyer!"

"Thought so! He and Damion would get along well!"

"I doubt it!"

"Waddya mean?!"

"It's hard to put two people together that both think they're the smartest in the room!" Terry laughed.

A mere fifteen minutes from departing *The Pub*, we arrived at a two-story craftsman-style home with a porch out front and a small lawn split in half by a brick walkway. On the right was a path of cement leading to a pair of wide garage doors.

Terry parked on the expanse of cement. JJ followed suit. We dismounted and walked across the recently-mowed lawn. A cat streaked across the sidewalk. JJ crouched, barking at it.

"I thought he stopped thinking we was a dog when he was four?" I asked Terry.

"He reverts back to it when he's nervous or excited. Or hungry." I gave a curt nod as we bounded up the porch steps. JJ appeared beside us once more. Terry let us in. "Mom's upstairs. Kitchen is on your right. Wait there; we'll surprise her." I barely heard him. I made my way in a daze to the kitchen. Everywhere were photographs of the kids: Little League, ROTC, high school graduations. Together, alone, usually with Katy.

I stopped in front of one. Damion's first grade spelling bee. I remembered that day. Damion had gotten second place because he spelled ladder with double t's. He was so upset with himself, so I bought him an ice cream. There he was with the ice cream... but not me. In fact, I wasn't in any of these.

I reached the kitchen. It was quaint, with a wooden table against one wall. I sat at it, facing a window that gave a good view of the lawn out front. I relaxed. It had taken twenty-three years, but I was finally home.

I felt the cold metal of a shotgun muzzle against the nape of my neck. I froze. There were only three people that could sneak up on me with a gun. One of them was my brother. The second was dead. That only left...

"Katy," I said affectionately, never mind the gun.

"You have to the count of five to either tell me who you are or get out of my house. Otherwise, I have the right to shoot you. And I will," her voice was deeper than most women, throaty like a saxophone. I glanced at the clock on the wall. Through the glass reflection, I could perfectly see my wife in a dirty checkered shirt and faded jeans. A tom-boy supermodel.

"One... Two... Three..."

"Last time someone counted up for my death, I had spent two months as the ringmaster in a traveling Cambodian circus only to find out the lion tamer was a Hanoi weapons dealer. Problem was, he found out I found out."

"Four..." her voice wavered.

"That was as far as he got, too. Unfortunately for him, my brother had to strangle him with his own whip. I'm hoping

44

the same doesn't happen here. That would be a horrible twist, for after all this time I only get to see you dead."

"Turn around."

"I can't. Chair and all," she put one hand on my shoulder and jerked me so that the chair scraped the floor. I faced my wife. She stared, shotgun lowered.

"I could have shot you."

"But you didn't."

"I… it's hard to shoot someone you thought died who-knows-where," her eyes held a defiant stance, verging on anger.

"I'm sorry about that."

"Is that it?"

"Not even close," she set her shotgun on the table. That was a good start. She pulled up a chair across from me. I glanced at her hands and smiled. "You're still wearing your ring."

"So are you. Just because you died doesn't mean my love did, too."

"Twenty-three years." I slowly shook my head.

"John… I… this is just so much to take in. I mean, look at you: you're alive."

"I'm back now and I ain't leaving. No more jungles, deserts, or any other Hell-hole. I'm here to stay." I got up and crossed the table. She welcomed my embrace, squeezing back. She smelled like paint and cinnamon.

"All you need is your first leather jacket and this is high school again," she whispered.

"Except that jacket smelled like cigarette smoke, gasoline, and cheeseburgers," she gently pushed away and looked at me. I felt the air shift as a hand moved toward my face. I instinctively grabbed her wrist. I winced as if the slap were successful. "Sorry. Reflexes," she pulled away.

"Twenty-three years..." she fumed.

"The mission failed. There was a cover-up. I couldn't get home."

"I told you not to go, John. We *begged* you to stay."

"I did what I had to do, just like before then and after."

"Would you do it again?"

"Not if it meant losing you." The doorbell rang. Katy stood and wiped away the forming tears.

"I'll be right back," she said. I took hold of her wrist.

"I don't want to leave your side."

"It's okay. I have a feeling I know who it is." The doorbell rang again. I regrettably let go of my lovely wife as she went to the front door. I heard it open a moment later.

"It's good to see you too," I heard her say, "come on in. There's someone I want you to see." A moment later, Katy entered the kitchen with a younger man. I gaped. He stopped in his tracks and stared with his light blue, pale eyes. I took in his sandy blonde hair. The hair he inherited from his grandmother.

Damion wordlessly turned around and walked away.

Seven
The Job

Peter. October 31st, 2009.

I stopped pacing in front of the van Johnny lent us and checked myself out in the side mirror. Black was the signature color tonight: black wind pants, black t-shirt, black jacket with black duct tape over the logo, grey (Wal-Mart was out of black) utility belt, and a black ski-mask stuffed in my back pocket, since it would be frowned upon to wear it as I drove in a black van. Society.

In all actuality, navy blends in best with the night, but seeing as how we're supposed to look like Johnny's muscle, we need to look like amateurs.

I entered the van, cutting myself off from the cold, crisp Los Angeles air. I turned the key in the ignition. As the van sputtered to life, I switched on the heater. Nothing happened. I sighed as I took off.

Most traffic was off the street for Halloween, so the address John gave was a mere thirty-minute drive.

He was waiting out front, hands clasped behind his back. I noticed, with annoyance, he was wearing a green beret and paint under his eyes like a football player. As long as he had a ski mask, it didn't matter.

I began slowing down. Before I stopped, he ran forward. In one swift motion, he opened the front door and swung himself inside before shutting it back. I drove onward. He grinned when he saw my utility belt.

"So, Batman, how's Robin?" My lips formed a straight line. As I drove, my fingertips tapped the steering wheel. He looked at me cross-eyed. "What? Catwoman got your tongue?" he chuckled. I pursed my lips. I was suddenly glad I had gone with the utility belt and not the fanny pack.

"What is that?" I asked, referring to a bulge at his shirt's waist.

"What, this?" he patted the bulge. "It's my piece. .44 Magnum. Can't leave home without it." I made a sound low in my throat. One of frustration.

"No guns. Guns lead to shooting, and shooting leads to killing. No guns means no shooting, no shooting means no killing."

"You seem tense."

"Tense? You could say that. I'm working on a job I barely have any info on, with people I haven't seen in action who don't know the game plan. This isn't extortion. This is a job. And you're cracking jokes. Tense. Yes, I'm tense."

"Don't worry: after this, you won't have to worry about working with amateurs again." I inhaled sharply.

"What?"

"After this job, I'm done. So are my sons. They're only involved so we don't have to hire more muscle. Keep it in the family, so to speak."

"Didn't you hear Johnny? He wants you to fight again."

"Peter: I'm happy. I have my family, the thing I've been searching for… for over a third of my life. I want nothing more. I got roped into that last fight because I respect Admiral Sanders, and I'm here with you now as a thank-you for reuniting me with my family."

"Oh, so we're even now, is that it?"

"Not even close. I owe you my life, Peter."

"So one more fight. I throw down all the cash I'm making off this job, you lose, and we call it quits." I watched him chew on his lip from the corner of my eye.

"One more rigged fight. There's no risk of me losing my family over it, so I guess I can help you out this once more."

For the next few minutes, he only spoke to give directions. I was fine with the silence, but he seemed uncomfortable for some reason. I needed my associates comfortable.

"So you're not living with your family?"

"No," he answered sharply.

"Oh."

"Yeah."

"Taking things slow?"

"Yeah."

"Met your daughter yet?"

"No, she has midterms."

"Oh. UCSB, right?"

"Yeah."

"Good school."

"Yeah."

"I'm more of a Berkeley man."

"You don't seem like a college guy." Finally, a complete sentence.

"What does a college guy seem like?" he shrugged. I cleared my throat. "That server the other day was cute, huh?" Another noncommittal shrug. "Cute," I repeated.

"I'm married, Peter."

"So you can't admit another woman is attractive?" Not even a shrug. "So in twenty-three years you never…?"

"Never. I was always a married man."

"And now that you're back together…?"

49

"Still no."

"Oh. Taking things real slow, then."

"The house on the left there. Park across from it."

"Why?"

"So Katy won't see us parked out front." I hit the brakes, sending us both lurching forward.

"Are you serious? You're having your first 'bring your sons to work day' for a B and E, and don't want their *goombah* mom to find out?" he stared at me, his eyes stone.

"Don't call her that."

"It can be a term of endearment," I answered quietly, treading carefully.

"Oh, so you're endear to my wife, now?"

"That's not what I-"

"Ssshh! Keep your voice down. Katy hears *everything*. Just don't call her that." I slowed my breathing as I parked across from the Washicha house. I regretted allowing John to bring those two. I had only agreed because they seemed willing to obey orders. That, and John agreed their pay would come out of his cut.

I watched as two silhouettes crossed the street. They had been waiting for us. One had the quiet determination of a man prepared to go to war with reason. The other, with a duffel bag strapped to his shoulder, bore a grace and insanity that insinuated he just wanted to go to war.

One of them sped up, still carrying himself with a grace that can't be taught, and went to the other side of the van. Each opened the door on their respective side. Once they buckled up, I took off. I glanced in the rearview mirror.

"You brought what I asked?" I asked JJ. He panted in response.

"That's a yes," John assured me. I grunted.

"The owner," I began, "has an advanced security camera system, twelve on the grounds, but no active monitoring. The images are rerouted to some sort of remote device, most likely the owner's private computer. He'll know someone was there. We'll just have to make sure he doesn't find out who.

"Then there's an alarm system at all doors and windows that, if not deactivated within thirty seconds, sends a distress signal to local PD and emits the usual sound. You know the one. That'll send the guard on the grounds straight to us. The guard is a rent-a-cop, albeit an armed one. Another guard is at a gatehouse to the neighborhood."

"So we make sure that doesn't go off," John said. "How do we get in?"

"The maid, straight from Tijuana, works today."

"And?"

"And you'll see." We reached Bel-Air Crest. Our vehicle clearly did not belong amongst the glitz and glamour. Parked to the left sidewalk was a sports car, to the right an SUV. I drove our humble piece of junk up to the gatehouse that could end the operation early if we didn't play our cards right. I rolled down our window. The gatekeeper eyed us suspiciously. I sighed in relief. He was new.

"Hi there," I said. The guard remained silent. I cleared my throat. "My sister-in-law is cleaning at 1454 Cobham. These are her nephews and brother. She needs to pick up her kids for trick-or-treating, but her car won't start." I motioned to the others. The night watchman beamed his flashlight on John, who squinted.

"You're the maid's brother?" I held my breath as John opened his mouth to speak. So far, all I had seen him do was throw a knife. I had no idea how he handled himself under pressure, especially when it came to the world of acting.

51

"*Si.*" John responded. The night guard waited for him to go on. "*La caro de mi hermana no esta functionando. Ella esun dolor, peroyo la amo.*" The guard stared blankly. It took effort to keep my jaw from dropping.

"Is that so? Anything else?"

"*Hay una sandia en mis pantalones.*"

"You got it, Buddy." The gate swung inward. "Good luck."

"*Gracias, pendejo.*" I drove into the gated community. As the wide expanse of black iron shut behind us and I rolled up the window, I turned to John.

"You speak Spanish?"

"Bits and pieces since I started needing it to order a burger. I also know some Russian and Lakota. You?"

"Five, including Spanish. Enough to know that you said something about a watermelon in your pants."

"Like I said: bits and pieces," he didn't seem fazed by how lucky we were that the guard didn't speak Spanish. Still: he didn't. So far, so good.

"Listen: whenever I cased the place, it was with binoculars. I haven't been up-close. Be prepared for anything…" I trailed off. "What's in the duffel bag?" I asked JJ. He unzipped it without a word, bending over and rummaging around. He sprang up a moment later, wearing a hideous animal mask. I hit the brakes and turned to face him.

"What the Hell is this?!"

"Look," John answered, "he's really been wanting to be a werewolf for Halloween. And this is my first Halloween with my son in a long time. So just let him wear the mask?" I sighed, rubbing my temples. John had warned me that this son in particular wasn't like other people. As if on cue, Jesse James howled for emphasis.

"Fine. Just tone down the… wolfishness. No howling. We

can't alert the guard. We don't want to hurt him. He pages one of his bosses every half hour with a status update. We don't want anyone rushing back or calling for someone to check it out."

"So what do we do with him?" John asked.

"We avoid him. If it comes down to it, we'll neutralize—I repeat: *neutralize*, not kill—him. We can steal his pager. We just can't take the pager with us, in case it can be tracked. If we're spotted, at some point in the night his bosses will know something is up."

"And we don't want them sending someone to check on him," John concluded. I nodded absently, my eyes scanning the street. I didn't have to check the address.

"We're here."

We gazed through a gate at a sprawling estate. It held a much more ominous feel to it than its neighbors. There was no single detail I could put my on finger that made it so. The grass was immaculately kept. The hedges leading up to the main entrance were properly trimmed. The house itself was ultra-contemporary, three stories, the top two stretching over the first at seemingly-random angles, with wall-to-ceiling windows at odd intervals. It was meant to almost be an eye-sore, not a spooky mansion. Yet the latter persisted.

A stone wall, approximately nine feet tall, wrapped around the property. It was meant for decoration, not defense or security. Two gates were near either end of the wall facing the street. At the end of one of the brick driveways was a worn-down Chevrolet. The maid's.

I parked half a block away from the house, on the opposite side of the street. The van had no particular purpose other than it was transportation and bulletproof. At least, that's what Johnny claimed. Hopefully we wouldn't be forced to find out.

No words needed to be spoken as Terry, John, and I slipped on our ski masks. John, before putting his on, silently removed his green beret and placed it on the dashboard. I reached over and pulled down the glove box, revealing four Nerf dart pistols. I handed one to each of them, sticking the fourth and final in my belt.

"Scissors?" I asked, my eyes trained on the mansion. The front door opened, revealing the maid. I heard the soft rustling of JJ sorting through the duffel bag. On the armrest between John and I, he placed everything from shears to nose hair clippers in order by size. I picked up a pair of surgical forceps and held them to the moonlight. The tip shone with a delicate sharpness. I set it in my utility belt as we all watched the maid walk down to her car.

"When you search for valuables, retrace your steps once you take out a camera, then head the other way. We don't want them to know how many of us there are. Gum?" I stuck out my hand. Through the glove, I felt the wet stickiness. I gasped and shook my hand, sending the pink candy on John, who hastily swiped it off. I grunted in annoyance, turning in my seat to glare at Jesse James. Terry looked apologetic. *Wrapped* gum." This time, JJ handed me a stick still in its wrapper, as requested. I unwrapped it, sticking the covering in my pocket and the gum in my mouth. I popped a quick bubble. "Maid's on the move. Time to go." I opened my door, not waiting on the others. I didn't have to. All three opened and closed together, as quietly as possible for van doors.

I briskly trotted across the street. The neighborhood was devoid of any children in costumes. One house down the street was having some sort of party. Other than that, the night was ours. With the others right on my tail, I blended into the shadows of the wall. We crept along, reaching the gate where the maid was leaving. A keypad was on the side of it. If we had the funds, I'd have a router and heat sensor so I could see the numbers used in the combination and have the possibilities simultaneously entered, the correct one ruling out the incorrect ones. Instead, I had a piece of gum.

The gate slid open. The four of us crouched down on the sidewalk as the Chevrolet purred away. As expected, the gate began to close too quickly for the four of us to pass through. It was not, however, fast enough. I spit out my gum into my glove and slammed it against the magnet that would seal the door shut, covering the entire metallic area.

As the maid took off down the street, the door bounced harmlessly against the wall, bounding back open. We hurried through and made our way up the drive while lights inside the house would turn off and the ones next to them would turn on as the eco-minded guard exited and entered rooms. Currently, he was on the west wing of the first floor in the dining room.

JJ and Terry fired their Nerf guns at various cameras against the wall. The Styrofoam darts whistled through the air, hitting their marks. Once we arrived at the front door, I reached in my largest compartment of my belt and pulled out a pair of walkie-talkies. I handed one to Terry and one to John. I'd need my own hands to be free.

I glanced at the front door's lock. It hadn't changed from a standard five-pin tumbler. Twenty seconds for an experienced thief. I latched open a different compartment in my belt and removed a bobby pin and a screwdriver. I jammed the screwdriver in the hole and aligned the bobby pin. I just had to mimic the key mimicking the pins. I felt more than heard the first pin give way. I used the bobby pin to keep it in place as I inched my screwdriver along.

Fifteen seconds later, there was an audible click. Though in this scenario, with my gloved hands slightly sweaty, it felt like much longer. I set my tools back in my belt as John opened the door. The others followed us in. Terry softly shut the door behind us. I motioned for them to head right

"East Wing," I whispered, "master bedroom is all the way down that hall to the left." JJ unzipped the duffel bag and handed me a toy monkey with cymbals, with cotton taped over the mini instruments. The brothers departed for the East Wing as John stayed behind and breathed down my neck.

I shrugged him off as I went to work on the alarm system. I removed the covering, revealing various wires and conduits. Surgical forceps in hand, I cut a green wire on one end meant to send signals throughout the device. All I had to do was send that signal somewhere else.

I clasped the monkey, my thumb removing the battery cover. It fell noiselessly to the ground. I put away the scissors, taking back out the aluminum gum wrapper. I gripped the wire, peeling away the plastic layer at the top with my fingernail. I then placed the wrapper over the exposed metal, squeezing it against the negative battery on the monkey. I flipped the monkey on. A few seconds later, it began its noiseless tune.

I set the monkey on top the alarm and we continued onward. Immediately to our left was a spiral glass staircase. We treaded up carefully in the dimness, the only light coming from the moon gleaming in through the glass windows. An eerie glow was cast over everything, giving the house an even more ethereal feel to it.

We continued climbing until we reached the third floor. We crept along silently to the end of a hallway.

We reached the end of the hallway. "Here's the study," I nudged open the door. Inside was a room as ornately gaudy as the rest of the building, much more so than a year ago, yet still with walls of glass facing the outside world. Statues and paintings were situated at odd intervals. One of the paintings was still a Degas. Hopefully the others would find similar art worth taking.

"How do you know this place so well?" John asked as I handed him the camera.

"I used to own it." John's head shot up. I heard a noise from outside. The rumbling of an engine. I hurried to the window and spotted a car entering the unbroken gate. A black sedan.

I sucked in my breath. The owner must have been back early. Unless this was some sort of ploy and Johnny set us up.

My eyes darted about. John's hand flew to his walkie-talkie.

"Boys, the mission has been compromised. Someone is coming in. Get out," he didn't wait for a reply before shoving it back in his pocket. "Here," John whispered. His voice boomed throughout the quiet house. He motioned to an air vent directly above the study's desk. He climbed on top the desk and ripped the metal grate off the ceiling, dropping it as he hoisted himself up. I heard exclaiming voices down below as our tricks were discovered. I picked up the grate, climbing on the desk after John. I raised an arm. He grabbed it, pulling me up. I set the grate back in place just as we heard footsteps approaching.

I covered my mouth so I wouldn't gasp. In came the last two people on Earth I had expected to see. I could feel John tense beside me.

"Do you know them?" I whispered. He nodded gravely, his eyes polished stone.

"One of them killed my best friend."

Eight
Back in the Jungle

John. October 31st, 2009.

The vent was hot and cramped, but that wasn't why I broke out in a cold sweat. Alexei Pomerov was enough reason for anyone to get sudden chills. The sight of him brought back memories. Memories of failure and desperation. And loss.

Pomerov hadn't changed in the last twenty years. If anything, he looked younger. More refreshed. At 6'5 and an impressive build, he was still an imposing figure. His eyes, a dark brown that in this lighting looked black, were piercing everything they gazed upon. His hair I recalled having streaks of grey. Now it was pure black with a matching goatee.

I slowly pulled out my revolver, gripping it tightly. The inscription dully gleamed. *De Oppresso Liber*. No statement better justified what I was about to do. I aimed between the grate. Straight at the murderer.

Peter's hand shot out and grabbed my wrist. He stuck a finger to his lips. I grimaced. My hand shook as Peter and I made eye contact. I relented.

"It was Johnny, Lee." Pomerov said.

"That may be, but you have no way to prove it."

"I do if they're still here." Pomerov sat at his desk, directly below us.

"Why would Black break into your home?" The man called Lee asked.

"Our relationship has been... strenuous. There's not enough evidence; this isn't like Richardson." My head shot up. Peter pointedly kept his gaze on the conversation. "You know as well as I do how much the Organization loves to argue."

"Indeed. Of course, you have my full support."

"Of course." Pomerov paused and sized up Lee. "And I know just how you can prove it."

"Are you referring to Joe's little problem?"

"That will resolve itself."

"You wouldn't consider him a threat?"

"Him? No. He may not be as loyal as some," Pomerov eyed Lee with a hint of suspicion, "but his reach goes only as far as his contacts."

"I see. And Black? He is loyal, despite this... strain?"

"As loyal as they come, for a rabid dog."

"At least he is not *The Panther*."

"A close second. I have an agent who will set tensions ablaze. As far as Johnny knows, I don't come in until tomorrow."

"Dad?!" Suddenly, Terry's voice exploded over John's walkie-talkie. "Dad, we're out. Where are you?!" Pomerov and Lee's heads shot up. Pomerov smiled, a stretching of thin lips in an upward direction. It held all the warmth of the tundra.

Both reached in their suits. I didn't plan on sticking around to find out what they were taking out. I began scrambling through the vent with Peter right on my heels. With each movement, a *thunk* resounded. They knew right where we were. We were sitting ducks.

In desperation we crawled side by side. A gunshot rang out. There was a *ping* as the bullet punctured the vent a foot behind us. Peter sucked in his breath. I gritted my teeth. This man had already taken too much from me. First my best friend, then my brother, and then, for the longest time, my family. I would *not* be next.

We made it to the next grate in a dark room. I elbowed it, causing a slight dent. I did so again. And again. The grating clattered to the ground. However, we did not exit. Peter understood what was going on as I climbed over the square hole. We now had given them a red herring to follow. Meanwhile, we would find another way out. One they couldn't hear.

We continued along the vent. From behind us came the sound of more gunshots, most likely from when they entered whatever room the grate had fallen into. We slowed down, not wanting to be heard. If we were lucky, they would think we had gone to that room and were either hiding or running.

We made it to the next opening. Glancing down, I saw it was filled with moonlight cast through a floor-to-ceiling window. I threw out an arm in the small space provided, signaling for Peter to stop. He did. I then grabbed the grate on either side and began to gently shake it loose. Eventually, it came undone and I slid it along the vent.

I went through the opening head-first. Once my waist was out, I cat-arched myself so that my hands could touch my feet and hung on to the vent, letting my feet fall out. I safely dropped to the ground, then reached up and pulled down Peter by his wrists.

My mind raced, but I didn't have time to ponder any of this. Right now, my focus was on what I do best: surviving.

Once we were both safely down, I had a look around. We were in a sort of ultra-contemporary lounge. A white couch was stretched out across from a giant flat-screen above an electric fireplace. Shouting came from outside. The private security team.

My head swiveled from side to side. Peter stood, mumbling to himself, his eyes darting about. I grabbed him by his shoulders and shook him none-too-gently. We made eye contact.

"Pete…" I uttered. "Look, you act like you're some kind of big-shot intellectual. Now is the time to prove it. My kids are outside. It would be too cruel of a fate to lose them when I'm less than a football field away. It's up to you and that brain of yours as to what happens next," he nodded, still slightly dazed. He was at least as spooked as I was.

Peter visually changed. His eyes hardened. His jaw set. I had seen men like that long ago who did the same before they went into battle.

"Option one: we try to take them out and die trying. Even if we don't, we'll be hunted until you, me, and everyone we know are worse than dead."

"That's not an option."

"And so we move on to option two." His eyes flickered to the couch as the shouting got louder. They were getting closer. "That couch. How high can you hold it?" I realized I was still grabbing his shoulders. I let my arms drop to my side as I examined the couch in question.

"If you could take one side at first, I'd be able to lift it above my head. Why?"

"We're going to need it," he gave no further explanation and I didn't ask for one. I took the back of the sofa, standing behind its midpoint, as he lifted the end facing the door. I gave a soft grunt as he let go.

"Now what?"

"Throw it out the window." I almost dropped it.

"What?"

"You heard me," he began fiddling behind the plasma screen.

"But there's no way to open them."

"Exactly." Now I understood. Peter was playing a risky game. I looked to the window. With a sharp intake of breath, I took a few steps forward, my muscles tensing. Without further ado, I hurled the couch at the glass. It shattered. For a brief moment, there was silence from outside. A few more shards came loose, leaving only a gaping crater. I heard the crash of the couch below, then the pounding of footsteps. I glanced at Peter, taking out my gun. I wasn't going to jump three stories. If I was going down, it would be fighting.

Suddenly Peter reeled back, giant TV in his hands. He took a few uneven steps in my direction, barely able to keep his balance. I took it in my arms as he pulled its wires from the wall and ran to the door. I stood exposed with a large flat screen in my arms as shouts came from the hallway.

"Pete..."

"Throw it out!" he yelled, no longer caring if we were heard. I tossed it. It followed the same path as the couch, still attached to the cables, which Peter had tied to the doorknob. That's when it all clicked.

Peter ran toward the window. Right before jumping, he firmly gripped the cable connected to the TV, which I saw was dangling several feet from the ground. He used it as a sort of grappling device, sliding to the ground. His feet smashed into the TV, which fell and broke on impact. I was right on his heels. With the rush of adrenaline I had, I barely noticed the rope burn I got through my gloves.

I heard a bang as they kicked open the door to the room we had just left. There were shouts of confusion, then, moments later, gunfire. As we ran, I risked a look back. It was difficult to make out anything except one point that caught my attention, one that almost made me stop cold in my tracks: a lone figure standing outside the front door, silently smoking a cigarette. He flicked it to the ground and stomped it out. No matter the distance, I still felt those cold, dark eyes. Watching me.

We burst through the broken gate and sprinted to the van. Our breath was coming in spurts like pistons. Terry was already in the driver's seat. The back opened and we hopped in next to JJ. We were barely seated before ours tires screeched and we were lurched back. JJ shut the doors as we sat there, panting. JJ joined us in our labored breathing, looking like he was enjoying himself.

We reached the gatehouse and were let through without any trouble. Once we were safely away from Bel-Air, I spared a glance at Peter.

"What about Johnny?" Peter, his face an unusual shade of red, stared at me.

"What about him?"

"Won't he be upset we were almost caught?" Peter gave me a level look. It was the kind of look that said there was something he knew that I didn't, and was judging whether he could tell me.

"This was a setup. To a degree, at least." I met his look impassively.

"Terry, remember that bar you met me at the other day?"

"*The Pub?*"

"Yeah. Head over there. I need a drink." I hadn't had a whiskey since the end of 2001, but after tonight, I needed one. I looked at Peter. "It will be easier for some explaining to be done."

"You got it, Dad." I watched as Peter sighed, laying his

head against the side of the van and shutting his eyes. I caught JJ staring at me. He held out a fist. I lightly bumped it. He shook his head. Understanding, I gave him my hand. He placed something in it, curling up my fingers with his other hand. I opened up my fingers. In the palm of my hand was a diamond ring. A very *large* diamond ring. He mouthed a single word to me. I gave a curt nod of comprehension. JJ's sharp eyes then glazed over and his tongue lolled like a dog's. Peter's eyes shot open without warning. His head snapped to the driver.

"What did you take?" he asked apprehensively.

"Some sort of Japanese sword. A small painting. A pretty big dia-" JJ began barking madly. Peter, startled, lost his balance and hit his head on the window. His gaze rested on my son. His eyes spoke volumes.

"He's my son," I reminded him.

"Which is the only reason I haven't already put a bullet in him. Or ten."

"Ten?" I scoffed. "You've never killed anyone in your life!" I exclaimed. He gaped at me. I inhaled sharply. I'd had my suspicions, but that was his business. I couldn't take it back now. Peter comically looked like he had gotten slapped.

"I... what did you just say?" I sighed.

"Peter, we both know you have never murdered someone. You wouldn't shoot the biker. You collect payments instead of performing hits. You dress too clean to want guts on your clothes."

"At least I'm no psycho. I don't go around like some sort of sociopath and murder whoever gets in my way."

"Fifty-four." I said. I slowly closed my eyes.

"What?"

"Fifty-four. I have fifty-four confirmed kills. You think I don't remember those men? Because I do. I remember all of them." I opened my eyes. He was looking at me, as if for the first time.

Terry pulled into the parking lot of *The Pub*. We all got out. I silently stuck the diamond ring in my pocket. Peter and I led my sons inside.

We headed over to my regular booth in the corner, where we could see everyone going in and out. It was one of the few spaces not occupied by creeps in costumes, though the same could be said when Pure Gore Fighting is here. Peter sat on the opposite side of me, Terry next to him. JJ took his seat beside me. After a few moments, Peter's lady-friend appeared. She smiled, mainly at Peter.

"A bottle of Jack Daniels and four shot glasses, please." I told her. These weren't the desired circumstances, but my sons would finally drink with their father. As she left, Peter drew her back.

"Actually, make it three shots. What wines do you have?"

"Well, we-"

"On second thought," he glanced at me, "it doesn't matter. I'll take some red wine and two glasses," she nodded and left. He and I stared at one another.

"I don't need whiskey to start talking," I told him.

"Neither do I."

"You first. You said Johnny screwed us over?"

"Yeah. Which of the two did you recognize?"

"The one with the goatee," he nodded.

"Alexei Pomerov." I perked up. He glanced at the boys. "You don't want me saying this in front of them."

"What I can hear, so can my sons."

"Maybe you don't care if you end up dead in a ditch, but I doubt the same goes for them." I hesitated, ultimately nodding to the bar. They sullenly left. Peter watched them take a seat. He cleared his throat. "A year ago, I led the most powerful criminal syndicate in the world." I let my emotions remain neutral.

Somehow, the news wasn't too surprising. *"Fratres Criminis.* Brothers of Crime, in English, though that hasn't been PC since-"

"Alexei Pomerov," I said. He cleared his throat.

"I was *Praetor* before being double-crossed by Alexei and Johnny, and I made more deals than Johnny Cochran just to stay alive. They said if I ever told anyone, I'd get a not-so-swift death. Now here I am," he looked at me as if he expected me to roar with laughter, maybe call him a liar.

"Alexei Pomerov," I said again. He narrowed his eyes. "He's young?"

"Younger than you. Johnny and Alexei had been thick as, well, thick as thieves. Clearly that's changed. Johnny wanted to leave a message, and was taunting me with stealing from my own home for kicks."

"At least he was honest when he thought Pomerov wouldn't be back until tomorrow." I motioned for my sons to come back. They cautiously sat at the booth.

Clare came back with the drinks. She did the math with the wine glasses as she poured and gave Peter a confused look. He handed her a glass. She half-smiled.

"I'm working," he slid his tongue along his teeth.

"Then quit," she shook her head, took the glass, and toasted him. I rolled my eyes.

"I'm off in half an hour."

"I'll wait," she flashed him a smile.

"See you then," she whispered. He nodded and took a long drink as she walked away. I filled up the shots. Peter licked his lips, tasting the rotten grapes.

"My final assignment," I began, "was to kidnap an Alexei Pomerov. My best friend, Carl Lowry, didn't even have time to yell in pain or prayer before Pomerov gunned him down." I held up my shot, making eye contact with Peter. "To Carl."

66

Nine
Grounds for War

Peter. November 1ˢᵗ, 2009.

"Talked?" John asked, incredulous.

"Yeah, you know. I took her to this nice place and we… talked." I answered, craning my neck to get a better look at *Valentina's* lounge across the street.

"You were talking a long time." I picked up my wine off the bar counter and took a sip.

"Clare's a conversationalist, what can I say?" A black Sedan pulled up to *Valentina's*. The valets, lounging against the wall a moment ago, now formed a human barrier so the car's occupant could enter the lounge without fear of assassination. I peered through the bar window.

"Is that him?" John asked.

"Nah, that's a *Capo*."

"A captain." John translated for his own benefit.

"You're catching on."

"Sure. It's like the Roman legions."

"*Exactly* like the Roman legions." I confirmed as I brought the wine back to my lips.

"Hey Pete, I have a question about your whole Dungeons and Dragons basement club." I swished the wine around.

"You mean *Fratres Criminis?*"

"That's the one." I sighed.

"Go ahead."

"Well, all of them are top-of-the-line criminal masterminds, right? I mean, that's how they became members?"

"That's right."

"Then how did a punk like Johnny Black get in?" I paused and took a look around.

"I'm not comfortable talking about this here, John."

"I'm not comfortable around old women who try to buy me a drink. Tough."

"The original spot for my successor-"

"Your successor?"

"Yeah, Johnny took my spot as a North American member." I drank some more wine to quench the bitter taste that had formed. "Originally, we chose a *Cartel* boss, Luis Cortez, but Alexei insisted on Johnny."

"And now Johnny is under Pomerov's thumb."

"Yet Johnny had us break into his house." I looked over my shoulder. Satisfied no one was eavesdropping, I finished my glass. John tapped my arm.

"What about him?" I glanced out the window. A convoy of identical black Sedans had pulled up. The valets desperately tried to figure out how to protect everyone. Before they found a solution, all Sedan doors simultaneously opened and a crowd formed, rushing inward.

"Yeah. That would be Don Luigi Beppo." If someone wanted to take out the heads of two crime families, tonight would be an opportune time. The Beppo Family bosses were meeting with top Black Outfit officers to discuss a ceasefire over their recent skirmishes, and sordid businessman Mickey Carbone was kind enough to lend *Valentina's* as a neutral meeting ground. Neither side wanted war; war leads to a depletion of resources and less business. So long as no one tried a surprise attack, everything would be fine.

68

"Well," John downed the rest of his iced tea, "it's about time for my match. Meet at *The Pub* after?"

"See you then. My money's on the other guy." John clasped my shoulder and left. Johnny had not been particularly disappointed we were almost caught—he was likely more worried we had seen Alexei's face, which, I assured him, we hadn't. All the cash from the job is going toward John's match tonight. I watched John exit the bar and shiver as the Los Angeles autumn wind hit him full blast. I chuckled. Louisianan. I turned back as the bartender refilled my glass.

The bar was filled with members of both sides, mostly mid-level guys not important enough to attend but not low enough to act as bodyguards. All wanted to be closer to the action, but not to each other. The air was tense as Outfit and Family members cautiously mingled with one another as various sports games played on flat screen TVs throughout the room. I kept to myself; I wasn't welcome on either side.

I sipped my wine for the next few minutes as I watched *Valentina's*. I had purposefully sat at the second right-most stool to prevent anyone from sitting by me: two or more people wouldn't be able to sit on my right, and John had previously ensured no one would sit on my left. No such protection existed anymore, as witnessed when a stranger sat on my right and ordered a whiskey. I sighed. He glared at me.

"Problem?" he asked in a faint Irish accent. I swished around the wine.

"Yeah, you're blocking my view, ya mick." His square jaw jutted out.

"Easy, lad. No one's at war here. For now." I studied him out the corner of my eye. He looked oddly familiar. His grey buzz cut made him look older than he probably was, but he must have been nearing 60. Yet if he was an officer, he would have been across the street.

"Look old man: I just want some time alone," I said. He scoffed.

"You're at a bar. That's not how it works." I finished my second glass. The bartender came to refill it. I waved him away.

"What's it like?" I asked.

"What's what like?"

"Working for Luigi," he stared at me.

"You assume too much." I squinted. I would remember someone with as unsettling a scar as he had—one that ran down his cheek from below his eye to his chin.

"You're telling me you work for Johnny Black?"

"I'm telling you that you assume too much. But it does look like we have the same employer," he took a sip of whiskey.

"You have a name?" I asked.

"Yeah. I do," he stood, finished his whiskey, and slapped a few bills on the table. As he walked away, his phone slipped out his pocket onto the floor. I knelt down and picked it up.

"Hey, you dropped your-" I stopped short as I saw what I held. He hurried over and swiped it. We made eye contact.

"Thanks," he muttered as he left. I stood there, paralyzed, as he walked out the door and took a right. My eyes followed him until he was out of sight.

I slowly sat back at the bar and mulled it all over. The nearest TV said it was almost eight. I still had plenty of time until I needed to be at *The Pub*. I suddenly felt the cool metal of a gun against the nape of my neck. I froze. He must have been back to ensure I didn't say anything.

"Move and you're dead," a voice growled in my ear. A different voice. A familiar one. I turned and saw the "gun": a phone.

70

"Joey?" he grinned toothily.

"I thought it was you, ya *mook*." I laughed as we embraced. "What are you doing here?"

"Same as you, I'd say," he said as he took a seat to my left.

"Long time no see, huh?"

"No shit," he took a long drag on his ever-present cigarette.

"No more glasses?" he exhaled smoke through his nostrils.

"I change it up with contacts every now and then."

"There's something else. New scar?" I stared at a small white line that crisscrossed his neck. He smiled and shook his head. He held out his arms wide so I could get a better look at him.

"I'm Made," he beamed. I gaped.

"You, Made? They must be getting desperate."

"I guess I could say the same of Johnny Black, huh, Pietr-" I cleared my throat.

"Peter."

"Oh yeah, yeah. So, *Peter*, I was actually hoping to talk to you about that."

"My name?"

"Your employment, ya *mook*. I have a bit of a-" He paused as his hand went to his pocket. He placed his cigarette in his mouth as he looked at his phone. "It's Eddie."

"Maroni?"

"Sadly." I chuckled. "Yeah?" From all the sounds in the bar, I couldn't make out anything the other end was saying. Joey's jaw dropped, causing his cigarette to fall onto the bar. He methodically rubbed it into an ashtray. "Eddie, don't come to me with this if you don't know." His voice held a slight tremor. He glanced at me, then looked around at the bar. The atmosphere was slowly becoming even more tense. I knew what he was about to say, and it had to do with the detonator

71

that had fallen out that stranger's pocket. The one I had held. Joey stared at me, fear in his eyes. "Get out of here."

"What's going on?" I asked, my hands already reaching for my money roll.

"Marc Beppo's car was blown up on his way here. We're at war."

Ten
Barroom Brawl

John. November 1st, 2009.

I sat in my corner of *The Pub*, enjoying a hamburger and a can of Coke. I just finished a tough match for Pure Gore Fighting. Tough to lose, that is. Now all I had to do was wait for Pete to deliver my cut.

Peter walked into the bar, still wearing slacks and a leather jacket from earlier. He sat down across from me.

"Took you long enough," I commented.

"Traffic was bad because of the explosion."

"Explosion?" he nodded.

"Marc Beppo, Don Luigi Beppo's son, was blown to bits after you left." I swallowed.

"Johnny's doing?"

"The Outfit's, at least." Peter wrinkled his nose.

"What? You don't like fresh burgers?"

"I don't find grease mixes well with all the sweat and hormones flying through the air." I shrugged and took a look around. The rest of the Company was going through their usual partying routine of drinking too much and breaking glasses. They'd pay for the damage.

"You have it?" he nodded, producing a stack of bills and handing it to me.

"For excellent work tonight." I didn't count it. Then he handed me another stack of the same size. "For excellent work *last* night." This one I did count, if only for the sake of what I said next.

"This won't do." Pete frowned.

"What do you mean?"

"I mean there's no way to split two grand into thirds."

"Thirds?"

"JJ, Terry, and me," he smiled.

"Do you have any cash on you?"

"Always."

"Give me twenty. That leaves six hundred and sixty for each of you." I frowned as did the math and reached into my wallet. "Thanks, man."

"Sure. We'll assume the twenty will cover the ring you took." My eyes widened. I stammered. Pete held up his hands. "Keep it. Better it goes to you than Johnny. Consider it a down payment on contracting your services for what I'm about to tell you." My costume didn't allot for pockets, so I placed the stacks between my legs.

"What's wrong?" I asked. Peter bit his lip.

"We're at war."

"We're always at war. We're America."

"No, John, *we are at war*. The Black Outfit and the Beppo Family."

"What does that have to do with us?" I took another bite of my burger, ignoring the odors Peter had mentioned.

"We work for the Outfit, John."

"No, *you* work for the Outfit. I'm an independent contractor who just finished his last assignment."

"No one will see it that way when we become cannon fodder for the Five." I tilted my head. "The California Five are the most powerful bosses in the state. Right now it's Johnny versus Luigi, but soon each Family will be forced to choose a side. This could turn into a long, bloody war unless one side quickly loses."

"So we go to war for someone we don't like."

"You got it."

"Sounds like me during the Carter years."

"Now's not the time for jokes, John. Listen, I met a guy today who works for the Beppo Family. I'm thinking we see how the tide turns, and if need be, we talk to him and switch over."

"Anything to save your own skin, right?" he pursed his lips.

"Yeah, that's right. You said it: we're fighting for someone we don't like. Don Beppo, the *Compare*, is a respectable man. We just need to wait and see how the tide turns."

"You'd rather live for an unjust cause than fight and die for a true one?" I scoffed.

"I'd rather live," he replied earnestly, "period. Neither cause is just, in any case. Just men fighting for power, as they always have."

"So we stay put until we know Luigi has a chance?" Peter began to respond, then glanced at someone quickly approaching our booth. *Rager*. He stopped in front of us in a huff and glared furiously at me.

"What's this?" he motioned to Peter, never taking his eyes off me.

"Peter Richardson," Pete replied, "apathetic to meet you," he stuck out his hand. *Rager* glowered at it. Peter licked his lips. "I'm Mr. Washicha's new agent." *Rager* seemed to have less... rage.

"Agent?"

"You see, John here is in the big-leagues now, and who knows when he will be wanted in a cameo? Or maybe a talk-show? I mean, everyone in the UFC has stories to share."

Rager's face turned purple.

"We're in Pure Gore Fighting!" he yelled. Peter's eyes widened. A few heads at the bar swiveled in our direction, but most stuck to themselves. Bar fights were common. We got angry, we fought, and we made up. I had never been in one with the Company. *Rager* took my Coke can and crumpled it in his fist. Caffeine drizzled over his hand.

"What, Washicha, you think you're too good for me? That I couldn't beat you in an honest fight, so you lose to make a little extra dough?"

"Sid, we've known each other since you were in HCW. You know that's not the case, man," he got angrier and angrier at every word. Finally, he sucker-punched me in the jaw. I sprawled out across the booth. My burger landed in Peter's lap. He stood up, staring at *Rager* disgustedly as he placed the burger back in my plate.

"You should quit before someone gets hurt." Peter said. Sid's vein protruded from his neck.

"Shut up!" he spat at Peter. Peter inhaled, then exhaled. Looks like I was about to finally see Peter in a fight.

"Hulk Hogan!" Peter yelled and pointed at a waiter in the corner. Confused, Sid turned around. Everyone had stopped what they were doing to gather round and watch the fight progress. Pete took a beer bottle from the booth next to us and swung it at Sid's head. Glass and beer flew. Sid stalwartly stood his ground.

He turned around, snarled, and grabbed Peter by the neck. They stared at each other for a moment. Peter uttered a curse as his hands went to *Rager*'s beefy wrist.

"Come on," Peter breathed, "don't do this. You have your whole life ahead of you. Look at that face. You could be the next star in a *Frankenstein* movie." By now, I had hopped out

76

of my seat and was ready to rumble. Sid didn't see me. I wrapped my arms around his neck, forcing him to let Pete go. Peter turned around to have another go.

"Stay out of this, Peter." As soon as Peter managed to scramble away and join the circle of spectators that had quickly formed, I released my captive. He turned to face me.

I growled. Rager lunged. I ducked and turned. His lunge turned into a roll and we faced one another once more.

It was my turn. I got inside his guard with my fist pulled back and hit him across the nose. Blood spurted everywhere. I may have broken it. He grunted, putting a hand to his face. When he pulled it back and saw the blood, he attempted a kick as I moved away. I held his swinging foot with one hand and slammed my elbow into his shin. He screamed and fell once I let go.

I sat back at the booth and resumed eating my burger as *Rager* howled on the floor. Most of the crowd had dispersed. A few were tending to Sid. Some were watching me uneasily, including Peter.

"You have your piece on you?" he asked. I shook my head.

"Surprisingly, no. Hard to get one of those to fit in my tights."

"Yeah. Keep the money: there are too many witnesses to hand it back now. Look: this is nothing. Just don't say anything when they arrest you. Don't put up any resistance. Once you get to the station, use your call on me. Tell me what they're holding you for and we'll go from there." I nodded again.

"Be sure to let my family know," he smiled wistfully.

Eleven
Damion Occhipinti

Peter. November 2nd, 2009.

I showed my credentials to the guard and he let me through to the interrogation room. Another one stood at the door. I pulled out a few bills—not as many as I gave to shut off the cameras—and stuffed them in his shirt pocket, jerking my thumb at the exit. He nodded and left. Thankfully, the Los Angeles legal system has always had an interesting inter-departmental relationship: the cops won't know they have a VIP suspect for at least another two hours: enough time for me to clean John's case. John was waiting for me, sitting on a bolted-down chair with his feet on the stainless-steel table without a care in the world. I sat across from him. He arched an eyebrow.

"I used my phone call so you could get me a lawyer and let my family know."

"I did both."

"Then where's the lawyer?"

"Sitting across from you," he rolled his eyes.

"You aren't a lawyer."

"I have the paperwork to prove it. That's why they let me in. I'm also a real-estate agent, stockbroker, bus driver, masseuse, and alcohol salesman."

"Bus driver?" That's the one that caught his attention?

"You'd be surprised what can happen." I lowered my voice.

"I know plenty about court procedures and legal... whatever. I'll get the judge to look at the case *our* way."

"You mean lie," he responded flatly.

"Bending the truth isn't lying," he tilted his head.

"Yeah it is. You aren't telling the truth, so you're lying."

"But I'm not lying. I'm just not completely telling the truth." John shook his head.

"Pete, am I gonna lose?" he sounded tired.

"Well, all we have tomorrow is the bail hearing."

"That's not what I meant."

"The case they're building is for skimming points and aggravated assault—"

"Assault? It was a bar fight."

"You snapped his leg clean in half. Look: they're stacking this against you. They could care less about you taking bribes or getting in that fight. That doesn't matter. What they do care about is that you're an older, newly-hired thug for Johnny Black. They're hoping you'll have dirt on the Outfit, and will give it up to go free."

"But I don't know anything."

"They don't know that. It's RICO."

"RICO?" I sighed.

"RICO: Racketeer Influenced and Corrupt Organizations Act. It's a domino effect Johnny Law uses to bring down whole families by arresting anyone remotely associated with a crime. They dig into this whole betting scheme and arrest you. Then they do the same to me that they're doing to you, thinking Johnny Black is behind it. Soon they'll have everyone in cuffs, only it'll never stick."

"Pete, isn't this room bugged?"

"Yeah. It just so happens that a guard turned it off for the duration of my visit. That's going into your fee, by the way."

"My fee?"

"I'm your attorney. What? You thought my legal services would be free-of-charge?"

"I thought I was your friend. That's all." My features softened.

"I am. That's why I'm here. You know what Johnny said when he heard? He said 'put a bullet in him.' Johnny doesn't like rats. He's afraid you're going to talk. But I said no. I would do this the legal way and get you acquitted. That's what I'm going to do. As a friend. A friend who costs money."

"How much are you thinking?"

"Once we win, I'll take my expenses out the four grand they took as evidence. Shouldn't add up to too much," he nodded. "Look: I'm carrying a wallet for you. You think I'd do that for just anyone? I hate wallets. No money roll. I'm carrying a driver's license, just for you."

"Is it yours?"

"You're missing the point."

"How is everything?"

"Well, you're suspended indefinitely from Pure Gore Fighting. Your family didn't take it too hard." Probably because I left out a few key details, such as "found at the scene of the crime."

"Peter, I'm going to ask you one more time: am I going to lose?"

"That depends on whether you're innocent," said a third voice. I turned in my chair to see another man standing at the doorway. Whoever he was, he had on a fairly nice navy suit and tie with polished yet worn black shoes. I rose and dusted myself off.

"Peter. Peter Richardson. I'm Mr. Washicha's attorney." The newcomer stared at my hand with obvious distaste.

"No, you are not. *I* am his attorney." I looked from his suit to my leather jacket and back.

"John, who is this guy?" I turned to face my client, who had turned as pale as the confused newcomer.

"This... Peter, meet Damion. My other son." I sighed and rubbed my temples. I stood up straighter, prepared to take charge.

"I'm sorry, Mr. Washicha-"

"Occhipinti," Damion corrected. Peter blinked.

"Mr. Occhipinti, I am Mr. Washicha's... I am my client's counselor. I didn't spend four years at Berkeley just to let someone else take one of my jobs."

"Really? You went to Berkeley?" he crossed his arms.

"Yeah, I did." I glared defiantly.

"How strange. I went to Berkeley, too, and their law program is three years, not four." I pursed my lips.

"That's quite a coincidence." I cleared my throat.

"Now, seeing as Mr. Washicha can't have two attorneys, I-"

"Actually," Damion interjected, "in the state of California, a client can have as large of a legal team as they so please. It was one of the first things I learned at Berkeley." I breathed in through my nose, out through my mouth. Inhale, exhale. Every time I was in John's company, I had to go through breathing exercises at some point. I tried keeping my voice down.

"Listen, ya *mook*, I'm tired of the formalities. I don't care who you are, you're here for a reason. Now, since I'm good at what I do, I'll let John hear you out before we kick you to the curb."

"Dad? Will you have me as a lawyer?" John grimaced.

"If you were to be my lawyer, would you actually help me win the case?"

"John," I said, "you aren't seriously thinking-"

"I'm hearing him out. Like you said. Damion?"

"That depends on whether you are truly innocent." Now it was John who had trouble breathing.

"So you won't help out your own dad?"

"My father died in service to country." They glared at one another. I tapped my foot as they had their staring contest. Damion blinked first. John looked like the matter was settled.

"Wait," I realized, "what about me? I'm valid. I know law. I can help."

"Pete, how can you possibly help more than a real lawyer?"

"Well, for starters, I can give you some legal advice: this isn't about innocence. Do you really think the jury gives one if you beat up some guy because you lost a wrestling match? It's all about your pitch. Your performance. Can you convince them that although you are guilty, you don't deserve to go to jail? It's this thing called jury nullification." Damion smirked.

"That's not at all what it's about. You look at the facts and determine what happened truthfully so the jury can reach the logical conclusion."

"Logic? Logic never did anything worthwhile. John, assert yourself to the judge tomorrow, then later to the jury. Get them to like you." I put on a meek voice and brought up my shoulders. "I am not a flight risk," I said, my eyes wide, "all my loving family is here, and I wouldn't leave them for the world." I made a rainbow motion with my hands.

"Except then," Damion intruded on my pep talk, "the prosecutor will say he's been separated for over 20 years. Then they can ask why, and after that it will come down to whatever happened in wherever twenty years ago. And, I'm guessing, his financials."

"Financials," I said even more meekly, "right. I was denied

my wages as a war veteran, and could not support myself, let alone my caring wife and infant children. I manage a small hole-in-the-wall retail store, where, although my customers were few, I managed to make enough income to get by. Oh, and the government left me for dead in the Middle East."

"How did you know about that?" John asked. I bit my lip. He sighed.

"Admiral Sanders," we both said. Damion shook his head.

"In the end, it comes down to one thing: you were caught with the money and there are two dozen witnesses who can say you assaulted Sidney Gerin." Now it was my turn to shake my head as I brought on my meek John imitation.

"Your Honor, I admit it: I hurt Sidney... whatever. But also acknowledge that I did so in self-defense. He hit me, and then he almost murdered a good friend of mine on the spot. As for the money, there is an explanation, and it is this: the man who handed me the supposed evidence is a dear friend who wishes to start his own business. I'm a possible investor, and he is just showing me what my monthly returns would feel like in a few years." I sat back, satisfied.

"People don't carry thousands of dollars in their pocket to a bar." Damion said. I looked to John for assistance. He shrugged.

"This guy's impossible," I declared.

"I'm only telling you what will be said in court. This is what we need to discuss: what they will say and what we have to counter. You can be the nicest guy in the world and still be locked away for a long time."

I pinched the base of my nose and began pacing. I snapped my fingers.

"John was going to quit Pure Gore Fighting!"

"I was?" John finally spoke up.

"That's the story," I said, running with it, "you were going to quit, and I was going to become your agent, just like we told that *mook*. Story matches up. The cash was an advance from your first gig."

"Which would be...?" I sighed, then began pacing again. I took two steps and then turned on my heel.

"I'll talk to Johnny. It'll take some convincing, but I might be able to get him to let you do a few special matches at his personal ring and go with the story. He'll want to get you out on the streets: a great shot and a fighter? Johnny will need you now that we're at war." John nodded along.

"Damion?" John pleaded, "Will that work?" Damion scowled.

"We will have to tweak it some, but yes, at its core, it could work. I don't even want to know what Johnny or what war you're referring to. I want you both to know that what you are doing is morally unacceptable and-" I held up a hand.

"My conscious isn't something I plan on discussing with you—or anyone else—anytime soon."

"So what will happen tomorrow?" John asked. I began to answer, but Damion got there first.

"They disclose your charges and hopefully set bond. There is one small problem that I don't understand: the prosecutor is District Attorney Fuentes." I gaped, plumping back down in my chair and burying my face in my knees. Damion went on: "I don't know what interest he has in a small case like this, but he does." I understood perfectly. It was just like what I told John: RICO. They truly believe this will be a groundbreaking case against organized crime. I sat up as a thought occurred to me.

"You're a public defender," I told Damion. He nodded even though it wasn't a question. "Public defenders are assigned to those who ask for them. John didn't ask for one; he asked for me."

"I did?" John asked. We both ignored him.

"I'm moonlighting." Damion said as he averted his gaze.

"For free?" he shrugged. John, who before now had been staring at the one-way glass against the wall, looked to his son.

"Did Katy put you up to this?" Damion met his gaze, jutting out his chin defiantly. "There you go, Peter: the boy was asked to help me out by his mother."

"I'm not a boy," he answered icily.

"Yes, you are. You're a boy until you prove you're a man."

"And I do that by helping my criminal dad get free?" John flinched.

"You do that by helping your father in his time of need, just like I helped you when you fell off your bike all those years ago."

"Yeah, that's right, Dad. I forgot about that. I forgot about you catching me when I fell, because you weren't there all those other times I fell. I fell hard, Dad. And you were never there." His eyes spoke of a world of hurt. I cleared my throat.

"If District Attorney Fuentes is coming after you, John, we need to prepare. I'll see about bail tomorrow. You'll have to spend the night here. Bail will be excessive, but I'll make some calls and have the money. We can start building your case after that. We'll end this without a trial." With that, I stood, nodding to father and son as I headed out the door.

Twelve
A Friendly Visit

John. November 2nd, 2009.

I sat hunched over in my holding cell. Lights weren't out just yet, and cat calls and yells were all around me. As I far as I was concerned, it was already dark and I was entirely alone.

This wasn't my first time in a jail. The guards were a different color, as were the walls and floor. Not to mention the food was better. But the POW camp was still just a jail.

I could still feel the humidity beating down on my sweaty body. It hurt to breathe. Dustin was tied down across from me, the scars on his body matching my own. Punishments doled out by the Cong for attempted escapes, and fresh ones for the murder of our old guard.

I'd been in this camp for close to two months. As soon as Dustin can walk, we are escaping. It isn't a possibility. It is fact.

They took another captive. From inside my bamboo cage I was forced to watch a fellow POW have stalks placed under his fingernails until each and every one, over the course of three hours, was popped or broken off. You can't survive that and stay sane. Or conscious. From where I sat, I wasn't sure if I could, either.

The red commander, taller than I recalled, emerged with two soldiers flanking him. One of his sentries unlocked my cage, which seemed to have grown. When I heard the mechanism click, I lunged.

I grabbed the commander by the neck. One of the Cong hit me with the butt of his gun. I let go as I fell. A barrage of kicks flew all around me as I lied on the ground. I wrapped my knees to my chest, trying my hardest not to whimper like an animal. They won't break me. They won't!

What had been North Vietnamese soldiers became two uniformed policemen. The commander became a man in a black suit, oddly familiar, with greased-back dark hair and Hispanic features.

"Bring the captain to Room Fourteen," he told the cops.

"How do you know my rank?" I asked hoarsely. He sighed a tired man's sigh, one of a man who used to enjoy what he did but now found little pleasure in it. Each guard grabbed one of my shoulders as we followed him down the cell block. One prisoner threw himself against the bars as we passed him.

"Hey Fuentes," he called, "what's a pretty boy like you doing at the precinct?" Others added their own jeers about how he should be campaigning and that he should pick on someone with his level of privilege. That's why he looked familiar: in front of me was District Attorney Isaac Fuentes. One of the cops opened the door to what I assumed was Room Fourteen—though it was identical to every other grey, metallic door—and Fuentes entered. I was thrust inside after him. The door slammed shut behind the two of us.

The room was dimly lit, spacious with a single table in the center and three chairs. I allowed Fuentes to escort me to a seat. His hands shaking slightly, he handcuffed me to the table as I sat. He sat across from me with two empty chairs next to him.

"Are the others for show?" I asked.

"Not quite," came the reply from behind me. Before I could

turn, I felt a hand grasp my hair as my head was launched toward the table. The room vibrated as my hands instinctively went to my forehead—my right hand stayed cuffed to the table. A man who held himself like a cop, older than Fuentes and more muscular, walked around the table.

"Careful, there," another voice said. I didn't bother turning. Another man in a dark grey suit strolled around the table. "Let's not bring in the wrath of the Fourth Amendment." The other man crossed his arms. The newcomer was clearly the oldest in the room. He had grandfatherly features and hair a grey that almost matched his suit.

"So, Mr. Washicha," Grey Suit began, "ex-Special Forces captain missing in action since 1986, the executor of over a dozen reconnaissance assignments, fifty-four confirmed kills, previously a valued member of a well-known fighting company, and now being held for a bar fight resulting in a serious injury for the other guy and for accepting bribery for a relatively-successful career. Is that correct?" I glanced at the camera in the upper-right corner.

"It's off, Numb-nuts," Big and Mean said. "And your lawyer isn't coming."

"We're giving you a chance to give your side of the story," Fuentes added.

"I was only promoted to captain after my brother turned down the offer. Twice."

"You mean your half-brother, Dustin MacManus Washicha, when he was recommended for promotion in 1973 and 1976?"

"Records like that are supposed to be confidential." I said.

"And yet here we are," Big and Mean replied.

"Look: I haven't committed a crime for over 20 years, and back then it had been sanctioned by the Government. But a man's got to do what a man's got to do." Fuentes bared his upper lip in obvious distaste.

"I understand. What size jumpsuit do you wear?" I chuckled.

"Come on. This won't stick. You know it. I know it. My lawyers will plea that I have been wrongfully mistreated and I'll get out."

"I... have some powerful friends, John." Fuentes said. "They want to lock you away for the maximum penalty. We have your professional history. You don't think we don't have your family's? Six years will be a long time to not be with your wife."

"I haven't been with her since 1986."

"What about your daughter, off at college? Don't you think she would like to meet her father?"

"How do you know she hasn't?" I demanded.

"I know plenty, John. But my friends would like to know more. If you tell them what they want to know, this will all blow over. You'll be one big happy family." I thought about that.

"What would you like to know?" The three of them smiled. The heads of Cerberus preparing for a meal.

"I knew you'd come around." Fuentes said. "You're smart. Too smart not to see the big picture. My friends are very interested in some... associates, you've been hanging around. Big, bad men they are certain you have seen commit horrendous acts," he held up his hands as I began to protest.

"They don't care if you partook in these acts," Grey Suit added, "they are much more interested in a few others: Marcus Dean, Johnny Black, Giuseppe Gregario, the man who calls himself Peter Richardson, and anyone else who comes to mind." I shook my head. "What? Is that a problem?"

"I don't know a Giuseppe Gregario."

"That's too bad, John. He's directly connected with over a dozen murders in the county, and indirectly connected with twice that. Our friends really want to get their hands on him." I peered at him.

"Who are your friends, exactly?"

"That isn't important. Now, you said you didn't know Gregario. What about the others?"

"I know them, sure."

"Isn't Richardson your lawyer?"

"He is."

"Did he go to law school?" Grey Suit sat. Big and Mean stood in a corner, watching.

"As far as I know."

"Where?"

"He told me Berkeley." I paused. "Won't you ask me this on the stand, anyway?" They seemed annoyed.

"Yes," Fuentes answered, "but my friends hope to dispose of that... formality. They would rather save the energy and have the case be dropped so they can focus their efforts on the information you give. But first, you have to actually *give information*. Now, what illegal acts have you performed for either Richardson, Dean, or Black?" I sighed.

"Fuentes, let me tell you something: Peter Richardson reunited me with my family. He got me to put twenty years of pain behind me in a matter of days. I've been spending my free time with my wife and playing ball with my sons, something I haven't done since they stood at chest-level, if that. Now, even if I did have dirt on him, even if he had been mowing down gangsters, why would I tell you?" Grey Suit pursed his lips, his face pinched.

"Because Peter Richardson was a notorious crime boss who ruled this city with an iron fist. All the hits in Los Angeles were orchestrated through him. Careers and lives were made and lost as he saw fit. He soiled ranks of cops, politicians, judges, lawyers; it didn't matter as long as he had power over them. Then he disappeared. Fell off the face of the earth. But people haven't forgotten. Our friends certainly haven't. He's dangerous, John. He's dangerous and he's using you. He gave you back your family because it suited his purposes. He knew after that, you would belong to him."

"I belong to no one."

"Really? Because the way I see it, unless you cooperate, you belong to *me*." I looked at Fuentes.

"Peter bought most of the officials in in the city in one form or another, right?"

"He corrupted them to their core," he responded.

"So tell me: how does such a young man become the district attorney of Los Angeles County when he is a few years out of law school?" he growled.

"Are you accusing me of something?"

"Just asking a question. Are you having trouble forming an answer?"

"Listen here, you-"

"I may be the one charged with bribery, but I can see that you're the one who should be locked away," he shook his head.

"It's a dirty business dealing with dirty people, John. You should know that."

"I'm learning more about it from you than the three weeks I've spent with Peter," he grunted. Big and Mean stepped up.

"Do you realize how miserable I can make life for you once you're put away for good?" Big and Mean asked as he leaned against the table, his face inches from my own.

"Do you realize how miserable I can make *you* once I'm *out* for good?"

"I guess we'll just have to make sure you don't get out," Big and Mean said.

"As soon as I do, I'll have a full investigation done on you. All of you," he barked a laugh and stood straight.

"Oh, really? A crook found guilty is always a crook in the eyes of our society. It's our word against yours."

"Then I'll just have to talk to Peter. I'm sure he has some other method to make you pay."

"That sounds an awful lot like a threat, Washicha."

"That's because it is," he nodded, glaring. I stared back. His eyes were ice. Mine were the Arctic.

"Guards!" Fuentes called. The door opened. I didn't turn around. "I believe it's about time Mr. Washicha here went to sleep. Don't make it too noticeable." Before I could move, something struck the back of my head. An explosion of pain went through my skull. I collapsed on the table, right back in Vietnam.

Thirteen
Between Black and White

Peter. November 3ʳᵈ, 2009.

I tugged at the lapels of my new navy-blue suit as I walked into *The Pub*, my new black loafers squeaking lightly on the wood. Clare's eyebrows, so light they were barely noticeable in the dim light, shot up. I chuckled. My ego dampened when I realized everyone in court would be wearing something similar. I shook my head. This wasn't about me; it was about John. For now.

I walked up to Clare as she took a table's order.

"-and no tomato," she confirmed.

"What about some Sherry?" I asked. She stared.

"What about it?"

"I'm sorry. I just can't take my eyes off of you."

"What?" I winced. Realizing I made the wrong approach, I reached into my pocket and showed her two tickets. Her eyes widened. "A Frankie Valli concert?"

"You said he's your favorite."

"I... he is."

"Read the ticket," she gingerly took one and examined it.

"Front row? Backstage pass?"

"We can meet him, Clare. Well, you can. Frankie and I are already acquainted."

"Peter, this concert has been sold out for months."

"A friend of mine used to have Frankie as a... client," she

hugged me. The few hundred dollars I paid Joey were already worth it. "There's a catch," she let go.

"Of course there is."

"I go with you," she beamed, snatching the other ticket out of my hand.

"I'll think about it," she said as she walked away. Her table's occupants stared.

Chuckling, I sat in what has become John and I's regular booth. Naturally, Clare was my waitress. I ordered a water and French fries, which were doubtlessly the least-messy items on the menu.

Five minutes later, Damion came in. I waved him over and he sat where John usually did. I tried to analyze him, to see any similarities between him and his father. There were none. I did note that he had a briefcase with him. I would need to remember to bring one to the preliminary hearing.

"Damion."

"Peter," he greeted stiffly.

"Actually, I would prefer the title of 'Mr. Washicha's real attorney,' if you would." His eye twitched.

"I wouldn't. Now, let's get down to business, shall we?"

"Hold on." Clare appeared with my water. I thanked her and she left. "Okay: go," he frowned.

"I don't see any possible way we can win this case. Our client is guilty, and so he will rightfully be found guilty. There's not much I can do." I took a sip of water.

"Clare!" I called out to her as she helped another table. She gave me a gesture to wait. I drank some more water. She came up.

"Yes?"

"Pop quiz: what do you call that thing where if a client tells his lawyer he did something, the lawyer can't tell anyone?"

94

"Oh, well that's the 'Duty of Confidentiality.'"

"So, Damion, what were you saying?" Clare began to leave.

"Next question, Ma'am," Damion intervened, "what if the lawyer knows his client is lying in court?"

"Well then that lawyer is obligated to tell the truth. Not that a lawyer with a wealthy client would ever do that." Damion grinned at me like he had won.

"Thanks, Clare." I said.

"Anytime. Honestly, I didn't believe you when you said you were a lawyer. Until I saw how you fought the other night," she walked away laughing to herself. I slid my tongue along my teeth and glared at the man who was supposed to be helping John.

"So have you talked to that friend of yours?" he asked, disinterested.

"Johnny isn't my friend. But yes, I talked to him. He agreed. But John will have to pay him, not the other way around."

"Good. He deserves it. Look: I was serious about us losing. Between the witnesses and the evidence, we don't have a fighting chance. Even though Sidney threw the first punch, John went beyond self-defense."

"How long can John go to prison for?"

"For assault and accepting a bribe in a sporting event? Maybe six years. We could haggle down to four, if we cut a quick deal. Fuentes is good at what he does, though. You need to face the facts that your buddy, my father, will be going to prison. He is guilty. That much is undeniable. The witness list keeps growing." I put my head in my hands.

"And yet all of them will also acknowledge that it was in self-defense."

"Not the bribery part." I shrugged. My fries arrived. I scarfed them down as Damion went on. "The only evidence besides injuries and witnesses would be the money found in his possession. That's something else we can't deny. If we go along with your idea, I can argue the point that so many witnesses who will undoubtedly have the same story don't need to be brought to the stand. That will stop Fuentes from pounding it into the jury's head so much." I finished my meal. I gulped down my water and wiped my lips with a napkin.

"I would have taken the money, honestly, except that would make things look worse."

"You mean it would make him look even guiltier than he is."

"Tomato…" I held out my hands like a balance scale. I checked my watch for what felt like the hundredth time that day. "Time to go." I got up and began to leave.

"Aren't you going to pay?" he asked. I turned.

"Hey, you're the bigshot lawyer, right?" he muttered something about being a public defender as he fished out his wallet. I added some bills as a tip for Clare. We left and I found out, unsurprisingly, that Damion owned a Prius. I went to the passenger's side. He didn't question it.

We drove to the courthouse in utter silence. Eventually, I decided to break it.

"Why are you so hard on your old man?"

"Why do you insist on helping him?" he shot back. I pondered that one.

"Because I know he has a good heart."

"That doesn't make him any less guilty.

"Of taking a bribe? Or of leaving you?" His eyes narrowed.

"Who are you? Doctor Phil?"

"Well, it seems obvious that your daddy issues make you bitter and wary of others," he kept his eyes on the road. I watched as his knuckles gripped the steering wheel until they were white.

"If we're going to work together, I'm going to need you to do me a favor."

"What's that?" I asked. He didn't answer.

"We're here," he parked and we simultaneously got out. I didn't thank him for the ride and he didn't so much as look at me. Still, we walked into the courthouse side by side. We went up the marble steps and through the columns. This wasn't Federal Court. This was the domain of District Attorney Fuentes.

I was stopped by a man in the hallway. Damion stopped with me and was waved on. Damion hesitated, but I assured him it would be okay. He left.

"I wasn't aware the FBI had jurisdiction in this case," I told Special Agent Vasquez. He smirked at me. In the past few years, age seemed to have caught up with him. He still had the dark features of his heritage, same knowing eyes, yet there were fresh wrinkles around them. His black hair had turned entirely grey.

"Notice the 'Federal' in the title. We can join whatever case we choose. For now, we're just auditing your friend's legal process."

"Friend? Which friend would that be?" I enjoyed playing dumb with Vasquez. I had done it for years, and it still managed to get to him. "Come on, Billy. You know my neighborhood. You've ridden through it often enough. Plenty of my old friends could be here."

"I'm talking about your client. John Washicha. Ring a bell?" I scrunched up my face.

"Washicha... Washicha... oh, right. You mean the one I was going see before you stopped me, an illegality in separating an attorney from his client? Yes, I remember him."

97

"So you're a lawyer now?"

"Straight out of Berkeley," he pulled out a notepad and pencil, carefully jotting this down.

"Where were you the night before last?" I hesitated. He knew I was at the bar. But I couldn't put myself at risk. Johnny would have no qualms with using my arrest as an excuse to whack me.

"I thought you were auditing?"

"Don't you know it's rude to answer a question with a question?"

"You mean like you just did?" I gave him an impish grin. He snarled.

"Do you have an answer?"

"I do."

"Well, what is it?" he raised his voice. No one spared us a second glance. This was a Los Angeles courthouse, after all.

"My answer is yes, I do know it's rude to answer a question with a question." I shouldered my way past him.

So the feds had an interest in the case. That was never a good thing. Especially if it's Special Agent Vasquez. Thankfully, John was the type to keep his word. No way would he give me up.

Damion was waiting for me at the door. I shrugged off his questions. He quit asking, though I could tell this wasn't over. I noticed he was holding two opened Coke bottles.

"This is your first case?" he asked.

"As a lawyer? You know the answer to that," he handed me one of the Cokes. "If you're nervous, drink this. The caffeine will calm your nerves and help you think straight," he handed me the one in his right hand. I thanked him and took a sip.

Damion was all right, after all.

Fourteen
Bail

John. November 3rd, 2009.

I sat at the defendant's table in the same clothes I had been arrested in two nights ago. Fuentes was droning on to the judge. Meanwhile, Peter was drinking a Coke and drawing on his hand.

"Pete, I didn't get the chance to tell you, but the other night I was interrogated."

"Why didn't you call me?" Both Peter and Damion asked. They glared at each other.

"They didn't let me."

"They?" Damion asked, prepared to write down a name.

"Fuentes and two other guys. Cops. They slapped me around a bit, asked a few questions. Gave me this nasty bump." I gingerly touched the back of my head.

"We'll get the case thrown out," Damion declared. I shook my head.

"They shut off the camera," I said. "There's no proof."

"Why would they do that?" Damion asked. Peter muttered something about RICO. He belched. A question was directed at us by the judge.

"Your honor, I need a moment to confer with my client," Damion said. Peter cleared his throat.

"Uh, yeah, so do I," he got in our small huddle at the table. "What are we conferring about?" Damion gave him a small glare.

"Were you paying attention at all?"

"Of course I was. But sporting legality isn't too interesting, so I drew Trampoline Man. You see, I don't like sporting or legality, so-"

"Trampoline what?" Damion asked. Peter looked at me like it was Damion who was off his rocker. Extra slowly, Peter sounded the words out. I detected a slight slur.

"Tramp-oh-lean Man. See you curve your hand, and above your pinkie you draw a stickman, and below the crease beneath your stickman you draw a trampoline. Now when you bring your fingers up and down, it looks like a man is jumping on a trampoline."

"That is the most-"

"Excuse me," Judge Taylor broke in, "but the question is a simple one: how do you plead?" Peter had an odd, mischievous glint to his eye.

"Well, you see, your Honor, that isn't a simple question."

"And how is that?"

"There are plenty of ways to plead. I could plead like this," he staggered from his chair, walking around the table, and got down on his hands and knees and wrung his hands together, "Not guilty, your honor! I didn't do it! Or," he got up and put the back of his hand on his forehead, "Oh, my," in a southern bell accent, "your most gracious Honor! I must plead to thy court not guilty! You see, I was a simple woman, raised on a simple farm, and Pa provided the best he could-"

"Enough!" The judge bellowed. "Are you here to make a mockery of this court?" Peter turned to me, unsure of the answer.

"John, are we here to make a mockery of this court?" I shook my head slowly, flabbergasted. "Your Honor, John says

100

we are not here to make a mockery of this court. Not guilty!" The judge sighed. Peter returned to his seat.

"Prosecutor?"

"You see, your Honor," Fuentes spoke in a soothing, velvety voice befitting a man comforting a rabbit, "John Washicha is dangerous and unpredictable. He attacked an unarmed companion in a bar. Sober, I might add."

"Objection!" Peter stood and waved. "Objection, your Honor! He hit John first. Thank you," he plumped himself back in his seat.

"Overruled."

"Your Honor," Damion moved on, "my client is not a flight risk. He is a respected member of his community." I raised my eyebrows. "He has worked hard all his life to provide for himself. He has worked harder for his family. He tried his hardest once the Recession began. He owns a small store that has a single employee who would be willing to testify to my client's generosity in the workplace, as well as his character. More importantly: he did not so much as start the fight. He is a patriot, a salesman, and a father of..." he stopped and turned to me, "three children." I winced.

"And let's not forget his wife!" Peter added, standing on wobbly legs. He made jerky movements toward the judge's stand, waving something in his hand. With a start, I realized it was my wallet. He approached the judge and flipped it open, rifling through the contents. I figured I had dropped it at *The Pub*. "Look at this picture, Judge. Now, would you separate a man from a woman like that? No one would. It's just cruel."

"Just how did you come into possession of the suspect's wallet?" Fuentes asked. Peter whirled on him.

"You!" Peter yelled, pointing at the District Attorney. Except he pointed with the hand holding the wallet, which flew across the room. Peter didn't seem to notice. "You. You have mistreated my client from the start! You've bullied him and prodded him like... like a person who prods another person! It's inhumane. No. Just no. He gave me his wallet." Peter turned to me and gave a dramatic wink. "It's nice leather. Yet he kept the money in question. Why? Because he wanted to prove that it was completely legitimate!"

"The Bail Reform Act of 1984 states that a defendant may receive pre-trial detention if he is a flight risk or danger to the community." Fuentes rebutted.

"Except," Damion countered, "that we have already determined he is neither."

"Now," Peter continued as if there hadn't just been a conversation after he spoke, "based on this evidence, I believe my client should be set free."

"So let me get this straight," Judge Taylor peered down at Peter, "the defendant handed you his wallet after he allegedly committed the crime?"

"Mhm..." Peter gave the judge a look that said he had never heard anything more obvious in his life.

"Tampering with the crime scene!" District Attorney Fuentes cried.

"Right..." Peter answered, wheeling around and waving his arms wildly, "because we all know that John cut the victim's throat with his credit cards. Or choked him with nickels. No, I got the wallet because he didn't trust the clowns of the legal system, which would be you, from keeping it. And he needs his driver's license to..." Peter drifted off, apparently unsure where he was going with this, "to drive!" I put my head in my arms.

"Mr. Richardson," Judge Taylor said angrily, banging his gavel, "that is enough. Save it for the hearing. You are making a mockery of this court!"

"No, I'm stating the cold hard facts! My client is innocent. He shouldn't be here. Case closed."

"Mr. Richardson, I am hereby fining you one hundred dollars for contempt of court," he banged his gavel again.

"Pennies, Judge. It's my client's money, after all."

"Well let's see how your client likes this: two hundred dollars!" Another bang on the gavel. I grunted. Damion chuckled.

"What's so funny?"I whispered.

"The lawyer you actually hired is drinking on the job."

"You're part Irish." I hissed. His features hardened.

"No, *you* are part Irish. My mother is Northern Italian." I growled.

"Can you cut that out? I'm your dad. Me. It took two of us to make you," he made a face.

"But only one of you to raise me." My hands gripped my knees. Peter wobbled back over and collapsed in his chair. Damion cleared his throat and stood.

"Your Honor, we apologize for our associate's lack of protocol. He in no way reflects our attitude toward the liberty of this court."

"Duly noted, Mr. Occhipinti. Bail will be set in the amount of twenty thousand dollars. We will resume on the fifteenth of November." Once more, he banged his gavel. Judge Taylor turned to the bailiff. "Call in the next case." And just like that, it was over. For now. Peter smiled toothily at me.

"Don't worry, John. I know a guy who-"

"You've done enough, Peter." I was surprised by how calm I was. I watched as Fuentes strolled over. He grinned as we made eye contact. He tossed my wallet onto the table. Peter swiped it.

"You know, if you give up your friend here, we could end this game," he told me.

"A game? That's what this is to you?" I leaned in across the table. He did the same. I could smell the cheap cologne rolling off him in waves.

"Life is a game." Peter remarked. "We, the players. In the end, it just comes down to a roll of the dice." Fuentes sneered at him.

"Looks like I won't need you, Washicha. I'm bringing Richardson in for public intoxication."

"Intoxication?" Peter chuckled. "I'm not intoxicated. Drunk, maybe. But definitely not intoxicated. Though, thinking back, I don't see how… all I've had today was a water and a Coke."

"A rum and Coke, more like it. Tell you what: I won't turn you in. When I put you away, you'll be in there for more than a night." With that, Fuentes left. The bailiffs detained me. I waited in a backroom cell alone, which I was thankful for. Twenty minutes later, I was told I could go; my bail was paid. I walked out into the main hallway, my shoulders slumped. I heard uneven footsteps behind me just as I put my hand on the   door.
"John," Peter breathed, his arm leaning on my shoulder, "I'm sorry. I don't know what's going on. I haven't-"

"Save it, Peter. There's no point. Just like there's no point in you coming back here." His face lit up.

"Because we won?"

"No. Because I'm firing you as my attorney." I passed through the door, leaving behind a stunned and thoroughly-wasted Peter. A moment later, as I walked toward the exit, the door opened again.

"Hey, Washicha!" Peter called, "And just how do you plan on leaving?!" I stared at him a moment, confused. Then it hit me: my bike was still at *The Pub*. I had no way to get home. No money to call a cab. I stormed over to him.

"Give me back my wallet." I demanded, holding out my hand. He fished in his pocket before finally pulling it out. I snatched it from his grasp. "Thanks." I muttered as I turned back around. I stopped and turned once more. "How are you getting home?" he waved me off.

"My apartment is only a few hundred blocks away. I'll walk. Could use the exercise. Clear my thoughts. You know how it is."

"Actually, no, I don't." I responded flatly. He shook his head vigorously.

"I figured the bail wouldn't be more than twenty-five, so I borrowed it from that friend I was telling you about. I'll need to return the extra five grand before the *vig* is piled on."

"Good friend, if he'll just fork over money like that."

"Well, I had to promise to pay it back. With interest. Of course, we get it back after the trial, so we won't pay much. You won't, that is." I stared at him.

"You borrowed money from a loan shark?" Peter gave a curt nod.

"Don't worry. Murray's a great guy. Well, that's a lie. But we'll be seeing him in a few days. I have something big coming up. Real big. I'll want you in on it. We'll pay off Murray, and then some."

"Count me out," he gaped. "I'm not a crook."

"And yet here we are," he made a wide gesture. I shoved him.

"It's your fault! All of this is your fault!" he sniffed.

"You're right. My fault. It's my fault that you have two lawyers. Otherwise, you never would have found your son. I thought we were friends, John." I sighed, softening up a bit.

"We are, Peter. But that's it: we're not partners. I'm done with your way of life," he nodded sadly, heading back into the courthouse. I didn't try to stop him. I'd wait for him out in the parking lot and then split a cab.

I spotted Damion walking down the marble steps. He must have left from a side door. I caught up to him at the bottom. He turned as I approached. "Three?" I asked.

"Yes, Mr. Washicha, you have three children." His voice was hard, like his eyes.

"Come on, Damion, what did I do that made you consider me dead?"

"Let's start with the fact of you not being there almost my whole life."

"You know why I wasn't there, Son."

"Well how about the fact of that when you could have come back, you didn't."

"I couldn't. I just couldn't." His eyes widened. But he wasn't looking at me. I peered over my shoulder. Peter was wobbling down the steps, about to break his neck. I sighed. "I'll go help him. I don't know why he'd do something like this."

"He didn't." Damion told me, a cold smile spreading across his face. "I put Everclear in his Coke."

Fifteen
Joey and the Gang

Peter. November 4th, 2009.

"-brash, irresponsible, immature, and sociopathic," I concluded my thoughts on Damion's actions.

"Are you done being a walking dictionary?" John asked, holding his cardboard coffee cup closer for warmth. I pulled out a folded paper to see if I missed anything.

"And a *mook*."

"Hey, I hired you back, didn't I?"

"He humiliated me."

"But admitted as much because he felt bad that I fired you." I remained silent as I watched Marc Beppo's funeral procession weave its way through the graveyard. We stood at the gates, dressed in the same bleak attire as the rest.

"Is this the one?" A newcomer asked from behind us. We turned, John already reaching for his gun. I held out my arm to stop him from attacking the large, bulky figure.

"Uncle Donnie? Where's Murray?"

"Mr. Gigante sent me in his place. Is this the one we've made bail for?"

"I can speak for myself," John said, "and yeah, I'm John Washicha," he stuck out his hand. Uncle Donnie grunted and grabbed it.

"Donnie Scarlatti. So the *vig* comes from your end of the heist?" John looked at me.

"A *vig* is interest," I told him, "lots of it."

"Yeah, it'll come out of my end," John told Donnie, who smiled. I winced. Murray Gigante has plenty of enemies, and uses Donnie as both collector and protector, which explains why Donnie's nose had been broken so many times. He already had a pug-like face, seeing the world through beady eyes that darted all over, as if he was constantly looking for either an escape route or dinner. Like his boss, Donnie was part of the "new wave" of Los Angeles *mafioso*: polished fingernails, whitened teeth, bed-tanned skin. It was like putting lipstick on a hippo.

"Where are the others?" John asked.

"Three are at the funeral," I replied, "and Leonardo-"

"Mr. Gigante asked Bianchi not to come. He's at retiring age, and all." Donnie said impassively.

"Leonardo was at retiring age twenty years ago," I replied through gritted teeth. Murray wasn't the one calling the shots here. This was Jimmy's heist.

A pair of footsteps padded the soft earth. We looked at the gates to see two Beppo *soldati* quickly approaching. John tensed.

"John," I said, "I want you to meet Joey 'Fours' Gregario and Eddie Maroni."

Eddie, stockier than Joey and wearing a bright blue shirt—no tie—that clashed with the somber occasion, stuck his hand out first. John grasped it and seemed satisfied with the handshake.

"Good to meet ya, John," Eddie said as he smacked on some gum. John seemed less impressed with Joey's, who wore thick-rimmed glasses.

"How was the ceremony?" I asked.

"Nice," Joey said as he lit a cigarette, "Marc's mother was

108

all torn up," he took a hit. "Don Beppo spent a fortune making sure it would be open-casket."

"And Marc...?" I let the question hang.

"Didn't look like he was blown out of his car, no," Joey said. We stood silent a few beats.

"So... where's ol' Leo?" Eddie asked.

"Not coming," Donnie rumbled.

"Shame," Eddie responded, "I haven't seen him since I had to pose as that drag queen from Florida." John gave me a quizzical glance.

"Eddie's a con artist," I explained. "a big earner for the Beppo Family."

"Don't forget Made," the last addition to our group said as he arrived.

"And this self-righteous *picciotto* is Jimmy 'Pips' Palermo," I said. John and Jimmy shook hands. "So," I said as it began to lightly drizzle, "what do you have, Jimmy?"

"Five to twenty mil in unmarked bills. Excess from the Cortez *Cartel's* money laundering racket."

"So you've been working at one of the Cortez banks?" I asked. Jimmy nodded. "The flagship here in LA."

"Can you picture that?" Eddie asked as he elbowed Joey in the ribs. "Pips, a banker."

"Get on with it," Donnie told Jimmy.

"Right, well, I've been a teller for a few weeks, and it looks like they keep track of the cash. The only time to hit it would be right before it leaves the bank in bulk at the start of the month to be delivered to Mexico."

"A few weeks, then?" I asked. Jimmy shook his head.

"The transfer is too secure. Lucky for us, it's tradition for the safe to be the centerpiece for the bank's New Year's Eve employee gala. Gets the civilian middle guys slobbering.

109

That's when we'll make our move"

"That's a long wait," Eddie commented.

"And a growing *vig*," Donnie said with a glance at John.

"What about security?" I asked.

"The Cortez brothers will be there, which means so will their security teams. Jose won't want the employees to feel secure, so they'll all be packing light. The safe, about six-by-four, is enclosed in a bulletproof glass chamber. The only actual bank security will be checking the list at the front door and manning the cameras from the first floor's back office.

"Live feed?" I asked.

"Five second delay with a three-month memory capacity. They have tapes spanning back years." I nodded thoughtfully.

"Don Beppo knows about this?" Eddie asked. Jimmy nodded.

"It's sanctioned to the point where I'll make my bones as soon as he and Tony Spits get their kick-up. Cortez is close with Johnny Black. We just can't get caught: aside from obvious reasons, we don't need war with another member of the Five."

"But Pete," John interjected, "we work for Johnny Black." Eddie and Jimmy chuckled. Donnie gave a heave that may have been a laugh. I cleared my throat.

"As of right now, yes. Joey here is making arrangements for us to switch over." Joey nodded. "So," I turned to Jimmy, "we need to steal from a safe in the middle of a party, using minimal force, with armed guards all around, and not get caught. How?"

"That's what I was hoping you could figure out, Pie-"

"Peter," I finished for him. "You want me to plan this thing?" Jimmy shrugged.

"It'd be nice," he said. My mind whirred. I did owe him;

bringing Uncle Donnie in on this had been a favor to me to settle things with Murray.

"What's the pay?" Donnie asked, breaking into my thoughts.

"After the *Compare* and *Capo* get their shares," Jimmy began, "and I pay Leo for forging paperwork, we'll split it an even six ways. This is more about me being Made than the cash." I shook my head.

"Six won't be enough," I murmured.

"What?" Jimmy asked.

"We'll need three to four separate teams. We have our grifter and strongmen, but our hacker? Our decoy? The driver? Even if we multitask, which I'm sure we will, we're looking at a nine-person job." Jimmy sighed.

"I'll talk to Bobby," Jimmy said, "Be on the lookout for the rest. The one thing we have on our side is time."

"Oh," I said as if this was an afterthought and not something I'd planned this entire time, "and no killing. If we're caught and they find out we've been sanctioned, we're looking at a long and bloody vendetta." Jimmy gave me a level look. He nodded.

I watched the funeral procession disperse as I began planning the heist that would put me back on top.

Sixteen
Johnny's Vendetta

John. November 8th, 2009.

What I wouldn't give for a bowl of gumbo. I couldn't even find a place that sold okra. Instead, I preheated the stove and removed a few strips of frozen bacon from the plastic package.

"Captain!" Vince called from downstairs. I turned down the heat and put on my jeans before heading downstairs.

Vince was, as usual, early, worriedly staring at the supply closet door. He held a pistol.

"Vince, what's-" Then I heard it. A faint, almost-constant rustling from that direction.

"It won't stop, Sir." I licked my lips.

"Here, give me the gun," I told him. He obeyed. Pistol in hand, I took a few cautious steps toward the supply closet. As I did, the rustling became louder. I gripped the door knob. In one fluid motion, I opened the door and hustled in, gun first, shutting it behind me as I flicked on the lights. The rustling came from the back corner, behind an ammunition crate.

I carefully crossed the small room. I leaped forward, gun pointed behind the crates. With a laugh, I tucked the pistol away in my jeans and picked up a yellow lab puppy.

"How'd you get in here?" I asked as I noticed he was a boy. He stared at me with sad yet playful eyes, providing no answer. I'll have to check the perimeter later.

I gasped. The pup's left ear had a scar running across it. I

112

petted him a few times and checked for any signs of ownership. There were none: no tag, no collar, no anything. He was as much of a stray as he could be.

I brought him inside and grinned at Vince's confusion, tossing him his gun. I scratched the little guy behind the ears and headed upstairs. Once in the kitchen, I flipped over the bacon.

I took a whiff of the frying strips and gagged. It wasn't the bacon that smelled like stale coffee grinds and mucus. I brought the little guy to the bathroom and started running the water. He whimpered. I set him into the tub. He squirmed and wriggled, but I was firm.

"Arf!" he lolled his tongue and grinned at me with those happy, sad eyes, waiting for me to take him out. I looked into those deep, sad brown eyes. That's when I knew: this pup was meant for me. The water went up to his side before I turned it off.

I left him to soak and I finished up with the bacon. I brought a slice to my new friend.

When he saw the meat he began pawing the side of the tub and getting water everywhere, whimpering constantly. He had no attention spared for anything except the food. I could see the clear outline of his ribs; I would hate to imagine the last time he'd eaten.

"Calm down, Scout." I blinked. That was a nickname my dad had for me when I was a kid. As I looked down at the pup and he looked at me, I came to a decision. "Well, that's your name then. Scout," he couldn't have been more than a few weeks old, so I fed him the slice in bits. Every time I put it near him, he would lap it up from my hand and stare back at where the rest was. He paced the water, unable to sit still in anticipation. I was faintly reminded of Peter.

113

I pulled the drain up and handed Scout the small remainder of the bacon. He panted when he finished as the last of the water drained away. He growled at the drain.

I toweled him off and walked into the kitchen. He followed me, still wet, and hopped up on the couch (getting it wet as well). He began eating the crumbs on the coffee table while I went back to the kitchen and ate my own share of bacon.

Finishing the final strip, I sat on the couch. Scout curled up in my lap. The History Channel was showing a special on Vietnam. I didn't want to see that. Any other war, but not that one. I shut it off just as *Enter Sandman* by Metallica played. I got up, with a whine from Scout, and grabbed my cellphone off the counter. I clicked the answer button as it went to my ear.

"John, it's Peter. We need you over here at Johnny's." I sighed.

"You know I have my own life, right?"

"You know you don't have another choice so long as Johnny is agreeing to host your fights so we can try and keep you out of prison, right?" I grimaced.

"I'm on my way." I went to the cabinet and took out two small bowls, filling one with water and hurriedly removing a slice of ham from the fridge. I ripped it into little shreds and put them in the other bowl. I opened the front door and looked back. Scout was lying on the couch, fast asleep.

I went downstairs and asked Vince to occasionally let Scout out.

"Should we put up fliers, Sir?" I blinked.

"Uh, yeah, yeah we should." Vince gave me a level look.

"His owners, if he has owners, will be worried sick." I sighed.

"Yeah. We'll put up fliers." I went into the garage and

114

clicked open the door as I hopped on my bike.

It wasn't long before I arrived. There were only a dozen or so bikes present, all parked neatly in front of the bar. I went in. I looked around, but didn't see either Johnny or Peter.

"Upstairs," the Haitian bartender called to me. I nodded my thanks and headed up. The door at the top was locked. I knocked. A moment later a small rectangle, barely visible against the wood, slid inward. Johnny's shades popped up. The rectangle shut and I heard a series of whirs and chains as the door was unlocked. It opened inward, revealing a sort of meeting room, with a wide table in the middle and two seats occupied by Peter and a stranger with greasy black hair and standard Black Outfit sunglasses. Johnny shut the door behind me.

"Like I was saying," Johnny said as I took a seat, "this lab has been on our turf for who-knows-how-long. That isn't good. If he's cooking on my turf, then he's dealing on my turf. If he's dealing on my turf, he's making money on MY TURF! I need the three of you to go down there and put a stop to it. No guns; the police need to think it was just a lab that caught fire. So: go to the lab, beat up the guys there, and blow the place to high Heaven. Got it?" Peter and the stranger nodded. I shrugged. Johnny scowled. "Well? Get to it." Peter and the other guy stood. I began walking down the stairs. Upon reaching the bottom, I turned to the man I didn't know.

"John Washicha. And you are?"

"Greg Sheffield," he spoke with a slight slur, not of the South but of one who combined his words. One who could take his time speaking because he knows others will listen. "You packing heat?"

"I've got a Magnum, but didn't Johnny say no guns?"

"Something... could always go wrong." I made no remark.

Things went wrong all the time in Special Forces. It was no different here on the streets. We began to walk-jog outside. As we did so, I studied our new accomplice from the corner of my eye. His muscles rippled down his exposed forearms. A slender scar that spiraled down the left side of his neck most likely hid an interesting story. A leg of his sunglasses had been taped and re-taped. His short, strong stockiness reminded me faintly of a bull dog.

"So, Pete, can you brief me?"

"You already heard most of it. The Beppos set up a meth lab on Johnny's turf and Johnny just found out about it. He wants us to take care of it."

"Where's the lab?"

"North side of Florence. Johnny arranged for us to borrow one of his SUVs. This won't take long." Greg eyed Peter.

"You don't look like a scrapper."

"And you don't look like a member of Johnny's elite guard," Peter shot back. "We all have secrets."

"How did you-"

"Standard tattoo peeking out your collar on the back of your neck." His hand immediately went to where Pete said. "Oh, right, I'm not supposed to know what the skull and bear tat means, am I?" Greg caught me grinning and glared through his sunglasses. Peter stopped as we reached the SUV parked out front. Someone was already in the driver's seat. Without another word, Peter got in on the passenger's side. Greg and I got in the back. With a roar, the SUV came to life.

I gave little thought as to what we were going to do. This was my third assignment from Johnny Black. Hopefully not many would follow—I just needed to keep Johnny happy so he'd grant me the fights needed to explain the cash found on my person at *The Pub*. But this was gang warfare. War is war.

Something I understood. As well as a person can, anyway.

"This is it." The driver grunted as we pulled up to a small apartment complex. "The lab's in the basement." Strange. Basements were rare in Southern California. The three of us got out. The driver stayed behind, keeping the car running in case things went South and we needed a quick getaway.

Reminiscent of soldiers on a mission, we strode to the side of the building, where two oak cellar doors were fitted between the ground and wall. Peter tried the handles.

"It's locked from the inside." Peter observed. "They don't want anyone coming in." I put a finger to my lips and removed my revolver. Johnny said no guns to make it look like an accidental lab fire, but the cops would have no reason to check for slugs outside. I examined the cellar entrance more closely. I just needed to break the pin.

I fired. The doors jumped up a few inches as the pin snapped cleanly in two. I ripped open the doors and charged into the basement, the others' footsteps echoing behind me.

Three men fitted in white lab coats and surgical masks were hunched over various tables filled with tubes and chemicals. All had the common dope-addict lack of muscle or fat. A fourth man stood in the corner, well-built with muscles protruding from his arms, shown off with a black muscle shirt. Security. All four had the deep tan of the Mediterranean. Peter took the lead.

"Surprised to see us? Don't be. You're cooking in Johnny Black's territory. You can leave on your own two legs or we can bring you out in stretchers. Your choice." The biggest one laughed.

"Cracking heads open makes for a good morning workout." The room itself wasn't too large. The tables made a rectangle, taking up most of the space. Peter grinned.

He grabbed a bubbling glass bottle by the neck from a table and adjusted his grip as he swung it at the nearest cook. It shattered. The mark screamed as the liquid seared his face. No one stopped him as he ran outside. Pete dropped the glass in the puddle he made.

"Batter up."

It was now three on three. The big guy whipped out a switchblade and made incisions in the air. Peter dramatically stepped over the puddle he just created. "Come on, boys," he waved his hands wildly, "Who's next?" In another situation, the sight of this arrogant mobster with his head tilted forward and his arms out like a bird ready to take flight would have been comical. Now, with the stench of burning flesh fresh in everyone's nostrils, I just wanted to get this over with. The others may not have known that Peter was putting on an act, but I had a feeling he didn't want to be here much longer, either.

One of the chemists—at least I assume that was the correct term—pulled out a phone from his pocket and began to dial wildly. As one, the three of us charged. Peter made a grab at the guy with the phone. I went for the bouncer, who swiped with his bladed advantage. I leaped back, considering taking out my own knife. Before I reached a decision, he turned the blade with his knuckles and gripped it with his palm like a butcher cutting lamb. He lunged forward, knife outstretched.

I ducked and swerved to the right, instantly turning with the motion to face my attacker. The knife was now plunged into a wall. That took care of that.

Out of frustration, he charged me with his arms wide. I met him head on and stood my ground. As we grappled at each other's shoulders, I monitored Peter from the corner of my eye.

He either knew an ancient fighting style I was unfamiliar with or he was making wild jabs without regard for where his hits landed. The thug lashed out with the hand holding the phone. Peter elbowed it and the phone flew into the puddle with a small splash.

It began to hiss as it became part of the puddle.

I cursed under my breath. And people were putting this in their bodies? With a grunt, my opponent forced me down on one knee. I groaned with the strain. He was trying to get me on the ground. I realized with horror that if he succeeded, my head would be taking the place of that phone.

The lump of sinew and muscle tissue in front of me was pushing me to a death that would make an open casket all but impossible.

Not today.

I wasn't a major science geek, but I knew enough for when it counted. Like now. If his force is directed at a downward angle, all I would have to do is stop fighting the force and increase it with my own, and with the change in movement I'd alter the angle…

And just like that, the juicer went flying over my head. I rolled to my feet. He missed the puddle. I huffed. I couldn't keep doing this. Peter, with a cut below his eye, was now by my side, his opponent thoroughly subdued with what may have been a cracked skull.

I took a labored breath. Before the juicer could charge again, I pulled out my revolver and took aim. He hesitated.

Peter, aghast, pulled my gun-arm to his chest so my fist pounded against him. He flew back just as I misfired with him still holding on. I attempted to yank my arm away, but his grip was tighter than expected. My aged fingers let loose another bullet. Finally, Peter let go.

I took a glance at our handiwork and felt a pang of guilt: Greg had taken a hit to the side. The thug that moments ago had been taking a beating from him was not seeking retribution just yet. Instead, he and his partner were running out, for the second shot had hit a glass beaker on a table and a fire had started, quickly consuming the other chemicals. I was instantly reminded of napalm with heat powerful enough to reduce a soldier to nothing.

"Let's go!" Peter shouted.

"I can't move!" screamed a wounded Greg. Peter painstakingly swiveled his head between the exit and our comrade, as if calculating whether we could get him out on time.

I rushed over. We were now so close to the flames I could feel the heat brush my arms. I threw one of his arms around my neck and tried to lift him. I grunted as I took on his full weight.

"Peter," I pleaded, "help." Peter half-reluctantly ran to our aid on the other side, even closer to the growing fire. Peter also grabbed the foot of the chemist he had knocked unconscious. Together we picked up Greg and carried his limp body outside, Peter dragging along the chemist up the stairs as well. There was no sign of the escaped gangsters. We set down Greg and the unconscious chemist on the side of the building. I watched Greg's chest rise and fall. He was alive. Hurt badly, but alive.

Seventeen
Fanabala

Peter. November 8th, 2009.

While John inspected Greg's wounds, I jogged around the building to the front. A small crowd of tenants had gathered, with the landlord directing them to stay out as they find the source of the smoke. I motioned for our driver to get out. Grudgingly, he did so. I turned on my heels and headed back to the others, certain he would follow.

He did. We reached John and Greg. The driver bent over to check on him.

"Is he okay?"

"No," I replied, stooping down to pick up a nearby brick, "and neither are you." Gripping one end, I swung the other side over the driver's head. He collapsed on impact. Greg stared at me, fear in his eyes. I dropped the brick. John gave me a startled look. I fished into my pocket and removed a small bag of methamphetamine, tossing it into Greg's lap. He was too injured to move.

"Pete, what in the-" I cut off John with a wave of the hand as I pulled out my burner cell and punched in a few numbers.

"Joey, it's me."

"Is it done?"

"I wouldn't be calling, otherwise."

"Good. Drop by a few days after your friend's hearing. We'll go from there."

121

"You got it." I hung up. Without further explanation, I walked off to the SUV. John caught up with me.

"Peter, what is going on?!"

"Business, John. Business."

"Could you elaborate?" We reached the SUV. I opened the front door and tossed in another bag of meth. As I shut it, I cleaned the handle with my shirt. No prints.

"Sure," I answered as I began walking down the street, "it's simple: that was our betrayal."

"Our betrayal?"

"The one that tells Johnny to go screw himself. The one that says we run with the Beppo Family. You had been right: we don't need to stick with someone we don't wanna be with. Beppo's different." I paused. "Your bike is at Johnny's?"

"Yeah."

"Let's go get it." I hailed a taxi. One immediately pulled onto the curb just as the first police cruiser showed. Greg and the driver would be blamed for the meth and the shooting: an open-and-closed case. They were at the crime scene with residue, weapons, and meth all on them.

We got in the taxi and I gave him the address.

"I'm thinking after we get your bike, we head over to this little bistro I know. The pasta is almost as good as the Old Country's."

"Thanks, but I have something at my apartment I need to take care of. I'm more of a grits guy, anyway."

"What are you saying?" I asked, a dangerous edge to my voice.

"I'm just saying pasta isn't as good as homemade grits," he told me factually. "Noodles can't compare to the texture and flavor." I shook my head.

"Noodles? Did you just say noodles? Noodles are chow

mien. That isn't Italian pasta. It isn't chicken parmesan. We're not talking about mac and cheese, John! We're talking about one of the greatest culinary dishes ever created! Linguini, angel hair, even bow tie beats grits a million to one." John grunted, the southern hillbilly.

We pulled up to Johnny's bar, elaborately named *Johnny's*. I pulled out my money roll and handed over a few bills as we got out.

"Pete, who are we even working for?" I understood what he was getting at. I had, after all, gotten him a new employer without consulting him. But I couldn't have let him in on it without risking the entire operation. Assuming he would have gone along with it in the first place.

"Luigi Beppo's a good guy. As good as these characters come, anyway."

"What do you mean?" I stopped at the door and glanced at him, choosing my words carefully.

"Is fire good or bad?" I could tell he was thinking back to the inferno that had just occurred. Or maybe his thoughts went back further than that.

"Bad. Fire destroys."

"Yet it can keep people warm."

"Where are you going with this?"

"Is snow good or bad?"

"Good. People love snow."

"Except when it turns into a giant blizzard and destroys everything in sight, just like fire can. You see what I'm getting at?"

"I think so. You're trying to say nothing is all good or all bad, right?"

"Right."

"Then why couldn't you just say so?" he muttered. I

ignored him as I opened the door to the bar. There were more bikers than before, but still not many. Most seats were empty. It was, after all, hardly a quarter past eight. Johnny—the only one here in a suit—stood between the bar and wall of the stairs with his back to us.

At the wooden stool next to him sat Marcus Dean, Johnny's right-hand man, with a sling and collar brace, wearing his signature eyepatch and a silk shirt unbuttoned two buttons too low.

"You can't?!" Johnny yelled into a phone. "What do you mean, you can't? I want him dead! I want him dead, and I want him to know he's dead before he's dead!" A small pause. "Yeah, that's right. Yeah, he did. Oh, he did? Look, last night two masked guys roughed up Marcus in his own home. Threatened him with a gun to the head and left him for dead. They beat on us, we beat on them. Just you wait: this is only the beginning." Johnny hung up with a grunt. He wore a satisfactory smile that changed into a scowl when he looked up and saw me.

"What do you want?" John's muscles tensed.

"Our money, that's what. The lab is gone." Johnny looked beyond us.

"Where's Sheffield?"

"In the back of a police cruiser, most likely."

"Something went wrong?"

"Everything went just right, actually. Ya know what? You can keep your money. Consider it our parting gift."

"What're you saying?" Johnny's asked, tense.

"I'm saying we're with the Beppo Family, now." Johnny barked a laugh.

"What? After you just took out one of their labs? That's not how it works." I put on a pained expression.

124

"Gee, you're right... good thing it wasn't a Beppo lab. It belonged to the Cortez *Cartel*. One of their only labs on this side of the border. Sounds like you need to check your sources." Johnny pulled out a gun. Half the bar followed suit. I restrained John's arm from reaching for his own. Instead, I undid the middle buttons of my collared shirt. Johnny's eyes bulged.

"You're wearing a wire," he said flatly.

"I am. Everything we say and do goes straight to the receiver my lawyer is currently listening to, Johnny Black." I put extra emphasis on his name. He sneered at me.

"Lawyer? What lawyer?"

"Damion Occhipinti. Say hi to Damion, John." John, shocked, said nothing. "So here's how this is gonna go down: we are going to walk through that front door." I re-buttoned my shirt as I spoke. "The *Cartel* already knows what happened, I'm sure. Greg and that driver have been picked up by the cops with all sorts of evidence; Cortez will know it was you. You can claim you were tricked or whatever you want. It won't matter. Even if he believes you, every second you waste talking to Luis is another second that Luigi can use to his advantage."

"And then," Johnny continued, acidic, "let me tell you what will happen: we hit you with everything we've got. We kill you. We kill John here. We kill his family. We kill your lawyer. We kill your lawyer's friends. We kill your high school girlfriends. Everyone dies. And as they're picked off one by one, you'll know each and every time that this was all. Your. Fault."

"All of whom are under the protection of the Beppo Family. Except my old girlfriend. You'd be doing me a favor, there."

"What about John here? He needs me for his fighter alibi to

check out."

"No, he doesn't. Don Beppo will host John in a fight, free of charge. Plus, once the books open up—which, considering there's a war going on, will be soon—I'll be Made. After that, you won't be able to touch me. Not without upsetting the Commission."

"Judas," he hissed. I was surprised Johnny knew anything from the Bible. Funny. That had been what I called him when he betrayed me what felt like so long ago. I kissed the palm of my hand and pressed it to his cheek. He allowed it.

"*Fanabala,*" I replied, "*fanabala et soldati. Fanabala,* Johnny Black." I turned and walked out the front door, John on my heels, leaving behind the only connection to my former life. Now that connection has been severed irreversibly. I didn't feel fresh and new and ready to start over. I felt like a part of me was missing.

We made it through the door. As soon as it shut, John turned on me. He grabbed the front of my shirt and pushed me against the wall.

"What the Hell, Peter?!" I remained calm, waiting for him to go on.

"Disregarding everything unethical you've said or done, you put my son in danger! You put my family in danger!" I shook my head slowly.

"They're under the protection of the Beppos, John. They're safe," he seemed to calm down a bit.

"Damion is working with you?" I bit my lip.

"Not exactly. I was sorta bluffing."

"What do you mean 'sorta?'"

"Okay, I was bluffing. The wire was for show. But it worked, and that's what matters," he let me go. We began walking toward his bike.

"Where'd you get the meth?"

"Swiped it off one of the tables when the fire started."

"And you stopped me from shooting that guy because…?"

"I didn't want to see him dead?" John nodded. I paused, then headed back to the neat line of bikes in front of the bar. I kicked over the first one, creating a domino effect. I ran back to John, who smirked.

"So they were tan because they were Mexican, not Italian."

"Exactly."

"And what did you tell Johnny just now?"

"*Fanabala.* Go to Naples. Meaning him and his men, *soldati*, can go to Hell."

"So… you now work for the Beppo Family now?"

"Yeah. Well, we do."

"No, *you* do."

"So do you, until we pay back Murray. We'll have to prove our loyalty, then we're in."

"Getting two of their enemies life in prison doesn't count as proof?" he got on his bike.

"Not in this game."

"What game is that?"

"The game of life."

Eighteen
The Hearing

John. November 15th, 2009.

Scout pawed at my leg as I straightened my tie. I looked down at him. He whimpered, staring up at me with shimmering eyes. I breathed a sigh of relief that his ribs were no longer visible.

I took a seat on the bed to tie my shoes. Scout hopped up and cuddled next to me. I sighed, dreading my upcoming court debut. Pete was no help at the moment; all he talked about for the last few days is the future newspaper headline: "Richardson Defeats Fuentes."

"Can you believe this?" I asked Scout, not really expecting a response. Scout started panting with that almost-constant grin. I petted him on the head. "A bar fight. Losing a match. Back in the day, no one would have bat an eye."

I went into the kitchen and grabbed his bag of dog food by the door. Next to it were two bowls, one already possessing gnaw marks and saliva. I filled that one with pellets. I didn't really believe in the stuff, but he needed a balanced diet. Besides, I was running low on ham.

I filled the other with water from the sink.

Petting him good-bye, I left. Soon I would need to get the little guy some toys.

I nodded to Vince as I headed out. Throughout everything, Vince never remarked on my questionable decisions. He was a good guy, no matter what Peter's "fire and ice" philosophy said. I hopped on my Fatboy and, with a screech of tires, took off.

Everything occurring was such a blur. Most important was my family. Then came this whole court case with the FBI watching like vultures ready to swoop down with RICO. A ghost from my past coming back to haunt me, Pomerov, was definitely worth including. Then there was the bank heist Peter was setting up. I could certainly use the money. I had no qualms with stealing from a drug lord, either. Lastly was this war with the Black Outfit, which brought me back to Johnny's promise to get rid of the most important one of the five: my family. After I paid back Murray's *vig*, I can leave Beppo and Black behind and focus purely on what matters.

I reached the courthouse and parked next to a blue Prius. That explained where one lawyer was. Hopefully Peter was already here, too. I hurried inside and searched for the correct room number. I was at least a few minutes late. I stopped in front of a pair of wide double doors and, once I was sure it was the number Peter had told me, went inside. I was relieved to see both of my lawyers. The left-most chair at the defendant's table was unoccupied. I strolled down the aisle and sat. Peter and Damion were in a heated discussion, to the point that neither noticed my presence. No surprise there.

"No you don't," Peter said, "a hundred bucks says I can. If I start to lose, I'll give you the signal to take over and you win." Damion snorted.

"I'll give you twice that if you manage it."

"Deal. I'm a lot better when some *mook* isn't sabotaging me with hillbilly moonshine." They shook hands. I was incredulous. I wasn't sure what they were talking about, but my son, who when he was six refused to cross the street with me because "jaywalking is against the law," was gambling! I tried to avoid gasping.

"How was last night?" I asked Peter. He grinned, slowly shaking his head.

"Clare had a great time. Valli's voice has changed, though."

"Hopefully for the better," he gaped, a hand to his heart. I chuckled. "What did you do after the concert?"

"We... talked."

The preamble to the court proceedings began. Peter was sober this time, but still barely paid attention. Damion scribbled away in a folder with his pen. My eyes began to wander around the room.

Fuentes kept coming back to *Rager*, who was the lone spectator, with a pair of crutches leaning next to him. He had no legal team of his own; he wasn't suing me. Fuentes and the others had gotten to him from the start. According to Fuentes, it was my fault *Rager* had a cast on his leg. But he was skirting the point. Apparently, I was also here due to "accepting an illegal act of bribery for my own selfish gain, against the ethics of participants of sporting events everywhere," as Fuentes put it. Peter was still working out details as to my fighting appearances with Beppo. Finally, *Rager* crutched up to the witness stand.

"Mr. Sidney Gerin, do you solemnly swear to tell the truth, the whole truth, and nothing but the truth?"

"Uh. Yeah." Peter tried hiding a grin. Sid wasn't known for being too bright. Peter began tapping his leg excitedly as Damion gazed intensely.

"Mr. Gerin," Fuentes slowly began, "where were you the night of November first?"

"I was at *The Pub*, celebrating with twenty other guys over my win." Peter and Damion stood together. Peter grinned at my son, who sat down sheepishly. Peter wove his way around our table, making grand gestures.

"I object! You're telling me that twenty other people were all celebrating YOU winning a single match?" Peter looked down, eyes wide. "Wow, you must have a lot of friends."

"Well… we were celebrating a few sets of matches."

"I see. How many matches? How many were you in? Who did you fight?"

"Objection!" Fuentes cried. "I'm doing the questioning here."

"Sustained." Fuentes could tell something was up. He seemed to be having a mental debate with himself. Finally, he reached a decision.

"That will be all."

"Mr. Washicha's counsel?" The judge asked.

"Finally," Peter sighed, "so, *Rager*-"

"Objection!" Fuentes again. "Legal names, please."

"Sustained." Peter shrugged, walking over to *Rager* and placing an arm on the witness stand wall.

"So, Sid, do you think you're a good wrestler?"

"It's fighting. And yeah, I'm pretty good."

"Good enough to beat my client?"

"Apparently I am."

"But you're saying you only beat him because he allegedly lost on purpose?"

"Yes. No. I could've beat him if he didn't cheat."

"Interesting. But Sid-"

"Stop calling me that!" he snapped at Peter. I didn't understand what Pete was getting at, making Sid upset for nothing. Peter threw his hands in front of his face, as if for protection.

"Objection, Your Honor! How do I address him if I don't

use his nickname *or* his real name?"

"Overruled. You're badgering the witness."

"Badgering. Got it. Anyway, Witness-Who-Is-Not-*Rager*-Yet-Not-Sid, why are you so confident you could beat John, my client, honestly?"

"Because he's a weak nobody." I scowled. Pete better have a reason for this.

"A weak nobody. Well, that's not very nice. As a matter of fact, it's downright mean. Would you call your bar fight with him… honest?"

"No." Peter frowned.

"And why is that, exactly?"

"Because it wasn't in the ring." Pete made a buzzing sound.

"Err! Wrong! It wasn't an honest, fair fight because you punched him first, square in the jaw, while he was enjoying a good meal! A good meal despite all the other smells in the air." Peter took a dramatic whiff. "And I think I know where those smells came from." *Rager's* eye twitched. His face was a dark reddish-purple. A vein throbbed against his neck.

"Because he was taking a bribe for losing to me!"

"So you're saying he lost on purpose?'

"No! Yes!"

"Which is it?"

"Yes, he lost on purpose! That's why we're here!"

"So you're saying he could have beaten you if he had wanted?"

"Yes! No!" Sid began hyperventilating. His eyes bulged.

"That's exactly what you're saying! You just said so! I can have the court reporter read back our entire conversation!"

"No! I know what I said!"

"Do you take performance-enhancing drugs?"

"Yes! Wait. No!" he buried his face in his hands.

"Sidney, if you don't answer truthfully, you will be forced to take a drug test." Peter whispered, loud enough for everyone to hear. Then added, seemingly to himself, "Juice-addicted moron." His quiet words resounded throughout the room. Sid snapped. He knocked down the witness podium and lunged at Peter with murder in his eyes.

The judge continually banged his gavel, but Sid didn't care. Ignoring his own handicap, he took two handfuls of Peter's suit and threw him to the ground. He prepared to pounce. I knocked over the table. Damion threw out an arm to block my path. Two bailiffs tackled Sid. He socked one in the neck before being tazered. *Rager* screamed.

Peter went on as if nothing were happening, talking directly to the judge. "You see, your Honor, a side-effect of steroids is temper tantrums. This is what happened the night my client broke this man's leg. He saw money and, knowing he wasn't better than my client and thinking the worst, attacked him." The judge stared at the scene before him with disgust. So did I. Judge Taylor cleared his throat as Sid was taken away.

"There is not probable cause to continue the assault charge. If you agree, Mr. Fuentes?" The D.A. grudgingly nodded. "Good. However, there is substantial evidence regarding possible bribery. Trial will begin the first of December, 2009." Peter, satisfied, dusted himself off, picked the table back up and helped Damion collect the papers that had scattered across the floor. Damion reluctantly pulled out a checkbook.

"Cash," Peter said. Damion fished around in his pocket.

"What's that for?" I asked.

"Your son said that I could never be a real lawyer. He said lawyers help people; I said lawyers make people feel a certain way. So we made a bet that I couldn't get Sid angry enough to attack me. I won." There was one piece of the puzzle that still didn't add up.

"How did you know about the steroids?" Peter grinned mischievously.

"I didn't."

Nineteen
A Friend of Mine

Peter. November 19th, 2009.

"Yeah, we'll be meeting Don Luigi Beppo himself today." I told John. Again.

"It's just that I thought the big guys like Johnny Black and Luigi Beppo followed a chain of command. That's what the movies say."

"The movies?" I scoffed, "This isn't a movie, John. I mean, they got that right. Sorta. But we're dealing with a special case: me. I used to be a Johnny Black or Luigi Beppo. Now, under special circumstance I never got Made into a Family, but I'm still a wise guy. Through association, you're getting the same special treatment."

"Don't I feel lucky?" he muttered. I grimaced. We walked up to the bistro. We had been told four o'clock. I checked my watch. Four minutes early.

I noticed a figure leaning against the wall next to the entrance. A guard to the Beppo stronghold could be expected, but this wasn't a Family member. He was resting his chin against his chest and slowly raised his head as we approached. He studied us intensely with his beady eyes.

"Mr. Gigante wants his money," Donnie rumbled. I sighed.

"We've been over this: Murray gets his money *after* the job, when we have the money." Donnie didn't so much as blink.

"He wants the money now."

"Well that's just not going to happen." I tried to enter the building. Uncle Donnie, surprisingly limber, blocked my path.

"Mr. Gigante says every week you don't pay, *vig* goes up."

"That's fine," I replied, "interest on the twenty-five thousand still won't exceed what he's getting from the robbery. It'll all be paid. You'll get your share, too. Maybe you could buy a new face. Some manners'll cost extra," he grunted.

"Funny," he didn't move.

"Why is money the only thing that ties us together?" I asked with false sincerity. "Can't we all just be friends?" he scowled, but lumbered off. Which meant his only purpose there was to talk to us, so he knew when we'd be here. Or he'd been waiting, hoping to get lucky.

I opened the door, letting John to go through first. Not that I thought there was a possibility this was a trap or anything.

I walked in and saw Bobby Mancuso leaning against the wall. It had been a long time, but Bobby was still the same guy I knew when I was growing up in the Old Neighborhood: same big ears, big head, and big mouth. He nodded for us to follow him. He stopped at a closed door with another gangster in front of it.

"You think Joey came to you by accident?" Bobby asked suddenly. I shrugged as the doorman patted us down. John tensed.

"Fate is funny." I motioned for John to let his gun be taken.

"Not fate. Me," he jerked a thumb at himself. "I'm the one who had Joey recruit you. You're welcome." I rolled my eyes. These kinds of gestures were common. Especially from the Old Neighborhood. "I didn't stick my neck out like that for nothing, Richardson. Don't screw this up, and I don't screw you up."

136

"What's that supposed to mean?" John asked, nearly puffing out his chest.

"Watch it, big guy. I'm protected."

"It's okay, John," I told him. "Bobby's a friend of ours."

"Yeah. A real pal..." John muttered as Bobby opened the door for us.

"Just let me do the talking."

We entered a private dining room. Two older men sat facing us with a large, bald figure in black standing behind them, hands clasped at his waist. The table was a large rectangular structure that could likely hold twenty chairs, but only five were present. It was clear who was in charge.

Don Luigi Beppo: nails freshly manicured, left pinkie ring with a diamond easily worth more than Johnny Black's bar, and dressed modestly in a tan three-piece suit. He was one of the most feared men in the state.

Hollywood affected gangsters in uncommon ways. They didn't have the same reverence or style that was seen in New York. Luigi, however, kept a tight ship to maintain tradition. I would have joined up with him ages ago, if hadn't been for *Fratres Criminis'* condition I stick with Johnny Black for half a year. That time was over.

"*Compare*." I said in greeting.

"And you are?" he asked. I glanced at Bobby behind us, who was supposed to do the talking for now.

"Peter Richardson, who was previously a friend of ours a few years back, and John Washicha. Both are friends of mine." Don Luigi motioned for us to have a seat. We did so, Bobby walking around and sitting next to Luigi and his associate, who wore thick square glasses. The Don waved forward the thug behind him, who leaned in. Don Luigi spoke a few words in his ear and he left through a side door. A few moments later a waiter came through the same door. Alone.

The waiter approached the table.

"What can I get you?" he looked at me. Aiming to impress my Sicilian host, I thought of something quick without looking at the menu.

"I'll take a bottle of spiced Sicilian red Zinfandel, and for my meal *gabagool* with thin, well-preserved cilantro." The waiter seemed confused.

"Gaba- what?"

"*Gabagool*. What's so hard to comprehend? The *gaba* or the *gool*?" There was no way this *mook* would mess up my shot with my future boss.

"He means capicola," Don Beppo interjected. Now the fool understood. Bobby studied me.

"I'll have what he's having."

"As will I."

"Same here."

"Me too." Great. Now the whole dinner was dependent upon whether I knew what I was talking about. The Don studied us.

"How do I know you two aren't stool pigeons?" I was incredulous. In shock, I spoke for myself. The question was directed at us, anyway.

"I've been in this game awhile. Long enough to know what happens to rats. Which I'm not."

"I'm not accusing. Merely… idle speculation."

"To be frank," Bobby, the Made Man in the room, spoke up, "the pair of you was asked to come here today so that we can learn what there is to know about the Black Outfit and what they plan, ya know? We can't be wasting resources in this war with Johnny Black. Now, we have one job for the two of you before we open the books," he sniffed. "How do you feel about contracts?" The question was directed at me, since John was not Sicilian and therefore could not become a Made member. Still, John answered, just like I told him not to.

"Where do I sign?" I covered my face. Luigi laughed, taking it as a joke.

"Anyway, who do we *whack*?" I added the emphasis so John would understand.

"Oh, yeah. Right. Who's the poor guy we have to kill?" Luigi pursed his lips and shot his unnamed associate a sideways glance, who leaned forward.

"Johnny was taken by surprise when he learned about... about the explosion," the stranger explained, "we figure, it must have been ordered by someone bein'... you know. Insubordinate. Someone who could get away with bein' insubordinate to Johnny, and probably someone not at *Valentina's*."

"Marcus Dean," I confirmed.

"If he gets put on ice, then they lower morale, and we get revenge for..."

"For my son," Luigi concluded.

"Why didn't you get your masked guys to do it, instead of just beating on him?" John asked. Luigi and his associate glanced at each other.

"I'm afraid I do not understand," Don Beppo said, "masked guys?" he seemed sincere, but he had years of practice faking it.

"Forget about it," I said. "So you want us to whack Marcus?"

"That's right," the stranger said. Bobby kept his mouth shut. Whoever this other guy was, he was clearly far above soldier status. "Despite the good that the two of you did for us lighting a fire between the Outfit and the *Cartel*, Johnny managed to worm his way out of it like he always does. The *Cartel* is a silent partner to him. There are rumors that Johnny plans on publicly allying with the Russian *Bratva* up north. You know how they are: they like to be on the winning side. If we take care of Marcus, they'll see which side that is." Don Luigi cleared his throat, folding his hands on the table.

"Here is my proposal," Don Beppo said, "you accept the contract, and in return you will each receive ten thousand dollars... and I will open the books." I knew this was a risky move, but I had to ask. We were talking about murder, after all.

"Would you suggest us getting some help?" Bobby stiffened. Understandable. This was his reputation on the line; if we needed help for our first real job it would make him look bad. Unless help would be needed. Going up against Marcus made it probable.

"You may bring whoever you need, affiliated or not. But you must kill Marcus yourself. Prove beyond a doubt your loyalty to the Beppo Family."

"Yes, *Compare*. I understand." I stayed perfectly still.

I can't do it. I can't do it. I can't kill anyone, even someone like Marcus. There is no way I can go through with it. But afterwards, Luigi will open the books, and I need him to open the books. That is my way in. My only way in.

Our wine arrived. The waiter placed five glasses on the table and half-filled each one. Don Luigi, the stranger, Bobby, and I all took ours and tested it, putting the glass up to the light to check for clarity, inhaling, then swirling it around to check the legs before all of us took a large drink and swished it around. John stared at us like we were *oobatz*.

"What are you doing?" he asked. I swallowed.

"What does it look like? We're testing the wine."

140

"Then why not just drink it?" The four of us chuckled together.

"John, you can't get the full value of wine if you don't test it out. How can you taste the faint tobacco and oak barrel if you don't experiment?" he rolled his eyes and stared at the wall. The man had no appreciation for fine wine. Don Beppo stared at me.

"Peter, before our paths part for now, I fear I have bad news... news that likely will not come as a surprise."

"What is it, *Compare*?"

"I understand the Black Outfit doesn't have beefs, so to speak. But that's the closest word I have for what Johnny has for you two. He swore he would see you both dead. Watch your backs. Watch them until he is unable to watch his."

Twenty
Johnny's Present

John. November 19th, 2009.

The rest of the afternoon was spent dining on Peter's idea of a meal, which had a few issues. Cilantro shouldn't be sliced thin as paper. And that capicola, Peter's *gabagool*, was more half-cooked pig than a proper ham. Either way, I would have preferred a juicy steak.

My phone rang. I excused myself from the table—to Peter's chagrin—and hurried over to a corner of the room, pulling out my phone as I did so. My eyes lit up as I saw the caller. Hurriedly I flipped it open, holding it close to my ear.

"John..." Katy said hesitantly. Silently I urged her to go on. "Why don't you stop by? We can talk." My mouth popped open.

"I... yeah. Yeah, I'll be there soon, yes," I replied, going for casual.

"Good-bye, John."

"Good-bye," she hung up first. I swallowed as I put my phone back in my pocket. I headed back over to the table, slightly unsteady. "I've got to go." I announced. Peter looked ashen, as if I was doing him some sort of grave injustice. Don Luigi took a sip of wine, steadily gazing at me.

"May I ask why?" His tone was light, but his eyes strongly suggested he wasn't really asking for permission.

"I..." How could I tell these guys? How could I explain all

my emotions and history and thoughts? "I have a family emergency." Luigi continued his gaze, then nodded.

"I appreciate a good family man. You may go." I nodded my thanks and headed out, stopping to take back my Magnum.

I passed by Joey in the front, taking a smoke. He gave me a slight tilt of the head as I rushed past him. I should have stopped to say hi, but I wasn't focused on courtesy. I stepped outside and spotted my bike.

Two men were standing near it. One was writing on a notepad as he examined the license plate. I rushed over. Both looked up at my arrival. One, with grey hair and now in a tan blazer, khakis, and sunglasses, had been one of my interrogators in the precinct. The other, none other than District Attorney Isaac Fuentes, wore a dark blue suit.

"Good evening, gentlemen," I said, strolling up to them, "may I help you?" The stranger removed his sunglasses and stored them in a blazer pocket. I glanced up. The sun was hidden by a barricade of clouds.

"That depends," the stranger said in a clipped yet soft fashion, "your trial is coming up. We're hoping you'll change your story." I grunted impatiently. I didn't have time for these clowns.

"And you are?"

"Someone very interested in your case."

"Glad to hear law enforcement spends their time watching the legal process instead of, you know, enforcing the law," he took a step toward me.

"How are you so sure I'm in law enforcement?"

"Aside from the obvious? Your posture, attitude, and bulge at your side are all pretty good indicators. Plus, those shades scream 'wanna-be hard-ass.'" He frowned.

143

"I have half a mind to put you away for a very long time, Washicha."

"Isn't that what you're trying to do now?" he chuckled menacingly.

"Not even close. Soon, we'll have you on racketeering charges. Those come with a much heftier sentence than skimming points. Unless, of course, you cooperate." I shouldered him aside.

"I'm going to let you do what the legal system does best," I said as I strapped on my helmet, "fail." I zoomed off. In my rearview mirror, I could see their heads together as they conferred. I grimaced. Both were definitely bad news.

So was that Don Luigi character. Sure, he was better than Johnny, but that didn't mean I had to like either of them. All of them were off, in my book. Joey, Jimmy, Bobby, Donnie: they were all insane.

Now those people were my associates. That gave me chills. A bunch of professional criminals, all just plain bad people no matter what Peter said. Sure, I'd killed people, but I didn't do it for money, I did it to protect the ones I love and the country I'm loyal to. Now I was getting paid ten thousand dollars to murder someone I barely know. Better than someone I do know, I suppose.

I arrived at the modern American-dream two-story, with two square windows on each floor and a pathway leading up to the house. I parked on the sidewalk and forced myself to slowly dismount and walk up the pathway.

That was when I noticed something was very, very wrong. I stopped dead in my tracks. I hadn't given much observation to my wife's choice in a home, but last time I checked, the windows on the first floor hadn't been shattered. Or one on the second floor. The line of bullet holes in the wall were certainly fresh. I ran up to the front door, Magnum .44 in hand, and discarded my helmet on the patio as I flung the door wide. They have to be okay. Who did this? They have to be okay.

I rushed in and was met by Terry, holding a Desert Eagle inches away from my temple. I held back my instinct to disarm him. Barely.

"Where's your mother?" I asked, staring straight ahead. He lowered the weapon.

"Bedroom."

"Situation?"

"You just missed it. Mom, JJ, and I were home, but we were on the second floor. Thankfully, no one was injured. A black SUV pulled up, began firing a round of what I made out to be both semiautomatic and automatic weapons."

"Submachine guns?"

"Some of them were Uzis, maybe. Nothing bigger."

"How many weapons did you make out?"

"Three, but I wasn't focused. I was too busy getting my gun while JJ brought Mom to the tub. I fired after them from the upstairs window, breaking it. I think the SUV was bullet-proof. After I fired, it screeched off."

"Luigi was right," I muttered.

"Dad… do you know who did this?" I grimaced.

"I think so, Son. I'm going to go see your mother." As I put away my Magnum behind my leather jacket, I went upstairs. Hesitantly, I opened the door. Katy was crying on the bed. "Honey?" she glared up at me, her eyes red.

"No! Get Out! Don't bring that–"

"Whoa! What did I do??"

"You know what!"

"Calm down. I didn't do this. Some bad people did, and

they made a big mistake involving you."

"I know." This was the closest I'd ever seen Katy to pouting. I sat down on the bed and embraced her. At first, she kept trying to pull away, but then she relented, weeping into my shoulder. I breathed in her cinnamon scent and tried to calm down.

They meant to hurt my family. It wasn't right. If you fight someone, then you do it on equal grounds and don't get third parties involved. Definitely not my family. Peter had made assurances that my family would be protected. As usual, I couldn't rely on anyone but myself.

Any qualms I had about the contract were gone.

"Listen to me: I know who did this. I'm going to make sure they don't do it again."

Katy escaped my grasp and looked up at me with her wide, innocent eyes, and said what she said years ago.

"John, please, we've had enough killing. I don't care if you go or not but please: be careful." I sighed as I calmed down.

"Katy, the Viet Cong couldn't kill me, the Soviets couldn't kill me, and by God this man won't kill me." Or touch her. I gazed into those beautiful green eyes.

"Please, John. I'm begging you: come back." I reached into my pocket and pulled out the ring JJ had given me. I'd been waiting for just the right time to bring it out. That time was now.

"Katy, have this in case-"

"No. You will come back, and then you will give it to me."

"I'll come back on one knee, just for you."

"Just come back," she pleaded.

"As you wish." I slowly kissed her. It was our first kiss in over twenty years and well worth the wait. Nothing had changed: if anything, her lips had become even softer and sweeter than I remembered them, as impossible as that seemed. The weight I had in my chest—the weight of trial, the mob, the thought of death—it vanished as my heartbeat quickened.

"Be back soon," she whispered breathlessly, still holding my gaze.

I nodded, unable to form any words. Or thoughts. I blinked.

"Stay here. This will all be taken care of," she squeezed my hands and I left, heading down the stairs. Terry was peering through the window with JJ lounging on an M16 next to him. Terry stared at me like a soldier preparing for the worst.

"What are we going to do, Dad?" I clasped his shoulder, admiring my boys' perseverance to stop what wasn't right. They weren't my boys. They were my men. But this wasn't their fight.

"No."

"No?" Terry seemed both intrigued and defiant at my response. I licked my lips.

"You're not coming. You two don't want to be in this any deeper than you already are." JJ stepped forward and, for what may have been the first time in his life, made sense.

"Father, they've attacked our household and we must therefore avenge our family's once-impenetrable fortress. Their swords may be sharp, but our wits are sharper, forged with the fire of vengeance we shall deal upon them." Terry was as shocked as me.

"JJ... how did you do that?" he asked.

"COOKIES!!!" JJ exclaimed, bounding into the kitchen. I shook my head, trying to remember what the doctor told us. Something to do with an improper synapse within his cerebellum connecting his cerebral cortex. Or something like

147

that.

I had no choice. I had to call Peter. One ring. Two.

"Peter, I need you at my family's house. Same place where you picked me and my boys up." There was silence on the other end. I could see Peter pacing in my mind.

"I'm going to need more than that, John."

"My house was hit with a drive-by. Black SUV. The occupants had Uzis and pistols."

"The Black Outfit," he confirmed my suspicions. "Is everyone okay?"

"A bit shaken, but yeah." I checked a clock on the wall. Twenty to seven.

"What time does Johnny leave his bar?"

"Around six on Thursdays to go clubbing."

"So he's not there?" Silence. "Peter?"

"No," Peter sighed, "but Marcus is." I felt my heart skip a beat.

"How many bikers will be there?"

"No clue. Most are off doing Johnny's dirty work this time of day. A handful. Maybe a dozen. I'll bring Joey and Bobby."

"Should Terry and Jesse James come?" Terry looked at me expectantly. I ignored him.

"I assumed they would."

"Will we need them?"

"We need manpower, and getting too much help from the Family will make us look weak. Look… meet me at *The Pub*. Johnny's boys may come back to your place. We want to face them on our terms."

"What about Katy?"

"They should leave her alone. They must have thought you were with her, or maybe they just wanted to get a reaction from you. In either case, she's not the target."

"Perfect."

"I'll be there soon," he didn't sound happy about any of this. I heard the click as he hung up. JJ reappeared, stuffing cookies into his mouth. I looked back to my men, who stared at me with hope in their eyes. I sighed.

"Okay guys, you can come. Grab your military gear if you still have it and meet me in the kitchen in ten. Don't tell your mother." They saluted me and hurried upstairs. I slowly followed them, heading into Katy's bedroom. She wasn't there. She never had been one for following orders.

I began to search for my gun collection. Katy wouldn't have left that behind. Tonight: this ends. One way, or another.

Twenty-One
Hammer and Anvil

Peter. November 18th, 2009.

I wiped my palms on my suit jacket. I hadn't had a chance to change from my meeting—at least if I died, I would be dressed properly for my funeral. I checked my watch. Seven o'clock.

The only customers in *The Pub* were me, Bobby, and Joey, who twirled a switchblade around his fingers. We knew what would have to happen tonight. The *Compare* had been very specific: I have to whack Marcus.

The three of us were at me and John's regular booth. From it, we could see anyone coming or leaving. Then they walked in.

John, especially grizzled, had the look of a man who didn't care if he, or anyone else, lived or died. The look of a real gangster. Then came JJ with an ignorant bliss of the situation. It was amazing, really; an attempt on his life—or at least his father's life—and he smiled and waved. Taking up the rear was Terry, bulkier than I recalled. John wore his standard military uniform, raising a few eyebrows around the room. Most went back to their drinks. Everyone was here for their own reasons, after all. The other two wore all black.

John, wearing grim determination like a mask, led the others to our booth with a dusty wooden briefcase in his right hand.

"Peter. Bobby. Joey," he inclined his head to each of us in turn.

"John. Boys," I nodded to each of them, taking his sons as one nod.

"Men," he corrected. I studied them.

"Men," I agreed. I shivered. It wouldn't be long now.

"Have a seat," I motioned across the booth to where Joey sat, alone. They sat, causing Joey to squish himself against the wall. Realizing this, Terry got out and pulled up a chair. JJ sat on all fours next to his brother as John set his briefcase in his lap. I took a deep breath, inhaling stale grease particles. "Marcus is usually at the bar on weekdays. Johnny has his guys all around the city protecting investments. Thankfully, he stretched himself too thin to leave his stronghold... well, strong. It's a club bar, so there shouldn't be civilians. There is the front door, along with one on the backside leading to the kitchen for deliveries and roughing up anyone that pisses Johnny off. We'll want to cover both."

"That place will turn into a mausoleum," John said. I sighed, leaning my head on my hand propped up on the table.

"John, think about it: most of them had nothing to do with what happened."

"I've thought about it. They chose the wrong side," he glared at the table.

"Johnny broke the code," I said, sparing a few seconds to glance at each man at the table. "He attacked an associate's family. Retribution is the only course. This war is about self-interest, and I say it's about time we protect our own." My eyes rested on John. He was toying with the clasp of the briefcase, studiously ignoring my gaze. I cleared my throat.

"It's not personal," Joey added for John's benefit. John snorted.

151

"He made it personal."

"Well, don't think about that," Joey said. "Keep your head clear. Think of the money. Think of being Made." John looked up, confused.

"John is Sioux-Irish," I explained.

"What's that have to do with anything?" John asked, slightly offended.

"Only full Sicilians can become Made in a traditional *Borgata*. Bobby introduced us as friends of his. He vouched for us."

"But he said you used to be a friend of 'ours.'"

"Meaning I was a wise guy. When Luigi said he would open the books, it meant I would be Made."

"And what's so special about being Made?"

"*Madonn'*, I thought you watched the movies. It means I'm higher on the pecking order. It means I get the better jobs, and therefore you get better jobs."

"But I'm not Made."

"No, you're not. But you're sticking with me."

"So I can never get promoted?"

"No, you ambitious *goombah*. The only reason I'm getting Made after one real job—and an important one, at that—is because of my special situation. Luigi knows having me as an important guy will help him with his respect." John crossed his arms.

"I didn't want the promotion, anyway."

"Can we get on with it?" Bobby asked. I took a shaky breath.

"Do you own a gun?" John asked me.

"Not since it was 'misplaced' at Johnny's bar last month. Seems there's no honor among thieves."

John took his worn and moldy briefcase and set it on the

152

table with a thump. He turned it to face me and—with a sharp *ping*—unlatched it.

Inside was a pistol older than the case holding it, surrounded by black Styrofoam with a straight grey clip embedded next to it. If I held it, I could fit the handle completely around my hand. It shined dully.

"My old Green Beret secondary weapon: the M1911 semi-automatic handgun. Seven-round clip, two-and-a-half pounds, .45 caliber. The standard pistol of the United States Armed Forces for 60 years, 'til 'Nam ended. It goes by 1911 Colt. I want you to have it." I frowned as I gently stroked the side facing me. On the side of the trigger was a small golden inscription. I squinted but couldn't make it out.

"De Oppresso Liber. 'From an oppressed man, a free man,'" John said. I slowly shook my head. I picked it up by the handle, bringing the clip with me. I slid it into the device meant to hurt others. No: to kill others. I carefully examined the weapon and found it to still be in good condition. I removed the clip and placed both back in the case.

"So: the plan." I said.

"I have an idea, actually," John replied. I arched an eyebrow, but nodded for him to go on. "We can't give the enemy much time to retaliate. I want to be breathing down their necks before they know we're there. JJ covers us from the outside. He and Joey will be at the back, Joey heading inside. If no one's there, JJ comes in, too. You, Terry, Bobby, and I will go right through the front door. We hit them hard and we hit them fast. But silence will be the key, until then." I bit my lip.

"Not bad, but we have to account for location. The bar isn't in the middle of the city. It's a rest stop. Silence isn't an issue. What kind of firepower did you bring?"

"JJ has an M16. I brought my Magnum and Terry has a

military-issue Desert Eagle pistol." I nodded thoughtfully.

"Hammer and anvil," I perceived. An old military technique that of course John would be familiar with: two infantry units attack from the front and hold the enemy as the anvil, while a cavalry unit maneuvers around them and charges from the rear: the hammer. The hammer smashes down and meets the anvil.

"You know military tactics?" he seemed impressed.

"The basics," I muttered. I resisted the urge to pace. "We can expect a dozen of them, mostly in the front room. The staff, which right now would be the bartender and two cooks, are Outfit members. That means two in the back and ten spread out in the front. They won't run or group together. They'll shoot. We have the element of surprise, but they still have power in numbers. Four men with pistols running through the front won't get very far, especially since we'll have to take the time to see the placement of everyone."

"So we get the placement beforehand," John countered. Joey blinked.

"And just how are we going to do that?" he asked.

"We count them," John said simply.

"What, just like that?"

"Just like that. We get them to come outside."

"How?" I asked.

"We shoot the place up and hide. They come out, look around, and go back in." I shook my head.

"Then they call for backup."

"Okay, then we take them out while they're outside." I thought about that one. They come outside, and they'll be sitting ducks. Except...

"They hear gunshots, and they'll run outside with guns drawn. The area around the bar is all gravel, with no place to hide. We could be on the sides of the building, but they'll still overwhelm us with numbers. Plus, there's no guarantee Marcus would go outside. We can't give him time to call for help or barricade himself in Johnny's office."

"You really thought that one through," John remarked. I spread my hands.

"It's what I do. This is a hit, not a battle."

"So what do you propose?"

"You're right about needing to count them. If we could get them all in one place, it would be a lot easier to take them down, too." I had an epiphany. I pulled out my cell and punched in a few numbers. The others all watched me with a sort of curious anticipation. It rang twice.

"*Johnny's.*" Andrew, the bartender, picked up in his regular Haitian accent.

"Andrew, it's Cade." I forced my voice to drop several octaves. "I'm making a poker run. How many boys we got tonight?" There was a pause on the other end. Either my ruse didn't work, or —

"Six are in. Abram and Ryan are in some intense pool. Count them out."

"Cool. Tell the rest to set up at our usual spot. You game?" he chuckled.

"Come on, man. I'm on duty. You know how Mr. Black is about stuff like that."

"But the Boss isn't there, is he?" I held my breath.

"Nah, just Marcus with some white dude in the office. But you know how it is: what one hears..."

"All right, man. See you soon."

"Aight," he hung up. John was obviously trying very hard to hold in a laugh. He failed. I snarled.

"Problem?"

155

"Nah, man. It's cool," he said in imitation of me imitating Cade. I glared. "Actually, there is one thing: what if Cade had been there?"

"Then I would have hung up and we would have moved on them without knowing anything. Anyway, there are twelve bikers and one unknown. Two cooks in the back, Marcus and an unknown associate upstairs. Six will be at a booth on the right side of the bar, ready to play some poker. Another two will be to the right, closer to the entrance, playing pool. Then there's Andrew, who keeps a shotgun under the counter. The rest will have pistols, mostly revolvers."

"Joey…" Terry began, eyeing Joey's glasses, "how good of a shot are you? Honestly."

"I'm good," he replied earnestly. "I'm alive because I'm good." John nodded.

"So you could take out two cooks by yourself?" he concluded.

"I'd say so."

"Good. Because that's the new plan. You have a silencer?"

"Is the Pope Catholic?"

"Use it." I wasn't used to John giving orders. I wanted to see where he went with this. "We want to hit them hard and fast. No time for us to pick up radios, not if we want the body count Peter gave to stay accurate. You go through the back, alone, and quietly dispatch the cooks. We'll all be at the front. If there's trouble, we come in. If we don't hear anything, we'll count to twenty and infiltrate. You hear us, you follow. We'll need you to take out the bartender. JJ will be firing through the window at the booth crowd. Peter, Bobby, and Terry will take care of the two at the pool table and provide cover fire so I can head upstairs. I know what Luigi said, but leave no mistake: Marcus is mine. In the movies, they say 'It's not personal, it's business.' Well this isn't a movie. Their business crossed into what's personal to me. Tonight, the two are one and the same."

John stood, his sons following him out the door. Joey grasped the golden Crucifix around his neck, gave it a quick kiss, and placed it in his shirt so it wouldn't shine. I shut the briefcase and clasped it, firmly gripping the handle in my right hand.

It was time.

Twenty-Two

De Oppresso Liber

John. November 18th, 2009.

Peter, Bobby, and Joey went in Joey's Cadillac while the rest of us were in Katy's pale blue 2004 Chevy Malibu. I got in the driver's seat while my sons piled in the back. Tonight revenge would be had. Not just for me, but for JJ. For Terry. For Katy.

The car rumbled to life. The others were right behind us as we drove off.

How Pete worked with these people for so long is beyond me. It just wasn't his nature. He wasn't... I wasn't sure what he wasn't. He just wasn't one of them. I shook my head. I might enjoy Poe, but I was no philosopher.

We were nearing the destination. I pulled out my phone and called Peter.

"Pull over up here," I directed. "We don't want our headlights to shine through the windows."

"I'll let Joey know," he hung up. I veered off the main highway, several hundred feet from the bar's parking lot. We wouldn't need a quick getaway: this was all or nothing. I cut the engine.

Everyone exited and shut the doors quietly. Peter, with a bulge at his side that wasn't there before, walked up to me. We put our heads together.

"John," he whispered, "I think I should go with Joey. You and Terry are better shots than I am, and we can't risk Marcus

158

going through the side door." Logical, sound, sensible. And a lie. I shook my head.

"We need you on the front lines. It has to be a full-out charge with everyone we can spare. You'll be okay," he nodded. If I was to be leading, then I would act the part. I studied Peter. "Listen to me carefully," I softly whispered, "don't use that unless you have to." I patted the bulge. He nodded as he gazed at the bar.

We removed the M16 from the back of the Malibu. I handed it to JJ, glad him and Terry were wearing body armor, but praying they wouldn't need it. I knew my sons had done dangerous things before, things that would have been illegal in this country. But tonight, I will stand by their side. As a father.

"Be careful," I said softly. He made a doggish growl in what may have been compliance. Terry stood off to the side, warily watching the building a football field away. I put my hand on his shoulder and looked him in the eye. His mouth tightened. No words needed to be spoken. We both knew that what was occurring was unethical, barbaric, hateful… yet necessary.

I began a stealthy crouch toward the front entrance. The others were right on my heels. The air was humid and chilly, yet that was all distant. Everything physical seemed galaxies away. This was all psychological, just like it had been all those years ago.

I felt rather than heard Joey break off from the group. His silhouette grew dimmer as he rounded the side of the building. I pressed myself next to the front door, Peter behind me, Terry and Bobby on the other side. JJ was off in the shadows, training his assault rifle on the window.

I began to count to twenty. I imagined Joey going in and taking out the cooks. On twenty, I unglued myself from the wall and banged on the door with my foot, preparing to imitate Peter's voice earlier (only, hopefully, better).

"Hands are full. Let me in," I said gruffly. I gripped my revolver tightly. Footsteps resounded on the other side of the door. It opened wide, revealing a large biker. His eyebrows knit together in confusion when he saw I wasn't who he was expecting. His eyes widened as I raised my gun, pressing the barrel against his forehead. I pulled the trigger. For my family.

The body was blown back into the bar. The door next to the bar counter burst open with Joey automatically firing at the bartender reaching for his hidden shotgun. He went down. Joey took up a position behind the bar. The two at the pool table began to overturn it for cover. I rushed into the room, the others behind me. Some bikers at the booth turned on Joey, but suddenly the window to their left shattered as gunfire pierced the glass, courtesy of Jesse James.

I dove, firing twice at one of the men behind the pool table. His body convulsed.I kicked down a circular table as I hit the floor. Terry crouched beside me. It was a tight fit, but Peter managed to hurry to our encampment, a blaze of gunfire behind him. A *very* tight fit. We couldn't give Marcus time to react. I had to get upstairs. Using the advantage of our adversaries' surprise at the exterior gunfire, I sprang up and fired again, hitting a man at the booth. He slumped against the wall. The others scattered behind two tables as Bobby shot off rounds from the doorway. We had them on multiple flanks, but they were split up into three groups and the element of surprise was wearing off fast.

I began to roll our table. Terry continued shooting from the side and Peter crouched between the two of us, assisting me in getting the table to the stairs. They were hitting the doorway hard, making it impossible for Bobby to come in. Everyone was in cover. This could drag out, and both sides would be looking for easy pickings. Finally, our table hit the wall against the stairs. I ran up, glancing back just as JJ entered through the window, firing. I grunted at him not following orders, but nothing could be done about it, now. He walked into the room, his weapon to his shoulder as he fired.

I sprinted up the stairs just as the door at the top began to close. I leaped forward, crashing into the wood. It burst open.

The room was filled with darkness except for the lightbulb above the stairs that didn't reach beyond the frame. My head slowly swiveled as I crept further into the room. I stopped as I bumped into what must have been the center table. The small sound reverberated throughout the room. I froze.

The door shut. I whipped around and fired, momentarily illuminating the room. From the corner of my eye, I could see handicapped Marcus huddled in a corner. The man who had shut the door was someone else entirely. I couldn't get a good look at him as we were plunged into total darkness. The sounds below had become muffled. I hunched my shoulders. If I couldn't see, then neither could they.

I heard a slight creak and then a *swoosh*.

Right on time, I turned, dropped my gun, and grabbed some sort of bat swinging toward my head. Moving with his momentum, I yanked it out the culprit's hands as I heard my Magnum hit the ground, taking the thin, wooden object—a chair leg—and hitting him in the side with his own weapon. I heard him hit the table. Hard.

I discarded the chair leg and scrambled for my gun. I groped toward where I thought I dropped it. I heard the hammer being pulled back. I stopped.

I lunged where I thought the sound came from, hitting someone with my hands. A gunshot went off, filling the room with a flash of light.

I heard the revolver skitter away. It was empty now, in any case. My attacker was an inch taller than me, with a grey buzz cut, a grey five o'clock shadow, and a black long-sleeve shirt with the sleeves rolled up.

That was all I could notice as the room once more turned to pitch black. I took several steps back, my heel hitting a chair. The air changed.

I blocked his kick to my chest with my elbow, in return dealing a punch to his abdomen. He, too, blocked it and came back with another kick, this one to the stomach. I grunted and grabbed his foot with both hands, swinging him around until his other leg hit the table, sending him flying.

Afraid of losing him, I jumped onto the table and covered the short distance to where I believed was the end of the table. I had to have been about a foot away from falling when I heard a faint whistling. A second later I was hit by what must have been a leather chair.

I was sent sprawling to the ground. I heard what must have been the metal of a boot knife being drawn. I hurled the chair off me and rolled for my life. Where I had been came the sound of carpet ripping.

I jumped to my feet and adopted a judo stance. My opponent's knife slashed the air in front of me. I began dodging his quick, precise swipes, unable to do anything except stay alive. One slice came dangerously close to my ear.

I got a cut across my arm. I clenched my teeth, sucking in breath as I decided upon a new tactic. After dodging a swipe at my neck, I made a jab at the man's jaw. He grunted and stepped back. It was now or never.

I sprung upward, bringing both my feet up into a ball and then out at his chest. The result: we both flew backward.

As soon as my hands touched the ground they brought me back to my feet. I gasped with the strain, but kept moving. I ran for where the door should have been, trying to find a nearby light switch.

I was successful, flipping it on and taking in the scene of destruction before me. Papers were scattered everywhere, as were my spare bullets. Chairs were strewn across the room. A massive cut dug into the carpet. The other man picked himself up and tried a flying kick. I held up my arms to absorb the blow.

On impact, we splintered the door behind us, tumbling down the stairs, each of us unable to get a grip on the other amid all the pain and motion. When we reached the bottom, we were a seething mass of wriggling limbs. He bared his teeth, murder in his green eyes. I gaped.

A pale scar ran down his cheek from what had been rusty brown hair a few decades ago.

The atmosphere on the first floor had changed. I distantly made out Terry and Bobby in a corner with JJ. Joey had his pistol trained on us, with Peter yelling at him to shoot. None of that mattered.

I called out to the man trying to kill me. He either didn't hear me or just ignored me, struggling to free himself. I unhooked my arm from his leg and rolled up my shirt's right sleeve, revealing a tattoo of the Special Forces symbol: two arrows crisscrossing another arrow encircled by a black ribbon with the words *De Oppresso Liber*—the same words on the pistol I gave Peter, and on my own. The twin to this man's Colt 1911. He gasped. A beat passed. Then another. He brought out his arm from behind my neck and showed me an identical tattoo in the same spot. My muscles groaned as we hugged.

"Just like Panama?" he asked, chuckling.

"*Exactly* like Panama," I replied. He grinned a wide, toothy smile that was most likely mirroring my own. It had been twenty-two years, but I was finally reunited with my brother.

Twenty-Three
Desperate Times...

Peter. November 18th, 2009.

"I felt... incomplete, after our last op," Dustin explained with his faint Irish accent. I recognized him from the bar by *Valentina's*, right before the war started. The one with the detonator. He worked over the bar, stitching up JJ with a pair of tweezers and some twine. JJ was stiff, unmoving on the counter. It wasn't that he was near death; he was simply told to stay still and was obeying. He learned his lesson about obedience after he had been shot in the shoulder a few minutes ago.

Joey and Bobby were outside acting as lookouts, and Terry—though excited about seeing his long-lost uncle—was searching the shelves for the most flammable alcohol so we could cover our tracks.

"It hadn't been our first failed op, but losing Carl... and, worse, no one cared, outside the squad. It was as if Carl had never existed. Pomerov continued to gain power. I couldn't stand it. So, once we got back, I set out to finish what we started.

"I spent seven years trying to discover who betrayed us. No luck. So I figured, if I couldn't kidnap Pomerov as originally intended, then I would have to eliminate him. For Carl. I headed to Moscow. After several months of careful searching, Pomerov found me, not vice versa. One of his agents contacted me and wanted to know if I was looking for work. I figured that I could get close to Pomerov if he thought I was on his side, so I signed on. Fast forward to 1998. Pomerov has a stroke and relinquishes all control to his son while he recovers. He never does. Foul play was plausible. So I now work for his son, also named Alexei. I figure I could get close to this one and topple the empire somehow, you know, crush his dad's dream. And so here we are," he spread his hands.

"That doesn't explain why you tried to kill me," John interjected.

"Or why you're even here," I added.

"This was supposed to be the assignment that got me close to the new Alexei Pomerov: he sent me 'on loan' to this guy, Johnny Black, to start—and finish—a gang war." I looked over to the door.

"By killing Don Beppo's son," I confirmed in a low voice.

"And injuring Marcus. Both sides had a bone to pick, and once I felt the time was right, I was supposed to assassinate Black so blame would be put on the other side. I guess that's not going to happen." I snorted.

"Probably for the best. You kill Johnny Black, you'd be dead before his body is cold."

"I can take care of his men, too, lad."

"I'm not talking about his men." All the pieces fit right into place. I began to slowly pace. "You had been nothing more than a patsy. Alexei was using you. You kill Johnny, and *Fratres Criminis* comes in for a swift execution. Alexei makes sure they don't get a chance to interrogate you. It will just look like Don Beppo sent you. Then Alexei gets rid of you as a loose end, no one knows he killed a potential threat to his power, and life goes on."

"What do you know about Alexei Pomerov?" Dustin asked,

certain I had no clue what I was talking about.

"I know everything down to his favorite color. Which is black, in case you were wondering."

"I wasn't," he responded flatly. I stopped pacing.

"So what did you do for Johnny?" I asked as I went over to assist Terry.

"Clocked certain members of the Beppo Family, and even a few Black Outfit members whose loyalty Johnny questioned."

"Like us." John summed up my thoughts.

"Not quite. I had no idea you were involved in this. Johnny must have ensured that."

"So what now?" I asked. "You can't exactly go back to Johnny, which means you can't go back to Alexei. You're dead."

"Then that's how I'll play my cards. No one expects any tricks from a dead man." I nodded slowly. He still wanted to go after those involved in a decades-old crime.

JJ whined. Terry, suddenly agitated, mumbled something about going check for a can of gasoline as he went into the kitchen. John went around the bar and began inspecting various bottles. Finding a suitable brand, he removed the cap and placed the neck against JJ's lips. He gulped greedily, but John took back the drink before too much was consumed. It was, after all, to dull the pain and nothing more. He offered some to his brother, who refused. John suddenly tossed the remainder of the bottle onto the floor, sending glass and fluid everywhere.

Dustin, finished with Jesse James, slid over the counter and began doing the same. They took bottles with high alcohol content and tossed them in random places across the room.

"So," John said, continuing his methodical vandalism, "what about your apartment?"

"What about it?" Dustin asked. I joined the organized carnage.

"Well, you're here. You can't go back to wherever you're living. I guess you'll want the shop back." Dustin stopped and rubbed his stubble-filled chin.

"Yeah, I guess I do need a place to crash. I had wanted to stay incognito—not even let Vince know I was here—but I guess that's pointless, now. That's where you're staying?"

"Yeah. I knew my family was in California. I figured, with your shop here, I'd stay in LA while I looked for them."

"Vince getting the checks I've been sending?"

"Yeah."

"Good. I like him."

"So you're the one whose been paying him?"

"Who else?"

"Pomerov must have been quite the employer," John perceived. Dustin shrugged.

"Not enough to curb old feelings. Anyway, I recall there only being one bed. Not to kick you out or anything, but where will you stay?"

"I have a feeling I'm going to be moving out of there shortly."

"How's Katy?"

"Shook up. There was a drive-by at the house today."

"So that's whose house Johnny was talking about. You must have really pissed him off. No one was supposed to get hurt..." he eyed his brother.

"No one was." Dustin nodded, reassured.

"It was supposed to trigger an angry response."

"It did. Aren't there rules about not touching someone's family?"

"There are," I answered. "Johnny Black doesn't seem to

play by anyone's rules but his own." Which would explain why Alexei wanted him out of the picture. Terry came through the door with a Jerry can. I hurled a bottle of vodka against the stairwell wall. Joey and Bobby came back in.

"Coast seems clear," Joey said, "no bikers, no cops."

"Will we have to lay low for a while? Stay out of sight of the police?" Terry asked as he began leaving a trail of gasoline. I chuckled.

"Lay low? First off, there's no evidence. If there is any, we're about to burn it to the ground. Second, cops don't give much effort to searching for gangbanger killers. They usually assume it's other gangbangers and just let the two sides resolve the matter themselves." Joey walked to the bar and placed a lighter on it.

"We'll use this. I need a new one, anyway."

"Is the kid okay?"Bobby asked, nodding at JJ. "We may need him again soon, the way things are going."

"He'll be fine," Dustin assured him, "just a flesh wound, in and out. Though I doubt John will want his sons in this sort of danger again." I hid a smile and looked to John, who had just thrown another bottle. The only one left was now in my hand.

"That's right." My eyes widened. "I brought the pair of you along tonight out of desperation and anger. It was a mistake on my part. One of you was shot because of it. I don't want that happening again." Terry mumbled something under his breath, but didn't openly protest. Jesse James proceeded to pant like a dog. Terry took his gasoline trail upstairs, behind the wall. A moment later, he descended, his face ashen.

"You look like you saw a-" Bobby stopped short as Terry was followed by none other than Marcus, a familiar revolver in his hand. It was aimed at the gas can. Everyone froze. Even JJ stopped his needless noise. For an instant, there wasn't a sound.

"John…" I began, "how did he get your gun?"

"I dropped it."

"And you didn't bother picking it back up?"

"I just got reunited with my brother, my son was shot, and you blame me for forgetting about dropping a gun?!"

"I do when the man I thought you killed is now holding it!"

"I thought he ran downstairs and you guys took care of him!"

"Which of these," I gestured to the bodies scattered around the bar, "is him?!"

"Obviously none!" he replied. I groaned.

"Enough!" Marcus barked. He held the revolver in his right hand, waving it about wildly like a caged animal, though we were the ones who were trapped. He regained composure and fully entered the room, the weapon steadily trained on the gas can. "Surprised to see me? You shouldn't be."

"It's empty." John said. Bobby raised his gun. Marcus carelessly fired at him. Bobby yelped and fell to the floor, cradling his foot.

"You dropped your bullets," Marcus remarked smugly. "If anyone in here moves, I shoot the can and we all go up in flames." John bravely took a step forward.

"If you do that, then you die, too," John answered, his voice surprisingly level. His eyes, trained on the revolver, gave away his true thoughts. Marcus growled.

"Desperate times, desperate measures." There wasn't much we could do. No one else was holding their weapon, and JJ's was on the floor, out of reach.

I glanced at John. He stared back with a hard expression. His eyes flitted to the final bottle of booze I held. I gave a slight nod.

"Now," our captor went on, "here's what's gonna happen: you give me the keys to your car, and I drive away." I held my breath.

Joey began fishing in his pockets for his keys, causing Marcus to shift his attention to him. That was all I needed.

I gripped the neck of the bottle and hefted it above my head, throwing it at Marcus's feet with all my might. Glass shards dug into his shins as the bottle's contents splashed on him. As Marcus's features twisted in anger and pain, John flicked Joey's lighter open to produce an amber flame and proceeded to toss it in Marcus's direction. I dove away from the imminent combustion. I winced as glass burrowed deep into my forearms upon my harsh landing on the wooden floor. I inched to the bar's opening, staying low, to where I could make out every detail of the scene in front of me. Marcus stood paralyzed with fear as the lighter flipped head and tail in the air in the air toward him. It was five feet away. Four. Three.

The flame died.

The lighter had gone out. I cried out in anguish, balling my hands into fists. Marcus grinned and raised his gun, pointed right at me.

I closed my eyes. This is how it ends: a violent death during a violent crime, just like all the other creeps and thugs of this occupation.

A shot went off. I took a sharp breath. Slowly, as I realized that I should have been dead already, I opened one eye. Then the other. I was alive. Marcus wasn't so lucky. I turned to find Dustin holding a twin of my own gun, raised directly at Marcus, who now had a crater in his forehead.

"Consider this my resignation," Dustin snarled. Marcus, eyes blank, fell to the floor. Shakily, I stood up and walked

171

over to John. Dustin fired again at Marcus's body, causing flames to start consuming it.

Everyone shuffled out into the blackness of the night. JJ was slung over John's shoulder and Bobby put his arm around me for support as he hobbled along. The hairs on the back of my neck stood on end. I turned around just as I was blown off my feet. My ears ringing, I saw Johnny's bar light up like a Christmas tree. Flames of all shapes and colors danced around the wooden building.

I wanted to stay and watch the flames lick away that building I had wasted six months of my life in, but there wasn't enough time to savor the spectacle.

I picked Bobby back up. As we walked over to the cars, I strayed from the main group to walk beside John. We were not in a hurry. No one spoke. The police would now be unable to avoid coming here, but we still could leave before first responders got a chance to spot us.

"Sorry about your gun," I told him. He shrugged.

"I live above a gun store. I can get another."

"You don't live there anymore," I reminded him, trying to lift the mood.

"No, I suppose I don't. I'll spend the night on the couch and work out what I'll do tomorrow."

"Today… was interesting."

"That's an understatement."

"It's not over."

"True."

"What do you think?" I stopped and turned to him just before we reached the cars. The others were waiting. Watching.

"What do I think of what?"

"Of what happened today? The job offer, the drive-by. This

massacre," he looked off to the distance.

"You know why candles aren't made of steel?"

"What?"

"I'm saying, do you know why they are made of wax? Why aren't they indestructible?"

"I don't know... so wax companies have business?"

"Maybe. But maybe candles were never meant to burn forever."

Twenty-Four
The Last Piece

John. November 19th, 2009.

I stared at the clock on the wall. Three. In the morning. I had lied awake so long I could make out the individual numbers on the dais. My sleep issues went beyond being on Dustin's couch.

Life is meant to savor, to enjoy. I learned long ago that a statement such as that is a hippie's nursery rhyme. Life is full of problems at every turn, and after you overcome one, you will have more waiting.

Scout was curled up at the foot of the couch, twitching his leg as he slept. A dog's life was so much simpler. Eat, play, and sleep. No responsibilities, no worries. But then what's the point? A person's problems—and their solutions—make them who they are.

I groggily sat up and swung my legs over the side, startling Scout, who began barking up a high-pitched storm. Frantic to not wake Dustin in the other room, I shushed him and he obeyed, settling himself back down where my head had just been.

After throwing on the clothes I had placed next to the couch a few hours before, I headed downstairs to finish building my Remington 870. I walked through the deserted shop and through a side door marked "Employees and Scout Only" into a small garage, where my workbench, Harley Fatboy, and

174

covered Model 841 Indian barely fit. Seeing the tarp over the Indian, the most trusted bike I'd ever owned, made me decide to put the Remington on hold.

I opened the garage door, inviting the freezing night air. I shivered.

No need for my new Magnum I had taken from the store as a business expense. It wasn't physical hurt I was worried about.

Getting to my Fatboy, I saddled up and rode off. This being Los Angeles, there were still plenty of people on the streets. Most of them were drunk or high, so I had to be careful in case one of them decided to suddenly run in front of me.

The cold air cut into my brain, waking me up and clearing my thoughts. I had it all. My brother. My wife and kids. Later today Peter and I would stop and see Don Luigi so we could get paid. The court case was going fairly well, all things considered. So why did I feel so empty?

Seeing the window-shattered, broken house, I felt a ping of guilt.

I parked, taking off my Vietnam helmet and putting the keys in my back pocket. As I looked at the house, I noticed I could handle the boards and the basic overlay but I'll have to call someone about the windows. I picked up my phone and called Dustin. He picked up on the first ring.

"Oi. Waddya want, me brother?" I barked a laugh. His accent after he just wakes up was something few ever heard, but many would like to. "Check it out: the house will need some repairs. I was wondering if you'd like to lend a hand. You know where Katy lives?"

"It would scare you, what I know. You couldn't have waited until the more humane hours of the day? Like around... day?" I chuckled.

"Listen, if you want to show up around eight, I'm sure my boys would love to see their uncle when he isn't soaked in blood or booze."

"They'd have to see me on a Sunday for that to happen again. See you then," he hung up. I went up to house's door and knocked. After a few minutes, it cracked open. Katy poked her head out. Seeing who it was, she opened it wider and wrapped her robe more tightly around her body.

"John...."

"I'm sorry. Were you expecting a different gentleman caller?" she smiled.

"Come in," she moved aside. I walked in.

"I'm sorry. I couldn't sleep knowing those thugs could come back, so I thought I'd come over."

"You don't have to apologize, Sweetheart," she brushed my cheek. I held her hand, examining it.

"I know," she bit her lip.

"Do you want anything? Coffee?" she shut the door and locked it.

"It's almost four in the morning."

"Tea, then?"

"I'm fine. Really," her lips pressed together.

"Come with me," she took my hand and led me up the stairs, into her bedroom. She gently pushed me onto the bed and curled up next to me. We lied down together, not another word needing to be said. I kept my clothes on, even my jacket. I was more comfortable than I had been in years. I put my arm around her as she put her hand on my chest. "This should help you sleep," she said.

She was right. I slept like a baby.

When I woke up several hours later, I turned to see my high school sweetheart staring back at me.

"Hi," she whispered.

"Hey, Angel. Have you been up long?"

"Not at all." I had feeling she was lying to me. "What's the plan for today?"

"Me and the boys are going to fix the house."

"John…" she traced my cheekbones with her fingers, "you don't have to do that. I can call someone."

"I know I don't have to. I want to," she smiled. "Plus, it gives the boys more time to spend with their uncle." I sat up, preparing to stand. Katy bolted up.

"Their uncle?"

"Yeah, Dustin. You know. My brother."

"I… half-brother," she corrected.

"Feels like a brother to me. Anyway, we ran into him last night."

"What was he doing there? Wherever you went, that is."

"It's a long story," I said as I rummaged in a drawer against the wall, pulling out a fresh t-shirt and jeans. I grinned. She must have known I would come, eventually.

"John… is everything okay?" I paused midway through pulling off my shirt. I continued as if nothing had happened. Katy had made it clear that we needed to slowly adjust to circumstances, namely my resurrection and impending jail sentence. Going deeper, I knew she was afraid.

"Of course. Why do you ask?" she sucked in her breath.

"I wouldn't call a drive-by 'fine.' I wouldn't call our son being injured 'fine.' You're in the middle of a trial that you've never explained to me, and you spend all your time with that degenerate hood rat. That's not 'fine.'" I turned to face her.

"Peter isn't a degenerate."

"From what I can tell, he's the one who got you into this mess in the first place!" she seemed on the verge of tears. I strode over and wrapped my arms around her.

"He's the one who found you for me. He's the reason you're in my life again. For that, I can't thank him enough." I took my arms back and put on a fresh shirt. I began to pull the ring out of my pocket. Just as my hand enfolded it, I paused. I glanced at Katy, who had calmed down. I finished changing, feeling the ring burning a hole through my pocket, wanting to escape. Katy watched me with cool, questioning eyes. I know what was going through her mind: how much has changed in twenty-three years? I kissed her forehead and checked the time on my phone. "Dustin will be here soon. I love you."

"I love you, too." I gave her a reassuring smile before heading down to the kitchen. JJ was sitting at the table rubbing his wound while Terry searched the fridge.

"Hey boys."

"Hey Pops," Terry replied. "Wild time last night, huh?"

"You got that right, Son. Too wild for my taste. I'll bring you boys a little money for the candy store later."

"I like candy. There's been something on my mind, though," he said as I sat next to JJ.

"What's that?"

"How does Uncle Dustin know so much about medicine? And, more importantly, healing a gunshot wound? I mean, I get he was in the army and all, but he was a real pro last night. Mom didn't even notice JJ was shot. Just hurt." I was about to reply about Dustin's many talents, including shooting, drinking, healing, hacking, and sewing, when an old Irish voice spoke up behind me.

"Well it's simple, really." I turned. Dustin stood in the doorway, box of donuts in hand. I hadn't heard him come in. Actually, I could specifically recall the door being locked. He set the box down on the table. "When you're this one's brother you have to learn how to heal lots of wounds."

"I didn't get into that much trouble," I grumbled.

"Oh really now? Need I remind you, my baby brother, of the brawl of '67?"

"It wasn't that bad," he chuckled. Katy walked in.

"'Wasn't that bad,'" she laughed, "forty years ago, and I still have traces of blood on my skirt from your head being on it while your brother here fixed you up." My mask of amnesia broke. I smiled.

"Hey, Dustin," Katy hugged him, "long time no see."

"Katy, my darling."

"What happened, Dad?" Terry finally asked, picking up a donut.

"Let's just say some guys gave your mother trouble. I had been a bit of a hothead back in the day."

"That's right," she came around and put her arms around me "my knight in shining armor. Though I wouldn't limit it to just 'back in the day.'" She kissed my cheek. My grin grew.

"So what's up?" Terry asked, blatantly ignoring his mother's affection.

"Your uncle and I will replace the boards that were shot, while you two fill them in and repaint them. Assuming JJ can handle it?" I looked to Dustin.

"It was a clean shot. He'll be fine, so long as he uses the other arm." Katy's mouth formed a thin line of disapproval. I winced.

"It would be my honor," JJ suddenly announced, studying the donut on each finger, somehow fitting five on one hand. We headed outside and Dustin took a donut off one of JJ's fingers, laughing as he did so.

"C'mon, boy, get your head on straight. Four is enough." Outside was a trailer laden with enough plywood and tools to build a new house, with plenty left over to fix ours.

"Nice job, Dustin. Home Depot?"

"Nah. I have a friend from Derry who owns a shop."

"A Northerner?" I remarked. Dustin shrugged.

"Irish is Irish."

"What's Ireland like?" Terry asked as he picked up a gallon of paint.

"One of the most beautiful countries God has ever graced us with," he answered as he finished his donut.

"You like it that much?"

"Not as much as ol' Ma did," I said.

"Oh, let me tell you lads," Dustin said in an impeccable impersonation of Ma, "there is no finer or greener country than the land of Éire."

"You have to give Ma credit, though: she's the only woman who could make cabbage edible."

"Oh, aye, you aren't lyin', Baby Brother." A taxi drove up and out came none other than Peter in a different suit from the night before. In this weather, I could understand it. My bare arms had goose bumps. He had purchased a new pair of sunglasses and was wearing them now, though it was fairly cloudy. He strode toward the group of us.

"Here to help with the house, Peter?" I asked, knowing he had no interest in manual labor. I wasn't even sure if he knew the difference between a Phillips and a flathead. Or what they were, for that matter.

"Not this time. But we have two meetings to get to in the next four hours."

"Two?"

"I'll explain on the way."

"Hold on, Pete. I can't leave my family to do all the work."

"Well have them take a break until you come back. Should

be around one." I looked to Dustin. Peter, noticing him for the first time, walked over.

"Good to see you, Dustin," he extended his hand. Dustin grasped it.

"Same here." They gave a single shake. Peter pulled out his cell.

"You mind punching in your number? I like how you handled yourself last night."

"I don't see why not," he took the phone and dialed away. As he did so, a black SUV pulled up in front of the house with the passenger's side facing us. The front side window rolled down, revealing a familiar man with grey hair, sunglasses, and a dark suit. I could make out Peter muttering curses under his breath.

"Who is this guy?" I asked him. He began to hastily walk toward the van.

"G-man to the core," Peter said, barely above a whisper. "FBI." I nodded, unsure what this meant. We reached the window.

"Where were you last night?" The FBI agent asked the pair of us, without introduction.

"I don't remember," Peter responded.

"Don't remember? Why is that?" The man looked like a panther preparing to pounce.

"Because last night I got wasted at my apartment. Can't remember a thing." The stranger that Peter apparently knew took a dramatic whiff of Peter's clothes.

"Strange. I don't smell alcohol on you."

"I said last night. Not this morning," Peter replied. The agent growled.

"What happened with Johnny Black?" Peter stared blankly.

"Johnny Black... oh, he's the baseball player that sprained

181

his wrist last game, right?"

"I heard you stopped working for him," he went on as if Peter never spoke.

"I never worked for a baseball player."

"And last night his bar was attacked. Strange coincidence, don't you think?"

"Either the Red Sox wanted revenge from the other day or he's having bad luck. Not much of a coincidence."

"John?!" Katy called from the front door. "Who's your friend?!" The agent peered down his glasses at my wife. I didn't like the look he gave her. He glanced at me.

"We'll speak again soon." The window rolled up. Peter glared as they sped off. We headed back over to Katy.

"Special Agent Vasquez," Peter explained as we crossed the lawn. "FBI's foremost authority on organized crime. I could have sworn he was supposed to retire a few years back."

"Pete, he's the guy." Peter stopped.

"What?"

"He's the one—one of the two—cops that interrogated me with Fuentes. Him and Fuentes were snooping around my bike at Luigi's bistro, too." Peter nodded.

"I should've known," he resumed walking. "Vasquez never did play fair, but I didn't think he would stoop that low." We reached Katy.

"Katy," I said, "there's someone I'd like you to meet. This is my friend. Peter Richardson." Peter grinned. He had a dazzling smile. He took her hand and gently pressed his lips to its back. I didn't mind. Neither, it seemed, did she. Katy apparently had completely forgotten about what she had just been saying about his degeneracy.

Another cab drove up. A young woman stepped out of the yellow backdoor as the driver hurried out to open the trunk.

He retrieved her suitcase for her and said something that made her tilt her head back with a melodic laugh. Terry and JJ ran to her, yelling her name. I froze. Violet.

She wrapped her arms around each of them. My brother started walking toward them.

"It's so good to see you, Vi," Terry said to her, beaming. "Meet our Uncle Dustin."

"How are you doing, my little lamb?" she stared at him, unblinking. I walked over. I made it just in time to hear what Dustin had doubtlessly heard many times before.

"But I thought you were... you know."

"It's hard to kill a Washicha. Just ask your father over there," he gestured to me as I took a step forward. I clasped my hands behind my back in an effort to hide my shaking hands.

She slowly shifted her gaze from Dustin to me as her hands began to tremble. Her face softened. She had been told over the phone to expect me. Actually, she was here on my account. But there's a difference between hearing and believing.

"Violet," I breathed. Her eyes were the same emerald as her mother's. She took careful steps in her white Converse toward me, her eyes never wandering. She stopped right as she reached me, her eye-level at my neck. I smiled at her.

I inhaled sharply as she slapped my cheek. She may look like her mother, but it was clear who had the quicker slap. I have been punched, beaten, whipped, stabbed, and shot, but no other pain stung as much as her slap. The pain of her bitterness made my chest tighten.

Then, she pulled me close in an embrace. With her head pressed against my chest, she let her tears fall freely. I lightly stroked her hair.

"They told me you were dead," she whispered.

Twenty-Five
Hit the Mattresses

Peter. November 19th, 2009.

"I just don't get how these people voluntarily work for one man without question," John said as we entered Luigi's bistro. "Like Ronald Reagan said, 'concentrated power has always been the enemy of liberty.'"

"Oh, so you're a Reagan fan."

"Of course."

"I'm more prone to Kennedy, myself." John stopped and gave me a funny look.

"Are you serious?"

"Yeah, I'm serious. He was one of our greatest presidents. Why wouldn't I be serious?" John chuckled and resumed walking. I shook my head.

"So how do you pronounce this place's name?"

"*Un Assaggio d'Sicilia*: 'A Taste of Sicily.' A Beppo Family jewel for generations, since they first came here from the Old Country." Bobby was at the bar, watching us enter. We casually walked over, and I noticed he had crutches leaning against the bar next to him.

"John, Peter."

"How's the foot?" I asked as I placed my arms on the cool marble of the bar.

"Lucky. Doc Morella fixed it up in no time, should be walking without the crutches in a week or two. How's your boy?" he asked John.

"Lucky. In a sling, but lucky." Bobby nodded.

"Don Beppo's in the back." I nodded my thanks and we headed in that direction. When we got to the door leading to the *Compare*, two bouncers in black casual suits came over. I placed my hands on my head and allowed them to pat me down. John was more reluctant.

"I don't think you guys need to take a step closer."

They hesitated—only for a second—before proceeding. John rolled his eyes, but allowed the search.

Finally, we were allowed through.

Don Beppo sat in the same private room as before, accompanied by the same stranger to his left, who wore large square glasses and a dark blue ascot. A different bulky man from our last encounter stood behind them with his hands clasped behind his back. Luigi spoke first.

"Ah, John and Peter. Please, have a seat. You remember my *Consigliere*, Andy Shapiro, yes?" We each gave a curt nod. Andy cleared his throat.

"We wanna let you know, Peter," Andy said in a raspy voice, "Mr. Beppo opened the books." I grinned slightly. "Wait for the call. After that, we figure, it's Mr. Beppo's best interest to not be seen for a while, ya know? That goes for the *Caporegimes*, too. No one knows where our pal Johnny is, we figure, why risk it? After last night, they'll want to... retaliate."

"Understandable," I responded.

"I believe a small gift is in order," Don Beppo said. He snapped and the brute behind him reached into his suit. John tensed, most likely recalling military maneuvers. The thug removed two large wads of bills, larger than anything I had made working for Johnny. He tossed one my way, then John's.

186

I tried catching it, but fumbled around for a moment before I clasped it in both hands. John smoothly caught and pocketed his.

"Here is a small bonus for burning the place down," he tossed a smaller—yet still significant—clip to me. This one I caught with ease.

"Thank you, *Compare*."

"Anything for a friend of ours. Now, as for you," he looked at John, who tensed, "consider your match problem settled. Four dozen witnesses saw you in my ring last night, *capisce*?" John nodded.

"I appreciate it."

"Good. We will speak again soon, eh?" Don Beppo made a dismissive motion with his hand. We left.

"So, Pete, where now?" John asked as we walked out, nodding to Bobby in passing.

"We're seeing the oh-so-honorable Admiral Matt." We approached his bike, but before either of us could get on, I caught the shadow of someone coming toward us. Uncle Donnie.

He must have followed us here and waited for us to come back out. He didn't seem to have anything better to do with his time. I sighed.

"What now, Donnie?"

"Murray wants his money," Uncle Donnie replied in his gravelly voice. His beady eyes continuously flitted between John and myself, unsure which of us to rest on.

"We've been over this. Murray gets his money *after* the job, not before.

"If the pair of you would stop messing around in these gang politics, we would already be done." I shook my head impatiently.

187

"We can't pull it off 'til New Year's. We're just passing the time."

"Do you have a plan?"

"Who's asking?"

"I'm right in front of you." I growled, unsure whether he was being difficult or truly didn't comprehend the question.

"Murray wants to know?" he paused, then gave a brief nod. "We're working on it. Jimmy is still gathering data. Leonardo had given him a degree high enough that he could get the job, but low enough that he can actually do what's he's there to do. Problem is, it's also too low to have full access to everything. We have a general layout of the building, security, and escape routes, but not the safe itself."

"Be quick about it." I glared at him, catching his eye.

"Don't tell me how to do my job," he grunted, but sauntered off to a waiting car. John shook his head as he watched him depart. He cleared his throat.

"So where are we meeting Admiral Sanders?"

"*The Pub*."

"Got it." John hopped on his motorcycle. I strapped on the helmet he gave me as I sat behind him.

We rode to *The Pub* without comment—not that anything could be heard over the roaring wind. Soon I'd need my own car. Upon arrival, I saw Matt's Lexus was already there.

We entered *The Pub* and I immediately picked out Matt in his casual suit and white Navy hat. He already had a beer and steak platter in front of him. Checking my watch, I saw we were more than a little late. He waved us over.

Matt stood and began shaking our hands. "Peter, good to see you. I see you're doing well." I glanced down and noticed I was once again wearing my suit. "Captain. Let me begin by saying you have found yourself an excellent companion. I've known Peter all my life, and can honestly say he is one of the best men of his kind out there." I raised my eyebrows at that. A compliment? It didn't sound like Matt at all. Something was up.

"Thanks, Matt," he sat as John slid into the booth. I followed suit. As usual, Clare came over.

"Iced tea, please." John told her.

"Water," I said. Clare bit her lip and nodded. She avoided making eye contact with me.

As she walked away, I followed her. She didn't seem to notice as she went into the kitchen. Just as I made it through the door, I laid a hand on her shoulder. She whirled around. The fright didn't lessen when she saw who it was.

"Clare, what's going on?"

"It- it's nothing. Really."

"No, not really. What is it?"

"Peter... you're a nice guy. You really are, but..."

"Oh. Is there a reason for... this?"

"A friend of mine that I've known for a long time proposed to me. I said yes." I was dumbstruck. What Clare and I shared wasn't anything serious, but that she got engaged while we were almost a couple hurt. It hurt a lot. But all I could say was one word. There was too big a lump in my throat for anything else.

"Oh."

"Are you okay?" I nodded.

"What... did I do something wrong?" she adamantly shook her head.

"It's really not you. It's not your job. It's me." I hardened.

"I'm a lawyer, Clare," she looked up at me, her eyes full of uncertainty.

"I saw the gun in that case, Peter. I don't know what you

are, but you're no lawyer." I sighed.

"You swear that's not what this is about?"

"I swear. Look... we had a good run. I know we did. But I'm getting my life together. I need something serious." Serious... I was willing to be serious. If I would have just been given the chance.

A cook yelled that an order needed to be delivered. Clare smiled wistfully as she turned away. I left. What more was left to say? It was over.

This was real. It was. I kept repeating that to myself as I went back to the booth.

I sat down like my relationship with my first true almost-girlfriend hadn't just ended. Both my friends stared at me, John with concern, Matt with curiosity. I attempted a smile. I felt how false it was.

"She okay?" John asked, jerking his head at Clare, who had just reentered with a tray.

"Ecstatic. She... uh... she's getting married."

"Not every day I see you at a loss for words. Are *you* okay?"

"I don't see why not. Just a fling." That was the strangest part of it all: what I said sounded true to my ears. John gave me a skeptical look, but that was all I was going to say on the matter. He knew as much.

"So Admiral," John said, "what were you saying?"

"Just that I've been transferred to paperwork duty here in Los Angeles, over in Anaheim. Makes it a lot easier for me to help you out. Waddya say?" The drinks arrived, courtesy of a different server.

"Matt," I began, "what's really going on here?" Matt rolled his eyes.

"You always can tell, can't you? Well I just-" he cleared his throat, "John told me about the job you guys are getting ready to pull off, and that you would look professional if you could get everyone supplied with military-grade weapons." I gave John a sideways glance. He grinned sheepishly.

"Matt," I said, "think for a second. Criminals already know how to get guns. John's brother owns a gun store; they can get it from him." Matt smiled.

"Come on. Just tell me the plan and what you'll be using, and I'll get you a better version of absolutely everything." I made a humming sound low in my throat. It wasn't that I didn't trust Matt. I just didn't want anyone else in on this thing.

"Anyone have paper?" I looked around, craning my neck. Matt pulled out a sheet and pen from one of those stylish leather briefcases that didn't clasp shut. He slid both over to me. I began making a rough sketch. "For whatever reason, the subterranean level doesn't seem to house anything. Safety deposit boxes on at lobby level, but we're going after the vault on the seventh floor. I say vault, but really it's just a large safe, capable of housing up to twenty million dollars in drug money. Which it might, in case you were wondering. Cameras are covered: we can place a bug in the system so we control what's seen. This is still early stages, but we'll definitely have to steal the entire safe—it's the ball centerpiece. So we need explosives, along with firepower, but not to kill." Matt's eyes lit up. I pushed my list across to him. He looked over it a few seconds and then reached over and took back his pen. He scribbled something down and tore off a corner of the paper. He passed it back to me.

"Go to that address, Level Six, on that date, and you'll get your Christmas present early."

Twenty-Six
Soldier of Fortune

John. November 21st, 2009.

I felt something warm and wet against my cheek. I opened my eyes. Scout was on my chest, licking my face. I dug into my jeans pocket and, opening my cell phone, I saw it was six on the dot. I sighed, picking up the growing puppy and setting him on the floor. He whined. I swung my feet over the side of the couch and stood, stretching. I had come over to the shop last night to help Dustin sort through some old files, and must have fallen asleep.

I stealthily crouched my way into what had been my bedroom. Dustin's eyes still shot open at my entrance, but he went back to sleep once he saw who it was. I threw off my clothes and took some out of my small oak dresser. Well, Dustin's small oak dresser.

I headed downstairs. Surprisingly, Vince wasn't here yet. I went into the storage closet and moved aside some wooden crates. Once I lifted the last one, I stared into a deep abyss of darkness.

Yawning, I hit the switch. The small room—filled with exercise equipment—glowed in a dim light. Not an inch of the room was wasted. Thankfully, unlike Dustin, I wasn't claustrophobic.

I got on the bench press, losing myself in the motions. Raise, lower, breathe. Raise, lower, breathe. Raise, lower-

I grunted, sweating. Raise, lower, breathe. Raise, lower, breathe.

I stopped after a few minutes and I took off my shirt, wiping my forehead with it. I got up, throwing the slightly-damp shirt over my shoulder and leaving the room, careful to turn off the light. I moved the crates back and left.

Huffing, I jogged upstairs. Dustin was up, frying eggs. He nodded in passing. I proceeded to the bathroom and hopped in the shower. I tried to relax my muscles. I could hardly breathe. I bathed, washing my hair carefully. There were more grey hairs every day, especially now that I'd stopped using my dye. After four minutes I turned off the water and toweled myself.

Heading back to the bedroom, I did as Peter had told me to do and put on my old officer uniform. He said it would be a good idea to play on the juror's sympathy. Other than that, he hadn't given me much to go off of. Other things seemed to be preoccupying him. He claimed it was this gang war and the upcoming heist, but I had my own suspicions.

My uniform: a symbol of freedom, of strength. It showed that there are people on this planet that stand for what is right and just. It proves that not everything is accomplished by a man behind a desk. And now I was using it to weasel my way out of prison.

But I had done my duty, and my country was repaying me in a way I had never imagined.

I fed Scout, shaking my head at just how much he had grown. Dustin offered me eggs. I mumbled something about getting a bite to eat on the way there.

I headed back down to the shop. Vince had arrived. I nodded in greeting as I left.

From there, I headed over to a nearby hot dog stand. It was

the only place on the block that opened this early. I bought a loaded dog and hailed a cab. Pete had had warned me motorbikes just weren't "professional enough." I'm not sure what he meant, but he was the lawyer, even if he never spent a day in law school.

Once I arrived, I paid the driver and got out. Among other cars in the lot was a blue Prius. No matter the outcome, today my son would learn something.

As I crossed the parking lot to the marble steps, I noticed a figure heading toward me from the opposite direction. Special Agent Vasquez, Peter had called him.

"Can I help you?" I asked gruffly as he approached. He grinned without revealing any teeth. A mild stretching of thin lips, at best. No longer hungry, I tossed the remainder of the hot dog into a trash can.

"Your son is a good man." I bristled as I do when any creep talks about my family.

"He's not the one on trial."

"I'm just stating facts."

"Actually, I think that's an opinion." I thought back to how Peter's smart talk got this guy riled up.

"You work for Johnny Black, right?"

"I've never worked for a baseball player. You have the wrong guy." I kept walking, making it up the steps and into the building. He followed me.

"Whatever you know about him or his people, or any of your acquaintances, you can just tell me and we'll make this all go away. You'll be a free man. You won't have to see your family on the other side of the glass." I stopped dead in my tracks. He nearly ran into me. I kept my anger at bay. He wanted me to show emotion.

"Look, maybe this guy Johnny did throw in a few games. I

194

don't know. I'm more of a football fan, myself. But I don't see what that has to do with me losing a match." I stormed off. I could feel his stare follow me.

I entered the courtroom and walked to the defense table. Peter and Damion were once more in the middle of a heated discussion.

"No, that's not how it works," Peter explained. "If you get a subpoena, they're just asking you to come. It's not an order. You don't have to go. Capone didn't."

"Capone ended up at Alcatraz." Peter frowned. I sat down. Peter turned to me.

"John, I tried my best to groom the jury-"

"He means *bribe* the jury," Damion interjected.

"But Fuentes fought back. Hard." Peter grimaced. "How's JJ?" he asked. I grunted. Damion didn't know about what occurred the other night, nor would he.

"He's fine." With me present, court was now in session. District Attorney Fuentes gave a long monologue regarding my unethical behavior and unsportsmanlike conduct, in which absolutely nothing was actually said that was in any way new. Meanwhile, Peter was sketching out the bank.

"Trying to set me free, Buddy?" I asked.

"Cute. Jimmy called last night with a fresh update."

"I call the defendant, Johnathan Washicha, to the stand." Fuentes called out. Pete stood angrily.

"I object, Judge! My client wasn't on that list!" Fuentes sneered.

"We have the right to ask the defendant to come to the stand in trial. This is trial." Peter looked to be at a loss for words. Damion rolled his eyes.

"Well… maybe he doesn't want to come to the stand." All eyes turned to me. I nodded and walked to the podium.

Before anything was said, I gave a statement that rang loud and clear throughout the room.

"I swear to tell the truth, the whole truth, and nothing but the truth. So help me God."

"Mr. Washicha-" Fuentes began. I cut him off with a raised hand.

"I've fought for this land enough to have earned the title Captain, if you don't mind." Not on our agenda, but I knew what I was doing. Fuentes looked to the judge, who nodded after only a small hesitation.

"Captain, why were you and Mr. Richardson at *The Pub* on the date in question?" I grinned.

"'Mr. Richardson' wanted to buy me a drink for a good match. I can't refuse a fan."

"What about the money, a total amount of four thousand dollars, which witnesses report he gave you?"

"My share in a business venture."

"I see. Now, you were in the service for seventeen years, correct?" I sat straighter. This was what I had been waiting for.

"Yes, Son, it is."

"And how long were you in Vietnam?"

"I got there in '73, and, if I remember correctly, I left 'Nam in '75. Afterwards, I served elsewhere."

"We will get to that later. A question of interest: did you or a peer murder Vietnamese civilians? Children, for example?" I smirked. He was trying to rattle me. This hadn't been the way I was hoping to get here, but it will have to do. I heard Peter scrape his chair back and watched his hands go all over.

"Objection! Your Honor, according to article 109 section C subtitled 'Rights of the Witness' paragraph three: any past crimes possibly perpetrated by the witness are exonerated if a specific time has passed and are in no jurisdiction with the current alleged crime to which is being prosecuted."

"Mr. Richardson," the judge sighed, "that is a very specific law per an area I've never heard of. It doesn't exist. In fact, it makes me question where you obtained your law degree."

"Berkeley."

"Berkeley? Really? Hm. Me too." Judge Taylor cleared his throat. "Mr. Fuentes, I suggest you move on." Pete sat down dejectedly. I grinned. My time to shine.

"It's fine, your Honor." I turned to the prosecutor. "You know, son, when I got back from 'Nam for leave in '74, I wasn't expecting a hero's welcome. I wanted to see my family and the land that I love. Along the way, I was spat on, cursed at, and—on one occasion—burned with a joint of marijuana. The Vietnamese treated me better, in some respects." I cleared my throat. "We are soldiers. This uniform I'm wearing represents something bigger than me. Bigger than you. Those who wear this uniform are meant to liberate, free, and protect. To answer your question: no I didn't kill any children. I'm no more a murderer or criminal than anyone else in this room. We were young like you, Fuentes, or old like me. And what we did, we did for you. We aren't monsters.

"You said that later on we would discuss my service overseas… other than Vietnam. Well, let's discuss them now. Iran, Nicaragua, Grenada, Russia; you name an oppressed country, chances are I was there. I used to fight for what you'd call honor or glory, but after a while, I fought because I had been taught nothing mattered more than three things: God, family, and your country. I understand you want to portray that I 'abandoned my country' by running away after a failed operation. You got it wrong. I didn't abandon my country. My country abandoned me. My squad and I were left out in the

197

desert with nothing and no one. Forgotten. Erased. Just a few files that needed to be shoved under the rug. We didn't exist. I'm not saying this for the hope of pity. I'm saying this because it's the truth: I am a soldier and a protector. Not a criminal."

Fuentes seemed unable to grasp the right words. Damion stared with wide eyes.

"Any further questions?" Judge Taylor asked the prosecutor. There was a pause, then a shake of the head.

"No, your Honor."

"You may step down, Captain Washicha." I nodded to the judge, then Fuentes, and went back to the defense table. The case was to be resumed January second.

I left as if I was just part of the crowd. I didn't wait for Peter. There was someone else I needed to see. I headed out to the parking lot. Just as I had hoped, Damion was leaning against his car. Waiting for me.

"Son."

"Dad. Nice speech."

"The best ones are from the heart."

"So I hear."

"Why don't we have a drink sometime?" he smiled gratefully.

"I'd like that."

Twenty-Seven
The Code of Silence

Peter. November 24th, 2009.

Joey began fishing in his pockets for his keys, causing Marcus to shift his attention to him. That was all I needed.

I gripped the neck of the bottle and hefted it above my head, throwing it at Marcus's feet with all my might. Glass shards dug into his shins as the bottle's contents splashed on him. As Marcus's features twisted in anger and pain, John flicked his lighter open to produce an amber flame and proceeded to toss it in Marcus's direction. I dove away from the imminent combustion. I winced as glass burrowed deep into my forearms upon my harsh landing on the wooden floor. I inched to the bar's opening, staying low, to where I could make out every detail of the scene in front of me. Marcus stood paralyzed with fear as the lighter flipped head and tail in the air in the air toward him. It was five feet away. Four. Three.

The flame died.

The lighter had gone out. I cried out in anguish, balling my hands into fists. Marcus grinned and raised his gun, pointed at my forehead. But I was faster. I pulled out my pistol and fired one single bullet, clear and true, at a stain on Marcus's leg. Stained with powerful vodka.

Marcus shrieked as he was engulfed in flames. He tried rolling on the floor, but there was too much fire. Slowly, his movement stopped.

Marcus was dead.

I killed him.

Panting, I woke up drenched in sweat. It was just a dream. Nothing more than a nightmare. I didn't kill him. Dustin killed him. This Life hasn't changed me. My hands are clean.

Looking out the dusty window, I saw the sun making its daily ascent into the sky. The phone on my drawer was ringing. I picked it up.

"Hello?"

"Peter, it's Tony Spits." I paused. Tony Spitolli? He was one of Luigi Beppo's top *Caporegimes*. This wasn't the wakeup call I was hoping for. I actually hadn't been hoping for any. "You still there?"

"Yeah. What can I do for you?"

"There's been a problem here at the bistro. We're calling you in." I tried to stifle a gasp. That's never something a wise guy wants to hear. It usually means that his Family is going to whack him. I kept my voice steady.

"No problem. I'll be there right away."

"And, uh, don't worry about your friend; we just want you. Wear your best suit." The line went dead. This can't be happening. What did I do? Did I upset Andy? Or maybe the *Compare* himself?

Regardless, I had to go. Refusing would mean betrayal. I couldn't run. I couldn't hide. I couldn't even fight. I opened my bedside drawer and took out the M1911 John gave me. I stared at it dubiously, biting my lip.

No. If I'm to go, I will die without blood on my hands. I carefully placed it back inside and shut the drawer. I took my suit off its hanger in my closet and brought it to the bathroom. I turned on the shower and set the clothes on the counter by the sink. They want me to wear my suit? I'll wear it. I'll be spick and span. I won't have a speck of dirt on me until they blow my brains out. Even then, I'll be neat enough to be buried then and there.

I stepped into the shower and gasped at the especially-icy water. I contemplated calling John, but there was no point. He couldn't stop the entire Family from coming down on me. I winced. They were going to come down on me. No one could do anything about it. What did I do? Did they find out I didn't personally pull the trigger on Marcus?

I shampooed, lathered, and rinsed. As the last of the suds went down the drain, I turned the water off and reached for a towel. I dried off and put on my suit.

I brushed my teeth quickly, combing my hair to the side with my other hand. I checked myself out in my mirror. I looked rather dashing. For a funeral.

I took a deep breath and left the apartment, leaving it locked just in case some sort of grave robber thought he'd find anything of value. Not that he would. All my cash was split between the toaster, inside an empty jar of peanut butter, and in my pocket. I walked outside and hailed a taxi. The electric chair was better than this. For one thing, I would get my last meal. For another, at least with the chair I knew I would just be electrocuted. These guys could do anything to me and aren't held back by the law.

I tried not to think about all the torture techniques I'd seen or heard about. It's incredible, the ingenuity with which Man devises ways to hurt his own kind, each method worse than the last. I had to stop thinking about it before I go back to grab my gun and choose my own ending.

Too late. The cab pulled up to *Un Assaggio d'Sicilia*. I grimaced, paying the driver with a considerable tip from my money roll. I wouldn't need it.

I got out, taking my last look at the outside world. This is it. I'd survived the most vicious crime rings of all time, only to fall to my own. I laughed. It felt good to do so. In fact, it felt outstanding. I couldn't stop. I doubled over, laughing my guts out. I may not like death in any form, but I'll welcome Him with a smile on my face.

I opened the door and went in. Bobby was at the bar, as usual, staring my way. Still grinning, I crossed the short distance between us.

"Hey there, Bobby," he frowned.

"'There somethin' wrong with you?"

"It's a possibility. Where to?" he grunted.

"The back. I'm supposed to lead you," he hefted himself up, grabbing hold of his crutches. I was right on his heels.

"Of course you are. I wouldn't have it any other way."

"What's that supposed to mean?" I shrugged mirthfully. I didn't realize it was possible to shrug mirthfully. But I did. Bobby opened the door. The room was pitch black.

"Come on, Richardson, a few more steps," he shoved me inside. The door shut behind us. I could make out someone else's breathing in the room. If they were going to do it, I hope would be soon.

The lights turned on. In the private dining room was the same table as before, only it was filled with occupied chairs. Don Beppo stood to the side with Tony Spits—overweight with an obvious toupee—on his left. I had been right; the table held exactly twenty chairs.

"What's going on?" I asked, staring at all the faces. Some I recognized. Most I didn't. Don Luigi laughed. It was deep and ended in a coughing fit.

"Andy told you the books were open. You must go through with the ceremony." I licked my lips. I did not realize until now how tense I had been. I gently exhaled, relaxing my shoulders and wiping away the cold sweat that had formed on my forehead. I wasn't going to die. I had given the cab driver a twenty-dollar tip. I would live. I'm alive. I lost twenty dollars for no apparent reason. All it took was a near brush with death to make me feel so acutely alive.

"But *Compare*, who is sponsoring me?" I wanted to beam. I didn't, and neither did anyone else. In fact, most of the men in the room gave me icy stares. I couldn't believe it. I was going to be Made. Untouchable. Indestructible, as far as the Family was concerned. Immortal. The guy that everyone else looks up to. A real wise guy.

"Bobby Mancuso, step forward," he did so. "How long have you known Peter Richardson?"

"Since he was a kid. Twenty years. Peter has always been a clear thinker, a listener, and knows how to follow orders," he grinned at me, giving a quick wink.

"Thank you. May the candidate step forward?" It wasn't a question. I briskly strutted to the Don's side. Tony came beside me, brandishing a dagger in one hand and a revolver in the other. Luigi continued, "We are your new family. Our bond is stronger than blood. Show me, if I told you to shoot both your parents in the head, which finger would you use?" Solemnly I held up my right trigger finger and held my breath.

Tony pricked my finger with the dagger's point. The Don held a small picture of Saint Francis of Assisi. My blood, one drop at a time, dripped onto the photograph. "This blood means that we are now one Family. You live by the gun and the knife and you die by the gun and the knife. Peter Richardson, do you swear that you will uphold the *Omerta*, the Code of Silence, even at the cost of your own life?"

"I do," he handed me the picture. I stared at him, then at Bobby, and finally at Tony, who now held a lighter. He set fire to the bloodied picture. I stared up, past the roof, into Heaven. I had delivered this ceremony enough times to know the words.

"As this card burns, may my soul burn in Hell if I betray the oath of *Omerta*. I enter alive, and I will have to get out dead." Don Luigi watched me closely.

"Kneel." I obeyed. "These men before me have witnessed your oath of allegiance," he clasped my shoulder. "Rise now, as a Made Member of the Beppo *Cosa Nostra*, as a brother and son." I rose, surveying everyone at the table, daring them to say a word. "Peter Richardson, you are now untouchable. Any grievance cast upon you by another will be seen as a Mortal Sin, and will be dealt with as such. We are your new family, and we will help you as you will us. Outside your Family, you are respected and feared. Everywhere, you are a Man of Honor. Uphold these values entrusted to you," he gently kissed me once on each cheek. He stepped back, allowing Tony to administer the same, with much more slobber. My new Family politely clapped. No one wanted to look too excited. Still, they had to clap. I felt cold hatred for these men who expect complete loyalty and obedience, who burned a picture of a saint because they considered themselves above whatever God there may be. And yet I gave them my loyalty and obedience. These people would look out for me; they would kill for me. I was torn between reality and what I wanted reality to be.

I took the available seat at the end, getting pats on the back and squeezes on the shoulder the entire time. I sat down between Joey and Bobby and couldn't decide whether to laugh or cry when I saw the meal: *Gabagool* with thinly-sliced cilantro. I grabbed a dinner roll and buttered it.

This truly was "The Life." It was a life that some people

killed for. Literally. Fast cars, flashy clothes, skipping lines at restaurants. The Sicilian, blue collar American dream. Yet I told them I would shoot my own parents. I can't shoot anybody.

This train of thought was ruining my appetite. I ignored it and enjoyed my meal. Enjoyed my Family. The family that I had been sure was going to murder me half an hour ago.

"I'm back," I whispered to myself.

"What was that?" Joey asked. I blankly stared at him. I had forgotten he's Made. He must have been invited since he's a friend of mine, as well as a "friend of ours."

"I said this is my favorite," he gave me a dubious look.

"Anyway... how's the job search looking?" he knew he could speak relatively freely. This room was one of the safest in the city as far as bugs were concerned, but that didn't mean they didn't pop up every once in a while. Bobby leaned in, listening intently.

"Pretty well, I think. I'm talking to a guy about it tomorrow. I'll be able to set up shop before the year is through."

"Any other spots open?"

"Two, but we're talking to one guy who's real good. Not much experience in the field, though. He's the brother of that friend of mine."

"Speaking of family, is your uncle in on this?" Uncle Donnie.

"Yeah, surprisingly. Not that friend of his. Or the painter." Leonardo.

"I figured," Joey replied. I took a bite of bread. "Is this as good as it gets being a typical wise guy?" Joey grinned, a glint to his eye.

"Not even close." My eyes gleamed. He chuckled. "What? Jealous of ol' Joey?" I sneered.

"Jealous? Why would I be jealous?" he threw up his hands.

"Take it easy. It was a joke." I gave him a crooked smile. I understood the humor, though that didn't stop my veins from pumping with what may have been anger. I sat there, surrounded by these violent sociopaths with their nice food and expensive suits, and I knew I was still alien to them. Worse than the fact that I knew it was that they knew it, too. I was in a category on my own, undefined by their principles and rules, though I followed every letter of every word.

Ever since I was a kid, all I had ever wanted was to be one of them. No, that wasn't precisely true. I wanted to be more than them. Perhaps that was what set me apart. Joey had asked me if I was jealous... I wasn't envious of their positions or their "in" status, when I'd always be an outsider looking in. I didn't feel envy; it's an emotion for the weak. Why strive to be equal? What I felt was raw ambition, at its core. It just isn't in my nature to willingly be satisfied with my position in life.Perhaps that was the greatest grievance of all: striving to be more than I ever could be. I had been somebody, once. Maybe if I could get back to that position and cement myself there, I would be happy with who I am and what I am.

What was I? I was a mobster like the others in the room, yet not of them. My hands were free of blood, but I was not held back by any sort of moral obligation. I simply... didn't kill. And so that made me lesser in their eyes, yet in mine I was greater. One day we'd see who's right.

Twenty-Eight
A Gift from Sea

John. November 26th, 2009.

I sat on the front porch with the rest of the men in my family—minus a certain son—with a sigh. We just finished patching up the house. Finally. I watched the sun slowly sink below the horizon.

Plenty had been accomplished: boards painted and replaced, shutters fixed, new windows installed. Everything had gone well... except today is Thanksgiving, and I am one son short. I sighed again, this time out of annoyance. Damion. I had thought I made progress with him the other day. Maybe I did. Still, he wasn't here. I pulled out my phone and punched in a few numbers.

Katy walked out with a tray of glasses filled to the brim—it was never too cold for sweet tea. She gave a small frown of worry when she saw I was attempting to call Damion for what must have been the billionth time. She handed out the tea and went back inside.

"Dinner will be ready in an hour!" she called out.

The line went to his answering machine. Again. I growled as his voice monotonously gave out his contact information. Those were no good for me, either: I had tried his pager and, for the first time, attempted email. Nothing. I put it away. The others avoided meeting my gaze. I searched my brain, trying to think of something to break the awkward silence. I placed the cool glass to my cheek. It burned with icy relief.

"That's it, then," I announced.

"Only one wee thing left to do," Dustin said. I gave him a sideways glance.

"What's that?"

"Go get the guy who caused this." Silence. I looked at the ground. Dustin had almost made it seem like a joke, but we all knew it wasn't. We all wanted revenge. We went after Marcus and the bar, but it didn't change a thing so long as Johnny was still out there.

"What are we waiting for?" Terry asked, standing and turning to me. "I mean, we already took out some of his crew, even his right-hand man."

"Who, if I remember correctly, almost killed us?" I argued. Terry didn't know the scope of Johnny Black's power. I'm not even sure I did.

"Dad, think about it: we have two decommissioned Navy SEALS and two legendary Green Berets. That's enough to make anyone pause."

"No, what we have is an old Green Beret who rose from the dead, an old Irish sniper, and two SEALS who admittedly aren't cadets, but still aren't prepared to fight this war. Look: I have faith in you—in us—but with just four soldiers," I stood up and clasped his shoulder with my free hand, "there's no way."

"To be fair, our old squad took on worse odds," Dustin interjected.

"True, but in this case we are out of our element." I never thought I'd back down from a fight. But my job was to keep my family safe, above all else. By showing Johnny Black we couldn't be pushed around, I had accomplished that. I wanted justice as much as the rest of them, but what I didn't want was to get slaughtered. JJ, as if sensing my thoughts, began gnawing on the medial gauze over his bullet wound. No, not the gauze. Just the skin around it. I shook my head and sat back down. Terry glumly did the same.

"How did he ever pass the mental exam to get into the SEALS in the first place?" I asked Terry, jerking my head at JJ. Dustin chuckled.

"Actually," Dustin said, "I may have had something to do that. I'd been to the Pentagon to work with some inside guys, and heard about you boys wanting to join. I eased the process a wee bit."

"Thanks, but I could have done it on my own." Terry said stubbornly.

"I know, boy, but think of your brother." JJ looked up at Dustin suddenly, the cloud of incomprehension lifted from his eyes. In a second, though, the apparent clarity was over. He went back to the skin around his gauze.

"You have Da's eyes." Dustin told Terry.

"Don't even get me started on that." I laughed.

"What was he like, Uncle Dustin?" Terry asked.

"Your Grand Da? He was... something, to say the least."

"He was either the greatest man you knew... or the worst." I explained.

"He was the one who gave us our first bikes, remember?" Dustin said.

"Which we had to make payments on," I countered. We laughed.

"Give the old man credit: he knew how to teach us a lesson."

"Even after he passed, I could still feel his hand slapping the back of my head and warning me about doing 'it' again."

"Sounds familiar…" Terry interjected.

"Hey, you didn't get the whippings we did. And dear old Dad had all the Native muscle behind the blows," I said.

"But I bet he never drag raced like you did," Terry pointed out. I winced. Katy had been right about not racing after the kids were born. Once, it had been a high school hobby. I had been out of practice when I suddenly decided to try it again, only to narrowly avoid getting jumped by several sore losers. Little Terry ran up to his daddy at just the right time.

"Thanks again for that. Though I have no clue where the cuteness went." I stood up as two black sedans with darkened windows stopped at the curb in front of the house. Directly in front of us.

"Dad..." Terry cautioned.

"I'm sure it's nothing." I gripped my Magnum in my belt loop behind my back, covered with a shirt.

"And to think, we just finished cleaning up," my brother said. A tall, familiar-looking man in a suit stepped out the lead car's driver's seat and sauntered up to us, serious and brisk. Dustin took the lead, meeting him on the lawn.

"Can we help you?"

"I'm here for Mr. Washicha." His eyes rested on me.

"Well, I'm Master Sergeant Washicha, those two young ones back there are both Chief Petty Officer Washicha, and, seeing how Captain Washicha outranks us all, you have to go through us first," he seemed unfazed by the veiled threat. The front door opened and Katy came outside.

"What's going on?"

"I'm here for John and Dustin Washicha," the portly driver said, never taking his eyes off me. I kept my hand on the revolver, but loosened my grip. There were too many ways to kill me for this to be an ambush. Still, better safe than sorry. Katy clung to my arm.

"It's okay. I'll go." Dustin and Katy looked unhappy with my decision. The driver nodded and headed back to the car. I gave Katy a quick kiss.

"I'll be back soon."

"Don't worry about soon. Just come back." I headed toward the car. Dustin grabbed my shoulder.

"What are you doing?" he hissed.

"Trust me, I'll be fine. You should know that." I gave him a hug and we hurried over to the car.

"You go in the other one," he told Dustin. Dustin hesitated, but acquiesced. I watched him safely enter the trailing vehicle before getting in the front one, where the mystery man was holding the back door open for me. I thanked him as I got in. He wordlessly shut the door. I groaned when I saw who was in the passenger's seat.

"Christ, Peter."

"Were you expecting someone else?"

"I dunno, Johnny Black? Fuentes and Vasquez? The *Cartel*?" Peter snorted.

"Why would Jimmy be working with any of them?" That explained why this guy looked familiar: he was the bank inside man I met at the funeral.

"Why the white?" I asked, motioning to their clothing. Peter tossed me a bundle.

"Put those on. We're going get that Christmas present Admiral Sanders promised us." I held out the clothes: a navy captain's uniform.

"That doesn't explain the giddup."

"Sanders' men don't know who they're giving these weapons to. If anything goes wrong, they can honestly say they gave them to other naval officers."

"So Sanders won't be there?"

"You know how he is. He's too nervous for that sort of thing." It seemed I didn't know as much about Admiral Sanders as I had thought. I finished donning the uniform. It fit perfectly.

"Why the second car?"

"We're setting Dustin up across the street with a sniper rifle. Nothing should go wrong, but we want to be careful."

"So," Jimmy said, "you fought?"

"Yeah. Yeah, I served."

"Vietnam?"

"Among others."

"Sounds like you have some good stories." I shifted uncomfortably.

"How long is this going to take? I have a Thanksgiving dinner to get to."

"We have another thirty minutes on the ride," Jimmy answered, "the exchange should be quick. So if you have any stories…"

"In '73, my squad was part of an op where we were captured by the North Vietnamese and taken to a POW camp. That way, the higher-ups could track us, free us, take out our captors, and free the other POWs. It was a real version of Hell on Earth if there ever was one. We were transferred before we could get rescued. Deep in the jungle. Probably Laos or the 'Nam-Cambodia border. The op was only supposed to be two weeks. It lasted two months."

"How'd Uncle Sam find you?" Jimmy asked.

"He didn't." I stared out the window. We drove awhile in silence until Jimmy broke it.

"So you have scars?"

"Sure, but not all are from the camps. Some are from being stupid as a kid. Da always said scars are God's way of teaching the stupid."

"You must be really stupid, then." Peter laughed.

"He also said those without any were too stupid to learn anything." Peter grimaced

"What kind of weaponry are we picking up?" I asked.

"Standard assault rifles and some explosives for the safe," Peter replied. "So a Thanksgiving dinner, huh?"

"Quality time with the family."

"Turkey and the works?"

"Spaghetti has been a family tradition since Damion was old enough to say it wrong. It's Katy's specialty."

"Really? Mine too. So that lying *mook* will be there?" I cleared my throat.

"No. No, Damion isn't coming."

"Oh. I'm sorry to hear that."

"Don't be. Would you like to come?" I paused. "And you, too, Jimmy?"

"Nah," Jimmy said, "I've got a thing to take care of."

"A thing?" Peter asked.

"Yeah, you know. That thing."

"Peter?" I asked.

"I… yeah, I'm in," he paused. "Thanks." We entered a parking garage and began driving up. It was nearly deserted. We reached the sixth level and parked in an isolated, dimly-lit corner. We got out. The temperature had dropped at least ten degrees from when I left the house. I shivered. Peter came around the car. I noticed in the dusk that, with annoyance, his uniform deemed him a rear admiral. A rank above me.

"This is the spot," Peter said. His voice faintly echoed in the dead silence of the garage. I scanned the rest of the level. We could see most of it from our corner. Jimmy had double-parked. From below came the screeching of tires.

Our sedan's twin entered and parked next to us. Joey and another guy from the funeral—Eddie, I thought—got out. A moment later, Dustin came out, too.

"Dustin?" Peter exclaimed.

"The sixth level next door was blocked off," Joey explained. Joey wore a suit while the other two wore starch-white uniforms identical to my own. We huddled between the two cars, shivering.

Peter opened his mouth to respond. As he did, the sound of inbound vehicles bounded off the walls.

"Showtime," Peter announced. Everyone around me— excluding Peter—pulled out pistols of various shapes and sizes. I did the same. A moment later, a black Humvee came up the ramp, followed by two SUVs. Another Humvee finished the convoy. I gaped. They brought actual armored Humvees. As a unit, the four vehicles turned slightly and screeched to a halt forty feet away, with each SUV close to a side of the garage, effectively blocking any escape on our part. All doors simultaneously opened. Boots pounded on concrete. Within seconds, we were surrounded by over a dozen officers with assaulted rifles. Before any of us besides Dustin and I could raise our weapons, they had theirs pointed right at us.

They wore officer white, but they didn't hold themselves like officers, except like the ones that went to Annapolis. They didn't have the same air of entitlement or command. They were disciplined like soldiers, but something about them was... off.

Three more men exited the first SUV. One carried a briefcase, another a folding table, and the third a long crate. We all watched as the table was quickly set up. The other two placed their items on it, with the briefcase facing us. The three soldiers stood at attention, evenly apart, behind the table.

They stared straight ahead. No one moved.

"Open it," the middle soldier suddenly ordered. Peter, Joey, and I cautiously approached the briefcase, Joey and I with our pistols slightly lowered. Peter unclasped the case, revealing a blank computer monitor. A moment later, a light flashed and a man's bearded face appeared on the screen. His spectacles shined in the near-darkness of his room.

"Gentlemen," he said with a thick Russian accent, "congratulations. You are witnessing history in the making. I have spent years developing these for you, and you shall not be disappointed." The soldier on the left side of the table opened the crate, revealing a silver minigun just over a yard long, with eight barrels as opposed to the standard six. I had encountered miniguns—very large despite the name—in the Cobra helicopters we used in Vietnam. Eighty pounds of pure carnage. Even the NRA can't approve of them: they aren't meant for recreation. They are meant to destroy.

"I present to you the C308 Crucifier. Titanium rotor and housing. Personally-devised synthetic casting. Twenty-two pounds when loaded. Three-oh-eight caliber. Five thousand rounds per minute. Capable of—well, allow me to show you." Suddenly we heard a deep rumbling from all sides. A tank descended from an upper level. We all watched with amazement as it stopped in the middle of the garage. The lid popped open and a solder hustled out. Two other soldiers exited the second SUV with Crucifiers. They jogged away from the vehicles, stopped, and aimed at the tank. Ignoring the assault rifles trained on us, we all rushed to the side of the SUV, struggling for a better view. I turned and saw Peter had not joined us. He stood, frozen, with a blank expression.

I turned back to the soldiers just as they began firing. The noise was deafening, awesome in the grandest sense. The tank

215

was hit so hard that it slowly began to roll backwards. Within seconds, it exploded. I shielded my face with my arm. What had before been an armored military powerhouse was now a heap of scrap metal. We slowly backed away, unable to take our eyes off the evidence of what we had witnessed. I stood next to Peter once more.

"Enough firepower to kill a god, one might say." The Russian giggled. My stomach lurched. "Load them." The three soldiers at the table marched to the first SUV. The two others with the death-machines placed the weapons back in their crates. We all watched as the five walked back toward us, each with a crate. My gaze remained fixated on the man on the screen. I heard the sedan trunks being opened behind me. A moment later, the soldiers went to the second SUV. They began removing more crates. "These are the only ten in existence. The exact specifications of the design are known to me and me alone." The crate on the table was closed and taken away to our awaiting sedan. "Keep them safe. Duplication would be difficult, nearly impossible without me." The three soldiers resumed their stations behind the table. "I trust your employer will keep his end of the bargain?" A barrel was lightly pressed against the Russian's temple. His eyes widened. The middle soldier began shutting the briefcase, but not before we heard a single gunshot.

The briefcase was latched and taken. The table was folded. The soldiers rushed back to their vehicles and zoomed off. Within seconds they were gone, leaving behind a smoldering tank and me wondering how I'd be able to eat a bite of spaghetti.

"Peter..." I licked my lips, "what the Hell was that?" he turned to me, stunned. His eyes were glazed over with fear. He swallowed, barely able to speak above a hoarse whisper.

"I don't know."

Twenty-Nine
Change of Terms

Peter. December 4th, 2009.

Marcus shrieked as he was engulfed in flames. He tried rolling on the floor, but there was too much fire. Slowly, his movement stopped.

Marcus was dead.

I killed him. "No," *I whispered desperately,* "this isn't right. It wasn't me." *All the faces around me began laughing hysterically. John, Joey, and the restpointed at me with grotesque grins on their faces.*

This wasn't how it happened. I didn't do it. Did I?

I shot up in my bed, gasping loudly. It was a dream. It was. I used my bedsheet to wipe the sweat from my forehead. Dustin shot Marcus. Not me. I exhaled. Thankfully, it was morning, so I didn't have to return to the world of dreams, where Marcus's death awaited me.

The phone was ringing. I covered my head with my rock-hard pillow. I wasn't ready to deal with this world, either.

The ringing stopped. An instant later, the persistent caller tried again. I grudgingly threw my pillow to the floor and groped around for my cell on the bedside table.

"What?" I answered.

"Problem?" Bobby.

"Are you asking or telling?"

"Does it matter?" he quipped. I sighed, sitting up.

"I guess not. What's up?"

"There's a small job I'm taking care of in your neighborhood."

"And?"

"And I want you in. I can't do much with this damn foot I hurt helping *you* out."

"Still on crutches?"

"Just got off, but it hurts like Hell. So look: payout is small, but so is risk. You know the bar about two blocks away from your place? The one with the drinks that are watered down more than the usual?"

"Yeah, I think so."

"Meet me there in twenty," he hung up. I stared at the phone with a frown. If Bobby weren't an old friend...

I got up, stretching and searching for my suit. As usual, it was hanging on my door. Next to the door was a set of crates containing weapons of mass destruction.

I sighed, rummaging around for an undershirt and socks. Those Crucifiers... they were incredible. But with that comes responsibility and the fear that I'll fail in my responsibilities. They were dangerous. Plenty of *Cartels* would pay big money to get their hands on just one of them. Ten, though? They have to be worth a fortune.

It wasn't too unfeasible that Matt would just give them away with no hesitation. This wasn't his first attempt to help me in my endeavors. Perhaps he had an alter ego that wanted to be a gangster, and so he tried to get as close to that life as possible. I wasn't Freud, but that was a possibility.

Fully dressed, I checked myself out in the mirror. They say that the meek will inherit the Earth... that may be, but for now, I'll just savor my vanity. Yet, upon closer inspection, I saw that my suit was slightly fraying at the edges. I contemplated changing into my spare. Or I could buy another.

The heist will provide for that. Then I'd buy be able to buy a suit for every day of the month. For the year even, if I had a place to store them. Which, considering I'd be moving out of this apartment, I would.

I briskly left the apartment, speeding past the out-of-order elevator to the stairwell, taking two steps at a time. Bobby may have said twenty, but I planned on being there in ten. I stepped outside and bought a cannoli from the local vendor. In the Old Country it's a cannolo, but America, like with most things, lost the actual word in translation. I stuffed it in my mouth as I continued walking, but came close to tears as I bit down, not realizing how hot it was.

I turned a corner and almost missed a step. My first thought was that, as usual, I was being paranoid. But this time, a black van was definitely trailing me. Feds. See, that was the difference in spying techniques between the feds and the crooks. The feds tried to make these large, bulky vehicles inconspicuous. Meanwhile, crooks painted something like "Mo's Paint Services" on the side, so when you see it, you just ignore it. Until you notice Mo has been following you for the last twenty blocks.

I turned into an alley. They made a mistake trailing me in my own neighborhood. I planned to go down here, ditch the van, take a right, and cut through a bar with a back entrance meant for this type of scenario. Right down the street from that exit would be the rendezvous with Bobby.

I strode through the alley, continuously turning my head to be sure no one had gotten out of the van to follow me on foot. It was doubtful. Definitely not crooks, then. Feds were above menial walking.

I turned back again when I was about halfway through the alley and walked right into a rather large individual. I bounced off, preparing for a fight. No one in alleys like these are here for tea.

To my astonishment, the large individual was none other than Uncle Donnie. He stared at me with his small, beady eyes.

"Terms have changed," he announced in his gravelly, monotone voice. I licked my lips, my face stone.

"Not exactly. The new Administration just needs a chance for their policies to fully be implemented. Though, I must say, I'm impressed you're attempting the whirlwind game of politics." Donnie did not laugh. Maybe he didn't get it.

He grabbed me by my shoulders and slammed me into the brick wall to my left. I grimaced and squeezed my eyes shut, but held back a yelp. Still holding my shoulders, he leaned in close.

"Murray doesn't want the money anymore," he whispered into my ear.

"Oh, really? That's good. Has he decided to become an evangelist?" Donnie growled.

"We'll take our payment in guns, instead."

"Well, unless you want peashooters, you're talking to the wrong guy. Now, John's brother owns a gun shop-"

"No," he gnashed his teeth. "There are certain guns Murray wants. Ten of them." My eyes widened. How did Murray, of all people, know about those?

"Look Donnie, I'm Made now…"

"Murray doesn't care."

Donnie and Murray had to be given a cut in the heist. They already knew about it, and we were in debt to Murray. The only way out would be to dispose of them both, which would be especially helpful since they also know about the Crucifiers. If I could escape this, I could hide out for a bit and get a friend to take care of them. One step at a time, however.

My phone buzzed in my pocket. Donnie cleared his throat.

"You gonna answer that?" I pulled it out and put it to my ear.

"Hello?"

"Hey man, it's John. I was wondering since, you know, business is slow right now, if you'd want to grab a drink or something?"

"I'd love to, but I'm a bit tied up at the moment."

"Oh. Okay..." he replied, confused. Donnie impatiently snatched the phone from me.

"Who is this?!" he boomed. I used that as my chance. I twisted myself out of Donnie's one-handed grasp. Forgetting the phone in his other hand, he made a grab for me. My cell flew straight to me. I snatched it out of the air and evaded Donnie's arms. I started running, feet pounding on the concrete, down the alley in the same direction I had been going, and pressed the cell to my ear.

"John?! You still there?!" I risked a look behind me. Donnie was slow, but he was coming.

"Peter, what's going on?" I would have sighed with relief, were it not for the need to conserve oxygen.

"Uncle Donnie knows about the guns. Not sure how. Murray wants in. He's following me."

"Who? Murray?" The urgency I felt was magnified in John's voice.

"Donnie! They want the guns as payment. Look, call Bobby. Tell him what's going on." I rounded the alley's corner.

"Bobby? Why Bobby?"

"He's a block over."

"You got it."

"Thanks!" I stuffed my phone, still on the call to John, back in my pocket. I was winded. It was becoming difficult to put one foot in front of another. Wearing a suit didn't help. I turned to my right, craning my neck to see that Donnie had rounded the alley corner. He knew where I was going, now. No point in running unless he got off my trail.

I went in the bar, firmly closing the door behind me. Several patrons looked up at the arrival of a man in a suit. All went back to their own business almost immediately. They knew what a Made Man looked like.

The room was filled with smoke and liquor. It was a wonder the entire place didn't burst into flames. I searched for a way to stand my ground. I had to act fast.

The bar crowd was milling around a pool table with most of the felt worn away. The table was directly in line with the door. I grabbed a stick from the shelf on the wall and headed to the decaying table, tossing a twenty on what remained of the felt. Two men took the bet. I nodded and set up the balls. I lined up my stick with the cue ball, preparing to break. My aim faced the entrance.

The door opened. I hit the cue at just the right angle, so that instead of hitting the other balls, it sailed through the air—straight at Donnie's face. In mid-air, right before impact, however, he caught it. He stared at it a few seconds. I stared at him. He looked up, locking eyes with me. I bolted, throwing my stick to the ground. They could keep the twenty.

I ran through the back exit, tripping into another alley and scrambling to my feet. The door banged open. I turned in a sort of half-crouch, prepared to spring. Donnie didn't waste time. He lunged at me, grabbing me by my collar. I winced, thinking of my suit.

"How do you know about the guns?" I demanded.

"Your friend told us."

"Why are you scared of me, Donnie?" he delivered a blow to my chin in response. Blood dribbled down from a corner of my mouth.

"You should be the one scared," he rumbled.

"Maybe. But, see, you lied. The only reason to lie is out of fear." This time, he drove his fist into my stomach. He allowed me to kneel in agony. Why was Donnie scared?

"I didn't lie. Your friend told us all about the Crucifiers."

"The FBI is on my tail, Donnie. They were clocking me when I turned into that alley and bumped into you. They're probably still following me. Following us." Donnie took a moment to process that. I made a run for it. He tripped me, sending me sprawling into a trashcan, spilling its contents over the ground. Donnie bounded forward, kicking me in the ribs. I grunted, rolling over several times, unable to catch my breath. He picked me up by the scruff of my suit jacket.

"Murray wants the Crucifiers. Give them to him, and the debt is paid."

"The debt will be paid when you help us out in the bank job and you get your cut with Murray's *vig*."

"That's a lot of risk. Murray likes to play it safe."

"You should learn from him," a low, powerful voice spoke from behind Donnie. I looked over his shoulder. Bobby was several feet away, pistol aimed at Uncle Donnie's head. Donnie turned to face him. "Not so fast. I have quite a happy trigger-finger." Donnie scowled. "Don't make that face again. Something that ugly... it gives me an excuse to blow your brains out."

"What do you want?"

"For you to let go of my friend there and go home. We'll forget this little slip-up and see you in a few weeks for the job." Donnie complied, grudgingly releasing me. He didn't say another word as he departed back into the bar, with only a glance back. Bobby kept his gun trained on him until he was out of sight. He kept aim on the door for a few seconds. Once Bobby was sure Donnie was long gone, he sighed, putting away the pistol and relaxing his callous expression. "What was that all about?" he asked. I shook my head.

"I messed up."

Thirty
The Same Game

John. December 6th, 2009.

I sat at my usual spot in *The Pub* and stared at the clock on the wall. Seconds away from being noon. He would be here in 5...4...3...2...1... the door opened wide.

In came my red-headed stepchild. Damion carried a briefcase and was wearing what he called a "casual" suit and tie. As far I was concerned, if you're wearing a suit, it's not casual. He straightened his already-straight tie and sat across from me. I folded my hands on the wooden table.

"Son."

"I've been going over some litigation. From what I can tell, Fuentes is running out of angles to hit you from, which means he'll try to find a new approach. One that we haven't thought of."

"That's great. Now why are we really here?" he cleared his throat.

"To hear a reason."

"Huh?"

"A reason. I want to know where the Hell you were when we waited for you to come back. Twenty-three years we waited day in, day out, hoping at the start and end of each one that you would walk through that door again," he cleared his throat and leaned forward, lowering his voice. "Do you know what that's like? Twenty years of watching Mom fall apart without you? Twenty years of wondering if you're alive or if I'll ever see my father again, when all the while you were in the same damn city as us?" My stomach dropped. I took a long pause.

"No. To be frank with you, Son, I don't," he seemed at a loss. I watched his features for any small change. He must have carefully rehearsed this situation. It was methodical, yet there was still a lot of emotion hidden in his words. A lot of hurt.

"It sucks, Dad. It sucks. You were here one day," he made a swiping motion with his hand over the table, "gone the next." Clare came to the table, avoiding my gaze. She wasn't rude. Just awkward. I ordered an iced tea. Damion gave me a curious look before ordering the same.

"Problem with my choice in beverage?"

"Not at all. It's just... that's what I usually get."

"But we aren't here to discuss our similar drink tastes," I said, more gruffly than I intended.

"No. No we're not. Look: all I want to know is where you've been. After that, we can go our separate ways." I shook my head.

"I want to be part of your life, Damion."

"I wanted that when I was nine, Dad. It didn't work out."

"You're right. It didn't. But this is our chance to make it right."

"It shouldn't be!" he slammed his fist on the table. Several customers looked over, but went back to their own meals. This was a bar. Everyone had their own problems to deal with. Damion realized his outburst and lowered his voice. "You never should have left. We begged you not to. So here's your chance," he spread his hands. "Please. Go ahead. Explain." I took a deep breath.

"Back in '86, you, Terry, JJ, and I were shooting at the range when I got a pretty important call from my detachment commander."

"I think I remember that." The waitress brought our teas.

"The Soviets were stockpiling weapons, and the Navy needed our help. The operation started off in Moscow. We ended up pursuing leads from there to Lebanon to Iran, and eventually to Afghanistan. There, we infiltrated the main camp. It was too easy," I shook my head. "Carl and I snuck in while the others led the soldiers on a wild goose chase. They were waiting for us, and the main target, Alexei Pomerov, shot Carl point-blank. I held him in my arms." I took a long pause, looking down. "He handed me his dog tags. Then I went after Pomerov." I growled. Carl Lowry had been my best friend.

"We lost him. Evac never came, and come to find out someone in the Pentagon shredded some papers to cover their own ass. We had to go through so many hoops to get back home... the four of us." We sat in complete silence. There was nothing he could say, and nothing I wanted to.

"I hope that answers your question." I got up and rushed to the door. No reason for my boy to see my tears. Just before I made it out, I heard him call out to me.

"Dad, wait." I turned. His jaw trembled. He crossed the room and motioned to our booth. "You haven't finished your drink." I gave him a sad half-smile. He returned it. We walked back over and sat down. I sipped the tea and gagged. I ripped open a few packets of Splenda and dumped the contents in.

"Why did you take the job?" he asked. I took another sip and grimaced. Better, but not the same.

"From what I can tell, the same reason you were a federal agent and now a public defender: to help people. To serve justice. We may have different views on just what justice is, but that doesn't change the fact. Look… that wasn't the first time things went awry. Vietnam hadn't exactly been a picnic. But back then, thoughts of children had been just that: thoughts. It was easier for me to feel invincible, especially with your mother's understanding and support. But with you guys… leaving was selfish. I admit it: I'm not perfect. But I try, Son. I really do. I did, and I'll continue to do so." I concluded. The words had flowed, unrehearsed. Nothing else was left.

"So once you were on your own, once you couldn't find us, you became a criminal?" I sighed.

"I knew you were probably in California. But moving costs money, and since I officially never made it home, I didn't have a soldier's pension. Katy had everything. At first, I worked in indentured servitude for a mercenary group, and they offered me a job, but there were no posts available in California. All I knew was that I had to be in this state. I lived in your uncle's gun store and joined a fighting company that goes on state tours, and everywhere I went I tried to get a trace. The fact that we had been living in the same city all this time…"

"You kept searching?"

"Every second I could spare. For you, your siblings. My wife that I love." Damion scowled with distaste.

"They refuse to receive government assistance—not even a disability claim on JJ. I send them what little I can spare. Violet's tuition, doctors for JJ… another three months, and the bank will repossess the house. I couldn't bear to see them every day and be reminded of it all. Be reminded of how this never would have happened if you stayed, like Mom told you to. Insurance helps, but it isn't enough." I listened to his story with concern. This was my family, and all this time I had been unable to help them. No longer.

"I'll give Peter a call. He may be able to work something out." Damion shook his head.

"I've tried legality, but those bankers have expert financial lawyers to back them up. I just have me," he paused. "Is he really a lawyer?" I added another packet of Splenda to my tea, stirring the cup.

"To be honest: I don't have a clue."

"Well, who is he, if he may or may not be a lawyer?"

"He…" I realized who I was talking to. "You'll have to ask him yourself."

"I have a feeling he doesn't care for me."

"Peter? Nah, he's like that with everyone." I decided it was the wrong time to mention the Everclear incident.

"Some friend you've got there, if that's how he treats you."

"Well, I guess he's different with me because I made him some money." Damion's face turned to stone. "So the allegations are true," he stated flatly. I sighed.

"Look, Damion…"

"I'm defending a guilty man."

"A guilty man who is your own flesh and blood. Well, unless you count what you told the court." Damion stood, pulling out his wallet and shelling out some bills. He nodded to me and pointed at my drink.

"Well, you finished it. I guess we're done here," he began to leave.

"Damion, wait," he walked out the front door, leaving me alone in the booth. I sat, frozen, for several minutes, feeling as if I had truly lost a son. Clare came to refill my tea. She turned to go. I had never really talked to her, but I figured now would be the time.

"Clare," she froze. After a bit of hesitation, she turned and looked at me. "I don't know much about your relationship with Peter, and I'm not really interested in details, except for one thing: why did you lead him on like that? Why'd you make him think he had a chance when he had none?" she sighed, a long, despairing exhale.

"You're asking me this, because…?"

"Because I feel as if I was just disowned by my son for the second time and I want to get my mind off of it." I motioned to the spot where Damion had just been. She sat, setting the pitcher down on the table.

"Look, I don't have long. But, honestly, he had a chance. He blew it."

"How'd he do that? If," I added quickly, "you don't mind me asking," she shook her head.

"He told me he's a lawyer. Lying about that was bad enough, but I didn't realize he was a crook until we went out a few times."

"He told you he's a crook when he introduced himself as a lawyer," she gave a faint, forced laugh.

"The lawyers I know use credit cards. Not cash for everything." I was incredulous.

"That's it? You ended it over his choice of payment?"

"What we had… it wasn't anything serious. I liked the guy, and I guess he liked me. But there wasn't much to it aside from that. Meanwhile, my friend I've known my entire life decided he needed a change. He, knowing nothing about my side interest, proposed. I said yes. End of story." I doubted Peter would like being referred to as a side interest.

"I'm not going to tell you that you're making a mistake by marrying this other guy without really giving Peter a chance. I can't. I don't know your fiancée. But I do know a thing or two about love. And if you don't love this guy…" She shrugged.

"He's a great guy, and I have strong feelings for him. Throw in that I don't have near those feelings for Peter, and it's no comparison."

"I understand that. My question to you is: is it love you have? Or the idea of love?" she stared blankly. "Do you love the thought of him, or the thought of a husband you've known for a long time?"Her mouth gaped ever so slightly as she furrowed her eyebrows.

"Zane Wyler is an amazing man, and I am lucky to have him. I have to go," she picked up her pitcher and stormed away.

"That wasn't what I asked." I muttered to myself. Now I'm 0-2 at this booth. All I need now is for Katy to come in and divorce me, and for Peter to whack me. I remembered I had to call him. I pulled out my phone. Just as I did, it started to ring. I checked the Caller ID. Speak of the Devil... I flipped it open.

"Hey, man." I said.

"Hey. Are you home?"

"Nah, I'm at *The Pub*."

"Perfect. Bobby and I are right outside," he hung up. He sounded... scared? Suspicious? A moment later, the pair walked in wearing nearly identical suits. I noticed Peter's was new; since he had that ceremony he wouldn't tell me about, he had redeveloped a taste for the finer things in life. Yet he still didn't have a car.

Bobby slid in the booth first, followed by Peter. Neither seemed inclined to speak. Peter squirmed a bit.

"Katy still upset over us being late to dinner?"

"More upset I haven't celebrated Thanksgiving with her in twenty-four years. I've been cooking family dinners every night for the past week to try and make up for it." We sat there in silence, which was eventually broken by Bobby.

"Eh, Peter, you wanna explain? You're the expert and all."

Pete nodded.

"We just got out of a private meeting with two big players: Andy Shapiro, Luigi's *Consigliere*, and Tony Spits."

"Tony Spits?"

"Yeah, don't worry about him." I could feel the reverberations of his leg bouncing under the table. "Look: *Fratres Criminis*, right?" I nodded, though there was no actual question. Peter waved his hands, starting over. "The Five are on the brink of war, and we are right in the middle."

"The Five?"

"You've heard of the five New York Families? Well the same thing goes for California."

"The whole state," I repeated, dumbfounded. War is never good, and with criminals there are no rules.

"You know some of them. The Cortez *Cartel* in the South, the Beppo Family and Black Outfit in Los Angeles, the *Bratva* here and in the Northeast, and the *Triads* in San Francisco and the Northwest. Mr. Lee, who runs the *Triads* in Hong Kong and has a branch over here in California, may be taking Johnny's side. Alexei may want Johnny gone, but he's still part of the Organization. Lee's hands are tied, as long as Johnny is alive. Alexei also has a small pull with the *Bratva*. Johnny cleared things up with the *Cartel*. That means that four of the most powerful crime families in the country will be fighting the fifth. We'll be slaughtered. We need to take care of loose ends." Bobby glanced at Peter. Pete didn't notice.

It's the same game as before: men telling me who to kill and I can't find a reason why.

Thirty-One
A Wise Guy's Way

Peter. December 15th, 2009.

Terry parked the car. John had told me about his impeding financial situation, and Dustin and I were trying to help them scrounge up enough to pay this month's expenses. Next month, after the bank job, they'd be able to pay everything off. And so my contribution was making Terry my personal driver. His mom wasn't thrilled about him using her Chevy Malibu, but she didn't have much of a choice. It wasn't like she had anywhere to be, anyway.

John and I got out. Terry stayed in the parking lot. Bobby had been very specific: only the two of us were to meet him. We entered the 50's diner, all linoleum. The wall facing the main road was all glass on the upper half, giving a nice view of the strip mall across the street, as well as Terry in Katy's car.

Even though we had arrived a little early, Bobby was already seated at a booth against the window, eating a burger. Watching us. I wasn't sure why he had called. He didn't give details, and I didn't ask for any.

His eyes followed us as we walked over and slid into the seats opposite him, John first. I felt the pistol John had given me rub against my skin as I got comfortable—I had started carrying it around in case Uncle Donnie and Murray decided on another attempt to shake me down. Bobby took another bite into the burger. Some of the mayonnaise dripped onto his light blue suit, similar to my own.

A waitress came our way. I shook my head and tried to keep Clare out of my mind. John smiled at her as he ordered a milkshake. I asked for a water. She left. Bobby set down the burger, carelessly wiping his hands with his napkin.

"Peter... I vouched for you." Bits of ground meat flew onto the table. "I have to take all responsibility for your actions. Is there anything you wanna tell me?" I slowly shook my head. He continued, "Look: those guns you told me about... they're dangerous, Peter. Real dangerous. Where are they?"

"Don't worry," I answered confidently. "I'm keeping them in a safe place."

"Seriously. Just tell me. We want to make sure they're properly protected." John stiffened.

"We? We who?" he asked Bobby. I leaned forward, anxious for his reply. We didn't want too many people knowing about this. If I had my way, no one would. Preferably not even myself.

"Word gets out fast. Lots of people want to get their hands on those guns. We don't want them falling into the wrong ones. Look, if it'll make you feel better, I'll buy them off you. How does fifty grand for all ten sound?" I stared at him. He was serious. Something about what he said was nagging at the back of my mind, but I couldn't figure out what it was. John, who had been thrumming his fingers on the waxed table, paused. I could feel him looking at me out the corner of his eye. Still, I kept my gaze steady.

"Thanks, Bobby," I said, "but no thanks. We could talk about this after the heist, if you'd like. We need the Crucifiers for it, but afterwards we can discuss this in detail. How's that?" Bobby sighed. There was nothing he could do about my decision without bringing it up with Tony Spits or Andy or—Heaven forbid—Don Beppo himself. I'm a Made Man now. He and I were about on equal footing. Otherwise, if he wanted to, Bobby could just kill me and search my place for them. Not that he'd find them there.

He wasn't distraught by my response. At least, if he was, he didn't show it. Instead, he slid out of the booth, muttering something about going to the bathroom. The waitress came back with my water.

"The shake will only be another minute," she informed John, "the blender's acting up again."

"No problem," he told her. "I have a feeling I'll be here a while." I shot him a look as she walked off.

"What's that supposed to mean?"

"It means that you two are going to keep debating or negotiating or whatever it is you're doing, and neither of you will give any ground. So I figure, what does it matter if my milkshake is a little late? I'll have downed three before we're done with this," he crossed his arms.

"Has Bobby been acting strange to you?" I asked John. He shrugged.

"I don't know him well enough to spot a difference."

"I haven't seen him in a while, but something is off. He always was a little different, in one of those ways you can't quite put a finger on, but this isn't that." Something occurred to me. "He never answered your question." John blinked.

"What?"

"He never answered your question. He said, 'we want to make sure,' as in plural. You asked who he meant by 'we.' He avoided the question."

"I figured he meant Luigi." I slowly shook my head.

"The Don's ire isn't something to mess around with. If there

236

was a problem, someone higher up than Bobby would have said something. Besides, that's a powerful threat. If he wanted those guns, he would have mentioned Don Beppo. Whatever is going on, it isn't sanctioned."

"You and Bobby have history?" I nodded. John's phone began to ring. He ignored it.

"We go way back. When I was just a kid in the Old Neighborhood, Bobby was like the dad I never really had. Even back then, he was Made. I knew he was the guy I wanted to be. He was sorta my hero, especially after that bloodbath in Chicago. He was Don Beppo's bodyguard, and probably the only reason they weren't blown away like so many others. I'm surprised he isn't a *Capo* yet." John listened with fascination. It wasn't hard to remember that he hadn't lived the same life as the rest of us. I took a sip of water, and choked. Ten guns. That was what was nagging at me: Bobby had specified ten guns.

As I began to set down the glass, it suddenly exploded. Glass shards flew in all directions, scratching my face. I felt a blow to my right side. I gasped; it was as if a train were redirected straight onto my path and had no plans to stop anytime soon. I was launched from my seat to the floor before I knew what was happening.

My eyes scrunched up with pain. Some liquid matted my hair to my head. I opened my eyes. My water had spilled onto the   floor.
John was on top of me, his eyes wild, darting all over. The other patrons stared at us, but that didn't matter. John was at least twice my weight. I gritted my teeth.

The glass upper-wall shattered into a million pieces. The rumbles of machine gun fire from outside replaced the silence in the diner. John rolled to the side. I was breathless. He settled into a crouch beside the booth.

"Your glass was hit by a bullet." I nodded, trying to grasp the situation. This was a set up. Bobby set us up. But why?

That didn't matter. We were pinned down by an assailant whose location was as-of-yet unknown.

Bobby came out of the bathroom. I noticed he had rubbed away his mayonnaise stain. He gaped when he saw we were still alive. But Bobby wasn't the type to hesitate. Neither was John. With the machine gun still firing but unable to reach us on the floor, John whipped out his revolver. Bobby held his pistol. Bobby shot first, wildly. There was no cover space; the tables were bolted to the floor. We had two choices: stay and hope John makes the first hit or run and risk getting blown apart by the anonymous gunner. I scrambled backwards, but John held my leg with one hand. I froze.

The waitress had left the blender running. John's milk and ice cream sloshed around in it. The firing from outside subsided. With the hand that held his Magnum, John swiftly aimed and fired at the blender. Milk and glass burst from it, covering the entire counter. Customers and workers alike screamed, crouching with hands on their heads. I noticed with disdain that some milk had trickled from the floor onto my suit. The blender's explosion momentarily dazed Bobby. John released his hold of my leg. I understood. I ran behind the far side of the bar, near the entrance. I couldn't risk running outside yet, since the gunner was most likely reloading. I wouldn't be able to make it to the car in time before he finished.

John was beside me. The only sound in the room was Bobby's footsteps as he slowly made his way toward us, having recovered from the shock of the small explosion. His shoes crunched bits of glass with each step. He began to shoot at the countertop right above us in time to his footsteps, forming a deadly rhythm, a lethal correlation between feet and gun.

The footsteps stopped. Two more shots rang out. I sucked in breath as even more glass rained down. He had shot the fluorescent lights directly above the pair of us. Not only that, but I could hear him shoot the other lights as well. Small shards littered my shoulders and back. The walking continued.

My mind was attempting to process too much at once. I had witnessed betrayals before, but usually I was one step ahead with a betrayal of my own. This... this was completely unexpected.

The Sun shining through what had been windows was now the only source of light, bounding off the glass all over the floor and creating a sort of seemingly diamond-encrusted linoleum. John whispered something at the floor. I don't think it was meant for my ears. Bobby stopped once more. I didn't understand why at first, but—maybe it was merely hope—I had an idea of what it could be.

"John," I clutched his shoulder, interrupting his prayer, "what type of pistol is Bobby using?"

"A Beretta M9 semi-automatic."

"And how many bullets does that hold?" he opened his mouth to answer, then caught on to what I was saying. He nodded.

"You've used up your clip, Bobby!" I called out. "You can't shoot us with an empty gun!" There was silence for a moment.

"My friend is on his way. Once he gets in here, you're both done for."

"I don't think so," John replied. "He has an M240 machine gun. Not the easiest thing in the world to carry. He steps foot in here with a pistol, I'll take care of him before you can say 'I'm sorry.' And believe me, Bud, you will be." There was no reply. Though I did hear a clip being removed.

Before he could reload, John sprang up, firing once. The shot missed, but it surprised Bobby enough for him to drop the clip. We sprinted out. John turned to fire again from the parking lot. I grabbed his arm.

"Don't. You could hit a civilian," he gave me a quick, level look, and nodded. We ran to the car. Terry already had it running. I slid over the hood and jumped into the passenger's seat. John got in the back. We took off just as Bobby stormed through the front door, shooting after us.

"Why didn't the gunner fire just now, when he had the chance?! Does it take that long to reload?"

"No," John responded grimly, "he was trying to get a better shot. The M240 is usually balanced on a tripod or some sort of variation. The shooter, I'm guessing on the roof of the strip mall across the street, couldn't get to us from his position. So he had to pack up and move out."

"What's going on, Dad?" Terry asked as he glanced in the rearview.

"Eyes on the road. This is not a drill. I don't have any data as of yet. Peter?" I stared out the window, trying to work this out.

Murdering a Made Man is punishable by death without direct approval from the Don or someone else that's very important in the Family. The gunman working with Bobby had to kill us and get away. Bobby would be able to say he was in the bathroom and got lucky; blame Johnny Black for the attack. That's what the diner scene was about. The blame. He could have easily done away with us privately. He wanted to make a scene. Make it public. Make it clear he was not involved. Now he had to get rid of us as witnesses. Whatever was going on, one thing was clear: none of this was sanctioned.

"Bobby must really want those guns," I surmised.

"Where am I driving to?" Terry asked. It didn't seem directed at anyone in particular.

"I know a few old warehouses…" I pondered8.

"No, I've got it. Terry, take us to the shop. You know where it is?"

"Uncle Dustin took me the other day." I could hear John slip something out of his pants. A moment later he began dialing on his cell. He put in on speaker. The other end picked up on the first ring.

"Aye."

"Dustin, it's John. Some guys are trying to kill us. We need you and Vince to close down the shop and turn out the lights." No reply.

"Dustin?"

"Can't do what you're asking if you're still yapping. I'm on my way there; I'll let Vince know to expect you." There was a click as he hung up.

"Dad, there's a black motorbike gaining on us."

"Pete, can you hand me a spare cartridge? It's in the glove box." I did as instructed. He was reloading his revolver as a bullet pierced the glass in the back. Terry swerved to the left.

"Here comes another one." Terry alerted us. I turned around and saw he was right. An identical driver had joined the first. The newcomer, I could tell from the blue suit, was Bobby. Both were now firing at us. The back window shattered. John seemed to be waiting on permission.

"Waste them." John nodded, rolling down the window. He leaned out, Magnum clasped in both hands. I ducked in my seat and turned to observe the action. John couldn't get a clear shot with the bikes constantly weaving through traffic. We veered right onto a small street. Soon John came back in the car.

"I'm out!" he yelled. I opened the glove box. No more cartridges.

Terry drummed his fingers on the steering wheel. The drivers had rounded the turn and were looking bigger and bigger in the rear-view mirror. One driver was on either side of our doors. They leveled their guns at our heads. Any second now, and they would shoot.

"Terry, brakes!" I yelled. He obeyed. Both bikers continued forward at full speed. Before they could change direction, Terry made a sharp left turn.

One driver followed; the other couldn't change direction fast enough and kept on his path. One down, one to go. Terry tossed John a pistol. The biker accelerated, catching up quickly. John fired a few rounds. Pistols were hard enough to shoot accurately without a moving target. The GPS said we were only a quarter of a mile away from our destination. I kept watching the gunman through the rearview. The tracksuit-wearing figure was only inches behind our rear.

"Brake!" Once again Terry stopped. We lurched forward. I would have been launched through the front window if I didn't have my seatbelt on.

The assassin hit our rear, abandoning his motorcycle as he flew several yards to the front of our car. He didn't get up, but we hadn't been going fast enough for him to be killed unless he broke his neck. Just dazed, maybe a broken bone or two. John and I exited the car, heading toward our injured assailant.

This guy has some explaining to do.

Thirty-Two
Friends?

John. December 15ᵗʰ, 2009.

We reached the shop. I had patted down our assassin. He came prepared: three pistols, eight cartridges, four knives, and a grenade—all now safely in Katy's glove box. We had left the M240 with his bike.

I picked the assassin up by his collar. He groaned. No one spoke. Terry brought the car around back while Peter opened the door for me as I carried the sorry S.O.B. into the shop. The door shut. The knob clicked as Peter turned the lock. The room was only lit by the sunlight pouring in through the windows. Vince stood in the center of the room with his arms crossed. I threw the biker down onto the middle of the floor. We crowded around him as Vince tied his hands behind his back with plastic zip-ties.

"Situation?" Vince asked.

"Standard mercenary, from what I can tell," I answered. "Experienced. Tattoo on the back of his right wrist I'm unfamiliar with-"

"It's the mark of a *Bratva* assassin," Peter explained.

"He was operating a standard M240, most likely on a tripod. Also carried a new M9, same as the guy who hired him: Bobby Mancuso, who set up a signal for us to be killed when he went to relieve himself. Our friend here tried to gun us down from across the street, but didn't count on Terry warning us by shooting Peter's glass of water. I couldn't get the details of his bike, but it's definitely foreign." Terry came in from the side garage door.

"The car is parked," he reported. The would-be assassin watched us with a cool, contemptible expression from his spot on the floor. Peter crossed the room, walking around our captive. He stuck out his hand to Vince, who shook it.

"Peter Richardson. You must be Vince. John's told me a lot about you. Look," Peter turned and motioned to the windows in the front of the store, "could those be drawn? There are only four places Bobby can check without running into people that won't be happy to see him trying to kill us. This shop is one of them. He'll be here at some point, so we need to be sure we're ready when he is. It doesn't help if he sees us through the window," he turned to me. "Can you take our friend here to the bathroom? Leave the lights on but close the door. Wait for me." I nodded. The thug must have still been injured from his flight, or more likely from hitting the ground; he barely put up a fight as we dragged him away.

"What about me?" Terry asked Peter. I turned my head, wondering how Peter would approach this.

"You go to the apartment upstairs and watch through the window. If anyone shows, yell down to Vince, who will be hiding behind the counter. Bobby will want to go through the garage or the back, so he won't see Vince. When he comes your way, Vince, take him out." I dragged the mercenary into the bathroom, ramming the door open with my shoulder. Peter was keeping Terry's role small. Good. I thought he could handle more, but I didn't feel like this was his fight.

Just as the door swung closed, it opened again. Peter came in, talking on his phone, completely ignoring the existence of our hostage.

"Yeah, just watch his house for me, will ya? Tell his wife you're a friend of a friend and doing him a favor." Peter paused, listening to the other line. "Exactly. Oh," he made it sound as if a thought occurred to him last minute, but I could see otherwise, "and don't trust anyone. You know how Johnny Black is. He'd send us a friend before a foe. Right, right. Call me back in half an hour." Peter put away his phone and finally acknowledged our tough little friend.

"I do not work for Johnny Black," the man said with an accent that sounded faintly Russian, possibly Eastern European. Peter smiled at him, a teacher explaining a new concept to a pupil.

"I know that, Dummy. But if I told my friends that their friend is trying to kill us, it would take a lot of time to settle everything. We could be dead by then." Suddenly, Peter brought back his foot. The presumed-Russian barely had time to flinch before Peter's shoe collided with his jaw. His body sprawled onto the floor. Next thing I knew, Peter had out the gun I gave him. *De Oppresso Liber* gleamed dully on the barrel. He crossed the short space to the Russian, who got up to a sitting position. This man, a hair away from death, watched with only mild interest. Peter removed the clip and tossed it to me. I grabbed it out the air and stuffed it in my pocket, unsure as to what route he was taking.

"Now, I don't know much about guns," Peter licked his lips, "is a bullet still in the chamber without the clip? I don't know. John, is a bullet still in the chamber?"

"Should be."

"Should be? Well, waddya say we make sure of that?" Peter sprang up and, with one hand, pressed the tip of the gun more firmly against the hostage's forehead, making as if to shoot. The Russian barely blinked. He had some iron.

"I'm interested in the results," he said. Peter flinched, even though he was the one holding the gun. "Go ahead. Satisfy my curiosity. Oh, that's right. You don't do that, now do you? You no kill?" Peter stared at him, his gun-hand steady.

"I killed Marcus Dean."

"Then this should be no problem. Go ahead. I want you to do it. Kill me." Peter gritted his teeth, glaring at the nonchalant Russian. Peter growled. In a fit of fury, he wheeled around. The Russian smiled. Peter whipped back around and hit the Russian across the face with his pistol. There was no grunt of pain. He simply fell to the floor. He sat back up with difficulty.

"Do you know what this is?" Peter asked, gesturing to a spot on his suit that was a shade off from the rest. "It's a stain. From a milkshake. You ruined John's milkshake and, worse, you stained my suit." Peter hit him again. A small trickle of blood ran down his chin. Peter glared at me as he put away the pistol. I pulled out my phone.

"Almost here?" I asked.

"Yeah," Dustin responded.

"I'm thinking Kuwait."

"Got it," he hung up. I could tell Peter was having a morality struggle, though he was attempting to maintain a certain level of poise. I could only imagine all the scenarios running through his head. Me? I've already had a betrayal that cost me everything. What was one that was merely an attempt on my life? Peter glared at the assassin.

"Do you know who I am? I'm Untouchable, that's who I am. You kill me, and my friends will buy two caskets, one for me and one for you. What makes you think you can waltz on in here and get away free?"

"Money," the apparent-mercenary responded. Peter

blinked, then kneeled on one knee. He leaned in close to the hostage, compassion in his eyes.

"I want to help get you out of this. I do. What's your name?" No reply. "Come on. I'm helping you out here. You know my name. You knew before I told Vince, didn't you?"

"Dillan Kamenev."

"Okay, Dillan: Bobby paid you to whack us?" Dillan gave his usual stone face. Peter grunted and stood.

"Doesn't good cop-bad cop take two?" I asked. He shot me a look I didn't particularly like.

"Your turn," he said. I chuckled.

"Why did you try to kill us?" I asked. Dillan stared at us. He tilted his head one way, then the other, determining how much to tell.

"It's what I was paid to do." Peter nodded. He knew that much. But he wasn't leading the questioning.

"Paid... by Bobby?" I continued. Dillan narrowed his eyes, but nodded.So Bobby wanted us dead, and didn't want to do it himself.

"Dillan," Peter said, "did Bobby give any reason for why he wants us dead?" he nodded. "Tell us," he demanded firmly. Dillan chuckled.

"Ah, Kuwait," I said fondly, "what a time." Our captive frowned. I gave a small, toothless smile. "Oh, you didn't know? If you don't talk to us, we're going to try a little experiment. See, I've always wondered: if you are in a wooden chair, and we have a wet rag in your mouth, and we put a current through the rag, will you fry like a burger on a grill? Or will it not work with a wooden chair?"

"What happens if it won't work?" he asked, curious.

"Maybe you'll catch on fire. Who knows?" he stared at us with cold, grey eyes. I glared, barely stopping myself from pulling out my Magnum and using the butt. Peter crossed his arms, staying behind Dillan.

"Would you like my mother's maiden name? My hobbies? The name of my pet possum?" I studied him. He was young, maybe early twenties.

"Your English is good. We'll see if you can talk with some amps running through you." The door opened. Dustin walked in, dragging a chair. Jumper cables dangled from his shoulders. Dillan gaped as Dustin closed the door.

"Washicha?!" Dillan exclaimed, incredulous. Dustin looked up. His jaw dropped.

"Kamenev?" Peter looked from my brother to our captive with shock. So did I. There was a small shout from the main shop. A moment later, the door opened.

Bobby strode in, silenced pistol raised. I shut the door with one hand and grabbed Bobby by the throat with the other. The gun clattered to the floor. Bobby, forced by the neck against the wall, bared his teeth. Peter snarled. Guttural, like an animal. I stared at the newcomer. Finally, as the situation was under control and Bobby struggled against my grip, Peter chuckled in an I'm-going-to-kill-you-but-let's-act-like-friends sort of way. Which, in reality, meant Dustin or I would kill him, if he had to die.

"Look who decided to drop by. This is such a pleasant surprise." Peter said. I glared, anger bubbling to the surface. I had finally been reunited with my family, and here were these crooks... all the same. They shoot at my family. They hide in the shadows like snakes waiting for their chance to strike instead of meeting on the battlefield.

"Can't... breathe...."

"John, let him go!" Peter ordered. I hesitated. A few more seconds and his bones would give way. Then it would be over.

I loosened my grip. Bobby gasped for air.

"Do you mind if I let Dillan go?" Dustin asked.

"What in the Hell is going on here?" Peter asked.

"Washicha and I worked together," Dillan explained, "in Russia. He asked for my services again just a few weeks ago."

"When we broke into Marcus's house," Dustin concluded.

"So you two… are friends?" Peter asked. Dustin and Dillan looked at one another. They shrugged.

"I don't want to kill him," Dustin said.

"And I don't want him to kill me," Dillan added. I looked to Peter, who shrugged. I guess sometimes business doesn't apply when it's personal.

"Are we… cool?" Peter asked Dillan.

"A friend of Washicha's is not a contract I wish to handle."

"Actually, I'm his brother," I said as Bobby tried to break free.

"Really? We should have drink sometime."

"You should see this guy after a bottle of Smirnoff," Dustin said.

"You hold your own like a Russian, Washicha." Dustin barked a laugh as he cut Dillan loose.

"More like you hold your own like an Irishman," Dustin retorted. Dillan rubbed his wrists, giving Bobby a nasty look as he left. All three of us glared at Bobby.

"Why'd you do it?" I asked. Bobby sighed. He was out of breath, and as he spoke, his voice was harsh. Defeated.

"We all do what we have to. Isn't that right, Peter?" Before Peter could respond, Bobby broke out of my grasp and darted for his boot, where I saw a .22 caliber pistol. A gunshot rang throughout the shop. Everyone froze. Bobby slumped against the wall and slowly slid to the floor. Dustin stood with a cool expression, smoking gun in hand.

Pete violently shook his head and started to pace.

"Okay, it's okay. No, it's not okay. Okay... Bobby wasn't going to tell us anything." Terry ran through the door. He blinked when he saw the body.

"I... Vince was shot." Terry reported, unsure yet unafraid. "Flesh wound. I'll give him a hand."

Peter snapped his fingers. "No you won't. Dustin will. You go get the car and bring it around front. Call your mom and let her know you're at the dealership and you're trading it in, courtesy of me. She'll thank me later." Terry nodded, confused, and left. Peter looked at me. "You have some shovels here?"

"I redid some foundation a few years back. I should have a spade or two."

"Good. We're going to need them."

Thirty-Three
An Unmarked Grave

Peter. December 15th, 2009.

Dusk was quickly approaching as we made our way to the dig site. The car ride was eerily silent. Terry was still driving the Malibu. Dustin had stayed behind to take care of Vince and tidy up. John and I both sat in the back, me directly behind Terry. Bobby was in the trunk. The only sound was the wind whistling through the bullet holes in the windows and a low roar from the annihilated back window. Getting pulled over was a risk we had to take: no one else had a car, and we couldn't let the Family know what was going on.

I racked my brain for any rhyme or reason for this betrayal. Bobby was loyal to the Family; why would he weaken it if he wasn't told to do so? And he wasn't told to. I was certain of that much. Men disappear from the ranks every now and then, and although most know what happened, the event itself is never pinpointed, and is rarely committed by someone outside the Family. Yet here Bobby is, trying to make a public execution with a hired gun. I pulled out my cell and punched in a few numbers. I raised it to my ear. With the roaring wind behind me, I could barely hear the ringing.

"Yeah?"

"Jimmy, it's me!" I practically had to shout to be heard. "Can you hear me?"

"Hardly. What's going on?"

"What makes you think something is going on?"

"The only time anyone in this business calls is when something's going on, that's why," he responded gruffly.

"Look, one day soon I'll call you up and we can go dancing. I just need some information." As a professional thief, I imagine he came across plenty of figures who drop tidbits, and works with others who know a friend of a friend who is the cousin to the guy I want to know about. "Dillan Kamenev. The name ring a bell?"

"Nah. Let me make some calls, and I might end up remembering him."

"Great. Should be a Vasiliev enforcer."

"Got it," he hung up. It's always a good thing to know who tried to kill you, even if I don't know the "why" yet. Hopefully the "who" will lead the way.

It began to lightly rain. I leaned forward so I wouldn't be soaked by the droplets falling through where the back window used to be. My face brushed against the driver's headrest. I used it as an excuse to figure out something that I had been bothering me.

"Do you always carry a piece?"

"No. Mom's been a single mother in Los Angeles. She keeps one in her glove compartment."

"Start carrying one."

"Does this sort of thing happen often?"

"Too often to be stupid. You've been promoted: consider yourself a bodyguard."

"Do I get a bump in pay?"

"Haven't you ever heard that pigs get fat while hogs get slaughtered? I'm offering you an invaluable position, and here you are, hoping for some extra cash when you'll be swimming in it in a few weeks."

"Right. Sorry."

"And don't apologize. It makes you look weak. These wise guys you'll be dealing with love to pounce on weakness."

"My bad." I groaned, slumping into my seat. I had forgotten about the rain, which had increased to a steady pour. I sat up straight.

I felt my phone buzz. I took it out and flipped it open.

"His real name is Anton Petrov. Back in Moscow he ran with Rex Taylor the bounty hunter. He got a murder charge pinned on him and Taylor gave him the new identity of Dillan Kamenev and moved him to the States, then severed ties. He joined up with a mercenary corporation, was let loose for reasons unknown, joined up with the Vasilievs about six months back, and still retains a sort of independent mercenary operation."

"Is Katerina aware of this independent operation?"

"From what I can tell, she tolerates it so long as there is no conflict of interest, and she gets her cut."

"Dillan doesn't give her details?"

"None are wanted." Good. That should avert a war between the Beppo and Vasiliev Families if any of this is uncovered. Hopefully, none of it will be.

"Thanks Jimmy. Still want that dance?"

"I'll settle for a drink. What's this about?"

"Come on, Pips," I tried to sound cheerful, "I didn't think you were the type to ask questions. Don't you know curiosity killed the cat?"

"I'll be waiting on that drink." I didn't wait for the click before putting the phone back in my pocket. Dillan was no more than a hired assassin, though more experienced than I realized. To work with Rex Taylor meant to get trained by Rex Taylor, giving him military training equal to if not greater than John's.

"Turn right up ahead," I told Terry. He nodded absently. We were several hours outside the city, nearly on the California-Oregon border. If I had my way, we'd be in northern Canada. This is one body that can never be found.

That Bobby attacked us first doesn't matter. That's not how it works. Bobby can't get touched by anyone, especially an outsider. If Dustin's murdering of Bobby gets out, he'll be six feet under, too. Terry, Vince, and John will join him for being associated with the offense. I might be able to use my status to get out of it, if I'm lucky. I'd rather it doesn't come to that. As far as anyone knows, John and I were the last to see Bobby alive. That already puts suspicion on us. The whole diner incident won't stay quiet, but witnesses can be talked to and confused, facts muddied. All they know is three men entered a diner—first one then two—a mystery man fired into the diner from outside, the three men pulled out their own guns, shots were exchanged, and the three men departed—first two then one. Who shot at whom is just a detail that can easily be mixed up.

The story we had rehearsed the first hour of the drive was clear, simple, and close enough to the truth that it actually could be, if anyone asks: Bobby wanted to work out a few minor details for the bank job. He asked to meet us at the diner. Someone—no doubt a member of the Black Outfit— tried to whack the three of us. Bobby returned fire so the two of us could make a run for it. We got in our car to go after the gunman, but he had already taken off. I called Bobby (I did so, in case my phone records are checked) and told him to meet us at *The Pub* in half an hour to get a game plan; he said he'd be there but afterwards he would be heading to Chicago. We showed up (we did make a short appearance). Bobby didn't.

254

The whole Chicago thing was to buy time, to sort of give several leads to anyone especially curious about Bobby's absence. It would take time to get people to scout him out in Chicago, and it would take time to find a body or a killer. Or maybe something happened on the way to Chicago. Who's to say? Not me. I don't know a thing about it.

"There. You see that junkyard on the right? Bring the car around the back of it. Try to stay on firm ground and leave light tracks so the rain'll wash 'em away." Terry did as he was told. Behind the junkyard was a clearing designated as the next dump mound site. Using the wire fencing that designated the perimeter as a guide, Terry drove us to it. He turned off the car as we got out.

John popped the trunk. Bobby's body was stiff, with two lifeless eyes staring glassily at us, right below a crater through the forehead. I shivered. Two shovels lied beside him. Without a word, I felt around in Bobby's pockets. Satisfied, I grabbed his cell and flipped it open.I blinked a few times, blinded by the brightness, and pressed the call log. Most recently was my call to him, and before that his call to me to meet him at the diner, made this morning. Right before that were two calls to a number with the Oakland area code. Preceding those were about two dozen calls Bobby denied in the last three days, all from the same number. Mixed in with those were a couple calls both to and from two other numbers, one of which was vaguely familiar. I hit the number from Oakland and pressed it to my ear. I had a feeling I knew who it was.

"You're alive?!" The other end answered, incredulous.

"Sorry to disappoint, Dillan. Bobby went away for a while. He left behind his phone." Silence. "You there?"

"Yes. Yes, I am here."

"Good. Now tell me: what was Bobby paying you?"

"Five thousand to accept the contract, plus the promise of a weapon he claimed could catch tens of thousands once the deed was done." I stared at the phone for a second, making sure I heard right. John gave me a quizzical look. I shrugged him off.

"Did he tell you anything about this... weapon?"

"Only that it is very rare. Very expensive. I almost turned him down."

"Why is that, if it's so valuable?"

"Because he didn't have it yet."

"We'll speak soon." I clicked "end call" and sighed, weary and stressed. Bobby promised Dillan one of the guns in my possession once we were disposed of. Meaning one of two things: either Bobby was going to kill us and steal the weapons, or if I said yes and he bought the guns he was going to kill us anyway. I took out my own phone and hit a few numbers with my thumb.

"What now?"

"Come on, Jimmy. Just think of that drink. Look, I need you to look into a few phone numbers for me, see who they belong to."

"What do I look like? A secretary?"

"You'll look like a man running for his life if I don't get the owners of those numbers."

"Yeah? And who's gonna make me run?"

"Not sure. Let me ask John. He's right beside me."

"Isn't he always?" I gave him the three phone numbers.

"That last one in particular is important." The one that Bobby kept ignoring. "You need any repeated?"

"I got it."

"So you'll get me what I need to know?"

"We'll see what I can do," he hung up. The discourtesy of

these *mooks*. Still, Jimmy is good people. I put both phones in my pocket.

Terry and I each grabbed a shovel. John picked the body up, holding it to his chest like an infant. We silently proceeded to the fence closest to the open land. I shook the fence to test its firmness. Satisfied, I tossed my shovel onto the other side and hopped over. Terry did the same. John tossed the body up into the air. He must have misjudged the distance or the wind resistance, because the corpse landed on the tip of the metal gate, where small spikes protruded. Bobby tipped our way and began to fall, but his arm was somehow stuck to the tip. Terry made a small sound in his throat. Or maybe that had been me.

John dislodged the body, and it landed at our feet. A moment later John hopped over.

Terry and I began digging. A light rain started up again. It worked to our benefit, both cooling us off from what would become back-breaking work and making the earth more malleable, though I couldn't say much for my suit. My phone began ringing. I passed my shovel to John and walked a few feet away as I pulled it out of my pocket. Once I did, I realized it was Bobby's cell, not mine. I answered.

"It's about time. Where the Hell have you been? What? You just think you can do your own thing?" he paused. "Look: do you want to end up like the others? Hello?" My own phone began ringing. Loud. I gasped and hung up. I answered mine as I checked the number on his. It was the same one that had been calling for the past few days.

"The one that called all the time is an unregistered burner cell."

"Can you trace the owner?"

"I can try, but it'll take time."

"How much time?"

"Hard to say. Whoever it is, they're real good at keeping things quiet. Could be a few days. Maybe a few weeks." I sighed. This would be the person who just called me. Well, called Bobby.

"And the other two?"

"One belongs to Chad Black, Johnny's cousin." I blinked. Lightening forked across the night sky.

"The last one?"

"Yeah, I got it. I double-checked it to make sure, but it definitely belongs to Murray Gigante, the loan shark." The same guy whose goon Bobby had pointed a gun at the other day. What is going on here?

"Thanks, Jimmy."

"Yeah, yeah. Just get me that drink."

"How about Monday?"

"Monday it is," he hung up. That's when it began pouring. I turned back to the others, who were hard at work digging Bobby's grave. Hopefully it wouldn't take long. As the dirt changed into mud, my hope disintegrated. We were going to have a very, very long night.

Thirty-Four
Katy Washicha

John. December 18th, 2009.

I headed downstairs from Dustin and I's shared apartment. It was getting crowded, having only been meant for one person—not two men and a rapidly-growing dog. I've been hoping once we all get our payday in a few weeks, I can find a place of my own.

I walked into the main store. Vince was counting the money in the cash register, meaning it was six in the evening: closing time. Even with his right arm in a sling, he remained as punctual and methodical as ever. The arm problem didn't deter him too much, anyway: Vince was ambidextrous.

"How are you holding up, Vince?"

"I'm managing, Sir. A good, clean wound. In and out."

"Good to hear. Well, that is… you know what I mean. Sorry again for getting you mixed up in all that."

"First time I've been shot at since I served."

"That's a long time."

"I almost miss it."

"Almost?"

"I thought I missed it. Then I realized how immature that was of me, once this happened. That immaturity reminds me of my youth."

"You still could have taken the week off. You know, to recuperate."

"Yes Sir, I do."

"Do you know how many times in the past twenty-odd years I've asked you not to call me Sir?"

"Four-thousand one hundred and ninety-two including that last one, Sir."

"Despite being... what? Ten years my senior?"

"Nine to be exact, Sir."

"Not only that, but you were in the Royal Air Force, you've been a good friend all these years, and you make more sales than me. You're the one who deserves the respect." His eyes clouded. He looked down at the register, but then changed course and met my gaze.

"When I fought for the Queen... I fought for thirteen years. I came back heralded as some sort of hero who had vanquished the tyrannies of our enemies. You fought for as long as I, and you came back as if you *were* the enemy. That willingness to accept no gratitude for service is what earns you the respect, Sir. Always remember that it is not our age that makes us wise, but the tasks we conquer in the process," he gave a small smirk. "Besides, the sales have little to do with my character and more to do with your slightly-unsavory appearance." I chuckled.

"And I wouldn't have it any other way."

"I know you wouldn't, Sir. Now, are you certain you don't want me to stay the night? That miscreant may have friends, and three able-bodied old men are better than two. I don't want this establishment to go up in flames while I'm away."

"For the hundredth time: no, thank you. First off, none of us are 'able-bodied' anymore, as I'm coming to find. Second, Dustin is-" my phone began ringing. I took it out and checked the caller I.D. I quickly answered.

"Hello?" I motioned to Vince that I needed a moment. He

nodded. I went into the back of the shop. I trusted Vince with my life. I just felt this was too personal for him to accidentally overhear.

"John..."

"Katy."

"Do you mind stopping by? There's something I want to talk to you about."

"Actually, I have something on my mind, too."

"So you'll come?"

"I'll be there in twenty."

"Thank you."

"Anytime." We both paused, each waiting for the other to say those three little words first.

"I love you," I finally told her.

"I love you too," she hung up. I went to see Vince.

"Would you mind going upstairs and letting Dustin know I'll be heading out?"

"Of course, Sir."

"Thanks, Vince." I touched the handle to the front door and hesitated. I turned around. Vince had finished up with the cash register. I gave him a quick salute. He gave a fraction of a smile as he returned it with his left hand. I nodded and left, hopping onto my bike at the curb. I zoomed off into the jungle of Los Angeles.

I couldn't imagine what Katy needed. It could be that the roof had begun to leak. It could be that Jesse James played with scissors. Violet got a boyfriend. Damion wants to talk to me. Or Katy never wants to see me again. Such lovely possibilities.

I came up to the driveway. I parked and walked up to Terry sitting on the porch stairs.

"Hey, Dad."

"Hey Terry," I sat by him, "what's up?"

"Nothing. You know. Just looking at the stars." I looked around. A few lights were just beginning to show against the dark blue sky.

I used to stargaze all the time. Just me and my thoughts.

"Where's JJ?"

"*The Pub*. Him and Violet are just talking, hanging out, you know. Normal stuff."

"When does she head back to school?"

"She still has like two weeks." Perfect.

"Could you join them? I need to have a talk with your mom."

"Ah, one of *those* talks. Gotcha," he headed over to his Harley Dyna Glide as I walked into the house.

"Katy?" I called out.

"Living room." I followed the sound of her voice and found her sitting on a couch. I went over and sat with her, putting my arm over her like old times. She didn't get closer. She didn't move away, either.

"Whatcha watching?"

"*The Outsiders*. Reminds me of you and your old friends." I watched it for a bit with her. Both of us were silent.

"No," I said suddenly, "see, there wouldn't have been any wait for a 'brawl' if one of us got hurt. Not with my friends."

"I remember how they were, Ponyboy."

"Best friends I ever had next to Carl and the squad."

"What happened to them? Carl? And Castle and Walker?"

"Carl... Carl didn't make it."

"Oh. I'm sorry, John. I know you two were close."

"Yeah. Yeah, we were. The rest of us just sort of parted ways when we got back to the States."

"You never gave me the full story of what happened with

262

that."

"And for that, I'm sorry. I will. Just not yet. Things need to get situated."

"Which has to do with why I asked you to come." I didn't move from my spot. Neither did she. "Look... this isn't easy to say. But when we thought you had... just... okay: the insurance companies and the government didn't help us out because there was no proof anything had happened to you. I had sold the house and moved out west because the memory was too painful, but real estate values didn't help our financial situation. Your savings went through four kids pretty fast. I got two jobs. But then Damion had college and law school... and Violet waited a few years before UCSB... I had to make a loan. Damion thinks the money came from the insurance companies, just like the mystery money we got every so often that kept us afloat for a while."

"You mean from Dustin."

"Right. I refused to hope it came from you. It still wasn't enough. So I went to what I thought was a legitimate financial institution. And it was. There was just more to it, as we found out. Turns out we borrowed from a loan shark." I thought of scumbags like Murray and Uncle Donnie.

"How much?" she shook her head, tears forming at the corners of her eyes. "Katy, how much do you owe?" she glanced at me.

"Two hundred thousand." My heart skipped a beat.

"When did you plan on telling me?"

"A few seconds ago."

"I..." I was lost for words. "That ties in to one of the things I wanted to tell you," she sat up.

"You aren't in debt, too, are you?"

"No, nothing like that. Well, sort of like that. I mean..." I took a deep breath, "those guys that shot up the house? They're part of a biker club led by a psycho named Johnny Black. I worked for him for a short time. Then me and Peter parted ways from him and… well, Peter's in the mob." I winced, waiting for some sort of repulsion. She instead gave me a level look.

"And you? Are you in the mob with him?"

"I can't be because I'm not Sicilian. But I help out, yes. And Katy: they pay. They pay well."

"Of course they do. The higher the risk, the bigger the pay, right? Just like it used to be. John, I love you, but you can't be this… bulletproof outlaw cowboy forever. Eventually you're going to have to settle down and stop riding."

"I know. I'm just trying to provide for this family and we have this big job coming up, a bank robbery. If this works out we'll be doing very well. The debt will be repaid and then some."

"John, there are other ways to make money."

"But that much? And I know how these guys work; you can't hold them off forever."

"How much are you making?"

"Enough. I don't think details are a good idea, considering who I'm working with. But combine my cut with Dustin and Terry's, and-"

"Dustin and Terry?" she jumped to her feet.

"They're part of this too, Katy." I stood. "They wanted to be. So did JJ, but I couldn't allow it because of his… physical condition. I knew you wouldn't approve, but don't worry."

"How can you expect me to not worry?" I grabbed her shoulders and gazed into her eyes. They were full of hurt.

"They're as safe as they can be. It'll just be this one job, and then we'll put all of this behind us," I guaranteed her.

"John, it's hard enough risking you. But three of my boys at once? That's too much to ask."

"They're trying to do like I am and help out."

"At what cost though, John? Their lives? Your life? It's not just you in this anymore. You know that. You ran with those guys in high school and fought beside them. You fought in Vietnam and God knows where else, and now you're asking me—when I finally have you back—you're asking me to go and let you fight again and have you die again? Why do you always have to be the one who's fighting?" she blinked. A tear plopped onto my shoe. I embraced her. She was right: all I had ever done was fight.

"Are you saying it's all I'm good at?" I sat and put my face in my hands, sitting forward on the couch. Katy sat beside me and put her arms over me.

"No, I'm not. John you're a good father, husband, and man. But you can't ask me to have you be a good criminal."

"I'm not. I'm asking you to have me be a provider again."

"Like this?"

"Not for long. Just long enough for us to be safe and get out of California."

"Then where?"

"I don't know… Ireland? Texas? Maybe to your family in Italy? All I know is I'm going to get us a nice little farm as far away from this kind of stuff as possible."

"Promise me? And promise me Terry will *not* take part in this… this bank job."

"I promise you both. I'll call Peter and tell him to find another guy. We will get away from this," she laid a hand on my knee.

"I believe you."

"There's one last thing: I've been putting together a

ceremony. Well, at least, I put it in motion. Peter's a surprisingly-good wedding planner. It's small, but we have the cake, the groomsmen, the decorations, the readings... all we need now is the bride." I got down on one knee, removing the ring from my pocket I'd been holding since JJ gave it to me. "So what do you say, Katy? Will you marry me again?"

"John, I need your honesty on this."

"Anything."

"When you look at me, are you seeing me? Or are you seeing the redemption you can find by making it all up to me? Do I, Katy Occhipinti Washicha, still mean something to you?" I stared at her. I knew what I wanted to say, just not how.

"No, you don't mean something. You mean everything," she knelt and gave me a firm hug. "But if you say no, don't worry. Peter says he can get a full refund."

"Save him the trouble. I say yes." My phone rang. I checked the caller ID. Unknown number. I denied the call. This night was for me and mine.

Thirty-Five
Friends.

Peter. December 18th, 2009.

I shivered. The heating unit wasn't turned on—it couldn't be. That was the problem with abandoned buildings.

Still, it was a nice place. The nicest for blocks, though that wasn't saying much. Harvard Heights wasn't the best neighborhood for admiring architecture. One day I would own this building. I could make it into a club, or maybe even a restaurant. Sure, a better place to live would be nice, but business before pleasure.

I tightened the hood on my fleece parka. It helped keep the cold air out of my face, but it wasn't much of an improvement.

The front door opened. The building's layout was a small anteroom at the front, immediately leading up a flight of stairs to the main room, where I now was. There was an adjoining office and bathroom. I wanted to own every square inch.

Several pairs of feet made their way up the stairs after the door closed. I grimaced. We had agreed on coming alone.

Three hooded figures approached. The leader, who I assumed was the one I arranged this meeting with, nodded. I copied him, keeping my own hood up. Faces didn't need to be seen. I cleared my throat.

"You were supposed to come alone."

"So were you," he jerked his head in the direction of Joey's corner. Joey, unseen in the shadows, did not stir.

"I'm not sure I can trust you, let alone others," I told him, ignoring his accusation that I broke our deal as well. He chuckled without mirth.

"Trust is a curious thing, no? But debt goes beyond trust. Beyond money. I always repay my debts." You can never trust mercenaries, but there are few others I can turn to with this. If I wanted this to go down quietly, that is.

"I understand. Well, you know what I want."

"The old men dead, yes. When?"

"New Year's Day. Both will be at a bar, *The Pub*, shortly after midnight." I felt Dillan stare at me with his cold, grey eyes.

"And we are agreed on the price?"

"We are. Once I divvy up the cuts, they will leave together. Take care of them. You can keep their shares. Just be discreet."

"I will."

"Listen to me very carefully: I want the old men dead. No mistakes. Both maintain regular contact with me. Dispose of them and your debt will be repaid. Do well, and perhaps we can work together in the future," he extended his hand. I grasped it. "We will not meet again soon. Not until any repercussions are assuredly dealt with once the deed is done." We shook hands. His was very firm, very rough. Dillan and his silent followers walked down the stairs. I watched their silhouettes depart. Joey appeared beside me. We stood together in silence until they were well gone.

"Now you wanna tell me what that was about?"

"It's like I told you earlier: I'm tired of loose ends."

"That doesn't tell me anything."

"It isn't supposed to."

"Anything else for the night?"

"Nah. Thanks for this."

"Sure thing. If we don't have each other's back, then who does?" he headed down the stairs. I heard the door close as he left. I was alone in the darkness. In the distance was the noise of cat-calls and all-night parties that often fill this part of town.

With a sigh, I walked downstairs. The entire place was bare. If it hadn't always been, it was now on account of the simplicity of the front lock. When I own this, I'll be sure to upgrade that.

I headed out the front door. There was no point in locking it. I headed toward the car I leased: a 2004 Corolla. I wasn't a fan of leasing, but this was out of necessity, and only until the bank job. After that…

I grinned. After that I would be back on top. Not like I used to be, but at least my name would mean something. I got in the car, turning the key in the ignition as I shut the door.

I felt something small and cold press against the back of my neck. I froze.

"Don't move or I'll blow your brains out," the intruder told me from the back seat. My eyes widened. It was the same man that had called Bobby's phone the other day.

"I wouldn't do that if I were you…" I told him slowly.

"Yeah? Why not?"

"This isn't my car. Once it's returned, the owner won't appreciate my brains on the dashboard." The mystery man dug his gun into my neck.

"Start talking."

"What is this, your first interrogation? Generally, you give me a topic, then I make a snarky retort, *then* you tell me to 'start talking,' usually with an 'or else' thrown in there."

"What happened to Bobby Mancuso?" I inhaled sharply, regretting giving Terry the night off.

"You should learn not to ask questions you already know

the answer to." I said slowly. The barrel dug more into my neck.

"And you should learn to answer someone pointing a gun at you. Now drive."

"Anywhere in particular?"

"Just stay away from the Washicha residence and don't try anything equally as stupid." I nodded, lightly pressing my foot to the pedal. Needing a destination in mind, I headed for *The Pub*. Another car immediately exited a nearby gas station parking lot and followed us.

"What do you know about the C308 heavy machine gun, nicknamed the Crucifier?"

"I'm no gun nut."

"Don't you read the news?"

"I'm not a big reader."

"There was a tank found ripped to shreds in a parking garage."

"And Bobby Mancuso heard about it."

"How'd you guess?"

"I'm just connecting the dots. You're working some sort of angle, and you can't narrow it down to what you want to know by switching topics. So you aren't. Bobby and these guns are related."

"You're pretty smart, for not reading."

"And you're pretty dumb for a cop," he hesitated. Bingo.

"Listen carefully: this did not happen. No one broke into your car. No one asked questions about Bobby Mancuso or the C308 Crucifier. In fact, you've never heard of the latter, and you can stop talking about the former. If you keep asking around about him, we'll see to it that the only thing you'll be asking for is mercy. Not just you. We'll take good care of those friends of yours, too. Joseph Gregario, for instance."

"I don't have friends. I'm a loner."

"What about girlfriends? Clare Angelou?"

"She's engaged."

"Hasn't stopped you before."

"Message received."

"Pull over." It just so happened that we were quickly approaching *The Pub*. I parked. "Remember what I told you."

"I thought you wanted me to forget?" I felt a ringing sensation as a pistol butt was slammed into my ear. I didn't hear the car door being opened or shut, but I felt the blast of cool air. I looked around just in time to see the car from earlier, the one that had been following me, speed off. I slowly counted to ten, waiting for my head to stop pounding. It didn't.

I turned off the car and ran into the bar, throwing open the door. I took a look around. Clare seemed taken aback by my abrupt intrusion—it was a public eatery, wasn't it? For once I ignored her as I went to the bar. I removed my cell from my pocket and peered at it.

"Is there a phone I can borrow?" The burly bartender nodded to a stool on the far right. I rushed over and punched in one of the two numbers I knew. It rang twice and switched off. I growled, trying again.

"Hello?"

"John, it's me. Are you alone?" he paused.

"Katy's here."

"Call back this number on her phone." I hung up. A moment later, the phone rang. The bartender glared at me. I ignored him as I picked it up.

"Peter? What happened to your phone?"

"Bugged. Yours is, too."

"I'm listening."

"A fed was in my car, and he started asking me questions about Bobby and the Crucifiers. At gunpoint."

"I don't think feds can do that."

"This one was incognito. A vigilante, maybe. Not acting alone."

"How do you know he was a fed?" I was getting impatient.

"He didn't kill me, so he wasn't with the Black Outfit. He knew about you, Bobby, Joey," I looked around, "even Clare." I hissed. "And he said Joseph, not Joey, so he wasn't from the Family."

"Vasquez?"

"No, I'd know if it was him. I can't be sure, but I think this was the guy that called Bobby's phone so many times. The one I told you about. Whoever this guy is, he isn't happy."

"Pete…"

"Don't say it."

"Look, you know more about this than me, and I hope you're right. But don't you think there is the slightest possibility that Bobby had been a rat?"

"No. No way." I replied without hesitation. "I grew up with the guy. He'd been pinched before and never snitched. He had been part of the Chicago incident, when you had wise guys giving each other up left and right. Bobby didn't."

"Okay. I'll take your word for it. Then why did this fed keep calling Bobby?" I wasn't sure what to say. I thought back to when he called Bobby's cell, but he hadn't said anything too revealing. He had been upset; I would have been too if so many of my calls were ignored.

"I don't know. But I'm going to find out."

Thirty-Six
Friends!

John. December 19th, 2009.

I woke up in Katy's bed to the sound of a shower. I had sensed her get out of bed and head downstairs not too long ago. As I turned over, I saw an electric clock that read 8:35 a.m.

I untangled myself from the mass of sheets, got up, and stretched. Slowly I walked over to the adjoining bathroom door and opened it. I peeked inside. There was too much steam to see much of anything.

"Hello?"

"Yeah dad?"

"'Morning, Terry. Where's your mom?"

"Kitchen. Do you need something in here? Sorry for stealing the shower, but JJ is using the one downstairs."

"It's fine, thanks." I shut the door. I grabbed a shirt from the floor and put it on. If there was one thing never instilled in me from good ol' Uncle Sam, it was cleanliness. I went downstairs. Today would be a break day—no work from Peter was scheduled, no court appearances, and Vince and Dustin had the shop taken care of. Just a day for me and mine.

As I headed downstairs, I heard the unmistakable sound of bacon frying. I bounded into the kitchen as if I had lost fifty years. Immediately I saw Katy and she gave me a good morning hug. I held her tight. We stood there, in the middle of

273

the kitchen, no sound but the sizzling strips on the stove.

"Do you still like Labradors?" I asked.

"Only the trained ones," she murmured.

"I have a semi-trained one over at Dustin's apartment. He could come around sometime."

"He can stay here as long as he wants, so long as you come with him." My heart skipped a beat.

"So you're not mad?" I whispered in her ear.

"How could I be? It's a one-time thing, after all," she gracefully unstripped herself of my body and slid the bacon from a pan onto five plates, each getting two slices, where waited two eggs on each. She took two of the plates and set them on the table. We sat down.

"It won't be long before this is all over." I said before I bit into a strip of bacon.

"I've heard that one before."

"Except professional crooks are in charge of this, not... oh wait, that's right. Professional crooks were in charge of my last job, too," she gave a small laugh, downing it with a sip of coffee.

"You always know how to make me laugh."

"He should have been a clown instead of a soldier," an Irish voice said from the doorway. I turned to see my brother.

"I personally think he's fine as both, Dustin."

"I didn't hear you knock," I told him. He held up the house key with a twinkle in his eye. "You need to get better at hiding things, Baby Brother. Mats are so... predictable."

"I put it there, actually," Katy informed him. "Would you like anything? Eggs? Coffee?"

"I'm fine, lass. Had some fried ham back at the shop. Vince is there now, as always." Still, he came and sat down on the left side of me, with Katy across from him to my right.

"So what's up?" I asked.

"Just stopped by to talk about that… thing," he eyed Katy warily.

"Whatever 'thing' you're referring to, she already knows."

"The wedding, mate."

"What about it?"

"Well, seeing as how I was the best man at the last one all those years ago, I don't think it's fair that I have the honor again," he said earnestly. "Give someone else a chance."

"That's very noble of you, Dustin," Katy commented. I nodded in agreement, though on the inside my gears were turning as I wondered who would take his spot. "Oh, let me tell Jesse James you're here," Katy said as she walked to the living room, "he wanted to show you his Irish impersonation," she left.

Without warning, the front door burst open. There was a trample of feet. Dustin stood, grabbing the pistol at his side. My hands automatically reached for my own, which I realized wasn't on me. I got up, knocking over my chair in the process as I went to the counter and picked up a steak knife. Whoever these intruders are, they aren't taking me down without a fight.

"Once we secure the Captain, he can take the second floor!" One of the intruders shouted to the rest. "Secure the vantage point. I want to set up a command center stationed in the kitchen, with the window blacked out. Let's see the set up." At that point, two men entered the kitchen, one about 6'4 and muscular, the other 5'10 and thin but still well-built with veins encircling his wiry biceps. They froze when they saw us. The knife dropped from my hand. I could hear Dustin murmuring to Mother Mary. Terry suddenly appeared behind the two men, nothing on him except a towel around the waist. His

Desert Eagle was drawn. Katy screamed from the other room. JJ came out the living room barking and wearing nothing but a sling—not even a towel—with a pistol. The intruders already had out weapons of their own. The wiry one whipped around. He and Terry faced each other as JJ nakedly faced the smaller one, daring the other to shoot first. Dustin didn't move.

"Identify yourselves!" The big one ordered with a thick Southern accent, his gun trained on Jesse James.

"You first!" Terry yelled back.

"Common Law private property clauses dictate the justification of defending one's life, home, or auto from trespassers with intent to harm or commit a felony on said property," JJ growled. Dustin looked at me, unsure what to say to that.

"John?" I shrugged. The larger of the two men kept his eyes on JJ, but spoke to me.

"Captain, what will you have us do?"

"Stand down," I told him. "All of you stand down." All four did so, Terry albeit reluctantly. I stared at the newcomers as they holstered their weapons.

"We've all come a long way since Afghanistan, haven't we?" Castle said.

"Yet you still look like the same old hillbilly," I replied. I moved forward and we embraced. Dustin was beside me as he did the same to Walker. We exchanged hugs all around. When all of us pulled ourselves apart (and together), I looked over to Terry. He still stood in the doorway, his pistol not quite holstered.

"Not to take away from the emotional moment here, Dad," Terry said, "but I think this question is somewhat pressing: who the Hell are these guys?" Castle in particular seemed taken aback by the question.

"You mean to tell me these boys here don't remember their uncles Castle and Walker?" Terry blinked in surprise. He went running towards them, his arms wide, wrapping them around the man that moments ago he had been pointing a gun at. JJ was doing the same with Walker, who looked slightly uncomfortable with JJ's nudity.

"Speaking of pressing questions," I asked, "how'd you boys find us?"

"Stories like that are best told over a drink," Walker answered, finally speaking up.

"It's hardly nine," I said. Castle stared blankly. He looked to Walker, who shrugged.

"*The Pub*?" Dustin asked me.

"Lead the way. Actually," I glanced over at JJ, "go ahead. We'll catch up," he barked in agreement.

They left, laughing over how bad things could have turned out. The door shut behind them. I sighed, in awe at the turn of events. I went upstairs to our room while the boys went to their own.I walked in to find myself at the wrong end of a shotgun. "You really should stop greeting me with that thing." Katy lowered it.

"Is everything okay?" she asked as she sat on the bed. She set the gun down beside her. I reached into a drawer and began putting on a pair of jeans.

"Better than okay. Those guys who barged in? Brett Castle and Justin Walker," she gaped, her eyes wide.

"They're alive?"

"Yeah. Who would've guessed? Aside from seeing more of JJ than anyone would've wished, they seem to be doing well."

"But how did they…?"

"We are heading to *The Pub* to find out. You're welcome to

277

come," she gently shook her head.

"This is your moment. Are you going to ask them to be in our...?"

"Yes, honey. Groomsmen, both." I kissed her forehead.

"And Terry as best man?" I shook my head.

"Peter," she gave me a look of disgust.

"HIM?! That thug who got you thrown in jail and might end up getting you killed?!"

"Let me explain."

"This better be good."

"If I choose Terry or JJ, the other will be hurt. Same for Castle and Walker. But with Peter..."

"No one feels left out," she concluded.

"Exactly." I brushed my lips against her cheek.

"John, I love this side of you," she said, rising and putting away the shotgun, then coming over and putting her hands on my cheeks. "The sensitive thinker." I finished buttoning up my jeans as she kissed me.

"Thank you, Sweetheart." I put on socks and boots. We hugged and kissed one last time before I left, hurrying down the stairs, grabbing my keys off an end table by the door, and shutting the door closed behind me.

Terry and JJ had already left. I hopped on my bike and took off, taking out my phone and punching in a few numbers in the process. It went straight to voicemail. "Hey Peter, it's John. Meet me at *The Pub*. I have an announcement to make and you're going to need to be there."

I was there two minutes quicker than usual. Peter, who lived closer, was just pulling up in that leased Corolla of his. Castle and the others were in a semicircle around the front door. I made my way over.

"Don't look now," Castle told me as I approached, "but

there's a suit following you. Armed." I turned and saw Peter.

"Is he a threat?" Walker asked, fingering his weapon.

"Negative," my brother replied. "He'd only draw blood if he cut himself."

"So what's he to us?" Castle asked.

"A C.O.," I told him. Castle craned his neck to get a better look.

"Him? A Commanding Officer? Over us?" Castle asked, incredulous, motioning to the six of us.

"Over me, at least." I responded.

"He's mobbed up," Terry chimed in, "my boss."

"You mean to tell me that you're involved with some guineas?" Castle asked.

"You have no idea," I mumbled as Peter joined the group. Castle eyed him openly. Peter gazed coolly.

"Hey John. Who are your friends?" No one responded. I cleared my throat.

"Let's head inside, shall we?" I opened the door and went through first. Terry and JJ were right on my heels, hesitantly followed by Peter, then the rest. We had to get a table instead of the booth, Peter and Castle on either side of me. We sat in uncomfortable silence for a bit, until Peter decided to break it.

"How's Katy?"

"Wait," Castle said, "Katy is alive?"

"You were in the same house as her not twenty minutes ago. When you two came in like bats out of Hell, she grabbed a shotgun."

"Well send her my regards." I nodded. I'd be sure to do so. "Jackie passed away a few years back. The kids move out. Walker's wife and daughter came here with him." Castle cleared his throat. "Hey Chief, you never did tell us this guinea's name," he jerked his thumb at Peter. Peter grunted at

279

the slur.

"John, who is this hillbilly trash?" Castle stared, unoffended.

"This is the loud, brash, and politically-incorrect ex-Staff Sergeant Brett Castle, my heavy gunner from the Green Beret days. Castle, this is Peter Richardson. I don't think any introduction is needed for him." Any animosity on Castle's end disappeared.

"Nice to meet you, Richardson. This boy to my left is the ever-so-magnificent Staff Sergeant Justin Walker, former spotter for the now-retired mick you have there," he nodded to Dustin. Peter seemed less offended after the "mick" comment, realizing Castle didn't single out Italians.

"What's your heritage, Brett?" Peter asked.

"Call me Castle. To answer your question: I'm one hundred percent bona fide hillbilly, as you called it," he said.

"Castle was born and raised in North Louisiana, Peter," I explained. "Now that we're on to your biography, Castle: what happened after we all went our separate ways?" A waitress I didn't recognize walked up.

"Seven shots of whiskey please, Ma'am," Castle said, "and a spare Styrofoam cup, if you have one lying around," she left before Peter could change his order to wine. Or maybe to a drink more befitting the time of day.

"Still chewing tobacco?" I asked.

"You know it. So anyhow, after all that mess went down in Afghanistan, Walker and I made our way to Chicago. Those mercenaries had a station over there, way we figured was we go work for them for a bit and get us a bigger job or something. It didn't quite work out like that. Seems they felt I owed them more than we had originally agreed, and for some time I was still in near-indentured servitude. Chicago was going through that extra-violent phase and we were hired by the state to maintain order, but made a little less than the average police officer. So Walker and I got out and opened a farm on the Louisiana-Arkansas border."

"Farming what, exactly?" Peter asked.

"Goats."

"Goats?" he barely held back a laugh.

"Laugh all you want: we made some good money. It was a good life. Simple. Then we heard through the military grapevine that someone was asking after our old captain here. We made sure it was really you, and we hightailed it over here."

"But that doesn't answer how you found out where I lived."

"Washicha isn't a common name. We used Yellow Pages."

"I tried that when I was looking for my family. It didn't turn up anything."

"Actually, Dad," Terry said, "I remember Mom not adding us until some years after we moved. You must have checked too soon."

"Anyway, we didn't know who was trying to find you, so we hurried over. I was fearing the worst, which is why we barged in like that." Peter's eyes were keen. I knew what he was thinking: who would be asking about me? The waitress showed up with our drinks.

"*De Oppresso Liber.*" Castle toasted.

"*De Oppresso Liber,*" we echoed and took our shots. Peter made a sound low in his throat. Castle looked at me.

"So Captain: what did you want to tell us?"

"Katy and I have decided to remarry." There was mild applause and cheers.

"I didn't know you were divorced," Castle said.

"We aren't. It's... complicated." Castle nodded. "The

wedding is on Christmas Day. I want you all as my groomsmen, except Peter." Peter glared at me. "He'll be my best man." That glare turned into shock.

"Whoa, wait," Castle interjected. "Him?" Castle spat in his cup.

"Guys, Dustin declined the position. You can't ask a man to pick between his two sons. I didn't even know two of the men at this table were alive when I woke up this morning, and I couldn't possibly be asked to choose between them."

"That is... a good point," Castle admitted, laughing heartily. "Another shot!" Castle demanded. We all cheered.

"I guess this counts as your bachelor party," Dustin added.

"As good as any." The waitress poured us all another round. Castle stood.

"Congratulations, Captain," he reached into the breast pocket of his unbuttoned flannel shirt. "Your wedding gift," he handed me a framed photograph. I held it with both hands, afraid it might disappear or evaporate.

The five of us: Castle, Dustin, Walker, Carl, and me, arms around one another with our bikes in the background. I remembered the day well. We were in New Orleans on leave during Mardi Gras. Behind the picture I felt something cold. I put the frame down on the table ever so carefully and in my hands were dog tags.

"Lowry, Carl D.," I read.

"Thought you might like to have them. I know you gave them to me and all, but he was closer to you." I was speechless. I mouthed a thank you.

"We miss him too," Walker spoke through the mournful silence.

"To Carl!" Castle toasted.

"To Carl."

Thirty-Seven
Let the Good Times Roll

Peter. December 21st, 2009.

Sitting across from me was one of the loveliest women I've ever known. What we shared was, if not love, close to it. And it was still growing, even though I had willed myself to see her less. Whether I saw her physically didn't matter; I saw her whenever I closed my eyes, if I wasn't careful. She had one of those appearances that grows on you. The kind that starts out as gorgeous and only gets better the more you think of her. The hair as bright as flames. The gleaming almonds for eyes. The untarnished soul.

"Look," she said to me, her eyes glimmering in the low light of *The Pub*, "you're a nice guy-" I gave a low chuckle. I met those almonds with my brown.

"Didn't we agree to be honest with each other?"

"Okay, you're a pathetic, egotistical jerk who has serious issues with showing how he feels. Better?" I gave a slight grin.

"Much," her words sank in. "Is that what it was? That I couldn't show how I felt? Because that can change," she began to extend her hand toward mine. She realized what she was doing and retracted it. I watched the diamond ring on it as if it were a snake prepared to strike. She followed my gaze.

"This shows it's a little late for change, doesn't it? But no, Peter, it wasn't just that. Zane... I've known him for so long. He's a great guy. Steady. You... you aren't steady."

"Not steady," I repeated, my mind whirring. How real was this, what I felt? Worse, imagination or not, how much power did it have over me?

"You're six years older than me. That's a big difference. Wouldn't you agree?"

"I think that if you were eighty-four and I was ninety it wouldn't be a big difference," she sadly shook her head.

"Men like you don't get to live that long," she got up and left. I sat there like a fool, wondering when or how my life took this turn.

Dustin sat down across from me. "Still taking it hard?" he cocked his head to the side. I shrugged.

"I haven't resorted to stalking her Facebook."

"Something you wanted to talk to me about? Something you couldn't say over the phone?"

"The fact that I couldn't say it is exactly why I need to talk to you: I have the understanding that you're good with technology."

"Thirty or so years ago I was an expert. A sniper can mean recon and the like."

"'And the like' meaning espionage."

"Call it what you will. Why?" I pulled out my cellphone. I quickly removed the back and slid it across the table to him. He examined it.

"It's bugged." I remained silent. "Fairly modern stuff, too. And it was added after the phone was made. See how it was added, not assembled? Recently, too. The rest of this has a coat of dust over it. "

"I'd say two weeks."

"You'd say about right. And it looks like it has GPS programming." I nodded. "I'm guessing you didn't put this on?"

284

"I have a good feeling about who did, and I also feel that John's is bugged, too." Dustin gave me a cool look.

"I don't like this. Any of this. I don't like what we're suddenly mixed up in."

"You've been mixed up in it for twenty years. This is your first breakthrough. I thought you'd be excited."

"I don't see Pomerov's empire going down in my lifetime. It's just... John lost it all. I don't want that to happen to him again. And now with Castle and Walker... I'm as excited they're back as anyone," he cleared his throat. "So you want me to remove the bug?"

"No. I want to use this to my advantage. So that the other end can only hear what I want them to hear."

"I can probably do that, but the GPS would stay. They'll still know where you are."

"I'm counting on it."

"And what about John?"

"He knows about it. He'll be careful about what he says. We can't remove his and not remove mine; that's too suspicious. I just want to feed them misinformation until the trial is over." Dustin's eyes widened.

"This comes from cops?"

"Not just any cops. FBI with discreet approval from our beloved District Attorney." Dustin nodded.

"Do you need to make any calls today?"

"Not that I know of," he took my phone.

"Good. I'll drop it off at your apartment tonight," he got up and left. Once again I was alone. Jimmy materialized out of thin air. Or that was how it seemed. Him, Eddie, Joey, and John—who stuck out like a hillbilly in a group of Sicilians— had been in another booth across the room, waiting for me to finish my business.

"Ready?" Jimmy asked. I nodded and stood. There were no drinks to pay for. He motioned for the others. They all made for the exit. We followed them out. Once outside, we stood around my car.

"Okay, Peter," John said, "what's this about? You said we're holding up a store?"

"I lied. I figured I might as well give you a bachelor party of my own," he shook his head.

"You really don't have to do this."

"I know. Now get in the car." I unlocked it and got in. John got in the passenger's seat while the other three climbed in the back. I started it up and got out on the street.

"Can you at least tell me where we're going?"

"*Valentina's.* Owned by Mickey Carbone. The one where Don Beppo and Johnny Black had that sit-down. Besides being popular, we know it's not bugged."

"Why would it be?"

"It comes with the popularity." I grinned to myself. Mickey had all of his establishments checked for listening devices twice a day. There was also an unwritten rule about no cops, and one about ladies and Made Men drinking free. It was that type of place. Mickey was that type of guy.

"Why the name if it's run by a Mickey?"

"Valentina was his mom. Once she passed, he opened up bars in different cities with each of her names. She's Italian, so you can guess there's a few. I know there's one in New Orleans, and another in Vegas."

"Don't forget New York and Miami," Jimmy chimed in.

"Right, right. So if you ever go to any of those cities, John, you should check it out. If they give you any trouble, just say who you are and who you know. That would be me."

"Yeah, got it. You're real important," he scoffed. I grimaced.

"Yeah, well..." I cleared my throat. "Matt wanted to come. He just didn't want it getting around that someone of his rank had been hanging around such unsavory characters."

"Admiral Sanders was in on this?"

"He's in on everything." I turned into the parking lot of *Valentina's*. Dusk was approaching, making the neon sign with the club's name really stand out. Already a line had formed; regular civilians waiting at a chance to carouse with Los Angeles's classiest underworld figures.

I parked and we got out. John started walking toward the end of the rapidly-growing line. I grabbed his arm. He looked at me. I shook my head and pointed to the entrance. The others were already heading that way.

We each nodded to the bouncer as we passed. There were a few scattered gawks from onlookers who had been waiting for an exorbitant amount of time. John looked slightly guilty about the whole thing. There was no reason to; this place was meant for us, not them.

Inside was one of Mickey's classier joints. In the center of the room was a square bar with two bartenders at opposite corners. Behind them was a crystalline glass shelf advertising all sorts of liqueur. A pianist played on a stage against the wall at the other end of the room. He showed all the signs indicating he worked for many mob bars: penciled mustache, dark clothing, mainly kept to his work except to sneer at the civilian customers. I hadn't been here for some time, but I recalled the stage being frequented by acts ranging from comedians to magicians to singers.

I watched John take it all in. The bar, the pianist, the chandelier, the patrons. I leaned toward Joey's ear and asked that he take John up for a glass of Scotch. The bartenders would turn up their nose at the slightest suggestion of peasant whiskey. Meanwhile Eddie, Jimmy, and I went to a set of booths as far away from the pianist as possible, which were set up specifically for clientele such as us. Not only were curtains provided for privacy, but the walls extending to the ceiling were utterly soundproof. Bouncers periodically watched them to make sure neither eavesdroppers nor the wrong type of crowd got too close. Were they bugged by the establishment? Unlikely. Mickey was a businessman, and his actual work was centered in New Orleans.

We entered the booth. Jimmy shut the red curtain. We sat down around a marble table. I sighed.

"There are more vagabonds than usual," Eddie commented.

"It's why Made Men drink free: to attract the vagabonds," I told him. I shut my eyes tight, reopening them after a few seconds passed. "I want John to have a good time tonight. Don't be stupid and don't make this about yourselves. Just chat him up and make him feel at home. He's a valuable asset."

"Yeah, yeah, you got it," Jimmy replied. We sat in silence a few moments.

"I'm still looking for two experienced guys for the heist. Jimmy, how are the Rothstein brothers doing?"

"They had a falling out after a job gone wrong. One lives in Vegas. The other is probably dead. You know you could always ask for-"

"Rocky Grotto is *not* working this job," I cut in.

"Come on. Rocky is one of the best thieves out there. He could do two guys' work."

"You know why we can't have him aboard. Not so long as I'm part of this." I motioned at myself for emphasis.

"You two should really patch that up. Well could you get in touch with *The Panther*?"

"Anthony wouldn't fly all the way over here to work with nine others for a few million."

"Even for an old friend?"

"We were business associates. Nothing more. How about Nini?"

"Dead."

"Frederick?"

"Retired."

"Tony's cousin? What's his name...?" I snapped my fingers to trigger my memory. Nothing came to mind.

"Serving a life sentence. Whoever we get on such short notice will need to be new to the game."

"We already have so many of those. Dustin is hardly an amateur , but at espionage, but John? He's a cowboy, not a thief. Add two more like him..." It hit me. "I'll take care of it."

"Speaking of taking care of it," Jimmy said, "I did some more digging into those numbers. That fourth number? A cop in the LAPD."

"Not a fed?" My brow furrowed in consternation. Local cops didn't usually have this level of secrecy; I had been sure we were dealing with the FBI. "Who's the badge?"

"I don't know. But that's not all: I got a friend of mine to put hits on all the numbers so that I'd know when they gave or received calls, with a timestamp. Murray had a few hits from his cell. The numbers... well, they were the same as Bobby's. He had been in contact with Bobby, Chad Black, and the mystery cop." I stared at the table. These four men were connected somehow. Well, not entirely.

"How about Chad Black and the cop?" Jimmy shook his head.

"They haven't talked. At least, not over the phone."

"Do you think the cop is on the take?"

"If he is, he doesn't show it. The burner cell is gone as of yesterday, but he hadn't called any other mobsters. He could be using a different phone, but-"

"But he would probably have all his underworld contacts on the same one. Could he be an informant?"

"Not for the Family. Besides, Murray's a loan shark. What would he need information for?"

"Well if it's not that, then what?"

"I don't know. I looked into the numbers the cop called. One of those numbers belongs to Special Agent William Vasquez." John and Joey entered the booth. I blinked. Both had drinks in each hand. One was handed to each of us, except Eddie. I didn't want his little problem to be a problem for us. Should I have brought him to a bar? Probably not.

By itself, the cop being in contact with Vasquez wasn't abnormal. They were both in law enforcement. There are any number of reasons why they'd be in touch. But when you consider that he called Vasquez off a burner cell, and with everything else in the mix, though... I looked over to John. He nodded to me.

"*Laissez les bons temps rouler,*" I declared, my drink held high. John smiled.

"Let the good times roll."

Thirty-Eight
Merry Christmas

John. December 25th, 2009.

"Last batch," Katy called as she entered the living room with a tray of cookies. She set them on the coffee table and took back her place beside me on the couch. JJ, out of his sling, hopped up from the floor and began devouring the still-steaming cookies. Castle, in a tuxedo similar to my own and likely worn just as often, shook his head with a smile.

"I'm glad to have such a special godson," he remarked before he took a swig of eggnog. I looked from Katy to Violet to Walker, seated in a plush chair across from him.

"You were meant to be Violet's," I told Walker. He shrugged.

"I always thought of myself as more of an uncle, anyway," Walker said. Terry grinned from his spot on the floor next to JJ, where he sat petting Scout.

"Good ol' uncles Walker and Dustin," Terry said. Dustin nodded approvingly from his spot against the wall. The doorbell rang. JJ took off in a frenzy, barking up a storm. Shortly afterward, he returned on two legs with a tux-wearing Peter, who carried a sack in one hand and a clipboard in the other.

"Sorry I'm late," he said, "but I come bearing gifts," he put the clipboard in the sack and began rummaging through it. He held up a crudely-wrapped present. "For a Mr. Jesse James." JJ pointed at himself questioningly. Peter nodded and tossed him the box. JJ caught it in midair and proceeded to carefully remove the ribbon with surgical precision. Once the ribbon was carefully folded and placed behind him, he ripped open the box and pulled out a bone. He examined it inches from his eyes, set it down, and saluted Peter with his good arm.

"According to Sir Isaac Newton in the *Principia Mathematica Philosophiae Naturalis*, 1686, for every action, there is an equal and opposite reaction. I appreciate your efforts greatly, Sir." Peter gave me a quizzical glance.

"He gave me his favorite bone last week," I explained. Peter nodded, pulling out various gifts and handing them to their intended recipients.

"No Damion?" Peter asked, gift in hand. I shook my head.

"Shame. I was hoping to mend old wounds."

"Moonshine? How'd you know?" Castle asked of his opened present.

"Lucky guess. One hundred ninety proof," Peter confirmed. Castle nodded approvingly.

"Not bad." Peter pulled another bone out of his sack and placed it near Scout's paws. Scout instantly began devouring it, similar to JJ next to him. Peter removed his clipboard from the empty sack.

"A spa day?" Violet exclaimed. "For me and Mom?" I finished opening my gift.

"No," I said, glaring at Peter, "for you and me."

"Deep tissue, mud bath, and matching mani-pedis," Peter said with a smirk. He removed a small can from his pocket and handed it to me. I grinned. War paint.

"This almost makes up for it," I said with a smile.

"Really?" Peter asked, incredulous.

"Not even close."

"Thank you, Peter," Katy said as she held up a book, "but what is it?"

"It's a catalogue for types of kitchen remodeling. Pick which one you want, and I'll have it done."

"I… I like my kitchen," she replied. Peter's eyes widened.

"Oh. Well, it also contains livings rooms-"

"I like that, too," she pursed her lips.

"Wow!" Terry exclaimed, "A book? Thank you so much, Peter." Peter examined his clipboard.

"We're four minutes late. We'll let you two get ready," he said to Katy and Violet. "*The Pub*?" Peter asked me. I nodded. We set down our gifts and got up as the girls headed upstairs. Outside on the street was Peter's leased car behind six motorbikes. Violet's bug took up the driveway. We walked to our respective vehicles.

"How did you know I like CCR?" Walker asked Peter.

"Same as Castle's moonshine: lucky guess." Peter paused as he opened the door to his car. He walked up to us as we got on our bikes. "How's life on the farm?" he asked Castle.

"Not bad. Could be better."

"Is there a booming goat industry in Arkansas?"

"If you're asking whether I pay taxes, the answer is none of your—or Uncle Sam's—business." Peter chuckled.

"John and I have a business venture coming up, if you're interested."

"I'll need more than that," Castle said.

"Robbing a *Cartel*-owned bank of its laundered money." Castle looked to Walker, who gave a slight nod.

"Count us in," Castle confirmed. I glanced at Terry and JJ to ensure they didn't overhear. JJ was happily gnawing on his bone. Terry was pointedly fiddling with his helmet strap. Both were still hurt that they wouldn't be participating, but understood their mother and I's concerns.

Peter nodded and got in his car, throwing his clipboard on the passenger's seat in the process. He took off. The six of us followed on our bikes. I scratched the back of my neck. I kept reminding myself that there was no reason to be nervous. I'd done this before. But that didn't take away the sweat forming on my forehead or the butterflies in my stomach.

We soon arrived at *The Pub* and began making our way to the entrance. The parking lot was practically empty; aside from it being noon, Don Beppo had rented the place out for the after-party.

"You guys go ahead," I said to my family and squad mates as I looked at Peter exiting his car with his clipboard. We met each other halfway. "That was awfully nice of you, giving those gifts."

"Your family is mine," he said as he flashed as smile.

"And Castle and Walker?"

"Might as well be your family, too."

"So you didn't give them gifts as a signing bonus for the heist?"

"John, they would have said yes, regardless."

"That doesn't answer the question." I crossed my arms.

"You're right," he said with a grin as he walked toward the bar, "it doesn't." I sighed and followed him. He stopped in front of the door and looked at the sign next to it. "How much do you think a place like this goes for?"

"What?"

"You know. If I wanted to buy it."

"No telling. It does a good business."

"I'm going to buy it," he exclaimed. "Assuming the heist is a success, of course."

"I have absolute faith in your genius planning abilities," I said, patting him on the back.

"Sarcasm is unbecoming of you," he told me as he opened the door. We headed inside.

"You're forgetting how little I care what's unbecoming of me. Besides: it isn't sarcasm." His eyes narrowed at my thinly-veiled compliment. The others had combined two center tables. We walked toward it. The employees, notably not Clare, were busy setting up decorations.

"Really? No sarcasm?"

"Well... maybe a little," he chuckled.

"That's the spirit." We sat next to one another, with Castle on my left and Terry on Peter's right. In front of each of us was an empty shot glass.

"Now," Castle began, "seeing as how we did this on the Captain's first wedding day, I figure it's a tradition worth following," he removed a giant flask from his tux jacket and filled each glass, handing the flask to Terry to pour for those on the other end. "Dustin, do you remember the toast you gave last time?" Dustin nodded and raised his glass. Each of us followed suit, Peter albeit hesitantly.

"*Do do shláinte agus grá do do bhean chéile.* To your health and love for your wife." We all took our shot. Those that were new to it—Terry, JJ, and Peter—made faces of varying disgust.

"What is this stuff?!" Peter croaked. Castle took a gulp from the flask.

"Moonshine!" he belched. "Made it myself." If Peter heard him, he didn't show it. He was busy checking the decorations against whatever his clipboard said they should be. His head shot up and back down as he read off the list.

"Pete, you know I'm the one getting married, right?" he spared me a nasty look before going back to his clipboard.

"Though I'm not sure what the bride sees in the groom," he

checked the clock on the wall. "We should go," just as he stood, a bell chimed. I looked to the front and arched an eyebrow.

"Ah, Mr. Washicha, good to see you so well-dressed," Fuentes said as he and Vasquez strode our way. Their heads methodically swiveled as they had a look around. My old squad, sensing the disturbance, scraped back their chairs as they stood.

"'There a problem here, John?" Castle asked.

"Well, if it isn't Staff Sergeant Brett Castle," Vasquez said." Former Special Forces, heavy gunner, thirty confirmed kills, and co-owner of a southern Arkansas goat farm."

"Who's this dictionary?" Walker asked.

"And look who we have here," Fuentes said, "Staff Sergeant Justin Walker. Former Special Forces, spotter for sniper Dustin Washicha, thirty-five confirmed kills, and co-owner of said goat farm with the aforementioned Brett Castle. And then we have Dustin MacManus Washicha, AKA The Irish Curse AKA Mike MacManus AKA Dmitri Gorbachev AKA Fred. Former Special Forces, sniper, sixty-three confirmed kills, refused promotion twice, and declared legally dead. On three separate occasions."

"This, lads," Dustin said as he poured himself another shot, "is the one—and thankfully only—Special Agent William Vasquez, one of the FBI's head field agents on *La Cosa Nostra*: forty years of service, refused nine times to be promoted to behind a desk. His most notable achievements include stabilizing Chicago after the 1984 incident and personally putting away twenty-eight Italian and Sicilian gangs," he took the shot. "You aren't the only one who does his homework, Mate." If either of them were fazed, they didn't show it. Peter smiled.

"Fuentes, Vasquez, good to see you know all about our friends here. I hope you pen their biographies well."

"All the biographies will end the same. That goes for you too, Richardson." Vasquez said, "Oh, and I was so sorry to hear about your little shake down in that parking lot the other night. I heard you got a little roughed up." Peter's mouth tightened. We watched Tweedle Dee and Tweedle Dum leave.

"MacManus?" Peter asked Dustin.

"Ma's maiden name," he answered.

"Someone needs to put a bullet in those two," Castle muttered. Then, louder, "Don't y'all have a guy who does that?" Peter sighed.

"Bad publicity," he replied. "The last thing we need right now is another crackdown."

"What in the Hell was that?" Castle asked. "I don't want feds looking at my record."

"Fed and district attorney," Peter corrected. "They want us to know that they're keeping tabs on all of us. That none of us are safe."

"Why?" Walker asked.

"John here is currently fighting for his freedom in court," Peter said, patting me on the back.

"What for?" Castle asked.

"Whatever they can pin on me," I said.

"So he's sending a message to scare you, saying he'll prove you're guilty." Castle surmised.

"Right on the head," Peter answered.

"Makes me want to kill him more," Castle added. Peter glanced at the clock. "We have to go," he said, already heading for the door. We were right behind him. "We're gonna be late." We piled through the door and half-ran to our respective vehicles. Peter's car raced to the street with six bikes behind him. Thankfully, Peter had chosen a cathedral near *The Pub*. We parked out front and ran up to a side door. Just as Peter and I were prepared to enter as the rest had, I saw a figure approaching from outside. The two of us didn't go in. Instead, I shut the door.

"I thought you weren't coming?" I asked Damion.

"I found time. This is for my mother, after all," he looked at Peter as if noticing a cockroach had just crawled over his shoe. "Are you also a licensed wedding planner?"

"I have the paperwork to prove it."

"That's not what I asked."

"No, it isn't. But a license is also not required."

"The business filings are."

"I'm doing this out of the kindness of my heart. Now," Peter flipped through the papers on his clipboard, "we are at capacity with groomsmen, though we could use an extra body manning the door..."

"I told Mom I'd come. I didn't say I would stay."

"Pete, give me a minute with my boy, would you?" he went inside, muttering something about the wrong floral arrangement.

"Your boy?"

"That's right."

"I'm a boy?"

"As far as I'm concerned: yes. Until you prove me wrong."

"I showed up, didn't I?" he crossed his arms.

"Showing up is great, but that's only half the job." I heard the door open behind me.

"Listen, Mom said-" I felt a hand about to touch my shoulder. I grabbed it by its wrist and turned around to see to who the hand was connected to.

"Oh, sorry Father." I said, letting go. He wiped off

nonexistent dust. Peter stood next to him.

"The bride seems to be missing whoever is supposed to walk out with her." I looked over to Peter, who flipped through some papers. He shrugged sheepishly.

"I will be, Father." I turned toward the voice. Damion.

"Join Mrs. Washicha in the front. Then we may begin." The priest left.

"Thanks, Damion," I told him.

"Like I said: it's for Mom." We watched him go. Once he rounded the corner, we headed inside. The others were anxiously crowded together in a back room.

"Gentlemen," I announced, "let's go get me married." They hurried out to the front as I joined the priest at the entranceway to the altar. We walked out and as an organ began playing. The crowd—many more than the 10-20 Peter had promised and made up almost exclusively of wise guys and their families—collectively rose. The groomsmen walked out one at a time with a bridesmaid around their arm, with Peter in a corner constantly checking his clipboard. As soon as Dustin, the final groomsman, took his spot at the foot of the altar, Peter set down his notes and walked down the aisle by himself, shaking hands with nearly every other person on the aisle ends. He was followed by Violet, our maid of honor. Then came the flower girl. who was one of the cutest kids I'd ever seen, with rosy cheeks and bouncy red hair like Little Orphan Annie. Peter had told me she cost five hundred bucks. She was six.

The doors to the cathedral opened wide. In came Damion, escorting Katy in a flowing white dress. With each step they took toward us, my heart pounded louder in my chest against the rhythm of the organ. After an eternity, they reached the altar. Damion lifted the vail, kissed her cheek, and shook my hand. We made eye contact. He took his seat.

"Will the best man present the rings?" I turned around and mouthed to Peter, "The rings?"

"What rings?" he mouthed back. I scowled. He chuckled, walking up and holding out his palm, which contained a wedding band and ring.

"Do you, Katy Occhipinti Washicha, take John David Washicha as your lawfully-wedded husband?"

"I do," she whispered. I felt my heart skip a beat.

"And do you, John David Washicha, take Katy Occhipinti Washicha as your lawfully-wedded wife?"

"I do." I said. My words boomed throughout the small cathedral. She held my hands in hers. I gazed into those gleaming emerald eyes as she spoke.

"John. We have been through everything between Heaven and Hell. I hope that wherever we are from now on between those two worlds, we are there together. I love you too much to lose you," she placed my wedding band back on my finger. I had felt naked without it.

"Katy. When I first met you I was a young, stupid hood with a motorcycle. Now I'm an old, stupid hood with a motorcycle." The crowd chuckled. "Everything I do, I do for you. Because I love you. Because no home is the home that you are: mine." I removed her old wedding ring and placed the new one in its stead.

"I now pronounce you man and wife. You may kiss the bride." I held her tight and did as instructed—it didn't take much prompting.

We walked out, past a sea of smiling faces. Men and women who barely knew us, who recognized true love when they saw it.

My bike, with tin cans in tow, was front and center. I got on and helped Katy hitch up her gown. She held my waist as we zoomed off to *The Pub*.

We were the first to arrive. I helped her down and we walked in, man and wife. In the short time since we'd been away, the watering hole had undergone major changes, the most notable being a baby grand piano near the bar. The pianist—the same one from *Valentina's*—was warming up. We quickly found our places—we were in the center of the room with placards reading "Mr. Washicha" and "Mrs. Washicha." Peter must not have realized that there were four Mr. Washichas present and that Katy was "Mrs. Washicha" before today. Still, he tried.

Peter entered. I got up to greet him.

"Can I plan a wedding, or what?"

"Stick to your day job," I said with a smile.

"Hey, I have the license, don't I?"

"Yeah, and I'm sure you're quite the masseuse, too," he dug in his jacket pocket and pulled out an envelope.

"Go ahead," he said. I opened it. My eyes widened. Inside were four checks.

"I didn't think you had a bank account."

"Read one," he replied, a smile playing around his lips.

"Pay to the order of six hundred dollars... Terrance Washicha... issued by Executive Entertainment International?"

"It's for a no-show job," he said, as if that explained it all.

"No-show job?" Katy asked as she put her arm around me and peered at the check, voicing my own wonder.

"John, Terry, JJ, and Dustin all work at a Beppo Family talent agency, as far as the government is concerned. It's an easy way to explain things to your bank or a real estate company or car salesman or whatever, because when jobless

301

people have lots of money, feds get suspicious. You get an alibi, plus a few hundred bucks a week for a job you don't do." I nodded and thanked him. Something about that seemed morally ambiguous, like I was stealing, but I was in no position to complain.

"How'd you get the piano in here?" I asked.

"It had to be taken apart and reconstructed. I guess that was a signing bonus, too, huh?" he winked and headed over to the pianist. Just as I prepared to sit down, I received a slap on the back. I turned.

"Admiral Sanders!" I exclaimed. He chuckled and held out his hand. I shook it vigorously, nearly knocking off his bleach-white cap.

"It was a lovely ceremony, Captain. I believe you pick up your gift tonight?" I looked around.

"The guns?" I asked. He nervously looked over his shoulder.

"Well of course," he said, his voice much lower.

"Actually, I think Peter wanted to talk to you about-"

"Hello everyone," Peter's voice boomed over loudspeakers, "and welcome to the Washicha... Washicha wedding. It is time for the happy couple to grace the dance floor with their presence," he beckoned to me and Katy. I nodded. We stood and walked to the cleared space by the bar. I held her close as the pianist began playing the instantly-recognizable *Tuesday's Gone*.

"What happened to *The Boxer*?" I whispered.

"This is what I listened to when you went missing. It always made me feel like you were there watching over me."

"I was and always will be. I'm not letting go."

"Please don't," she said as she held me tighter. "Besides, you don't like Simon and Garfunkel."

"It was a good song," I murmured as our lips touched. We danced there feeling as one with each other more than we ever had. I stared off at the wall.

"What's wrong?" she asked, concerned.

"Carl would have wanted to be here."

"Of course he would have. But you still have Castle. And Walker. Enjoy who *is* here." I nodded absently. I recalled *Tuesday's Gone* being rather long but unfortunately, like all good things, it came to an end. The small dance floor quickly filled. Out of the corner of my eye I saw Eddie begin to dance with Violet. Katy followed my gaze.

"I see him, too."

"That's one of Peter's friends."

"So are you. I'm dancing with you, aren't I? Let Violet have this moment. He's been giving her the puppy dog eyes since we got here."

"Fine. I'll trust you on this." Once the next song ended we sat. Peter stood and spoke into the mic, carelessly walking toward me.

"I have not had the pleasure of knowing the groom for long. Nor have I had the pleasure of being a wedding planner before. Or a best man. The reason, naturally, being that it's no fun. But seriously, John," he looked down at me with a twinkle in his eye, "knowing you, being able to call you a friend, has changed me as a person," he winked and looked at the crowd. "I know jokes usually accompany these things, but I have none save the groom's dancing skills. Now, we all know the groom as a big-government loving, Carter-worshipping, hippy-accepting liberal, and if that sounds like him, then you're at the wrong wedding. Bring it in, Jimmy." The front door opened. My jaw dropped as Jimmy entered, carrying a basket on which rested a cardboard cutout. He plopped it down next to the table.

"Is that..." I couldn't form the words.

"A Ronald Reagan gift basket?" Peter said into the microphone. "Complete with books, pens, pins, stickers, bumper stickers, his personal diary, Iran-Contra, and a life-size cardboard cutout? Well, see for yourself." With that said, the music resumed. Peter, who seemed to enjoy hearing himself talk, had made the shortest best man speech of all time. He sat next to me as I rummaged through the basket, laughing over every discovery.

Joey stopped by our table and handed me a white envelope. He breathed out a puff of cigarette smoke. Peter stood.

"No smoking," he told Jimmy.

"Come on, Peter..." Peter held up his hands.

"You'll thank me one day," he said as he escorted Jimmy out. Katy curiously opened the envelope. Her jaw dropped. She handed it to me. Inside was a stack of very large bills. Soon other such envelopes arrived from total strangers. The sizes varied, but the amount was never insignificant.

"At this rate, we'll be able to pay back the loan shark in no time," Katy joked. I draped my arm over her shoulders as she put all the envelopes into a pile. I looked over to the dancers then back into her eyes. They still took my breath away. For once, everything felt right.

Thirty-Nine
And A Happy New Year

Peter. January 1ˢᵗ, 2010.

I awoke with a pounding in my head and a stiffness to my limbs. I attempted to put a hand to my temple in order to steady myself, but found myself unable to do so. I tried looking down. The room began to tilt. It was impossible to tell how long I had been unconscious this time, but judging from the burning sensation in my throat, it has been at least three hours. That made four blows to the head.

I looked around. I was in a sort of bare dungeon-like area, entirely empty excluding a wall-length mirror facing me. That... and to my right the wall was filled with hanging tools. They didn't seem to hold any occupational comradery: there was everything from a surgeon's scalpel to a butcher's cleaver. The one thing they all had in common was the lethality. They looked as if they were sharpened regularly. If this was an interrogation room—and judging from the tools, it was—then that mirror would also serve as a window on the other side.

Staring at the mirror, I saw that my hands were bound to a wooden chair. I struggled against the thick rope, to no avail. I grunted in pain. The sound reverberated throughout the room. A moment later, a door from behind me opened. In was thrust a shackled and bloodied John, who fell to the floor several feet behind me. He struggled to get to a sitting position. Finally, he succeeded. I watched him through the mirror. He stared back at me through it.

"What happened?" I asked, though I had a pretty good idea.

"They were waiting for us."

"Murray went with them. He double-crossed us."

"Castle is-" The door opened. A well-dressed man came into the room, mid-forties. I glanced down at my own attire: a bloodied and rumpled tux. I growled.

"This doesn't concern you, Jose."

"Oh, but it does. You tried to steal my brother's money. From *my* bank."

"Where's Johnny Black?" I asked, knowing this clown was nothing more than a patsy. He sneered.

"Johnny? Don't worry about him. He's looking after your other friends."

"We have no beef with you, Jose. Your brother took the wrong side. You don't want to make the Beppos your enemy."

"I don't? As I recall, you were the ones who stole from *me*. Not the other way around." Someone else came in. Johnny Black.

"Enough, Jose. Let yourself out. I've got it from here." The bank CEO left without another word. The door shut behind him. Suddenly, Johnny ran forward and kicked John in the ribs. John rolled to the wall, groaning. I refused to let my fear show. It wasn't over yet. I had a feeling John agreed with me. "Now then," he smoothed over his suit. "Care to tell me what happened?" I wrinkled my nose.

"Not particularly. Maybe after lunch." Johnny snarled, pulling out a revolver and holding it at arm's length. I felt the cool metal tip rest against the nape of my neck. "On second thought, I'm not that hungry." In all actuality, it didn't matter if they knew the whole story. They probably knew most of it anyway, and if they didn't they would get it from someone else. Telling them or not telling them wouldn't help my chances here. The only thing to do would be to stall. Not for the hope of a miraculous cavalry arrival or anything like that. Just a few more minutes to gloat over how I got here. To show Johnny how I outsmarted him before he blows my brains out.

"That's what I thought. Now where do you intend to start?"

"I hear the beginning is a good one," he pulled back his gun. I braced myself. It didn't help. He slammed his fist into the side of my head, sending my detained body crashing to the floor. My head felt as if it were on fire. I distantly tasted blood. Johnny grabbed the chair and set me upright. I began telling him our tale, with John occasionally chiming in.

"Last night, at precisely eight p.m., a limo showed up at a particular bank. A man stepped out, very charming and handsome, who tipped the driver generously and asked that he drive around for the next hour. The limo had been rented for the night, and wasn't needed until later.

"The man, Peter, showed his bank staff identification to the bouncer, who let him through. The bouncer, as anyone who worked at the bank would know, was not part of the normal security team, nor were most of the armed men there that night. The others were upstairs with most of the other guests—some remaining in the lobby—on the seventh floor, for the party.

"One staff member already upstairs, who had been working there for several months as a teller, was speaking with several coworkers about the safe in the center of the room. Its namesake must have been true, he said, to flaunt it so. No one at his level except himself knew the amount, but they all saw it. It was enclosed in a floor-to-ceiling glass case for the employees to admire and slobber over. The executives, especially the bank's owner, sneered at their near-groveling. The money didn't precisely belong to the executives, but they knew it only held a few million.

"The employee, whose nametag read 'Jimmy,' excused himself so he could grab some punch. Meanwhile, the man from the limo—Peter—entered the seventh floor from the elevator. Few recognized him, but no one questioned it. The bank had lots of workers, after all. Including all of the guests—mainly spouses—it was impossible to keep track of everyone.

"He left the elevator and headed to the punch bowl, smiling and shaking hands with those he encountered. As the man with the nametag 'Jimmy' laid eyes on him, the newcomer brushed some nonexistent dust off his tux with all five fingers extended. Jimmy gave a slight nod of understanding and excused himself from the posse. The other man poured himself some punch and found a specific group he wished to mingle with. He walked up to three men, shaking hands with an African-American first, giving him his brightest smile. The recipient stared back with a mixture of shock and disgust.

"'What the Hell are you doing here?' Johnny Black asked. Peter chuckled.

"'It's a party, Johnny. Lighten up.' The other two stared at the newcomer, who knew them both by name. 'Jose. And if it isn't Luis Cortez. I gotta say, I wasn't sure if you'd be here tonight. I'm glad you are. I hear it'll be a blast.' Luis stared with confusion.

"'You are-'

"'Someone who would rather not be named. Yes, that's me. Nice party, by the way.'

"'I… yeah.' Johnny grabbed Peter's shoulder, pulling him to the side.

"'What are you doing here?' Johnny whispered furiously.

"'What are any of us doing here in this great game of life?' Johnny growled in reply, motioning to several strong-looking men lounging in a corner. They hurried over.

"'Please show our guest every courtesy I have to offer.' Peter brushed his hand off his suit.

"'Yes, show every courtesy to me. I am, after all, a Made Man with a powerful boss who I'm supposed to call later tonight. He knows where I am, and will be very upset if he doesn't get that call.' Johnny's eyes widened.

"'Disregard that. Just… keep an eye on him.' They nodded and went back to lounging. 'I don't know what game you're playing, but it won't work.'

"'Life is a game, my friend. If you want to win, you always have to stay twelve steps ahead of the competition.' He grimaced, but went back to his friends. Peter began chatting with some others as Jimmy, noticing that almost five minutes had passed, headed to the storage room with a cup of punch in hand. No one paid him any mind; several other men had gone in there alone throughout the evening, followed shortly by female companions.

"But this employee didn't have anyone following him. He acted as such, going to the control panel in the back and opening it with his key. Inside were various switches and wires. Jimmy splashed his cup of punch over all of it, causing the single bulb in the storage room to flicker. Outside, the mood changed. It went from confusion to almost fright as the lights—and TV—went out.

"There were exclamations of power outage and mention of the transformers coming on in twenty seconds. The saboteur checked his watch and saw that they were right on schedule. Just another forty minutes. He left soundlessly, shutting the storage room door behind him as he joined the crowd with his empty plastic cup.

"Moments later, the lights came back on as the transformers started up. Johnny went over to Peter.

"'What was that?'

"'I believe they call that a power outage.'

"'How'd you do it?'

"'Johnny, I'm flattered you think so highly of me that I can perform acts of God, but the truth is: I can't.' Johnny grunted, storming off. Peter headed over to a large group gathered around, chattering about whether the outage had any danger to it.

"'I'll call my brother. He's an electrician who should be at a party right down the street. He won't mind giving us a hand.' And so Peter got on his cell. The man he called, however, was in fact in a van parked on the side of the building. The van had held five armed, masked men, in addition to the driver, but the five had left once informed that the building was powerless. They had stealthily entered through a side door, heading up to the sixth floor to wait, unseen. With the power out, their weapons didn't activate the metal detector. The door, electronically locked and therefore without need for a guard, held no difficulties for them.

"They, like the other guests, wore their Sunday best. Unique to these five was the minigun of .380 caliber that each carried. None wanted to be seen with such a lethal weapon. At least, not yet.

"The driver, whose nameplate read 'Dustin,' drove to the front of the building. He parked, getting out the white van and opening the back doors, where he took with him a briefcase full of nifty tools. He explained himself to the bouncer, who radioed his division's boss upstairs. The boss had heard rumor just a few seconds ago of someone's brother coming to make sure everything was fine, and so ordered for this newcomer to be let through. After speaking to several guests—the few hanging out in the lobby—Dustin headed to the back, which housed the camera room. A guard, probably the only official on-duty one in the bank, was lazily watching his many screens.

"'I was called to fix the power problem.'

"'And you are here, because...?'

"'I just told you: I'm fixing the power problem.'

"'But why here?' He motioned around him. 'In this room?' Dustin sighed dramatically.

"'This room is hooked up to the majority of the building, right?'

"'Yeah, but this isn't the power room.'

"'Are you an electrician?' Dustin asked suddenly.

"'No.'

"'Really? Are you sure? Because you're acting like you're an electrician.' The guard scowled, but had been told to do whatever necessary to ensure the guests had a good time. H hefted himself from his seat. Dustin swooped down to the central computer and began typing away. He paused, clicking his tongue against his teeth.

"'What's the problem?' The guard asked.

"'The mainframe refuses to manually reboot. I'll have to use an automated device.' He reached into his briefcase with the guard now interested. An interested guard meaning that every movement was closely followed. The supposed electrician removed a small USB device, thrusting it into the side of the computer. A loading icon appeared. A moment later, the screens went off. Dustin banged his fist against the table. 'You have a virus. A very stubborn one, aye.'

"'Can you get rid of it?' Instead of responding, he removed the USB and began typing some more. The computer screen reappeared, then the security camera screens. Dustin stood, swiping up his briefcase.

"'Whatever was there should be gone. I wouldn't reboot the main system until tomorrow, though. Best to let it rest.' The guard nodded. Dustin left the room, then the building. He jumped back in his van and drove around the block, coming back to his original spot on the side.

"'We're all clear.' He spoke into his transmitter. Jimmy, on the seventh floor, checked his watch. Twenty minutes left. He looked to the giant flat screen set against one wall, counting down until the ball drops. It was 11:40 over in New York. It wouldn't be long now.

"The guard watching the cameras didn't notice that the same activities occurring twenty minutes ago were filling his screens. Therefore, he couldn't see the final newcomer arrive in a tux with an ice chest that had to be checked at the front. It contained several bottles of champagne laid upon plenty of ice. This man also had supple identification claiming he was an employee and had been for six years. Six being the floor he was assigned to.

"He entered the elevator and pushed the button for the seventh floor, moving aside the top grate as the doors shut. The man in the elevator, whose identification read 'Eddie,' attempted to push the ice chest up through the tile. It was too heavy. Eddie then spilled the chest over the elevator floor, sending ice and bottles everywhere. Now much lighter, he once again tried and succeeded to get the chest on top of the elevator. He climbed up with it.

"Just feet above him, the doors separating the elevator from the sixth floor slid open. No alarm went off. The elevator

312

systematically stopped. Five men stood in the gaping hole. One of them, a grizzled veteran, set down his gun. He held out his hands for the ice chest, which was tossed to him. He gave it to one of his compatriots. He then reached for Eddie himself. Eddie grasped his hand and the ex-soldier pulled. Eddie joined his associates. He looked around him, noticing a large X over four tiles on the ceiling in the center of the room.

"'I guess that marks the spot.'"

Forty
Murphy's Law

December 31st, 2009.

"Peter walked up to the trio of bosses again, punch in hand.

"'This is such a lovely gathering, fellas. That centerpiece really completes the room.'

"'The glass surrounding the safe is bulletproof,' Jose informed him. 'And we have associates watching your every move. I wouldn't try anything.'

"'Try anything? Why would I do that? That safe can only hold… what? Five to twenty million dollars? What good is that to me? Besides, I'd need a crew to help me out. Someone on the inside. An opportune time to strike, preferably not during operating hours. A way to get into the security system. That's too much work.' Peter's inner thoughts were what a mistake these idiots were making. His whole point of being there was that they'd watch him and no one else, like a game of Color Monte or Shells. They had just admitted the gambit had worked flawlessly. They hadn't kept their eyes on the pea. The three men's eyes got wider by the word.

"'Do you know who I am?' Luis Cortez asked. Indeed Peter did know exactly who he was. It was hard to be in this line of work and not know. Luis Cortez: head of the Cortez *Cartel*, a leading contender in the California Five, primarily dealing in narcotics, weapons, immigration, prostitution, and systematically wiping out the competition. He had lost a position in *Fratres Criminis* to Johnny Black by a very small margin. It was also his money within the safe.

"'All I see is a big, hairy Latino with a need to show off his wealth. Men like that usually don't keep their cash for long.' Luis growled. He made eye contact with Johnny's friends in the corner. They walked over. All of them had a sort of deadly grace in their step. These weren't typical thugs. They were some of the Black Outfit's elite. Peter recognized Chad Black, Johnny's cousin and a prominent captain, among them.

"'Chad,' Luis said, 'we've changed our minds. Please take Robin Hood here out back. Nothing too drastic. Just make sure he knows to show respect when it's deserved.' Chad gave a quick, derisive nod. Peter chuckled as one Black employee grabbed his shoulder none-too-friendly.

"'Remember this, Luis: money brings power. This...' Peter motioned to the impatient employee, 'won't last without the funds to see it through.' Luis scoffed.

"'I can see the fear in your eyes. Fear brings power, and power brings money. '

"'I don't fear you. I fear what Big Guy over here is about to do to me since you can't handle me like a man.' Luis grunted.

"'You want to see a man? I'll show you a man. Let's go, boys,' Luis began to escort Peter, with Johnny's entourage following, to the elevator. Just as they passed the glass encasing the safe, the countdown for the ball drop began.

"'Wait,' Peter told them, stopping dead in his tracks, 'this is my favorite part.' They relented. These were crooks who had him exactly where they wanted him. It wasn't like he could escape. Even if he could, they would be able to find him. He had willingly walked into their fortress unarmed. He was fair game. The countdown continued. Everyone in the room shouted the numbers on the screen, caught up in the

315

excitement.

"'Five! Four! Three! Two! One!' There was an explosion of cheering as the ball made its descent. Champagne corks popped.

"Another explosion began. At first it went unnoticed amid the celebration. Yet the noise in the room quickly died down as the occupants realized the floor was shaking. Someone yelled something about an earthquake. But an earthquake wouldn't be accompanied by a sound like artillery fire. Luis turned and saw cracks were appearing in the glass that he had claimed was bulletproof. These cracks were stemming from the floor, which was beginning to crumble. Suddenly, it gave way. The glass shattered. The safe, with nothing to support it, fell to the sixth floor. Peter jerked away from his captor and leaped into the newly-formed hole, following the debris. He landed on the safe, momentarily losing his balance. He held out his hands to steady himself before jumping down, away from the gunfire. Amid the confusion, only one person in the room above moved. Jimmy shouldered and shoved his way through the crowd, heading for the stairs.

"It didn't take long to get a reaction from the crime bosses. Johnny Black began shouting for his men to jump. None obliged, especially considering the artillery hadn't yet stopped. Luis Cortez, who had never been afraid to be a hands-on guy, had pulled out a gun and was heading for the elevator.

"Five of the men on the floor below were firing with their Crucifiers at the door to the safe. Soon they would get lucky and hit it just right so it would open. If not, they would simply obliterate it and take whatever was inside. Three didn't much care if the money ended up in shreds—two were helping out a friend and squad mate get back at someone who had tried to hurt him. The third was that squad mate. Of course he wanted to pay back his family's debt, but that could be done a number of ways. This was for revenge, and to help out a friend.

"Peter and Eddie were busy opening a secret compartment in the ice chest. They removed eight parachutes and had them strewn over the floor, each at someone's feet. Jimmy calmly entered from the stairwell and picked up the eighth, then went to the chest's secret compartment and removed two carefully-folded duffel bags.

"The safe door opened. They had been firing at it for perhaps ten seconds. Three of them stopped. Two began firing at the windows against the wall, obliterating them. Inside the safe was, as expected, stacks of fifty thousand dollars each, banded in stacks a few inches thick, adding up to perhaps ten million. It was simple enough for Jimmy to swipe them into the bags. Everyone put on their parachutes. The firing ceased. Chad Black and his friends ran in from the stairwell. Luis Cortez was unable to join them—for some reason the elevator wasn't functioning properly. The eight thieves ran to the broken windows just as they began to be shot at. They all jumped. Together, they opened the parachutes, guns still in hand. Five headed toward a van that started upon seeing the parachutes activate, while three circled above an awaiting limousine out front. All landed near their respective vehicles and threw down the parachutes. All got in the vehicles, which promptly took off.

"The van, occupied by four ex-soldiers, a hitman, and a loan shark's extortionist, drove straight to a local watering hole. The limo, which was occupied by a con artist, a thief who until tonight had been employed at the bank he just helped rob, and the mastermind behind it all, began to circle the city. When Peter got in, he took his cellphone off the seat he had

317

been in earlier and put it back in his pocket. Eventually, as hoped, the limousine was pulled over. The back door opened. None other than Special Agent Vasquez poked his head in.

"'Take a step outside,' he beckoned to Peter without further introduction. Peter, who had been afraid it would take longer for Vasquez to catch up, happily obliged.

"'Is there a problem, Officer?'

"'You know damn well I'm no officer. I am a Special Agent for the FBI and will accept no other title.'

"'That's funny. My friends call you a lot of things, but 'Special Agent' isn't one of them.'

"'I understand that you have been riding around town for some time now.'

"'And how would you know such a thing?' Peter asked, even though he knew that they had been tracking his phone, which he had purposely left behind.

"'Sources. Sources also indicate that a certain bank was robbed only minutes ago. Would you know anything about that?'

"'How could I? I've been riding around for hours, as you say.'

"'Yet you stopped for a short time in front of the bank in question.'

"'Wait, you mean Jose's bank was the one hit?!' Peter didn't put too much energy into his performance. There was no point. Vasquez knew he was lying. 'Yeah, I stopped there to say hi to some old friends. Only for a minute or two. Surely not enough time to rob the place.' Vasquez stared at Peter, who met his gaze coolly. Both knew that his story could be true. Witnesses would confirm his presence if asked, but that wouldn't be necessary. All Vasquez needed was the GPS in Peter's phone—the one he didn't know Peter hadn't kept with

318

him—to get at least a partial truth. "'Are we done here?' Peter asked smugly. 'Or would you like to search the limo for money and guns?'

"'That won't be necessary.' Vasquez grumbled. He began to walk away. Suddenly he whirled around. 'What did you just say? How did you know guns were involved?' Peter didn't answer at first. He had made a careless mistake.

"'It's a bank robbery. How else would it be done? I assumed there were guns just like I assumed money was stolen. Regardless, I have neither on my person.' Vasquez waved him off and got back in his car. Peter got back in the limo. The driver rolled down the window separating them.

"'Company policy says if we get pulled over, the customer will have some forms to sign.'

"'No problem. I'll head over tomorrow afternoon. Could you drop us off at *The Pub*? It's a local watering hole.'

"'Sure thing.' Peter knew Vasquez wouldn't call the bluff. Which was good, since he did actually have his pistol wedged between the seats, although it hadn't been used. He tucked it in his tuxedo.

"The others were already at *The Pub*. In addition to the occupants of the van—Dustin, John, Castle, Walker, Joey, and Uncle Donnie—was Murray Gigante. They had requested a private room in the back, and had paid well to ensure they wouldn't be disturbed. In the center of the round oak table were two duffel bags. They had left the Crucifiers in the van with Castle, who had taken over driving and was trying to find a place to park. That wasn't the easiest thing to do on New Year's Eve/Day.

"Peter, Eddie, and Joey entered the back room. Everyone, minus Murray and Donnie, cheered upon their entrance. Peter cut them off with his hands.

"'All of you did well, and have earned your cut. We're looking at about ten million, so nine hundred thousand for each of us along with Leonardo and Don Beppo, and one hundred thousand for Murray. Remember to wait a month or two before spending too much. We don't want to attract attention. But the real problem isn't the cops; it's the *Cartel*. They know I was involved, but they were bound to suspect me anyway. Naturally they'll look to my friends and business associates. Keep your heads down.'

"Castle was unable to find a place to park at *The Pub*, so he went to an alley behind it. Seemingly out of nowhere, cop cars filled the area. They were heading for the bar. He also noticed two vans, not belonging to cops, drive up to the other alley mouth. Castle pulled out his phone to call John.

"'Mr. Castle?' A voice called from the darkness. Castle set down his phone, unsheathing his hunting knife from his boot as he peered out into the night. A figure appeared, walking along the side of the van until he was at the window. Castle rolled it down.

"'What do you want?'

"'I just want to know whether all ten C308s are in the back of this vehicle, Mr. Castle.'

"'Who are you?'

"'A friend of Bobby Mancuso.'

"'You're with those suits, Vasquez and Fuentes.'

"''With' is a very loose term. We know each other, yes.'

"'I'm not helping you.'

"'Then you're no use to me alive.' Castle opened the door, prepared to spring with his knife. The mysterious man opened fire, not stopping until his clip was empty. Castle's corpse slumped against the van. The shooting had alerted the Black Outfit on the other side of the alley. The figure wiped his gun with a cloth he kept for such purposes and gently set it in the body's hand. He then promptly headed to the front of *The Pub*. If all went according to plan, it would look like their friend betrayed them and they had no choice but to gun him down. Sure, the caliber of bullets and the number fired would match the gun the body held, but he'd make sure the police didn't look too closely. No one outside this group would suspect the real traitors. Soon the group itself would be so far on the defensive it wouldn't have time to make accusations until it's too late.

"The men in the back room heard both the sirens and the gunshots. Peter began erratically cursing. Chairs scraped back. Peter, John, and Uncle Donnie ran to the front as the others scrabbled for their cuts. Clare walked past with a tray of drinks. Donnie shoved her out of his way, sending her and her drinks crashing to the ground. Peter didn't think. He simply reacted, a primal protective instinct. He took out his gun and fired off a volley. He aimed for Donnie's head.

"The bullet grazed his shoulder. Uncle Donnie reeled and turned on Peter with a pistol of his own as John took out his revolver to back up Peter. Donnie wasn't sure which of his adversaries to aim for. Before any of them could react, the front door burst open. Cops swarmed. The trio forgot about their dispute and put away their guns. They went into the back room, which was in chaos. Murray and Jimmy were arguing about what to do with the money, some of which was scattered about the table as several thieves tried to personally ensure their cut was taken care of and others intervened.

"The back door opened. Half a dozen men leveled their weapons at it. Dillan Kamenev came through, saw what was going on, and blinked.

"'This way! I have a way out!' No one questioned him. All

of them except Murray, Uncle Donnie, John, and Peter followed. No one noticed those four stayed behind. Peter and Murray threw the scattered stacks back in one of the bags. Murray took hold of it. Peter grabbed his wrist. Murray met his eye.

"'We don't have time to argue about this. You know where to find me when this all blows over.' Peter hesitated for a second, then nodded. Murray slung the bag over his shoulder.

"The others had come across Castle's body. There were cries of outrage and despair, but they had to keep moving. They began running down a sidewalk before two vans drove up on either side of them, forming a V. They were trapped between the vans and the building. Black Outfit members got out the back. All of them, including Walker and Dustin, had no choice but to surrender.

"The back door closed back by itself. Murray flung it open, John on his tail. Yet instead of heading right down the alley as the others had, he took a left toward the first vans to arrive. Peter, the last to exit, hesitated, preparing to follow Murray. Before he could, however, Uncle Donnie whirled around and punched him square in the jaw. Peter hit the floor, unconscious."

Forty-One
Back to Black

Peter. January 2nd, 2010.

Johnny Black lounged against the mirrored wall with his arms crossed, eyeing me warily.

"You don't get to be a man in my position without having some level of intelligence," he told me. I gave an uncommitted shrug with just my shoulders. "I understand it all except for this: all of that was possible without showing your face. You could have had your friend sneak around without casting suspicion on yourself. Yet you chose to let everyone know who was robbing the place. Why?"

"It wasn't about the money. There are plenty of places begging to be robbed with less security and a bigger payoff. Sure, it was Jimmy's idea and all, but I could have said no. I knew it was risky. I knew I could have played my cards safer somewhere else. But I wanted you to know I outsmarted all of you. Proudly." Johnny motioned wide with his arms.

"This conveys your... pride?" he chuckled. "You must be a pious man." I snarled.

"The money is still gone. Cortez lost out on ten million dollars."

"The ten million you gave to Murray Gigante?"

"That ten million, yes."

"I suppose you're right. Cortez will be very unhappy about that. Little will he know that half the take is being given to me

323

in thanks for getting rid of you and your little entourage." I blinked. My mind raced. Sweat, which had long ago beaded my neck, now ran down my back accompanied by convulsive shivers.

"Murray was working with you?"

"More like *for* me. Our informant seems to have been slightly off about the C308s: he said there would be ten of them. Murray counted five." The Crucifiers? What did they have to do with any of this?

"Why did you want them?"

"Why would I want destruction incarnate at my fingertips? Take a guess. I'd wipe out my competition. Evidence would literally be blown away, so the guns would be practically untraceable by law enforcement. From my understanding, they don't even exist." That was obvious enough. I tried a different tactic.

"And you two were in on it with Bobby Mancuso." Johnny shook his head.

"Bobby worked for me and me alone. Murray knew nothing of it," he faced the mirror, staring at himself.

"Then explain why Bobby and Murray exchanged phone calls leading up to his disappearance." Johnny whipped around and hit me across the jaw. My head jerked to the side. It took me a moment to recover. When I looked at him, he acted as if nothing had happened.

"Do *not* command me. As for Bobby and Murray, I'd suspect they were double-crossing me. Going behind my back hoping to get the guns themselves. I'll still get my share. As we speak, my men are breaking into your apartment to steal the remaining five." At this point, I wasn't worried about the guns. Especially considering they weren't at my apartment.

"So you, Murray, and Bobby all wanted the Crucifiers. You

were working with Murray and Bobby separately, while Murray was working with you and Bobby."

"Everyone wins. Murray's profit off the bank job is fifty times greater, I get to remove you and your friends with cause, and Bobby would get the guns. When he said that was all he wanted, I dug a little deeper. He had the chance at some serious cash. What were a few guns? Then I found out what these bad boys are." Johnny shrugged. "Anything else?"

"I have something," John said from the floor. I saw him in the mirror. He had regained much of his color from earlier. "I have to make an appearance in court today for my trial. I don't think they'll be happy if I don't show up."

"No, they won't be happy. With you. They'll never find the body. Believe me: I'm not worried."

"Believe me," I retorted, "you should be. Remember what I said in my little story about a GPS on my phone? It's still active. Soon FBI will be crawling all over this place. It won't help if you have two dead bodies on your hands." That made me wonder just where we were being kept.

"Except your phone was left at that bar. They have no way to follow you here." If he was expecting me to show fear, I made sure he would be disappointed. I had suspected as much.

"Where is 'here?'"

"A subterranean level of my old bar that survived the fire. Thanks for that, by the way."

"Anytime," John and I replied simultaneously. I continued, "That explains why we couldn't find you: you were where we already checked. I bet you were here the night we attacked the bar. Hiding. Like a coward. Almost in plain sight." Johnny growled. I was trying my luck.

"Except not in plain sight at all. Underground," he paused,

as if unsure whether to confide something in me. "We're not too different, you and I. I was never a patsy, but we have our similarities. I had Murray and Bobby trailed as a matter of course. Something else turned up. My boys reported that a young Russian mercenary was also following Murray. They say this same mercenary was there tonight and had tried leading the rest of your gang to safety. When we closed in, he somehow managed to escape. This boy is the same one my guys saw helping Bobby try and take you out. A strange arrangement, but I've seen stranger. It's business, not personal and all that. Yet I ask myself, 'Why is an enforcer for the Vasilievs following Murray—an associate of Peter, who is one of his recent employers?' The answer was simple: just as Murray was double-crossing us, we were both double-crossing him. Neither of us trusted him. It's in our nature, this distrust."

"I'm nothing like you," I spat. He shrugged.

"You can tell yourself that all you want. You can tell *me* that all you want. Just know you won't be able to tell anyone else," he set himself up for another punch. I braced myself. The hit connected with my chin. I flew back and hit the floor. I heard a crack. At first, I had assumed it was my skull. It turns out it was just a chair leg breaking off. Johnny moved on to John, squatting above his head. John stared at him. Even shackled hand and foot with a revolver lazily pointed as his chest, John maintained his composure. "You know, Washicha, it's almost too bad you'll die here. Almost."

"Oh yeah? Why's that?" John asked monotonously. Johnny leaned down and whispered something into John's ear. I couldn't make it out, but whatever it was, John didn't like it. It was as if this energy that had been festering inside him was suddenly released in full force. In other words: he snapped.

I watched, bound to the fallen chair, as John whipped the chain of his wrist shackles straight up, crisscrossing his hands in the process, effectively forming a noose around Johnny's neck. Johnny shot up, releasing his grip on his revolver, sending John to his feet. Johnny's back was right against John's chest as the chain tightened. Johnny furiously beat against John's ribs with his elbow. I began worming my way toward our only hope: the gun.

Johnny took one last desperate shot by forcing John backward. John lost his balance and had no choice but to keep tripping back. Add Johnny's own weight, and the momentum was frightening. John's back hit the mirror, shattering it. He fell through the hole into the next room. Johnny might have ended up with a torsion in his neck, but he turned at just the right moment as John fell. Johnny was now free. His eyes darted throughout the room, searching for his gun. I winced. There went our only chance of survival.

John, cut and even more bloodied from the glass, sprang up from the other room and threw himself through the hole. He tackled Johnny, who went down. John began smashing Johnny's head into the ground. Johnny's elbow shot up, catching John in the nose. John sprawled to the floor. Johnny used this chance to get on top of John. He began giving John left and right hooks, forcing his neck to bend at unnatural angles.

I grasped the revolver between my cuffed hands behind the chair. I turned the chair as Johnny continued to wail on John with no attention spared for me. I faced the wall, but the revolver faced the fighters. I watched them through a particularly large shard of glass lying on the floor with no thoughts of morality nor consequences. Only survival.

I fired the gun. Combine my poor marksman abilities with

my inability to either hold it properly or see my target clearly, it was no surprise that I missed entirely. However, the bang did cause Johnny to look up from his beating. John used this distraction as an opportunity to escape. His shackled hands were above his head on the floor. He interlaced his fingers, using all his might to deliver a blow with both hands to Johnny's abdomen.

It knocked Johnny over, who. albeit large and powerful, was weakened and distracted. That blow must have sapped most of John's energy: he was already old, and combine his earlier beating with the long night he's had, it's hard to imagine how he's still standing. Yet he jumped up and shuffled over to me best he could with his shackled feet. He set the chain on his feet right on the muzzle. I fired. There was an audible *ping* as the chain snapped in half. He went for his hands next, but I saw through the shard that Johnny was up and ready.

"John!" I warned. John turned just as Johnny pounced. John took a step back to brace himself. His foot landed on my hands. I cried out in pain, releasing the gun. Johnny and John collided, rocketing to the floor. One of their bodies managed to break off another chair leg as they soared over me. They began scuffling on the floor, neither able to get a good hit in. I could no longer see the revolver. I tried to feel around for it. Nothing.

Johnny leaped over my body. I watched through the shard once more. Wherever the gun was, he ignored it. Instead, he sprinted for the wall of tools across the room. John was right after him, diving for his body. The distance was too great for a full-on tackle, but John did manage to use his chains to trip up Johnny's foot. Johnny fell. John began climbing on top of him one move at a time. Johnny struggled to resist. In a sudden surge of power, Johnny shot his knees to his chest in a would-be fetal position. John flew over his head. Johnny got back up and proceeded toward the lethal tools. John unsteadily rose to his feet and struck Johnny with both hands. Before Johnny could react, those chained hands were at the back of his neck. John forced Johnny's head down just as his knee went up.

I wasn't exactly sure what happened next. Maybe it was the force. Maybe everything was hit in just the right way. Maybe the chain was rusty. But next thing I knew, John's shackles were scattered on the floor in bits and pieces instead of a clean break like when I shot the feet shackles. John was now free. Johnny, on the other hand, was still reeling from the blow. He went down on one knee, one hand to his bloodied face and the other on the ground. When he stood, however, he was holding the gun. He aimed it at John's chest with one hand, the other still holding his face. Despite now having the upper hand, he took several unsteady steps back. Blood trickled down his fingers.

"You do not know the smallest inkling of power," Johnny told him.

"I don't have to," John replied coldly. Johnny stared at him.

"You just don't get it: Alexei has a plan. A beautiful plan but one I was never meant to know about. You think this is all about my biker gang? A slight because we're on opposing sides? This didn't start here. Alexei's plan didn't start here. This started decades ago, in '86." John's eyes widened. The year he lost his family.

"You were never meant to know about it?" I asked tauntingly. "You? His prized lapdog? His rabid pet? You belong to him."

"I belong to no one," Johnny growled. "I'll see you in Hell," he spat out some blood.

"Tell the Devil I'll be a little while," John spat out his own. Johnny chuckled.

"It was fun while it lasted, Sarge. Yet all good things must come to an end," he cocked the hammer. "Goodbye." My broken chair leg, which I had inched myself toward and now firmly grasped between my bound hands, struck the back of Johnny's knees. The majority of the wood broke off from my hands. He fired as he fell back, the bullet harmlessly hitting the ceiling. In an instant, John was on top of him. He yanked the gun from Johnny and flipped it around, holding the barrel. John began smashing the butt against Johnny's skull. His other hand held Johnny's throat. They were only a foot or so away from where I was lying. I saw every gruesome detail through a shard. That was good. If I had to see it all first-hand, I may have lost it. At one point, a drop of blood landed on my arm. Except it didn't feel like blood. It was more solid. My body's first reaction was to try and vomit. Nothing came up.

I yelled repeatedly for John to stop, that Johnny was well-past dead by this point. He didn't let up. He kept pounding what remained of Johnny's face. There was a primal glint to his eyes—and one of remembrance. It was all emotion, present and possibly past. I could only imagine what was going through his head. I could clearly see what was going through Johnny's.

The door to the interrogation room opened. Throughout the entire exchange I had wondered why no one was breaking this apart. My only possible answer was that they suspected Johnny wanted to handle this himself. Yet now that Johnny was dead...

Half a dozen armed men entered. But they weren't Johnny's crew. I gaped. Leading the party was Dillan, who was followed by Dustin, Walker, Eddie, Joey, and Jimmy.

Everyone except for Murray and Uncle Donnie. And Castle.

Dustin and Walker pried John off the corpse. I could see silent tears forming in John's eyes as he glared at the unrecognizable body. Joey went over with a key and removed my handcuffs.

"We'll explain on the way," Dillan said.

"On the way to where?" I asked.

"It's daylight. Your friend's trial starts in an hour."

Forty-Two
The Trial

John. January 2nd, 2010.

We all piled into an SUV Dillan claimed was on standby for cases such as this. I would have preferred he tell me it was stolen. He handed me and Peter our guns as we got situated. "Where to?" Dillan asked.

"My house," I told him. Sitting in the front passenger seat, I punched the address into the GPS. "I need a change of clothes before the trial."

"What happened?" I asked Dillan as he began driving.

"I did as Mr. Richardson asked and waited at *The Pub* for Donnie Scarlatti and Murray Gigante. Once they got their share, I was to follow them and kill them." I blinked. Peter hadn't told me about this. "But a strange man was hanging around the alleyway where I had been hiding. He then shot your friend Brett Castle."

"Did you get a good look at him?" I asked. Dillan shook his head.

"It was dark. Whoever he was, though, he was no friend of the Black Outfit. He bolted when they came to investigate the shots. He held himself as if he were a..."

"Were a what?" I prompted.

"Back in Moscow I was trained to pick out policemen, in case one of them was undercover. He held himself like one of them." A cop? Special Agent Vasquez, maybe? But Peter had said he warded him off when the limo was pulled over. "But when he left, I couldn't follow because the Black Outfit would catch me. I figured you'd rather me help you than go after the targets."

"And you had no idea Murray was working with the Black Outfit?" Peter asked.

"None. I had been trailing them, as ordered, and found nothing out of the ordinary. It took a full day and some payoffs, but I found where they were keeping you. Then it was a matter of waiting for the right moment to strike."

"All by yourself?"

"I did not have much of a choice. I wanted to avoid a war between my own Family and the *Cartel* or, worse, the Outfit." Dillan slowed to a stop in front of my house. I exited quickly, running as fast as my injured body could carry me. I flung open the front door, which should not have been unlocked, but that was not my concern at the moment. I bolted upstairs into the bedroom.

Katy was sobbing on the bed. She looked up at my approach. Her face instantly lit up. She rose, pausing for a bit when she saw the blood caking my hands. She threw her arms around me. I was careful to embrace her with only my arms.

"I thought you were dead," her eyes glistened in the pale yellow light. "You're all beat up, but... you're alive," she whispered against my chest. My heart constricted at the word "alive."

"Castle," I murmured. She looked up at me with those emerald eyes.

"What?"

"Castle is dead," she stared in shock. I gently removed her arms from around me. She didn't protest. I dropped onto the bed. All the adrenaline came to a halt. I realized just how tired

I was. A part of me just wanted to forget about the trial and sleep. To forget about all of this.

"I... he was with you?"

"He was," she gritted her teeth.

"Didn't I tell you not to go?! Look at what has happened, John. You've almost been killed who knows how many times. The house was attacked. JJ was shot. And now... Castle. All for—what? Gangland politics and money?" My mouth went dry.

"We didn't get it," she froze.

"What?"

"We didn't get the money," she turned around, unable to look at me. "But the guy who attacked the house, the one we've been afraid of, Johnny Black, he's dead, too. We don't have to worry about him anymore," she whipped around. I flinched. Tears ran down her cheeks.

"We only had to worry about him in the first place because you crossed him, because—because of *Peter*," she hissed. "If it wasn't for him, none of this would have happened."

"Peter didn't get Castle killed. Castle went in of his own accord. But I'll find out who did this to him, and I'll take care of it."

"No, John. Castle was my friend, too. But you need to let this rest. You don't need to get any more involved than you already are. Enough is enough."

"Katy, don't you see? I'm fighting my hardest to get out of this. I'm almost there, too. Look, I have to be in a courtroom in half an hour looking presentable. I know this is a lot to take in. I'm trying not to focus on it this second. There will be time for grieving later. But right now, I'm trying to close one chapter of this life, this game. Soon I'll close the whole book." With that, I grabbed my plain black suit and accessories from the closet and hurried into the bathroom. I discarded the bloodied and torn tux I was wearing. Peter had gotten it off a truck, anyway. I ran the shower and stuck myself under the cold water. The droplets burned against my skin. A mixture of sweat, blood—most of which wasn't mine—and dirt swirled down the drain. I cleaned my hair and got out, missing large areas of wet skin with my towel. I put on my suit.

When I got back into the bedroom, Katy was gone, replaced by Scout lounging on the bed. "Katy won't like you there," I told him. He whined. I sat beside him and petted his head. We sat there awhile, dog and owner. The others were waiting on me and my throat burned with thirst, but I needed this. Scout and I made eye contact. He whimpered.

"I know, Boy. It will all be over soon. One way or another." I left, leaving the door open for him. I bounded downstairs into the kitchen and opened the fridge door wide. I rummaged through, fitting as much unpackaged ham and bottles of water as I could into a crook in my arm. I left the house and tried not to drop anything as I opened and closed the door. I failed. I stooped to pick up the ham. If the others felt how I did, they wouldn't care if there was a little dirt. Or, looking at the ham, a lot of dirt. They opened the car door for me. I climbed in. Jimmy, sitting next to me, began dispersing the food. I glanced back to see Eddie chugging a water bottle. I put my hand on his knee.

"Slow," I said. He wiped his mouth with his sleeve and nodded. I opened my own bottle and took a sip. I struggled to not make the same mistake. Dillan stared at me a moment.

"You clean up nicely."

"I know."

"You still look like crap."

"I know," he nodded to himself and drove off.

"So what about Gigante and Scarlatti?" Dillan asked.

"Murray made a lot of powerful enemies by double-crossing everyone," Peter answered. "Half the city will be looking for him, if it isn't already."

"And the money?" I asked. Peter hesitated.

"We'll have to wait and see."

"Looks like I won't be getting Made for some time," Jimmy added.

"Well," Peter said, "you'll have to lay low for awhile, anyway. Cortez will try his best to track you down. Those safety precautions we put in place should slow the search, but Luis is resourceful. Besides, the books are still open: you'll have another chance soon."

"For now," Dillan said, "here we are." Whether he was referring to our present state or our arrival at the courthouse, it was hard to say. He parked and we got out. I heard Peter mention something to him about the debt being repaid and that they would stay in touch, and he'd get a bonus if he found the contract. Something like that. Dillan drove off. A moment later, Peter was beside me as the six of us walked into the courthouse.

My family—my *entire* family—greeted us at the door. Damion must have been frantic that I hadn't been answering my cell, which was still at *The Pub*. I stopped short when I saw Katy.

"I hope you don't mind, but the kids had already left to support you, and you didn't take your keys, so I drove your bike," she handed the keys back to me with a smirk. She didn't mention that she no longer had a car because of me. "I don't have much time to explain," she explained, "but I understand you're doing all of this for me. All of you are, in your own way," she cast an accusatory glance at Peter that showed she didn't mean "all," he shifted uncomfortably. "But right now you need to get in that courtroom and win," she gripped my shoulder and smiled. I smiled back.

"I never got to thank you for sending this one to help me." I motioned to Damion. Her features went from a strange hopefulness to completely blank.

"What do you mean?" she asked.

"Damion said that you are the one who got him to help me when I was first arrested."

"John, I didn't even know about this until you told me," Katy said. Damion cleared his throat.

"I didn't exactly say that," Damion said sheepishly.

"Damion... did you lie about being forced to help me?" I questioned.

"I didn't lie. You assumed Mom sent me here," I gazed at my son. From the start, he had helped me of his own accord and made sure I wouldn't know. Why, I'd find out later.

I looked at Violet and felt a pang of guilt. One of her few encounters with me was at my trial.

Our reverie was broken by the arrival of Special Agent Vasquez. There were various outbursts from our party, ranging from "Not this *mook* again" to "A badge can't protect you from an explosion." That last one came, surprisingly enough, from the quiet Walker. Katy and Damion got closer to me. Peter took a step forward. I threw out my hand to hold him back. It was my turn.

"You ever read Mark 14:72, Vasquez?" he scowled.

"'Immediately the rooster crowed the second time. Then Peter remembered the word Jesus had spoken to him: 'Before the rooster crows twice you will disown me three times.' And he broke down and wept.' One of my favorite verses."

"And so once again I'm denying you. Peter, fittingly, is

337

denying you too." If he was fazed by our unwillingness to cooperate, he didn't show it.

"The GPS in your cellphone says you were at *The Pub* last night. In fact, it says you're still there." I motioned to where we were, indicating that it was clearly wrong. "There was a murder last night. While you were there."

"And if another one occurred right now, I'm still there?"

"No, but your phone is."

"Which means I may or may not have been there when the murder happened." I shouldered my way past him. The rest followed. I didn't turn to see what Vasquez was doing. Whether or not he knew who killed Castle, he knew it wasn't me.

"Johnny Black is missing." Everyone stopped. I turned my head to look at him.

"They better find him quick. He has the game coming up."

"The game?" Vasquez asked, befuddled.

"The baseball game. We're still talking about the pitcher, right?" I kept walking. We entered the courtroom. Excluding Peter and Damion, the others dispersed to find seats. Katy kissed me on the cheek. I gave Violet a quick shoulder squeeze. We approached the defendant's table and sat with me on the left, Damion in the middle, and Peter on the right. A clock on the wall said we had arrived just as we were set to begin.

"All rise," a bailiff called. Judge Taylor entered and sat in his usual spot. His eyes bore down on me.

"Be seated."

"Pete," I said, "I want Damion to handle this." Peter gaped. "Just trust me on this."

"If we lose..." Peter breathed. I watched Damion carefully.

"Do you think you can do this, Son?"

"I got it, Dad." I nodded. I looked at Peter.

"Relax," I told him. "You're about to win your first case. As a lawyer, that is." That didn't stop him from silently pouting.

"Ladies and gentlemen of the jury," District Attorney Fuentes said, pointing at me, "this man is no less than a danger to society. He was caught red-handed and ensured the most important witness could not speak here today."

"Objection!" Damion called. "It was agreed that the assault charge has been dropped. Besides, the restraining order is there for a reason." The judge nodded.

"Sustained."

"Cheating is, on all levels, unethical," Fuentes went on as if he had never left off. "At the professional level, such a heinous act is even worse. Mr. Washicha has been unemployed for-"

"Objection," Damion said, "my client has been the manager of a firearm and firearm accessories commercial business for years. He has had a relatively steady income and until recently has only had to support himself. There was no desperation in his financial situation, and since the only possible gain from this is money, there is no motive."

"Since the defense is so inclined to speak over me, how about we give them their time now?" Fuentes asked the judge. Ever the showman, Fuentes gave Damion a wide flourish.

"Very well," Damion said. He seemed meek and rather unsure of himself. I suddenly had my doubts in choosing him over Peter.

Forty-Three
"Friends"

Peter. January 2nd, 2010.

"I couldn't help but notice, District Attorney, that you did not mention my client's rather impressive service record," Damion began, with a quick glance at Peter.

"His desertion is a matter for the military courts. They appear uninterested in pursuing it."

"That's not what I said. You failed to mention his invaluable service to his country, putting others' lives before his own, something he continues to do to this day. Mr. Washicha-" Damion paused, "my father has, as I have been recently informed by my mother, lost his two closest friends in the line of duty. Protecting his family. Protecting everyone in this room. Did he lose that match on purpose? I don't know. I wasn't there. But I do know he received nothing for his service to his country. The question isn't whether he did it, instead it is a matter of whether it was right. Around the time this crime allegedly took place, he was reunited with his family," he looked back at John. "And I am proud to see him, point to him, and say 'that's my father.'" He came and sat back at the table. "I love you, Dad." I heard him whisper to John.

"I love you too, Son." I looked away. I didn't want to see that. Besides, it was none of my business. It just so happened that I ended up looking at the jury instead. And it just so happened that I saw their doubt. And it just so happened that

340

I had been in enough courtrooms with doubtful juries to know how this would end. Damion's spectacle had helped, and doubtlessly helped his relationship with his father, but it wasn't enough.

"Told you jury nullification was the way to go," I told Damion. He rolled his eyes.

"Does that conclude your closing statement?" Judge Taylor asked. My eyes darted into each jury member's face, searching for a belief of innocence. Or at least a belief in not-guilty. There was some, but not enough. I looked over to John, past Damion's head. He was too busy with his admiration for his son to notice the possible conviction. "Will that be all?" Judge Taylor asked, impatient. I licked my lips. A small cut on John's chin caught my eye. "Well?" I stood.

"No!" I asserted. He arched an eyebrow, as did Fuentes.

"Then please proceed. Try not to make a mockery of my court in the process." I gave a single nod. I stared at the floor as I wondered how to articulate my thoughts. My eyes rested on John's face. That's what I had to focus on—John's face. I walked around the table and cupped his face in my hands, moving it about so that the light hit it at the right angle.

"Don't move from that spot," I whispered. He nodded awkwardly, confusion and a hint of anger in his eyes. I addressed the jury. "Don't you see those bruises? Those cuts? Isn't it obvious how he got them?" From the silence in the room, it wasn't obvious at all. "His fellow fighters. His ex-coworkers. Of course, John has too much loyalty and honor to admit such a thing, so he won't give names. But that's how this country's legal system works: he's guilty no matter what this court says. Professional fighters are harassing him mercilessly due to the charge alone. You would be doing him a favor by putting him away." I reconsidered that last part.

"Almost."

"Objection! Is there any proof that those marks actually came from Pure Gore Fighting?" Fuentes asked skeptically.

"Only deductive reasoning and that, upon closer inspection, those bruises couldn't be accomplished in a simple barroom brawl. This was an experienced, powerful fighter. Possibly more than one. Besides, who else would harm my client without John wanting to confess to the perpetrator?" I looked back to John, who smiled at this ingenuity. He may not have been experienced with the politics surrounding organized crime and the legal system, but I could tell he understood enough. Fuentes couldn't spring the "Surprise! This is all about the *Mafia* because no one really cares about skimming points" card until he had John cornered and ready to make a deal. If he did pull that card, everyone would instantly be on the defensive and his only hope, John, would either be dead or worse. On the other hand, he could admit that John's bruises came from fighters harassing him, thus making John seem vulnerable. Juries like to help someone vulnerable. I trapped him with his own game.

"No, there is no one else that comes to mind," the district attorney grudgingly admitted through his teeth. Joey, Jimmy, and Eddie began cracking up in the back. The judge pounded his gavel.

"So," I said, "here's what we have: a loving family man and veteran in a stable financial situation, with no criminal record, who allegedly decides to make a few quick bucks by rigging his fight. He is then confronted about it. He denies the claim, maybe because—gasp—he's innocent. He is thrown into a fight. It doesn't end there. He's hounded by police and his fellow fighters alike for something he didn't do. He is then assaulted—badly, from the looks of it—and is being thrown in prison with the only evidence being he was too good to lose and he had some money that was easily explained. That is what the prosecution is saying, correct?" I stared at Fuentes, daring him to speak.

"I…" Fuentes looked lost. "They claim the money comes from a front for a known crime lord."

"So there you have it, folks: even the prosecutor admits that the money may have come from somewhere else. If they could back up that claim, my client would be here on another charge. The reason he isn't? He's innocent. And that's all there is to it." I sat. "The defense rests."

"Prosecutor?" Judge Taylor asked. Fuentes didn't speak. The judge leaned in. "Isaac?" he asked softly.

"I… we have proof that he was in the same restaurant as a murder victim last night!" Fuentes announced. Judge Taylor, obviously tired of all the finger-pointing, looked to us.

"Defense?" I shrugged and leaned back in my seat.

"If it's true, charge him." Judge Taylor looked from me to Fuentes to back and again.

"The prosecution rests," Fuentes mumbled.

"What was that?" I asked. "I didn't hear you."

"That's enough, Mr. Richardson," Judge Taylor said. He looked to the jury, who were much more convinced now. Admittedly, I may have been the one to win them over, but Damion lit the fuse. Judge Taylor announced that the jury would leave to deliberate and there would be a short recess until a decision was reached. We filed out with everyone else. In the large marble hallway, the spectators chattered amongst themselves. John and his family were engaged some sort of personal, heartwarming talk. I stayed away, especially when I heard John thank Damion for practically winning the case.

Eddie, Joey, and Jimmy gave John their best and left. They

had seen enough trials to know where this one was heading. I almost offered to pay for a taxi for them, but I had decided to refuse payment from John for my legal services. I'd give him his fight earnings later. He'd need them.

Walker walked up to me. He didn't say a word at first. Just crossed his arms and watched everyone with me.

"John has been telling me about you," he said suddenly. "He told me that in half my age worth's of years you became the most powerful crime lord in the world." I shrugged. "Without killing anyone. How'd you pull that one off?" I shrugged again. What else did John tell him about? My non-existent love life?

"Most people avoid that topic with me. Let's see... I was sent on assassination jobs. Everyone trying to 'earn his bones' has to do it at some point or another. My targets always ended up dead. I never pulled the trigger."

"Then how?"

"I looked for... uh... algorithms. Chinks in the armor, if you will. In any organization there are always some types of weak points. People unhappy with where they are, thinking they deserve more. People who have problems that need to be resolved. Businesses that are suffering. Somehow someone else always ended up doing the dirty work for me. That and I never pissed off the wrong guy on a bad day—just the right guy on a good day," he smirked.

"Thanks for the advice, Professor." We went back to watching the crowd. A few minutes later a young woman in a power suit approached the pair of us. It was obvious her attention was directed at me. She didn't seem inclined to speak.

"May I help you?" she bit her lip.

"No. Well. I mean. Not me, no. Not really. But Clare..." She now had my full attention.

"What? Has something happened to her?"

"I... I don't know. Look: we had been in Phi Alpha Delta together for undergrad. I got my law degree last semester and we stayed in touch. She mentioned you a few times."

"Really? What did she say?"

"She..." the lawyer shook her head. "It doesn't matter. My point is, recently she's been... aloof. Distant. Paranoid."

"And you know the reason." It wasn't a question. My nerves were on edge as it was.

"I do. At least, I think I do. Her fiancée, Zane. He's a hothead. I'm scared for her. I could be wrong, but whenever she posts something, makeup covers some areas more than others. Today I got a text saying she didn't show up for work. I just thought—you know—you might want to check on her."

"Check on her," I repeated. "Right." I pulled out a roll of cash and unfolded a few bills. "Thanks," she stared at the money.

"Keep it. Making sure she's safe is thanks enough," she left as suddenly as she came. I watched her go. She certainly wasn't cut out to be a lawyer.

"Clare's that waitress friend?" Walker asked.

"Is there anything John doesn't tell you?"

"Not much. If he didn't, I wouldn't know, now would I?" he had a point. "What are you thinking?"

"Well, you're thinking how it would be a bad idea to pay Clare a visit because nothing good will come of it. I'm thinking about how good coffee sounds right about now." I gave him my cheekiest smile. "Come on, I'm not stupid. What could I do?"

"Good. John is a real man when it comes to women, but even he wouldn't want to see you deal with something like that." I knew he was right. John, finally disentangled from his legion of adoring fans, walked up.

"What was that all about?" he motioned to the perky lawyer who had just turned a corner.

"Just a fellow lawyer who thought Damion was cute. I guess his looks came from his mother." I waited for Walker to call me on the lie. He didn't. Not yet, anyway. "Want to grab some coffee?"

"Isn't it stale?"

"Probably. Let's go." I steered him in the right direction. I just had to get him away from the others for a few minutes. We found a coffee vending machine. I bought us each a drink. Once the coffee spurted into cups, John took a sip. He made a face.

"Yep. Stale." I ignored his light accusation. I remained calm despite the warzone going on in my mind.

"You ever heard that saying that you can tell a lot about a man from his key ring? It's one of those psychology things where they psychoanalyze you."

"No way," he said, interested.

"I'm telling you. See, I'd imagine you have only a single key, a sign that you're simple yet that in itself is complex." Just as I hoped, he reached into his pocket and pulled out his key ring. He held it up for me to see.

"House key, garage key, shop key, and bike key," he pointed to each one. "Four keys." I gently took the ring, examining it closely.

"So your bike means more to you than your shop, since it's a larger key."

"No, no, *this* is the bike key, and *this* is the shop key. Though the bike does mean more," he pointed again. I peered at them closer. His face loomed right over mine in an attempt to see what I did. Steam rose from my coffee cup. Nice and hot. I suddenly coughed violently, sending my cup—and the steaming liquid inside—straight into John's face. He gave a yelp of surprise. Or maybe pain. I yelled something about getting napkins and ran, ignoring the stares of those around me. If that *mook* laid a hand on her...

I made it outside and saw I had heard correctly: Katy brought John's bike. I carelessly put his helmet over my head. The key turned in the ignition.

"PETER RICHARDSON!!!" John came into the parking lot. He did not look pleased to see me. "You—YOU'RE STEALING MY BIKE?!"

"I'll return it!" I yelled above the roar of the engine. I drove off. At least now it wasn't the coffee he was upset about. I'll return the bike later and he'll be fine.

I reached the condo complex Clare told me she'd moved into and jumped off the bike just as it came to a stop. I ran toward the wide glass doors, leaving the keys in the ignition, and threw down my helmet. This wouldn't take long.

Ten feet from the entrance, I stopped and composed myself. I hadn't come here with a plan. I just knew I had to see if she was okay.

I walked in with a nervous expression. There was a single clerk behind a desk. Columns and marble floors gave a distinctly Greek impression.

I approached the clerk. His nameplate read X. Gibson. The two names I knew beginning with "X" were Xavier and Xander. Xander was generally short for Alexander, which starts with an "A." I took a 50-50 shot.

"May I help you, Sir?"

"I think so. I was coming visit a friend, but there was a man in a van around the corner who said he had a package for an

Xavier Gibson and he refuses to go out in the cold. Are you Xavier?" I tried not to eye his nameplate.

"I am." I didn't exhale with relief, though I was close.

"I'll wait here, if you want. You can get your package and come back," he nodded and discreetly left. He looked back once he reached the door. I gave him a thumbs-up. Right when he went through the doors I scanned the callbox logs for the various occupants and where they could be reached. Wyler: Room 405. I grunted and ran to the stairwell, where I proceeded up the steps. No need for the clerk to come back and I be trapped in the elevator. Unlikely, but possible.

I reached the fourth floor and quickly found 405. I steadied my breathing and knocked three times.

The door opened inward a fraction of an inch. What I knew to be Clare's almond eye poked through. When she saw me, she gasped and tried to shut the door. I understood her anxiety: her eye was blackened. I used my shoulder to bang open the door. Clare screamed. I barged in. Sitting in an armchair, watching a soccer game and drinking a glass of LaCroix, was Zane Wyler.

Even though he was sitting, I judged him to be around 6'1, with a goatee and adjacent mustache. He was well-groomed and surprisingly muscular. At my approach, he jumped up. I marched forward until we were perhaps two feet apart.

"Who the Hell are you?" he demanded.

"That depends on one thing: what happened to Clare's eye?"

"She fell."

"In that case, I'm your worst nightmare." I ripped the bottle from his hand by the neck and swung it over his head. Glass and sparkling water splashed everywhere. Unfazed, he gave a right hook. I jumped back and tried to remain calm. I wanted him angry. Angry people made mistakes. I was angry, sure. But I knew how to control my anger. Sort of. His anger was hot. Mine was ice cold.

He took out a pocket knife. The blade swung open. He lunged. I moved to the left. Without missing a beat, he continuously swiped at me. I breathed heavily, but didn't receive so much as a scratch. Or if I did, the adrenaline prevented me from feeling it. He wasn't much of a fighter. His rage didn't help. Clare stood to the side, crying. Whatever she screamed was indistinguishable with the blood pounding in my ears. His knife made contact with my chest. We both stopped. I put a finger to the cut. It came away with a reddish tint. Very shallow.

In one fluid motion, I took my gun out of my tux and held it by the barrel. I proceeded to whack the *mook* on the side of the head with the butt. He fell like a log, dropping the knife. I didn't stop there. I bent over and hit him in the same spot another seven times. I could hear Clare yelling for me to stop. I lost count of how many blows I landed. He tried to block the strikes with his hands. I smashed his fingers along with his skull. Eventually, he just stopped trying. Still breathing heavily, I stood. I gave him a good kick in the ribs and, as an afterthought, spat on him. I turned away and made for the door. Clare stared in shock. Once I reached the door, I turned back around, pointing at Clare.

"Don't hit her again. Ever. Again. Or I'll be back, and I'll be using the other side of the gun." Changing my mind, I went back to him and stomped on his head. I removed my money roll and dropped a few bills on his chest.

"Go buy the lady some flowers. Nice ones. A dozen roses. Don't make me come back, ya no-good prick." I stomped on his head one last time, leaving behind an unconscious Zane and weeping Clare. I put away the gun as I slammed the door shut. Several residents poked out their heads. I kept walking. This time I went into the elevator. I gently pressed the button for the first floor.

Forty-Four
The Scene of the Crime

John. January 2nd, 2010.

"We declare the defendant, Johnathan David Washicha, not guilty," the foreman announced. The courtroom broke out in cheers. I stood and shook Damion's hand. Fuentes glared daggers at me. I laughed. For a moment, I forgot just how furious I was with Peter. We joined the crowd as it shuffled out. Damion was on one side of me, Katy on the other. After Peter decided to take his legal fee in the form of my bike, a correspondent for the Beppo Family showed up. He—who never gave a name—had managed to swipe both me and Peter's phones from *The Pub*. He said both were debugged and to call Don Beppo when Peter got back. Then he left.

Since then, Peter's phone rang nonstop. I was tempted to answer it, but instead chose to respect his privacy. Besides, I had to hear the verdict. Damion had done an excellent job. Peter, too, but Damion... I smiled to myself. Damion. My son once more. I clasped him on the shoulder as we exited. Peter was lounging against a column. My eyes hardened. He gave me a small grin, spreading his hands and shrugging as if to say, *"What could I do?"*

I left my family and Walker to talk amongst themselves. I faced him. He didn't speak. Rage boiled inside me, but I kept it at bay. For now.

"They found me innocent," I told him. He nodded.

"Congratulations."

"Thanks. You were a big help."

"I got you there in the first place."

"You also got me back to all those loving people over there."

"And caused one of those loving people to die. I have a conscience, John. I may not have known Castle well, but his death was my fault."

"Is that what's bothering you?"

"No. Yes. Ugh!" he exclaimed. His phone started ringing again. I held it up for him. Someone had called thirty-six times in the last twenty minutes. He snatched it. "You want to hear what's wrong?" His head swiveled this way and that. "Follow me," he led me to a secluded corner, then answered the phone, putting it on speaker.

"Clare, I did what I-"

"Peter! He isn't breathing! Zane is—he's dead! You killed him... you killed him! Peter Richardson, you killed my fiancée!"

"Calm down. You're hysterical. He was hitting you."

"You killed him! Don't you feel bad? Feel anything?"

"I didn't mean to."

"You didn't mean to? Is that all you have to say?!"

"Look... I'm sorry, okay? I was just so upset. And when I saw your eye... I snapped. I didn't mean to kill him, though." Something told me a part of him did mean to. But at the same time, I still believed it was an accident. He had a lot to answer for. The kid had of guts, taking my bike. And now this. Peter stood there, scanning the room. Something about him was different... he had changed his clothes.

No, that wasn't it. He did, but something else was off.

It clicked. I had seen the same happen to men in warzones.

The jaw jutting out, the eyes coldly defiant. Murder is too much for some to handle. He didn't know how to react.

"I gotta go," he ended the call.

"You killed him," I said quietly.

"Apparently so."

"You took my bike because you found out he was hitting her," he gave a slight nod. I waited for him to speak.

"I couldn't take it. 'Do you feel bad,' she asked. Do I? I don't have a clue. I mean, I feel terrible. But it's more of a hollowness. A lifetime of crime and my first murder is caused by a domestic dispute?" His first. I did not know if I thought there would be a second. He continued without pausing, "That's the greatest joke of them all. Now I'm a common criminal," he stopped, realizing he was ranting. "I feel bad that I hurt her, but not that I killed him. I could have stepped on her toes and feel as bad as I do now, and kill someone unrelated and not feel a thing. I mean... you know what I mean. It's because it's *her*. I'd still probably grieve if it were someone else, but I murdered someone close to *her*. He beat her, sure. But my point is," he took a deep breath, "I made her unhappy."

"That's called love," I told him. He turned away. "A man stopped by after you left. He asked that you give Don Luigi a call. It sounded important," he nodded, punching numbers in his phone. He took it off speaker-phone and held it to his ear.

"*Compare*, it's Peter," he listened intently. Whatever was said, it didn't last long. Still, Peter's face fell. He hung up and looked at me. "We have to drop the Crucifiers off at a warehouse by the docks. Then we're supposed to meet Don Beppo at the back entrance to *The Jaded Dragon* over in Chinatown. I don't like this, John. I don't like any of it."

"What can we do about it?"

"Do as we're told until I get a better idea."

"Works for me. Where are the guns?" he grinned sheepishly. "Pete? Who did you give the guns to?" His grin grew wider. It hit me. "You have *got* to be kidding me," he slowly shook his head, still smiling. The sleep deprivation must have hit him. I sighed. "Let's go," he wordlessly made for the door. I followed him. Damion stopped me.

"Dad."

"Son. Thank you, again."

"Look… I don't know if what Peter said about the fighters beating you up is true. Actually, I'm almost certain it's not. But what I said is. I'm sorry."

"I know just the way you can make it up to me."

"How's that?"

"Share a drink with your old man soon. On me," he gave me a wistful smile.

"I'd like that."

"So would I, Son. So would I." I caught up to Pete, giving Katy a kiss on the cheek as I passed her. Fuentes and Vasquez were out in the parking lot. Neither spoke. They just watched us get on my bike. I hesitated. "Pete. I need my keys."

"Oh, right," he fished them out his pocket and handed them to me. The Harley started up with a roar. We took off. "We'll need to stop by my place and get my car!" Peter shouted above the wind. "To put the guns in the trunk!" I nodded. We rode a while with neither of us saying a word. It made me more than slightly uncomfortable.

"I don't blame you, Pete! You did what you had to do!" I wasn't sure if he could hear me, but I went on. "If it had been Katy I would've done the same." I threw that last sentence around in my head a bit, unsure whether to elaborate. I wasn't even sure if he was listening. I stopped at the light just as it turned red. "When I was a sophomore in high school I saw these four football players picking on this girl. She was beautiful. I mean absolutely stunning. They were messing with her just because she was new in town and they had nothing better to do. Well, I went up to them, asked them to stop, and-"

"Let me guess," Peter replied. So he was listening after all. "you somehow managed to beat up all four guys at once and you and the girl lived happily ever after, right?" I chuckled. At least he was listening. The light turned green.

Soon, we arrived at Peter's apartment building. I parked on the curb. "No, it wasn't some miraculous victory. I got my butt kicked, and as I was lying there, bloodied up, the girl put my arm around her neck and brought me to the nurse. Her name was Katy.

"I hadn't been much of a charmer in those days, but she did most of the talking for me. Next thing I knew, we had a date that night," he didn't respond.

We went in and headed straight for the parking garage. Peter didn't say anything to me and I didn't say anything to him. We both got in either side of his Corolla and he began driving. Peter, naturally, couldn't play the quiet guy for long.

"There's one thing I don't get."

"Only one?" he shot me a look that said he was trying to keep a conversation going.

"None of Bobby's actions make any sense. Betraying both of his independent partners, talking with a cop, trying to kill us before the bank job..."

"Pete, I've learned over the years that people rarely make sense. You'll never get the whole story," he vigorously shook his head.

"There has to be some sort of logic to it all. I'm just not

putting the pieces in the right order. Or maybe I'm missing a piece." Just then, a wave of exhaustion hit me. The only rest I'd gotten in the past thirty hours or so had been from a short unconscious stupor with the help of Johnny Black. I was tired physically, mentally, emotionally... I was just plain tired. I wanted this to end. But it couldn't. Not yet.

"I just want to know who murdered my friend."

"I'm getting people on that. We'll talk to Don Beppo about a search put out on Murray and Uncle Donnie. I have Jimmy looking into getting an insider in the LAPD to keep us updated on the case. Joey is scouring the weapons market for any sign of C308s."

"Murray didn't kill Castle."

"That doesn't mean he wasn't involved. I'm trying, John. I am. I just have nothing else to go off of at the moment."

"No, you don't get it: Murray didn't kill Castle. Uncle Donnie didn't kill Castle. Both of them were inside when it happened. The Black Outfit scared the murderer off, so whoever he was, he wasn't one of them. Who does that leave?"

"Dillan."

"You can't be serious."

"I'm not, but that doesn't mean he isn't a possibility. Maybe it was one of the *Cartel*."

"A *Cartel* member that arrived alone, left alone, *and* stayed away from the Outfit?" he stayed silent. I could see why. The killer had similar enemies to us. That made it look like whoever it was, was a friend. Or acted like one, at least.

Peter parked in front of a modern condominium complex. We got out the car and headed inside. The lobby was deserted except for a clerk behind a lavish counter. He looked up at our approach.

"You!" he glared at Peter. "You have some explaining to do." Peter took out his handy dandy roll of cash. He let a few bills slide onto the counter in a pile.

"These are not the droids you're looking for." The clerk, clearly confused, put away the money. Peter began to leave. He stopped and turned back to the clerk.

"Are there cameras in here?"

"In the lobby, elevators, and hallways, yes." Peter tossed him the rest of the roll and headed for the elevator.

"Didn't you hear him, Pete? There are cameras in the elevator."

"Relax. I'll make a few calls. The feed will be erased or — more likely — misplaced before the cops arrive."

"What makes you think they aren't already here?" We got in the elevator. Peter hit the button for the fourth floor.

"No crowds in the lobby, no cruisers, no investigator asking random passerby if they saw anything."

"The murder must have taken place over an hour ago. The cops could have come and left by now."

"Clare wouldn't have called the cops."

"Her fiancée is dead, Peter. She very well may have done just that."

"She didn't," he denied vehemently. The doors opened back up. We marched up to room 405. Peter knocked. There was silence from within. He knocked again. No one came. This time he tried the handle. The door opened. Inside was Clare kneeling over the slightly-mangled body of who I presumed to be Zane Wyler. She glared at our entrance. Tear streaks stained her cheeks. Her eyes were red and puffy.

"Get out, Peter. Just get out."

"And what if I came to pay my respects?"

"Get. Out," she stood, balling her fists. "You've done

enough."

"You were the one who wanted me to say something. Well. Here I am."

"And what do you have to say?"

"I… did what was best for you," he said, his eyes pleading.

"That's for *me* to decide, Peter! Not you! Not like this!" she searched her immediate vicinity with her hands in the shape of claws. She hefted up a framed picture of her and Zane from a nearby coffee table and hurled it at Peter. It hit me right below the eye. I grunted and held my face.

"We came for those packages I left you. You still have them, right?" she jutted out her chin. "Clare, where are those packages?" she rolled her eyes.

"In the bedroom closet, beneath the shoe boxes." Peter motioned for me to go get them. I went as he continued to try and soothe her. I found the bedroom easy enough. Facing the bed was the largest flat-screen I'd ever seen. On the other side of the room were two doors. I tried the first one. Inside was an assortment of women's clothes.

I began rummaging around. Toward the back I found a pile of shoe boxes. Knocking those aside, I found a stack of five rectangular prisms underneath. The Crucifiers. I put two of them under one arm and three under the other and went back into the main room. Peter had managed to coax Clare away from the body.

"I'm going to call some people to fix this," he consoled her, "I'm sorry. I'll make it right somehow, okay?" she didn't respond. "I have to go." We made for the door.

"Why?" she asked. We both turned. "Why did you do this?" Peter turned back around and walked through the door. He shut it behind me, then leaned against it on his back as if it were the only thing keeping him on his feet.

"Because I love you," he muttered, his eyes scrunched shut. He popped them open, staring at me.

"Let's go." We went into the elevator. He hit the button for the lobby. The ride down was eerily silent except for the cheesy elevator music. It cast an almost humorous tone on recent events. Almost.

ABOUT THE AUTHOR

Born and raised in Patterson, Louisiana, Parker Fulton Felterman has always been fascinated by mysteries and crime films, from *Scooby-Doo* to *Goodfellas*. Upon graduating from the Louisiana School for Math, Science, and the Arts in 2017, Parker enrolled at Carnegie Mellon University in Pittsburgh, where he pursues a BFA in Drama. Parker's other writing endeavors include his first novel, *The Revolver*, and two produced scripts that he also acted in: *Shades of Shadowlawn* (which he also directed) and *Between Time and Space: An Existential Odyssey of Do-Overs, Hellhounds, and 80's Rock Hits*. Parker's interests include current events, the stock market, wine-making, nature (especially the river), and anything that can hold his attention for longer than a few days- a task easier said than done.